VASILY MAHANENKO

THE KARTOSS GAMBIT

*Books are the lives
we don't have
time to live,*

Vasily Mahanenko

THE WAY OF THE SHAMAN
BOOK 2

MAGIC DOME BOOKS

THIS BOOK IS ENTIRELY A WORK OF FICTION.
ANY CORRELATION WITH REAL PEOPLE OR EVENTS IS
COINCIDENTAL.

The Kartoss Gambit
The Way of the Shaman, Book # 2
Second Edition
Published by Magic Dome Books, 2017
Copyright © V. Mahanenko 2016
Cover Art © V. Manyukhin 2016
Translator © Natalia Nikitin 2016
All Rights Reserved
ISBN: 978-80-88231-07-3

ACKNOWLEDGMENTS

THE AUTHOR WOULD LIKE TO THANK EVERYONE WHO MADE THIS BOOK POSSIBLE:

- ❖ Joshua Millett
- ❖ James Patterson
- ❖ Greg Bray
- ❖ Jonathan King
- ❖ Sean Harrington
- ❖ Darius Parisienne
- ❖ Andersen Byron
- ❖ George Olive
- ❖ Julia Pennoyer
- ❖ Janine Johann
- ❖ Randy Bauman
- ❖ Jeff Bascom
- ❖ Dwight Shaper
- ❖ Jackson T. Potter
- ❖ Ronald Hobbs
- ❖ Caleb Peace
- ❖ Jonathan King
- ❖ Oren Eini
- ❖ Margaret Copeland
- ❖ Ross Dupont
- ❖ Leroy P. Michaels
- John Regier

- ❖ Joshua Glenn
- ❖ Cole Johnson
- ❖ Skilgar Wulfsson
- ❖ Jesper Rasmussen
- ❖ Bartosz Iwiński
- ❖ Andreas Persson
- ❖ Aaron Weingrad
- ❖ James Patterson
- ❖ Patrick Scifi
- ❖ Maickel Hagemann
- ❖ Steven Daly
- ❖ Zachary R. Franks
- ❖ Alex Fnkl
- ❖ Karty Kannan
- ❖ Smrty James
- ❖ Pieter Sleijpen
- ❖ Allan Miller
- ❖ John Justin Green
- ❖ Bill Kluender
- ❖ Ng Chin Leng
- ❖ Cory Cinquini

TABLE OF CONTENTS:

CHAPTER ONE
AT THE FRINGE OF THE EMPIRE

I BOLDLY STEPPED INTO THE PORTAL and prepared myself for long struggle with the Governor. The three months I would be forced to spend entirely in his power were no cause for celebration, but I had no intention of surrendering, crawling on my knees or cowering like a kicked dog before this fumble of the developers. That sweaty toad can kiss my ass and forget about the Orc Warrior figurines, for all his attempted bribery: peace, love or lots of dough. Potential use of physical force against me wasn't much of a worry. I was sure that the freed prisoners couldn't be casually punished or tortured – we did have rights, after all, even if these were somewhat curtailed. It was worth bearing in mind that the system was fully aware that the sensory filters were disconnected, so I had little to worry about and... What on earth is this?

To the player located in a prisoner capsule! You have earned 'Respect' with the Pryke Mine guards and are being transferred to the main gameworld.

You have the option of taking part in the adaptation scenario: 'The Governor's Castle'. Time to be spent at the location 'The Governor's Castle': 2 months 26 days. Role taken: 'Castle craftsman'. Conditions: eight hour work day, a weekly salary, the results of the daily labor go to the Serrest province; every seventh day is a holiday, development of crafting professions (up to level 30 inclusive) – at the expense of the Governor.

Reward for taking part in the adaptation scenario: Respect with the Serrest Province, two items of the 'Rare' class.

Should you decline, you will be sent to a random settlement in the Malabar Empire and your reputation with the Serrest Province will fall to the level of 'Hatred'. Do you wish to take part in the adaptation scenario 'The Governor's Castle'?

Judging by the shimmering portal that surrounded me I wasn't going to be taken anywhere until I made the choice. If that's the case I had time to think about it, weighing up all the pros and cons.

First. An adaptation scenario... How much more adaptation can I need? I get it already – I'm a loser and a wretch, who only gets handed truckloads of compulsory adaptation instead of the standard game and normal communication with other players. That is definitely a minus.

Second. There's the close proximity to the Govertoad, even if just geographically. I'm sorry Mr. Digital NPC, our encounter was a mistake and mutual love is definitely not on the cards. You just wanted to use me... Right, my thoughts are getting in a mess again... In any case, the Governor's personality amounts to two fat minuses.

Third. I am a business-like person and should think things through rationally. It would be foolish to simply walk past such a pile of freebies: the salary, the development of an unlimited number of professions, the character level being my only limit. I could be learning Smithing, Alchemy, Enchantment, Cartography and level up in many other things at the same time, all justified by the conditions of the scenario. Definitely a double plus.

Fourth. If I refuse, I'll get Hatred with Serrest. This is a clear minus or rather a plus towards taking part in the scenario. There are just forty provinces in Malabar and to lose access to one of them is a very short-sighted choice.

I think that's it. I don't know about anyone else in my place, but for me the choice was clear. I didn't want to limit my freedom to one holiday a week. If that's the case, I'd say 'Good luck' to the Govertoad - he'd have to make do without me. I was all but crestfallen when I jumped into the portal with the flashing message that for two months and twenty six days I'll be stuck in the Governor's castle. Things turned out a lot less dire - the system simply provided advance information of the scenario, naively thinking that I would go for it. After all, it came with so many freebies and big bonuses... They can dream on!

I confidently selected the 'Refuse' sign, small as it was next to the larger 'Accept', and in an instant the world was filled with color, sound and the fragrant scent of a pine forest.

To the player located in a prisoner capsule! You have declined to take part in the adaptation scenario and were sent to the settlement of Beatwick. Time to be spent at the settlement: 2 months 26 days. Maximum time you can spend outside the settlement: 48 hours. If you are found outside the settlement beyond the allotted time, you will be teleported back into the village and a record of violation of the parole conditions will be made. Three violations annul your parole and you will be returned to the mines to serve the remainder of your prison term.

Have a pleasant game!

Compulsory quest accepted: 'Visiting the Village Headman'. Description: go to the headman of Beatwick to be allocated living quarters for the next three months. Deadline for completion: 12 hours. Penalty for failure: 3 violations.

I made a few steps towards the village visible in the distance, but was stopped by another message:

Your reputation with the Governor of the Serrest Province has fallen by 22000 points.
Current level: Hatred. You are 12000 points away from the status of Enmity. Due to receiving a maximum negative value, your bonus for daily reputation gain is invalid.

So they did land me with that after all. That's right – I knew what I was signing up for: the maximum value in negative reputation. Although... A negative reputation is a reputation nonetheless. In Barliona there are four levels of negative reputation: Mistrust, Dislike, Enmity and Hatred. From Neutral reputation to Mistrust there are minus 1000 points and to Dislike another 3000. Then it's minus 6000 until Enmity and 12000 until Hatred. I was given the maximum in one go! When I played my Hunter, I managed to get Exalted, the maximum positive reputation, with only one faction and that only after playing for a couple of years, while now in just three months I went straight to Hatred! Yes, of course a Shaman knows no half-measures, with reputation it has to be at the maximum, with crafted items – only Legendary ones, and with girls only those who get you locked up in prison. Just one thing was bad: now Serrest was lost to me – as soon as I get spotted by the guards there, I'd be immediately sent to prison 'to assess the situation'. Then it's spending a day in the preliminary detention cell and then teleportation to the borders of the province. The next time I'd spend two days in the cell. After that it's three and so on without a limit. The most unpleasant part was that a reputation like that is almost impossible to improve - you need the personal intervention of the Emperor.

Visions of the lost carefree life in the Govertoad's castle floated up on the fringes of my consciousness, but I quickly dispelled them and headed to Beatwick. At the first glance it was a pretty standard average village; judging by the chimneys it had at least seventy households. The wooden houses, roofed with wooden shingles, the barking of dogs, happy shouts of children running around after a madly screeching cat that had something tied to its tail - all of this was a picture of normal village life, which I remembered from the times I had gone to visit my parents. The enormous stockade of thick logs around the entire perimeter protected the village from the dark forest that stood about a hundred meters away. The strange expression 'forest of masts' involuntarily popped into my head - the trunks of the pines, as straight as spears, shot up into the sky, hiding the sun with their thick canopy and creating deep twilight beneath. Fallen pines, shrubbery and hazel thicket, together with other kinds of trees, made the forest quite literally impassable. Only rare paths, probably hacked through by the locals, lead into the depths of this wonder of nature. Despite such surroundings, life was not restricted to the interior of the stockade – up until the very edge of the forest there rolled wide yellow fields of some kind of cereal crops, green meadows, where cows and sheep grazed, and hundred-meter-long vegetable patches that had villagers bent over them with their hoes. The village theme was played out to the full. Thick black smoke and the ringing blows of a hammer came from the smithy that stood near the road to the village. Great: there was a place here for leveling up. The only drawback for me was the red band on my head: without it Beatwick would have all but rolled out a red carpet for me as a free citizen of the Empire. Right now though, I'd be lucky not to get dogs and pitchforks.

I took a deep breath in the fresh air and headed at an unhurried pace towards the village gates, looking out for any special aspects of local life. My main task was to find the local Headman and 'register' my presence in the village. If I only knew where to look for him. This was no Pryke mine, where the orc always sat behind his desk – here the Headman could be running around anywhere.

As I made my way towards Beatwick, I tried to take note of every detail that could be of use in the next three months.

I saw how the smith, large as a bear, came out of the smithy, lifted a small barrel of water and, breathing out a loud 'Eehh!', emptied it over himself, snorting and giving off a lot of steam. He stood there for a couple of seconds giving me an unfriendly stare and loudly breathing in the cool air, then he lifted the anvil from the ground as if it was a feather, shot me one more glance and disappeared back into the smithy. With that I felt my plans for leveling up in professions take a nosedive: I hate heat. For me it's better not to work at all than be sweating buckets, my tongue hanging out as I gulp in the sizzling air.

A group of three bearded men were actively swinging the scythes and giving me extremely unfriendly glances. Their small foreheads, menacing and, at the same time, unintelligent eyes made them look very similar to Neanderthals, whose pictures I remembered from history lessons. They only lacked some animal skins on their backs, otherwise they'd be a spitting image of them. When I walked by them I could hear muttering that didn't sound at all like Barliona's common tongue. I could bet that these three had some kind of a quest connected to them: either they were the quest givers or they would provide some kind of related information. If I asked the locals, it would probably turn out that these guys weren't from around here.

An interesting-looking tree caught my eye...

"Watch out!" the clear voice of a child tore me away from contemplating the local sights. I turned towards the source of the sound and opened my mouth to ask what happened, when my forehead was struck with something large, hard and very painful. Bam! The peaceful county landscape was enriched by the image of a flying Shaman, sending curses on anyone and everyone. My flight came to a stop almost immediately – inside a fresh haystack. With some effort I dug my way out of the green entanglement, spitting out grass and brushing it off my coat. What the hell!? I habitually looked at my Hit Points, and cursed once again. 40% of my Hit Points were gone! What have I done to deserve this? The answer came soon enough, but left me somewhat perplexed. It was a huge cartwheel, tied around with a rope and framed with metal sheets. Riiight. Something like that could send you off for a respawn in no time!

"Are you all right?" a small out-of-breath boy, his face red, flew up to me, barely older than seven, by the look of it. "I was... my tooth... the wheel! It's so heavy! And there you were! And it rolled the wrong way! Took my tooth with it! And then – 'Bam!' And you're flying! Into the grass – 'Whack!' Did it hurt?" He was looking at me with such concern and guilt, trying to tidy up his messy ginger hair with fidgety hands, that I was totally unable to get angry at him. "You won't tell mum, will you? Our blacksmith is good at pulling teeth, but he's so busy all the time, so I have to do it myself," the little boy started to explain, fitfully gulping in air between words and flashing the gap where his tooth use to be.

"Now I have no tooth, like Bald Bobby," the kid continued to chatter and it dawned on me that the wheel that sent me flying was the local replacement for a dentist, when the smith was too busy.

"You really won't tell mum? Otherwise she won't let me out by myself again, only with my sister! And she's such a bore – that's not allowed, don't touch that, keep away from the dogs! Yuck! How can you be so boring? I remember how we went to the forest..." It seemed like part of this NPC's settings stated that if silence lasted for more than a minute he'd immediately vanish from the face of Barliona. It didn't matter what the topic was or whether anyone was listening – he just had to keep talking. "Right, stop!" I interrupted his tale of venturing into the forest and gaining victory over the great vicious rabbit, "Do you know the village Headman? If you take me to him, I won't say anything to your mum," I could use a guide at the start, and the boy must know each and every one in the village.

"The Headman? Who doesn't know him? Everyone does! Five coppers and I'll take you to him right away. He's always hiding, so you can hardly ever find him," the kid was grinning and stretching his small hand towards me, with an expectant look.

"Here you go, you young extortionist," I threw five copper coins into his hand and they immediately disappeared, as if they had never existed. Of course, I could have made the boy take me to the Headman for free, but five coppers weren't going to break the bank and this way I might get some kind of a quest out of his parents (or a good hiding, if it turns out that one mustn't give the kid money under any circumstances.)

"What's your name, then?" I asked the young rascal, who was fussing around the fallen wheel and trying to decide which was the best side for getting to grips with it.

"I'm Clouter," the lad replied quickly and started to redden from the effort of trying to lift the wheel.

"Quit fibbing, there isn't a name like that. Let me help," I came up to him and put the wheel upright. It really was heavy. "Where will you roll it now?"

"I'm Clouter," said the little guy insistently, wiping his nose with his sleeve, "I don't like Avtondil. I won't be called that. Everyone has good names, only I've got a stupid one. I always get a beating for it from the Straighters. No need to roll it, just push it that way, it'll get there by itself." Avtondil... no, Clouter pointed towards the village, "with luck it won't hit anyone this time."

"And who are these 'Straighters'?"

"They are from the neighboring Straight Street, Al Spottino's gang. Watch out!" Clouter screamed after the rolling wheel and shouted to me: "We'll meet down the-ere!"

Clouter tripped up a couple of times, tumbling down the hill, but immediately got up and continued running after the wheel, shouting at the top of his voice. I chuckled at his goofiness and was about to follow him when I was suddenly turned around, lifted off the ground and thrust into the enraged bearded face of the blacksmith:

"Why are you bullying Clouter, you thug?" before I could answer anything, the blacksmith took a good swing and sent me flying again. It's not like I was expecting a royal welcome, but this was too much. These flights were beginning to wear me out with their frequency! I got up from the ground and quickly glanced at my Hit Points. Oh boy! I only had 18% of Life left! A blacksmith's punch hit much harder than the wheel! I saw that I might not survive a second blow and started to summon a Healing Spirit on myself.

"What's with the dancing? You're a warlock!" It

was just as well that the Tambourine sped up the Spirit summoning - I managed to completely heal myself only a second before my next flight. This was some blacksmith! Strong as a bear. I tried to get up, but my feet gave way and I slumped to the ground, seeing a semi-transparent message appear:

Dizziness! You lost concentration for 10 seconds.
Skill increase:
+10% Endurance. Total: 60%.

"Stop, Mr. Slate!"

"Leave it, Clouter, stay out of the way. Can't you see that we've had a killer-warlock land on us?"

"He's no killer! He helped me to bring the wheel back to the village and he wanted to see the Headman!"

"The Headman, you say?" Slate loomed over me and then with one hand lifted me off the ground. No-one would believe me if I told them that I got caught between a Slate and a hard place in Barliona! Quite literally. "What did you want from the Headman?"

"I'll be living here for three months," I croaked through a half-strangled throat. Well, well! Playing as a Shaman I was beginning to discover Barliona from a completely different angle: I would have never thought that if you press on the throat, the player would start to croak like that. He won't be getting suffocated - just a status bar would pop up, stating that he didn't have enough air. But the rasping is not something I've noticed before. The blacksmith let go and I fell on the ground like a sack of potatoes.

"Going to live here, eh? Then why are you loitering here as if you're trying to snoop around? There's no Headman around here," without waiting for my reply the blacksmith turned around and went back to his smithy. By the looks of it, my first encounter with Beatwick residents was far from a success.

"Don't be upset," fired off Clouter. "Mr. Slate is nice, he just probably failed to make something today and that made him all cranky. Let's go together, I've finished rolling the wheel. See where it's crashed into the fence? It can stay there."

By the wooden gates I found the local guards - two red-nosed men with puffy eyes. They were doing their best to stop themselves falling to the ground by propping themselves up against their spears. They clearly weren't doing so because they were tired or spent too long at their posts, but from uninhibited imbibing of spirits. The scent of syrupy homebrew wafted a few dozen meters away from the duo, and several bottles strewn across the ground were clear pointers to what the brave upholders of law and order were really up to. You couldn't say much for their overall appearance either: a short chainmail that reached down to the middle of their beer bellies, sitting on top of a simple tunic, studded thick trousers and worn bast shoes made the guards' appearance so 'terrifying', that even if an enemy decided to invade the village he was doomed to laugh himself to death first.

"Halt! Hic! Who goes there?"

"I'm on my way to the village Headman, I was

sent to live here," I gave the simple reply. It looked like the local Headman was someone well-respected and referring to him might open doors.

"To the Headman, eh?" the second guard started to mumble in a drunken voice. "Tell him that the gates are in safe hands, we're watching them like hawks. No enemy will get past us!" The guard straightened out, showing what a strong warrior was guarding the village. He was so overwhelmed with emotion that he lost his balance, took several steps backwards, hit the stockade with his back and slid down, having lost his support from the spear.

"Hold it, Wilkins!" the second guard hurried after him, totally forgetting about the unfairness of things like balance and the force of gravity. I shook my head in resignation at the sight of such guards and was about to head into the village, but then caught sight of the opened gates, which had previously been hidden by the plump guardsmen. They were made of common wood, but one side had been scarred by the four-digit claw of some unknown monster. Moreover, this had been done from the side of the village, as if someone wanted to make an opening into the world outside. I wondered whether there was some quest connected to these gates. Was it to find and destroy the monster? In that case I would be offering my services to the Headman.

"What happened to your gates?" I asked Clouter, when we approached a large house located right in the centre of the village.

"Nothing's wrong with our gates."

"But what about the marks that look like they were made by some claws?"

"That's a prank played by the Straighters. Each night they sneak past the dosing guards and cut the gates with knives. Anyone getting caught gets dragged in front of the Headman and anyone who doesn't gets a ton of honor and respect. For example, I've never been caught yet!"

"So how many times did you sneak to the gates?" I asked, disappointed, and just trying to keep the conversation going now. That could have been such a great quest!

"So far zero times, but I didn't get caught either, right?" the kid gave me a toothless smile and pointed towards a brightly-painted house. "We're here now. The Headman's sitting inside, as usual." He then took off so fast that all I saw were his flashing heels. "And don't forget," Clouter shouted after running a good distance and turning around, "Not a word to mum about the wheel!"

"So you've been sent to live with us?" the Headman asked me, as he carefully rolled up a paper and hid it in a draw of his table. As soon as I set my eyes on him it was clear - this was someone who liked order, a pedant and, at the same time, an NPC who was very sure of himself. I couldn't say why, but his appearance really put me in mind of one of the advisors of the Malabar Emperor. He had the same commanding face, framed by a short goatee, and penetrating watchful eyes that took note of every detail; in general, he was a complete picture of one of Barliona's good officials. He was the complete opposite of the Govertoad and it was no surprise that such a leader had the respect of the people in the village.

"Yes, for almost three months."

"No need to stand, take a seat. We have to decide what you'll be doing here," the Headman gestured me to an armchair and then leaned against the back of his own, looking at the ceiling, as if trying to think of how I could be of use to his village.

I sat in a soft and rather comfortable armchair, which was clearly not of a local make. It was strange that the house of an ordinary NPC should have such furniture, Headman or no. Reluctant to interrupt his thinking I began to examine the village leader's 'office'. It was a separate room in a residential house. An enormous wooden table, like that of the Pryke Mine governor, stood in the middle of the office and was a prime example of a well-ordered work space: everything was in folders and neat piles, with nothing out of place. He really was a pedant. A few modest-sized glass cabinets with books and scrolls, a fireplace and a luxurious thick carpet were the other furnishings of the local leader's office. I was about to shift my gaze back to my host, when it was caught by a relatively small painting: there was the Headman, two grown men, an attractive young woman and a smudge of paint that covered the fifth person in the picture.

"We have no inns, so we'll have to assign you to lodge with someone. I think Elizabeth wouldn't mind, her house has been on the empty side for two years now," the Headman began to fill out a paper, which he then handed to me, "here, please relay my request to her. Furthermore, before I decide what type of work to appoint for you, I need to know what you can do and the level of your skills. I need exact numbers."

I opened my stats and began to read out my professions and their levels. It's just as well that he didn't demand that I should tell him all my stats - I was reluctant to reveal that I had Crafting even to an NPC.

Stat window for player Mahan:					
Experience	285	of	1400	Additional stats	
Race	Human				
Class	Beginner Shaman				
Main Profession	Jeweller			Physical damage	57
Character level	14			Magical damage	555
Hit points	680			Physical defence	230
Mana	1850			Magic resistance	60
Energy	100			Fire resistance	60
Stats	Scale	Base	+ Items	Cold resistance	60
Stamina	58%	30	68	Poison resistance	60
Agility	24%	7	7		
Strength	55%	18	21	Dodge chance	6.40%
Intellect	16%	56	185	Critical hit chance	2.80%
Charisma	40%	6	6		
Crafting	0%	3	4		
Endurance.	60%	10	10		
Not selected					
Free stat points			0		
Professions					
Jewelcrafting	61%	12	12		
Mining	61%	12	13		
Trade	25%	6	6		
Cooking	20%	5	5		

"A Jeweler, a Miner and a Cook," said the Headman thoughtfully. "Totally useless professions in our parts. We have no Precious Stones, you'd have to buy them in town, which is two days' travel away on a cart. Mining might have been useful, but we have only one vein, by the smithy, and it's worked by our blacksmith Slate every day. You're not advanced enough to work an Iron Vein in any case. You could, of course, travel to the Free Lands. That's not far from here. You can get Tin and Marble veins there, but our forest is a dangerous one. Few would go there without decent protection. The Cook profession doesn't even bear mentioning: our Mrs. Potts can teach any cooks - even one of the Governor's - a thing or two. So that's that."

Free Lands nearby? Where the heck did I end up? Is this place really in the middle of nowhere?

"You don't happen to have a map of the Empire? It would be good to know where I was sent to serve my free settlement time," I asked the Headman. He squinted, giving me a long piercing look, and then replied, "Yes, there is a map."

He cleared the table, took a scroll out of one of the drawers and unfolded it. It was an enormous map of the Empire, about a meter by meter and a half. Where did he get such a wonder?! Such a map costs around ten thousand gold! "We're here," the Headman pointed his finger at the very edge of the border with the Free Lands. I bent over the map and quietly swore under my breath. 'Middle of nowhere' would be putting it mildly.

After the unification of all the countries took place and one language was adopted, the real world was split into five large regions, along the continents: Eurasia, Africa, Australia and the two Americas. In parallel with reality, five great continents were formed in Barliona, with each being divided roughly into three zones. For example, on our continent there was the Malabar Empire, Kartoss and the Free Lands. Malabar was where the players lived. It contained the main resources, quests, factions, cities, including the capital, and also some yet unexplored lands. Thus the area where I now found myself had not been completely mapped yet - even on the Headman's map it was sketched out very roughly. Kartoss, the Dark Empire, headed by the Nameless Dark Lord, was about five times smaller than Malabar in territory, which didn't stop it causing a great deal of trouble with its constant incursions and raids. But you had to give this Empire its due: it abounded in unique objects and resources, which were often sought out by high-level players. It is interesting to note that both a raid group of a hundred players and a loner that secretly snuck into Kartoss had equal chance of getting loot. It was impossible to play on the side of the Dark Empire, although many times the players signed petitions and held demonstrations, asking to be permitted to play for the dark side of Barliona. The Corporation kept promising to develop this feature, but, as far as I knew, nothing was ever done in this direction - Kartoss remained the realm of the Imitators. And, finally, the third zone on every continent, which took up almost sixty percent of all the areas accessible for play: the Free Lands. Rare independent towns with their own reputation rating, villages made up of two-three dozen houses, great forests, endless steppes, impassable bogs and mountains that rose up to the sky. In the fifteen years of Barliona's existence only thirty percent of the Free Lands territory had been mapped, with the rest remaining a veiled mystery. Naturally, there were some enthusiasts who dropped everything and dedicated themselves to exploration and travel, but they either failed to produce maps of the explored areas or chose not to share them with the rest. Or, which is most likely, they sold the maps for crazy money to the leading clans. For the majority of players the territories of the Free Lands remained uncharted. One could only guess what quests and achievements they contained, although the Corporation representatives have repeatedly encouraged the players to stop battling Kartoss and explore the Free Lands, saying that these held the 'best bonuses' in the Game. The developers even placed all the new Dungeons, one opened every half a year, inside the still unexplored parts of the Free Lands, to give players an incentive to spend their time on making their way there. But I digress, a lot...

I had been sent for settlement to the farthest reach of the Empire, on the border with the Free Lands, which here took the form of impassable woods, bogs and mountains. There were no towns or villages. On the map, almost exactly by the spot labeled Beatwick, there were several icons indicating free mines in this area. I should go there and check them out. However, what really dampened my spirits was that the nearest Imperial town, Farstead, was a really long way off. Two days on a cart is not exactly next door, if I understood the scale of the map correctly. Considering that I cannot leave Beatwick for more than two days, a visit to Farstead was out of the question.

"Had a good look now?" inquired the Headman and then rolled up the map and put it back in his table. "We may not be in the centre of the Empire, but there's still plenty to do here."

"Do you have any assignments for me?" I asked out of habit, knowing full well that the red band on my head wouldn't make me seem particularly trustworthy in the eyes of any NPC. I had to spend around a week in the village for its residents to get used to me and get less wary of my headband and only then start seeking out any quests. But there's no harm in trying.

"Of course there are, but I can't give them to just any stranger," replied the Headman, confirming my thoughts. "First live here for a little while, make some contribution to the village and then there'll be assignments for you. Although... there is one. Recently a pack of wolves has appeared in the woods. They've become bold and started raiding the herds. The shepherds said that they are lead by an enormous Wolf. If you do away with the Wolf, we can see about other assignments. In any case, it is high time for that pack to be culled, it's no good for it to be roaming the woods in such numbers. But bear in mind – I won't take your word for it. I will need proof.

Quest available: 'The Hunt for Grey Death.'
Description: A pack of wolves lead by an enormous alpha wolf has appeared in the lands around Beatwick. Destroy 10 Wolves and the great Grey Wolf. As proof that you've completed the

assignment bring back Wolf Tails, which have 100% drop rate from each mob. Quest type: Common. Reward: +100 to Reputation with the Krong Province, +200 Experience, +80 Silver. Penalty for failing/refusing the quest: -100 to Reputation with the Krong Province.

"I'll take it. I'll go after the wolves tomorrow, first thing in the morning," I said as I accepted the quest. "But I have a few more questions. How many..."

"Wolves first, questions later." The Headman cut me off in a tone that indicated that the matter was closed. "Now Tisha will take you to Elizabeth, to whom you must remember to give the letter. Go on the hunt tomorrow and after that we'll talk. Tisha!" called the Headman, and a couple of moments later the girl from the painting flew into the room.

"Let me introduce you, this is my daughter Tiliasha. This is Mahan, he'll be living in our village for three months. Take him to Elizabeth, he can stay with her."

"Just call me Tisha." The gentle voice of the girl was in tune with her beautiful appearance. "Let's go, I'll show you the village," she then moved gracefully to the door and gestured to me to follow her.

Quest 'Visiting the Village Headman' completed.

It was a large village. From the side of the hill I counted around seventy houses, but in actual fact there were one hundred and three households. Quite a lot, especially by frontier standards. The village followed a standard layout: the central square, where the Headman's house stood, and three streets: Straight, Crooked and Serpentine. The kids from these streets were always in the process of trying to establish who was the best and strongest, so fights were fairly frequent. Tisha also told me about the gates - a year ago her father carved three claw marks into them in order to put some fear into the kids, who were really beginning to get out of hand, making it look like there was a werewolf in the village. But the plan somewhat backfired: everyone was too scared to set foot outside their homes for a whole week. So he had to come clean about it. Then it became a tradition among the youngsters: if you wanted to prove yourself - you had to carve some claw marks into the gates. During the day the gates were guarded by a couple of drunkards, who were no good for any other job in any case, but at night the more serious guards took their place - either her brothers or hired hands, free citizens of the Empire, same as myself. The same in all but the red bands, that is. I couldn't stop myself from asking if there were any free citizens in the village right now, and was very disappointed to hear the answer that the last such person came through the village half a year ago.

Tisha's own story turned out to be quite interesting. She had come to the village together with her family just two years ago, immediately after the death of the previous Headman, Elizabeth's husband. Before that Tisha used to live in a large city. Her father held quite a high-ranking position, because a carriage use to take him away early in the morning and in the evening a large crowd of richly dressed people would gather at their house, lock themselves in the study and hold long discussions. Then something happened and father gathered the household and came here to the edge of the Empire.

"So the gates are guarded at night by your brothers? All three of them?" the thought of the painting with the smudge wouldn't leave me alone - something was amiss here. From the time of my initiation I had decided to put more trust in my instincts.

Tisha's face darkened, she fell silent and walked for a while through the village without saying a word. She then regained control of herself and said in a serious voice:

"No, not three, just two. But they only do it once a week. Never ask me about my third brother. I don't remember him myself, but we do not speak about him in the family. All that I know is that he betrayed our kin and our homeland and father banished him from the family forever. Not a word more about him. We're here. Elizabeth lives in this house," Tisha turned around and quickly vanished around the turn in the road. Oops. Looks like all my ambitious plans to seduce her have just been destroyed. Now I won't get anything other than a mere greeting out of her until I increase my reputation. A pity. But, in general, she did share some very interesting information with me. Banishment from the family is a very serious act for an

NPC. I can't imagine what had to have happened for a former high-ranking official to personally banish his own son. Once I level up my reputation to Friendly, I will certainly ask the Headman about the painting myself. I'd bet my life that the story behind the banishment is quite a complicated one and must have a quest attached to it. Assignments like these are exactly in Barliona's style - improving players' social skills by getting them to reconcile families.

"But you said you wouldn't tell mum anything about the wheel," an upset child's voice pulled me out of my thoughts. "You promised!"

"Firstly, I promised no such thing and, secondly, I have no intention of telling anyone anything. What are you doing here?" It took a little while for me to spot Clouter hiding under the porch.

"What do you mean? I live here. With my mum and my sister," replied the boy, crawling out of his hiding place.

"Then it's you that I've come to see. Is your mother home?"

"She's home, all right," Clouter looked around, gave it a thought and started to crawl back under the porch. "But I'm not going in there. It's porridge for dinner and I hate it. If mum sees me, she'll take me by my ear and sit me at the table. I'd best stay here for a while."

"How can I help you?" a low woman's voice made me look up from Clouter's hiding place. Judging by the squeaking of the floorboards the kid was trying to signal me that he wasn't there and that I really had no idea where he might be. With a wise mother's smile Elizabeth looked under her feet and then asked a completely unexpected question: "Excuse me, I wonder if you've see a ginger boy around here? I've baked his favorite pie, but it will get cold soon and won't be as tasty. I'll have to give it all to Dawnie, like the porridge."

"You gave the porridge to Dawnie? For real?" after hitting his head a couple of times on the floorboards, Clouter ran like lightning from his hideout and stood before his mother, eyes shining. "Is it a blueberry pie?"

"Of course, it's the blueberry pie, just as you like it. Run along while it's still hot, you rascal," Elizabeth ruffled his hair, as the kid ran past her and then turned to me again, "So, how can I help you?"

"I was sent to you by the Headman. He said that I could come and live with you for three months. Here are the papers," I handed Elizabeth the letter. If her behavior with her son was so natural, I shouldn't have any major problems with this NPC.

"Three months, eh?" muttered Elizabeth, scanning through the paper. I couldn't help wondering what the Headman wrote in there. I didn't manage to have a look in his house and then was too busy talking to Tisha. What if it gave me a boost to Intellect? You never know. "The nights are warm at the moment, so I can give you the summer house. Is that all right with you?" my landlady looked me over. "Are you going to live here as a freeloader or as a help?"

Was there a quest in this for me? I may have to do it for free, but a quest is still a quest!

"I don't like being a freeloader. If you need anything done, just tell me and I'll do it: whether it's fetching the water, chopping wood or digging the garden..."

"No, my laborers can do all that well enough. The Headman said that you aren't new to cooking," Elizabeth paused and I froze in expectation. A profession-based quest! It's a dream for any player! You can't even imagine the kind of bonuses you can get there! Elizabeth hesitated, but then appeared to come to a decision and said: "I'm not a rich woman, so I can't feed another mouth. You will be completely responsible for feeding yourself?" she then glanced at my red headband and added: "I also ask you not to come inside my house uninvited."

Attention to the player! You have been denied access to the main house of Elizabeth, the widow of the former Beatwick Headman. If you breach this restriction, one violation of your parole conditions will be recorded. Have a pleasant game!

Elizabeth turned around and went into the house, leaving me on the porch in a state of complete depression. I had already gotten all excited about getting quests and a friendly attitude to me... How could I have forgotten my red headband status? With that any NPC will treat me warily and with suspicion. A former criminal, what do you expect? What if I start killing everyone left and right, or pickpocketing and nicking their money? Who knows with these ex-cons!

So it looks like earning levels wasn't going to be such a simple task after all. And I had all these plans to gain a dozen or two in the coming three months by doing various quests... A pity. I'll have to do something about that, that's certain. And as soon as possible too.

The summer house, kindly provided to me by Elizabeth, was astounding in its simplicity and Spartan feel. Its entire collection of furniture consisted of one bed, which took up half of the free space. That was it. There was the earthen floor, which remained cold even in today's heat, grey wooden planks for the wall and narrow windows right by the ceiling, which had trouble letting even the moonlight through. Great place for spending the next three months. I threw myself on the bed and started to make plans, just to keep my brain occupied.

First. I'll have to do the quest with the wolves first thing tomorrow. Extra experience and reputation with the Krong province should help me win Elizabeth's trust and move into the big house. I had little desire to be stuck in this cage for three months.

Second. I had to solve the problem of how to visit Farstead. Getting there on a cart wasn't an option - it would take too long. So I had to find another way. The Headman said that a caravan travels to that town from time to time. I had to make an arrangement with its leader to buy a scroll of teleportation from Beatwick to Farstead. The return scroll I could buy there. Judging by the distance to the town, the scroll could cost around eight or nine hundred gold. It's quite a lot, but I had to get to the Bank of Barliona and get my hands on the possessions of my former Hunter character. There should be at least eleven thousand there just in gold, not counting all the leftover equipment. Although all of it was focused on boosting Agility, I could use even that. It would be like plate mail compared to what I had on now.

Third. I had to find out about the mines that I'd seen marked on the Headman's map. He did warn me, of course, that it's dangerous to go it alone there, but I really mustn't let an opportunity like this get away. If I understood correctly, the closest deposits of something or other are located a couple of hours' walk from Beatwick. I didn't really feel like sleeping, so if I left now I'd be back by the morning. This will also give me a better idea about what I can count on in terms of leveling up professions.

Fifth... there is no fifth, I'm done planning. Now is the time for action - to go and look at that mine. But first I had to look through my bag, since I haven't really had time for that until now. After the Dungeon it was quite full of things I haven't even looked at. I threw the contents of the bag right on the floor, lit a rushlight, put it into a small hole in the wall and began the inspection. There were the chess pieces. It was a pity that each Orc Warrior took up an entire slot in the bag. The thought of having to drag all thirty-two figurines around with me left me somewhat stumped. Where on earth will I get a bag that big? Then there were seven rings with a +3 stat bonus and four rings with a +2 bonus. They were the ones I failed to sell at the Pryke mine and were now outdated. There was no point of keeping them for later for a potential sale at an auction. Junk like this wouldn't even sell for five gold. I'll have to offload them with a normal NPC merchant. I didn't even look at the chainmail gloves, dropped by the last boss of the Dungeon. These belonged to the members of my future clan and I had no intention to turn into a rat. Why expose myself to extra temptation? What if I liked them and didn't want to part with them? Twenty three pieces of Malachite, one hundred pieces of Copper Ore and sixty eight Copper Ingots would all come in handy for leveling up my Jewelcraft until I solved my ore supply issues. There was my old friend, the Mining Pick. And, finally, there was the large pile of various skins, tails, meat, claws and other junk, which had dropped from the rats and spiders of the Dungeon. I fought off the impulse to gather it all up and sell it without even looking at it - the first completion of a Dungeon gave quite a good chance to get a considerable bonus even from simple mobs, so I didn't want to throw away something potentially useful. As I sorted through it all, I set aside a Spider Eye, horrible in its look and feel. Its properties remained unidentified, and I did not have the Wisdom stat, which would help in this task. It's not like I needed it in any case. It was much easier to go to mage NPCs in any town and identify the object for a couple of gold. I also set aside twenty two Rat Tails with 'Used by Alchemists' property and twelve Spider Mandibles, with the 'Used by Armorers' property - I would go around the relevant shops trying to sell these goods later. Just look at my thoughts running ahead - 'go around the shops'. I haven't even sorted out the teleportation scroll, but I'm making all these plans for the town anyway. The rest turned out to be total trash, with only the Rat Meat being potentially useful for leveling up in Cooking.

After going through the items, I put them back in the bag, got a solid grip on my Mallet and went out into the night. The owners of Barliona know very well that many of the game's players only appear during late evenings. For this reason the nights here are very light and generally have very good visibility. I took a couple of steps from the door and cursed. Just my luck! It looked like Beatwick was on that unique list of places where the rule about lighter nights did not apply. Pitch black darkness covered the village like a blanket and it was impossible to see anything even a couple of meters away. Thus my plan to go to the mine fell through quite thoroughly. I had no desire whatsoever to trudge around in this dark. I sat on a bench, leaned against the wall and closed my eyes. There was an almost complete silence that seemed to arrive in the village together with the dark, broken only by the rustle of the forest and the quiet chirping of crickets. There were no dog noises or shouts from crowds of NPCs, which were now peacefully sleeping in their houses. It was an ideal night to go out by yourself and breathe in the crisp, clean air, which contained hints of pine resin, fir needles and a tangy whiff of an animal. An animal?! I immediately opened my eyes and saw just a couple of meters away an indistinct cloud, out of which two red eyes were staring at me. What the...? I selected the indistinct cloud and tried to see in its properties what

I was dealing with.

Object properties: hidden.

Hidden? How's that? Concealing a mob's properties was impossible in Barliona. Or at least it was until just now. The entire game is built upon the ability to read them, which allows the players to devise combat strategies with the mob or a boss. I had to get into the manual or on the forums to see who is able to hide their properties and whether this was even possible. But that's for later, right now I had other matters to deal with - what does this thing in front of me want? I had little doubt that its intentions were anything but nice and friendly. As a rule, in Barliona if a mob is aggressive, it's sure to have red eyes. Neutral or friendly mobs would have eyes of any other color but red. The two red lamps looking straight at me did not make my immediate future look very promising.

Trying not to make any sudden movements, I got up from the bench and started to shift sideways towards my door. I had to cover just a couple of meters. With every small step I took the strange thing also shifted sideways, always keeping a meter and a half in front of my face. I don't think I'm liking this anymore. Maybe I should attack it first? Attack is the best defense, after all. I was about to summon a Lightning Spirit on this incomprehensible something, but then my hand slid against the door knob. The thought of testing which of us was tougher was evaporated in a second - a door, despite its humble status, was a great obstacle against mobs. No-one abolished the principle of 'My home is my castle' - even in Barliona.

I carefully slid my hand behind my back, slowly lowered the door handle and quickly dropped inside the house. Immediately turning around, I tried to slam the door shut with my whole weight. Just as I was making my first move the beast lunged forward and began to push hard on the closing door from the other side.

Damage taken. Hit Points reduced by 30: 260 (Door hit): 230 (Physical defense). Total Hit Points: 650 of 680

Skill increase:

+10% Endurance. Total: 70%

+5% Strength. Total: 60%

I was just a couple of centimeters away from completely closing the door. I strained all I could, heaving my whole body against it, but the beast that was pushing on the other side just wouldn't let me do it. Moreover, gradually, centimeter by centimeter the door began to open. At some point a mist-covered appendage slipped through the crack that formed. Inside the house the mist dissipated and I could see four sharp claws in the twilight. What is this, an overgrown wolverine? The claws dug into the door and left deep marks - exactly the same as those on the village gates. Was I suppose to think that this is the way the local youth got its kicks? It'll become a running joke if it gets around the village tomorrow - how the Shaman got scared by children's pranks. I was about to stop resisting, but then a message popped up:

Energy level: 30. Stop, you angry Shaman!

This was the automatic message I put in place back at the mine to stop myself biting the dust from the Energy loss. This was no joking matter. It's not like the local kids would have the strength to demolish my Energy in a matter of seconds. This is something else.

But what this something was I didn't get a chance to find out. A couple of seconds later a message flashed that my Energy had gone down to zero and I froze like a broken doll. Unlike in the mines, in the main gameworld Energy can be easily restored from zero, even without the aid of water. But until it is restored to at least ten points, the player freezes like a wax figure.

Another blow on the door threw me far back into the room and already mid-flight I saw some grey shadow speed after me. There was no mist around it, but in the darkness of the room I couldn't make out what it was. Only one thing was clear - the beast had two arms and two legs. Or four appendages, to sum it up. Why did I put out the lamp before leaving? That way I'd know what I was dealing with now. There was a flash of four sharp claws: a sharp pang of pain and the surrounding twilight became even darker. So, my house is not much of a castle, it would seem. Though it's not like it's really my house - I was getting ahead of myself.

There was a flash and it seemed to me that I

almost immediately found myself at the entrance to the local cemetery. A very symbolic respawning point. A small temple stood a few meters away from me, shading me from the bright morning sun. Looks like that unidentified beast did get me in the end, and the compulsory twelve hours from the moment of death went by in a flash. Great.

I was about to head to the temple when I found myself staring angrily at a message that popped up:

Attention!

In connection with your death, your level of Experience has been reduced by 30%. Current Experience: 199; points remaining until next level 1201

I checked my purse. That's right, it now contained only three thousand gold. The other half was lying in the summer house. I could only hope that no-one had come in and laid their hands on it. It should have been somewhere behind the bed and not really visible from the door.

But what was it that got me? Despite the fact that I had 680 Hit Points and 230 Physical defense, the beast sent me for a respawn with a single blow. I looked into the combat logs, hoping that this feature had become unlocked since my leaving the mine. Yes! Now we'll read what it was that swatted me. I switched on the filter for the damage sustained in the last thirty hours and saw several lines:

23:45:23 Damage taken: 28 (258 'Door hit' - 230 'Physical defense'). Hit Points remaining: 652.

23:45:26 Damage taken: 28 (258 'Door hit' - 230 'Physical defense'). Hit Points remaining: 624.

23:45:39 Damage taken: 28 (258 'Hit against the wall' - 230 'Physical defense'). Hit Points remaining: 596.

23:45:41 Damage taken: 24762 (24998 'Unknown' - 230 'Physical defense'). Hit Points remaining: 0.

I looked at the messages dumbfounded. That was some swatting! Twenty five thousand damage can be inflicted by a mob that's no less than level 70. But where would an aggressive mob of such a level come from in Beatwick and why on earth did it decide to pay me a visit?

"Were you looking for something, my son?" a voice sounded nearby and made me turn around. A small, plump and pink-cheeked priest of some god was standing by the temple, thumbing through the prayer beads in his hands. A black robe covered him from head to foot, but failed to conceal the size of his enormous stomach. "Do you want to receive a blessing from Vlast? In that case you have to become his novice. Are you ready?"

So this was a temple of Vlast. The god of winemaking. He was an analogue of Bacchus, Pan and other such gods from the real world. I went into the manual to read the main limitations imposed by serving this god and was surprised to see that there were none - any NPC or players could become this god's novice without any restrictions. This didn't concern just the novices, but you could even become a priest just a few months after becoming a novice. There were no additional costs or donations to be made. All you had to do is drink a glass of wine or homebrew every day and thus receive your divine blessing. Although if you failed to drink it, you'd incur a divine curse, not a pleasant thing, as a rule. This meant that you'd have to atone for your sins with two glasses of homebrew. All right, I was never that interested in Barliona's religions as a Hunter and as a Shaman had even less need of them. Of course, Vlast is a convenient god for leveling up the Faith stat, but there are just too many complications in this field. Not my thing. Now it was clear, however, where the priest got his large stomach - probably from saying all those daily prayers with his parishioners and anyone else who dropped by. With the devout aid of wine and homebrew, that is. I bet those guards I met by the gates yesterday were also his active novices.

"No, thank you. I respect Vlast, but I am not ready to become his novice. You have my thanks," I bowed to the priest, receiving a similar bow in response.

"As you wish. Vlast doesn't force anyone to serve him. Only someone with true insight could fathom the real depth of his teaching. Can I help you with anything else, my son?" the priest run the standard phrase by me.

"Yes. Holy father, can you tell me if there are any

monsters in these parts that roam about at night and bring grief and destruction to the local people?" the incident with the respawn wouldn't let me be. I was dying to find out what dealt me all that damage.

The priest stopped fingering the prayer beads, looked around and then gestured me to follow him:

"Enter into the temple, my son. This isn't the place to talk of such things."

There was nothing interesting inside the temple. There was the altar with the depiction of a rather chubby Vlast, whose bleary-eyed gaze stared into empty space, and a couple of benches. That's it. The place was totally Spartan. The priest went behind the altar, took two cups from somewhere and handed me one of them.

"Vlasts' commandments do not permit one to start a conversation without wine passing one's lips first," the priest said in lofty tones. "I see that there's a reason that you asked me about the night monster," he began as soon as we had drunk a couple of draughts. It was ordinary wine and did not give any stat bonuses - just a 'slightly tipsy' debuff after drinking it. "I can see that this trouble has not passed you by. Yes, there is trouble in our land. People don't like talking about it and everyone's pretending that nothing's happened. You've seen the claw marks on the gates, yes? The Headman had to make up a story, saying that he was the one that scratched them on - just to calm the villagers down. But every seven days the claw marks appear again. It's just as well that the local kids got it into their heads that they are the ones getting up to this, so people stopped worrying. And the fact that every seventh night either a cow or a sheep disappears from the common herd - everyone blames the wolves for that. But no-one gives a thought about how wolves would get through closed gates. The whole village is surrounded by a solid stockade, which not even a mouse would squeeze through. Only the Headman and his sons know the truth, since they spend nights trying to catch the elusive beast. It's been evading them for two years now and they've only glimpsed the monster's red eyes a couple of times. From afar. Your help would be invaluable. Would you take this on? If you could at least find out what beast it is that roams Beatwick, you would receive an ample reward.

Quest available: 'Night terror of the village'
Description: Once every seven days a monster roams Beatwick, which brings trouble and destruction to the residents. Find out who is the night terror of the village. Quest type: Rare. Reward: +400 to Reputation with the Krong Province, +500 Experience, +80 Silver coins, a Rare item from Headman's Stores. Penalty for failing/refusing the quest: -400 to Reputation with the Krong Province.

"I'll take it. I'll find out who is hiding under the guise of the beast," I accepted. Now it all became clear. The beast's properties could not be seen, because that was the nature of the quest. So it looks like I'll have to find out about it the normal way and not the one that only players could use. All right, I'll postpone this matter for a week, when it's time for the hunt once again. Our first meeting with the beast ended with its complete victory, but we'll see how things go from here.

"Thank you, Mahan! If you need help, you can ask for it straight away," the priest thanked me and I headed for the village. It was now time to collect my dropped cash and go wolf hunting. There was leveling up to be done.

CHAPTER TWO
WOLVES AND OTHER THINGS

"WHEN DID YOU MANAGE TO GET OUT?" asked Elizabeth as soon as I stepped into the courtyard. "I thought you were having a lie-in until noon, but it looks like you're quite an early bird."

"I thought I'd take a walk," I said, side-stepping the question, reluctant to bring up the monster. "I decided not to wake anyone, climbed over the fence and went to check out the local surroundings."

"How did you avoid getting mauled by Tiny Tim?" she asked in surprise.

"Tiny Tim?"

"Our dog. We let him out into the courtyard every evening. He's been taught not to jump over the fence, but he won't let any strangers into the courtyard either. That's him sitting over there, see?" Elizabeth pointed to the far end of the courtyard, where Tiny Tim was living inside an enclosure, the meter-high wolfhound that he was. He was growling quietly and giving me a decidedly unfriendly look. Where were you, my friend, when I was being sent for the respawn? Probably sitting in your little hole and sniggering at my expense. I suddenly had a feeling that I really had to 'have a chat' with Tiny Tim. It was silly, of course, but since my initiation as a Shaman I have made a habit of trusting any sudden hunches.

"Can I get to know him a little better?" I looked questioningly at my landlady.

"Of course, just don't tease him. It would take him just a couple of bites to rip through the wire, I don't want any trouble. Our Tiny Tim is well-trained and shouldn't attack without good reason, but it's best not to tempt fate."

I assured Elizabeth that I wouldn't do anything to the dog and walked up to his enclosure. Looking around to make sure we wouldn't be disturbed, I squatted and looked straight into the wolfhound's eyes. I couldn't explain why I did this, but felt that this was the right thing to do. Giving off a quiet growl, Tiny Tim came right up to the wire. I was hit by a pungent animal smell. We stared into each other's eyes for a couple of seconds and then suddenly...

The rest of the world went grey, became covered with a mist and a ringing silence surrounded me. It was as if someone turned off all sound with a wave of the hand. A shadow separated itself from Tiny Tim and walked right through the wire as if it wasn't there. The dog's shadow walked at a relaxed pace around the courtyard, like it owned the place. I looked at the real Tiny Tim. He looked at himself, eyes wide, mouth open and tongue hanging out. He was the embodiment of doggy surprise. At this moment the dog phantom took a couple of steps and then suddenly cowered to the ground, tail between his legs, and began to backtrack. I never thought that dogs could backtrack, especially with their stomach to the ground. I could be mistaken, but weren't they not supposed be able to do that? All right, we'll write it off as the whim of the developers. The phantom crawled through the closed door of the enclosure, made his way to the dog-house and when his back was against it seemed to try to dig himself into the ground.

"Did something frighten you?" I asked quietly. My voice sounded like a thunder clap. What could have made such an enormous dog run away in fear and try to dig itself into a hole?

Something mist-covered and formless appeared next to the dog. For a couple of moments it loomed over him and then suddenly this silent drama was broken by the squealing of the real Tiny Tim. The wolfhound fell to the ground, tail between his legs, covered his face with his paws, made a puddle and generally looked so scared that I involuntarily drew back, stumbled and fell on my backside. The darkness around us dissipated and the dog's squealing was joined by the noises of the surrounding world.

Update of the 'Night Terror of the Village'

quest

The monster that roams Beatwick by night terrifies even the largest and most vicious dogs. Keep this in mind during your search

"What are you doing to Tiny Tim?" Clouter appeared next to me. "He's scared of you! Go away! Mr. Slate was right - you're a warlock! Don't be afraid Tiny Tim, I won't let him hurt you," Clouter put himself between me and the enclosure and looked ready to fight for his dog.

I had little desire to explain anything to this small NPC, so I got up and went to the summer house. As I guessed, my gold was behind the bed. I automatically threw it into my bag and lay down on the bed. The wolves won't be going anywhere and now I really had to give the forum and the manual a thorough read. The place where I ended up was becoming very interesting and I had no intention of playing the hero and trying to find out the monster's secret all by myself.

Let's think. What does a search for 'Beatwick' give us?

Let's look in the manual first. It's a village on the border of the Empire, Krong Province. I already know that. Number of residents, livestock and other NPC statistics do not interest me, next. Yes, there we go. The Headman died recently in Beatwick. Cause of death remains unknown. He was replaced by the Farstead industrial association representative. There are no quests linked to Beatwick residents.

The last sentence left me dumbfounded.

According to the manual there were no quests in the village. As it stands, I had already collected two: 'Night Terror of the Village' and 'The Hunt for Grey Death'. Something wasn't tallying here.

I made a search for the quest titles. Right, such quests do exist. However, their description made me think: 'Variable quest, not linked to a particular location.' So, there are no quests, and yet they do exist. That's just stupid. To the manual again. Search: 'Variable quest.' Description: a quest given out by an NPC depending on your progress within the scenario.

Now I became totally confused. What scenario? Why would there be a playable scenario in Beatwick, a village in the middle of nowhere? There aren't even any players around here to do that.

Right, moving on to the forum. What can we find out about 'Beatwick'? The forum also offered little comfort. My search came up with only one message that was over a year old:

'Stupid village! In the middle of nowhere, gryphons don't fly there, the portal to the nearest town costs a grand in gold! The devs have gone batshit crazy setting such prices! In Farstead I got a quest to deliver a package to the Headman. I spent two days on a cart, that's just nuts! I even logged out for that time. Right, so I got there and delivered it. I decided to have a look around at night, and it was bad enough that you can put your eye out it's so dark here, the village is being roamed by a Vagren. A level hundred one! And I'm only at thirty! I couldn't even hit him. He dodged all my attacks, the

bastard! My advice to you: it's a waste of time. I had a look around the village by day and there wasn't one quest to be had! What's the point of villages like that if there's nothing to do here for real players? One good thing is that I've done the quest and got some rep with the Province.

BTW, the Headman has a cute daughter! But she won't fall for flowers or presents. Daft NPC!"

A new search, this time in the manual:

Vagren. A type of Werewolf that keeps its consciousness after a shape-change. A Vagren can change his appearance any time at will, independent of the phases of the Moon. It is one of the few races that cannot be chosen by players. Race characteristics: faster movement when in Vagren form, ability to cause fits of panic in dogs, + (Level) to armor due to thick hide. The appearance of a Vagren is provided in the illustration.

I was looking at a tall humanoid dog, or rather, a wolf. The paw-like hands ended in four great claws that looked the same as those I saw last night. So there's a Vagren roaming Beatwick, is there? Then Tiny Tim's reaction was understandable. A panic attack is no laughing matter, especially if you're looking at a hundred-level werebeast. It's a pity that I can't go straight to the priest and share the information I just obtained. He would simply be unable to hear me, even if I was shouting in his ear: the quest hasn't been completed, so you can't hand it in. Never mind. I have a week to think of some way to catch this fleabag. My revenge for the respawn will be terrible.

As I left the house I glanced at Tiny Tim. He had now recovered and was rampaging around with Clouter. Having allowed himself to be mounted, Tiny Tim ran around the enclosure like a veteran racing horse and Clouter was laughing at the top of his lungs, grabbing his ears like reigns.

"What to do with him!" a stout woman that came out of the house threw her hands up in resignation. Judging by the kitchen apron she was the local cook. "He's making a horse out of the dog again! Marianna! Go calm your brother down, before he breaks his neck," she shouted inside the house. I didn't stay to see how it all ended and quickly headed out of the village.

If I understood the Headman correctly, the wolves appeared in the forest not far from the grazing herds. That's where I needed to go.

My initial wolf-hunting impulse petered out after about three hours. I haven't come across a single wolf, even of the mangy, sickly kind. Finding nothing better to do I started killing anything that moved. A level two grasshopper? A Lightning Spirit on you! A three-level toad? Got one for you as well! There was no experience at all or even loot to be had from this and these animals didn't even count towards the 'Bane of the Animal World' achievement. But to stave off boredom I continued to repeatedly terrorize the surrounding insects. Oh, there's a mouse running there. Just hold on, I'll get you now!

Damage taken. Hit Points reduced by 220: 450 (Arrow hit) - 230 (Physical defense). Total Hit Points: 420 of 680

Despite the excruciating pain in my shoulder, I dropped to the ground and rolled sideways. The place where I initially fell was immediately hit by another arrow. What the hell?

I kept tumbling, without even looking where I headed, and hit a small tree. Ignoring the fact that I lost some Hit Points from the collision, I rolled behind the tree and caught my breath. Phew! Now I could breathe and look about. Nice wolves roam around Beatwick - ones with an arrow-shooting habit. I had no time or inclination to look through the logs (it would become clear who was attacking me soon enough), so I took out my Tambourine and summoned a Healing Spirit, replenishing my Hit Points. Now I was ready for a fight.

A minute went by that seemed like eternity, but no more arrows came. Could this be it? I lifted myself over the grass and had a look around. Silence, not a soul to be seen. So where did this strange shooter come from? And, most importantly, who was it?

The reply came in the form of an arrow that hit me right in the chest. What the ...!

Critical damage sustained. Hit Points reduced by 670: 900 (Critical Arrow Hit) - 230 (Physical defense). Total Hit Points: 10 of 680

I fell to the ground like a sack and fitfully gasped for breath. That hurt a lot! If I get hold of the bastard, I'll tear him limb from limb! At least I didn't have to take the arrow out: it had already vanished from this world, leaving only a memory in the form of pain behind. I summoned two Healing Spirits, getting myself back to full Hit Points, and stayed quiet. This clearly wasn't a player attacking me, since no message appeared telling me that I was being attacked by a PK-er. So it looked like some mob was out looking for fun. Well, we'll see who has a latent death wish in Barliona. A mob can't sit long on one spot; it really must go and see the result of its shots. Imitators, what do you expect? Stupid and predictable. The main thing was to lay low until that time. Although, truth be told, he's a good shot, the bastard. Nearly killed me! I even had my Endurance go up to level 11. So much for my worries about leveling up. Yeah right. All I had to do was wander some distance away from the village: I'd be hit by more than my fill of leveling up.

I didn't have to wait for long. Five minutes later I heard soft steps, sliding quietly over the grass. Well, well, you wannabe-Legolas. Just wander over for a chat. I was lying with my face to the ground, afraid to stir. The main thing was to get the mob to come as close to me as possible and then we'd see if this archer was much of a warrior. An NPC wouldn't fire a finishing shot at me, the scripts wouldn't allow it, and he wouldn't be able to use his bow up close. I learned all this very well when I was playing my Hunter. If this stranger had all his stat points in Agility, judging by how he managed to critical me, he shouldn't be much of a close combat fighter. And I'll use that against him...

The footsteps stopped right by my head. That's it, whatever it is - it's here. I was about to jump, when I was checked by the painfully familiar 'aroma' coming from my opponent. It smelled of sweat, dung and some sort of musk. A dark goblin! Any player who had ever made a raid into Kartoss would never forget this pungent smell of the main fighting troops of the Dark Lord. But what was one of them doing in Krong? He'd have to walk almost the entire Empire to get here!

The goblin standing next to me muttered something in his 'dark' language, sounding annoyed and clearly surprised that no pile of money was lying next to me. He grumbled thus for a little while and turned around to walk away! It's time! I jumped to my feet, selected the surprised-looking red-eyed minion in front of me and summoned a Lightning Spirit. Take that, you green-mugged bastard!

Damage inflicted. 209: 555 (Lightning Spirit Damage) /2.14 (Opponent Level /Character Level) - 50 (Inner resistance to Spirits)

So this green piece of slime is level thirty, too! Never mind, we've beaten bigger goons than you into a pulp - the main thing was not to let him get away far enough to shoot. As if hearing my thoughts the goblin gave a shout and started to make tracks fast. Where do you think you're going? Getting a better grip on my

Tambourine, I went after the dark minion - like in the good old times, when I tried to make it into Kartoss by myself. Although that time I was the one running, with the Wild Pack - the main fighting force of the Dark Empire pitted against the players - at my heels. They did get me in the end. I just couldn't run and at the same time take aim and shoot at three-hundred level-mobs. Now, however, I had one big advantage in that I could summon Lightning Spirits as I ran. The main thing is to keep an eye on Energy while I'm singing them songs.

The Goblin went into the forest, trying to choose hard-to-reach places. Being small, he slid under the branches very easily, which was no simple task for me. The tree branches would not just knock the breath out of me, taking off my Energy, but hit me in the face, competing with the goblin in reducing my Hit Points. Before he reached the trees I managed to get that pointy-eared menace almost down to zero, but his life bar, though flashing red, refused to disappear. I saw that I would never catch up with the goblin inside such a forest and stood every chance to lose him, so I stopped and started to summon a Lightning Spirit. I needed just three seconds to...

The arrival of an arrow again took 220 Hit Points off me. Oh no, you're not getting away with it this time, you bastard! Take that! The last words of the song about the Shaman flew off my lips, the goblin yelped and his frame went grey. At last!

Experience gained: +200 Experience, points

remaining until next level: 1001.

Skill increase:

+5% to Intellect. Total: 23%

Achievement earned!

The Defender of the Empire level 1 (19 Kartoss minion kills until the next level).

Achievement reward: damage dealt to all the members of the Kartoss Dark Empire is increased by 1%

You can look at the list of achievements in the character settings

With some difficulty I struggled through the branches to the goblin's body and picked up twenty gold, an ordinary bow and a dozen crooked arrows. My loot had no stat bonuses, so I decided to sell it to an NPC trader. I had little desire to be seen by the other players with this rubbish - just so they could have a laugh at my expense. Never mind - a couple of extra gold coins wouldn't burst my pockets. After I summoned a Healing Spirit on myself, increasing my Energy and Hit Points, I had time to think. I just couldn't get my head around what just happened: what was this pointy-eared and bad smelling character doing in the neighborhood of Beatwick? And, more importantly, why on earth was he so keen to hunt me down? From what I can remember of specific traits of dark goblins, they never hunt alone. Usually they form a pack - the larger the better. And now this naive mob decided to attack me one-on-one. This was all very strange.

I shook my head in disappointment that I hadn't come across any wolves today, got up and headed back to the village. I will try a different direction tomorrow: perhaps I'll bump into the pack there, even if the Headman did clearly say that the wolves were roaming around somewhere in this area. Well, we'll see, I guess. The main thing was to avoid having this quest becoming a dead weight. I was extremely reluctant to lose any reputation, which, as experience showed, my Shaman would have considerable difficulty in raising. I did, of course, have some hopes for the daily +5 to reputation that I was receiving thanks to the First Kill, but having to wait a couple of years...

I barely made two steps, when I heard a twig quietly snapping behind me. That couldn't be the goblin coming back to life, surely. I turned around. I closed my eyes, waited a couple of seconds and opened them again. Nothing changed. A stupid thought popped into my head that I should continue walking straight as if nothing happened. So much for my being upset at not being able to find the pack. There they are, the lot of them, with their level twenty leader, who was nearly as tall as me. Trying to do anything when you are surrounded by ten wolves is pretty pointless. One thing was comforting - the eyes of the wolves weren't red, a fact that stopped me in my initial impulse to summon a Lightning Spirit and bring down at least one mob before respawn. While the wolves were deciding what to do with me, I had to figure out how to get the heck out of here. I quickly glanced at the surrounding trees. That one I would never climb, the branches are too thick and close, that one is too small to take my weight, that one is full of some kind of thorns... Ah! We have a tree! Too bad it's twenty meters away. The wolves wouldn't let me get to it in time. After assessing the situation, I froze like a statue. How did that song go? "How sweet to be a Cloud, And not a floating... Shaman. Every little cloud, Gets kicked in the..." I didn't have time to think of where the cloud was going to get kicked. The leader of the pack came up to the body of the goblin, growled at it and then pierced me with a stare. I was having quite a day for staring contests with my canine brothers!

For the second time today the surrounding world went grey, becoming covered in mist, and I saw a short 'film sketch' potentially titled 'wolf genocide' with a mob of dark goblins in the starring role. A band of small green-skinned bastards, armed with bows, took over a mine (a Tin one, judging by the ore veins), which was home to a pack of wolves. At the time of the attack the wolf cubs were seized and put into cages. An attack group of twenty wolves tried get the cubs back, but failed. An enormous female, most likely the leader's mate, fought until the very last moment and, in the end, the wolves took her off the battlefield wounded with many arrows. Half of the pack died at the mine, without ever freeing a single cub. The show was over and the world returned to its normal state.

Quest available: 'Last Hope Step 1. Saving Grey Death.'

Step 1 description: Save Grey Death,

grievously wounded in the fight against the goblins. If the she-wolf dies, the leader would not survive his grief and will die together with her. If you complete the quest chain the wolves will leave the lands surrounding Beatwick forever. Quest chain class: Rare. Reward for completing Step 1: 250 Experience. Reward for the quest chain: Hidden. Penalty for failing/refusing the quest: None

'There are no quests in Beatwick', I chuckled as I accepted my third in two days. It's a pity that I wouldn't be able to carry out the Headman's assignment and get all those wolf tails. I had no desire whatsoever to attack the wolves now. I was ready to suffer through being ignored by the village residents for two months if completing a rare quest chain was at stake. I'll go and catch that Vagren if the worst came to worst. It was decided - I would help the wolves.

I followed them to a small cave where the wounded she-wolf was lying. Though you may as well have called her a giant hedgehog: almost twenty arrows were sticking out of her in all directions. How she managed to survive this remained a complete mystery to me, but her fitful breathing was a clear sign that she continued to fight for her life. The enormous wolf came up to her, licked her nose, squealed something and gave me an expectant look, as if to say 'Now you do the healing.'

Strange. Could a Rare quest be so easy? For a healer this was elementary- select, say the healing incantation and get the Experience. Maybe I made a mistake in choosing not to hunt the wolves - I might have had more to gain from helping the Headman. I just needed to summon the spirits five or six times to completely heal the pack leader's mate. And you get 900 Experience just for that? There must be a catch here, I can feel it!

I selected the she-wolf, summoned a Healing Spirit and immediately saw what the matter was. The summoning had an unexpected result. No, the Spirit did get summoned and duly entered the wolf, giving her part of its strength, but all of the Spirit's strength, focused on the healing, was transferred to me in the form of damage. All five hundred and five units of it. It was just as well that part of the damage got deducted by my resistance, but the situation was still far from ideal. The one small blessing was the lack of pain.

After restoring all my Hit Points, I took a moment to think. By the looks of it, the wolf had to be healed by non-standard means. But, in that case, which? What are we going to do with you, gorgeous? I have no bandages and the Spirits are bouncing off you. Should I feed some special herb to you? I read over the quest description one more time, but it didn't say a word about how to go about completing it. Nor did it contain a requirement stating that the quest could only be done by a healer. This meant that it could be accepted and completed even by Warriors and Hunters, who were unable to heal with anything other than bandages and potions.

Lost at what to do next, I stroked the heavily breathing she-wolf. Even if she was an Imitator, it was hard not to feel sorry for her. Especially that...

Please confirm that you have read the rules for completing the 'Last Hope' quest chain

The big sign 'Read the Rules' was beaconing and trying to catch my eye, so I pressed it right away. Let's see what rules they are talking about.

Access to the 'Hidden quests' section granted due to the possession of the 'Last Hope' quest chain

Attention! During the 'Saving Grey Death' quest sensory filters are turned off by 50%. Please note that during this quest you will be feeling real pain

Your reading this has been put on the record. Should you decide to take legal action, this will be taken into account during the examination of the complaint

Please confirm that you would like to continue with the quest 'Saving Grey Death'

Filters to be turned off? I just don't get it. What do sensory filters have to do with healing the she-wolf? All right, I agree. Keeping in mind that I can feel all 100% of the pain, perhaps a miracle would happen and for a while the pain I am able to feel would actually be reduced by half. That would be great. All right, I'm prepared to feel the pain, what else?

Damage taken. Hit Points reduced by 220:

450 (Arrow hit) - 230 (Physical defense). Total Hit Points: 420 of 680

  Update of the 'Saving Grey Death' quest. Step 1': 1 of 20 arrows pulled out

No way I'm going on with this! Breathing heavily, I got up from the floor, where I collapsed from the pain that suddenly hit me. Could my 100% sensory input have been topped up with another 50%? The pain was so great that my muscles all began to spasm! I quickly summoned a Healing Spirit on myself, caught my breath, sat next to the she-wolf and had a think. Or rather made it look like I was having a think, because other than the thought 'I will not be able to take twenty hits like this in a row', my head was completely empty. This was crazy. No way the developers would come up with a quest that could only be completed through that much pain. They just couldn't. There must be some kind of a trick to make the arrows slip out themselves. I just have to think harder.

The pack leader came up to me. He sniffed the arrow I took out and looked at me as if asking: "What's with the hold up? Get back to work already." How can I get back to work, you old grey, if it hurts so much? I can't take that many hits, I'm sorry. Although... Maybe it really hurts only the first time and it gets easier afterwards? Harnessing my willpower and realizing that I was beginning to look like a real masochist, I touched the wounded she-wolf.

Update of the quest 'Saving Grey Death. Step

1': 2 of 20 arrows pulled out

I was on the floor again when I came to myself. Like hell it's easier! I even blacked out! My Endurance ended up increasing by 20% - I'd get it to level twenty soon, if I keep taking the arrows out this way. A stalemate, by the looks of it: a pain either to give up or to keep going. And to keep going was way more than I could handle.

The brainstorm that I tried to summon up petered out without a result. I just didn't understand what I had to do and how. That's it, time for a rest! I should come out of the cave and get some fresh air - perhaps then some useful thought would strike me. I couldn't even make a wild guess at how to take out the rest of the arrows. Well, no. I could, of course, but I had very little desire to go down that path.

Searching the manual was no help either. First I was told that I could access the 'Hidden Quests' section, where I read that to complete the quest I had to heal the she-wolf, having pulled all the arrows out of her first. Did I rejoice too soon at gaining access to the manual? Even the hard-core trolls on the forums were silent about this quest. That's it, time to go for that fresh air and do some thinking.

Either the floor was slippery or my legs hadn't quite recovered from my previous arrow-pulling, but the unforeseen happened. When I was getting up, I lost my balance, which made me fall down again - on the wolf that was standing next to his mate. I muttered something like, 'sorry, old grey, I didn't mean it', and started to get up again. The wolf just snorted, but didn't growl. Knowing that I was crossing all bounds of impudence, I leaned on the wolf with one hand, while my other hand accidentally touched the she-wolf. Perhaps subconsciously I still wanted to complete this quest...

Update of the quest 'Saving Grey Death. Step 1': 3 of 20 arrows pulled out.
You transferred the received pain

The pack leader, whom I was leaning on, yelped in surprise and jumped aside. Just as well that he decided not to attack, I'm just not ready to battle a wolf pack here and now. But that doesn't matter right this second. What does is that I'm already holding three arrows out of twenty.

I summoned a Healing Spirit on the leader, and gestured him to a place next to me. No slacking off now. I'm not going to do all the work for him.

After the eighth arrow the pack leader was done. Each time he jumped aside, but proudly came back, until, after the eighth hit, he simply lost consciousness. At least he was breathing - I was beginning to worry I had left the pack without a head. Now just ten arrows needed to be pulled out, but where would I get another volunteer?

As if by magic, an ordinary wolf wandered into the cave. 'I wonder, would the transfer work on them as well?' The wolf came up to me, sniffed the unconscious leader and then stared at me. So, shall we try it? I touched the wolf and then the wounded she-wolf. It worked! Though the wolf was finished after just one arrow. He yelped, jumped aside, his legs gave way and he slumped to the ground. I healed him, just in case, and left the cave in search of a new victim. And why not? These weren't real wolves, but Imitators, let them suffer for their leader. It's not like I should be the one doing all the work.

I had to pull out the last arrow by myself. I ran out of wolves in the pack. I did not dare invite the she-wolves, who had less Hit Points than the damage caused by the arrow. They were women, after all, even if they did have tails: how could you put them in harm's way? So, I had to simply take the pain.

Update of the quest 'Saving Grey Death. Step 1': 20 of 20 arrows pulled out.

Quest completed. Experience gained: +250 Experience, points remaining until next level: 751

After I got up from the ground, where I fell when the pain hit, I got my breath back and summoned three Healing Spirits on the she-wolf. Now I could consider the quest completed. Grey Death is alive. She opened her eyes, lifted her head, looked around and immediately jumped to her feet. I did not quite understand what happened next. First an angry growl shook the cave. All the wolves came to themselves and jumped up. Then the she-wolf's eyes began to go blood-red and she lunged at me. At the same time the pack leader tried to jump in front of her. She crashed into me, taking off half of my Hit Points, but immediately her mate flew at her, pulling her off me and not allowing her to finish me off, while the rest of the pack ran from the cave, out of harm's way.

The she-wolf got up again and was about to attack me, but the pack leader stood in her way. The wolves had a growl-chat between themselves, with the tone of her growl being higher and accusing, and his calm and reasonable. Just like an experienced husband talking to a wife who's having a bad day. I felt myself out of place in their family dispute and tried to quietly follow the example of the rest of the pack and sneak out of the cave, but then a message popped in front of me:

Quest available: 'Last Hope Step 2. Freeing the wolf cubs'

Step 2 description: Free 10 wolf cubs taken prisoner by the dark goblins. If you complete the quest chain the wolves will leave the lands surrounding Beatwick forever. Quest chain class: Rare. Reward for completing Step 2: 550 Experience. Reward for the quest chain: Hidden. Penalty for failing/refusing the quest: None

Both wolves went quiet and stared at me. Both. Are they waiting for me to make a decision? Of course I'll accept the second Step. I would be getting more experience from it and would do some leveling up fighting the goblins. I just had to get an idea of where they were.

"Settled down now? Time to show me where those green bastards set up camp," I said at last. In normal life saying something like this would sound ridiculous, but Barliona is not the real world and here even wolves, if the occasion really calls for it, could easily have a chat with you. The pack leader growled something in reply, came out of the cave and trotted off in the direction of the forest.

I gathered some green branches, made something resembling a shrub out of them and saw a fairly predictable message:

Attention, a new stat has become available to your character: Stealth. Stealth allows you to camouflage yourself in your surroundings. You become difficult to see both for mobs and other players. Once you reach the maximum level of stealth it will be almost impossible to spot you. There is some chance that you would be able to completely drop out of combat

Do you accept? Attention, you will not be able to remove an accepted stat!

If I was still playing my Hunter I'd go for this stat in the blink of an eye! I liked roaming around Malabar forests alone, so I had to run away from mobs quite often. Having this stat would have meant quite a different ending to my trip to Kartoss. But by the time I started to read up on the advice of veteran raiders, I managed to reach level 33 and fill up all four of my free stat slots – though, admittedly, the stats I picked were also quite useful for a Hunter. I had no desire to reroll my character, so I camouflaged myself by using special elixirs. Their property of running out both in terms of time and supply was something I learned in a hands-on fashion - at the most inappropriate moment. Well, no point digging up the past. But I would not be picking Stealth for my Shaman - the last slot had to be filled by something focused on attack. All my stats were either crafting or defense-based. I could end up with a poorly balanced build if I wasn't careful.

After disguising myself as a piece of shrubbery, I was lying just a few steps from the edge of the mine, which was, in fact, a great big hole. However, smoking the goblins out of this hole was not going to be a simple matter. Those guys dug themselves in quite well - the only entrance to the mine was closed by enormous wooden gates and from below spikes were stuck into the ground all along the perimeter, preventing you from simply rolling in. Four hastily-made wooden watch towers stood around the mine boundary, with two lookouts in each - level thirty goblin archers. About a dozen green-skins got on with the everyday task of gathering Tin Ore. A separate tent, standing right in the centre of the mine, belonged to some big boss, since its entrance was guarded by a warrior. Near the tent there were about ten cages with the squealing cubs inside. It was just as well that we didn't take the she-wolf with us - she'd run right to them and try to free them. A few meters from the cages lay the bodies of the ten dead wolves. The goblins didn't even bother clearing them away - they'd disappear by themselves in a couple of days. I suppose it was possible to take the tails off them, which I needed for the quest. At least I'll get it half done: perhaps the Headman would accept it, even without Grey Death's tail. By the way, I first thought that to be the name of the pack leader, but the truth turned out to be quite different.

I immediately discarded the idea of a heroic surprise attack on the mine and systematic clearing out of the goblins. The archers on the towers wouldn't let us get even close to the gates and jumping down on the spikes was a guaranteed respawn. So, once again, I had to do everything from ass backwards.

I crawled back to the forest, took off the shrub camouflage and went to read the manual. What did it say about dark goblins?

A Dark Goblin. A humanoid race that lives only in the Kartoss Dark Empire. It is one of the few races that cannot be chosen by players. Race characteristics: +(Level) to Agility, reduced Hit Points and Strength. When they see an orc female, they completely lose their head and do everything in their power to seduce her. The appearance of a Dark Goblin is provided in the illustration.

I didn't bother looking at the pictures of Dark Goblins, and immediately started to search for the appearance of an orc female. I found it. Oh boy! How could this two-meter green hulk with bulging muscles and a bone pieced through the nose be the object of passion for the meter-high pointy-eared munchkins?

It's a pity that I don't have any friends with orc characters or I'd ask them to help me seduce this green rabble. As it stands, I might as well be painting myself green... Paint!

A light bulb lit above my head! There is only one trader in Beatwick and although he doesn't have that many wares, he must have some green paint. It's a completely standard item. I would borrow or buy a skirt off Tisha. I'd pad out all the right parts with dead grass, paint myself the right color and would look just like a female orc from afar. A wig would come in handy too. That's it, then. I would return to Beatwick and buy everything I would need.

Having assured the wolves that I would return very soon, I ran back to the village. To my surprise the trader didn't have any green paint. I prepared myself for being completely disappointed, but the trader suggested that I should approach the merchant that came to the village just a couple of hours ago. I ran as fast as I could to the central square, where a large crowd of people had already gathered.

The first thing I did when I got to the merchant was sell all the junk made up of the skins, tails, meat and claws. I had to clear out my bags, and my Greed Toad wouldn't allow me to simply throw away even useless things. After giving it some thought I added the goblin's bow and arrows to the pile. The merchant, a dwarf judging by his personality, but a human by his outward appearance, quickly fingered through my pile, seeming to barely give it a thought, paused for a couple of seconds over the bow and arrows, even lifting his eyebrows in surprise. Judging by his reaction he knew very well who dropped such unusual items.

"Four gold," he said finally, "there is absolutely nothing of use to me here – I'll have to resell it all. Is that all right with you?"

I nodded, agreeing to the price.

"Do you wish to buy anything?"

"I do. I need green paint, a lady's leather skirt, a lady's leather tunic, a dark wig with long hair and a portal to Farstead," I fired out in one go. I had no time for any extra politeness at this point.

"The paint costs two coppers," said the merchant, entirely unsurprised at my strange request. "The tunic and skirt – two gold each, the wig – twenty, and the portal to Farstead - a thousand gold. Payment upfront, I don't do credit."

Instead of shocking the merchant with my request, it was my turn to be surprised. Where would an ordinary merchant get all these things? All right, the paint and the clothes I understand. These are saleable goods that many would buy. A wig, willy-nilly might also be lumped in with saleable goods, but a portal scroll – certainly not! A thousand gold for players and NPCs under level forty is really a lot of money. Until you are able to go through Dungeons, money is usually in short supply. The quests handed out by NPCs bring little profit and low level items are hard to sell. As if reading my mind (or just seeing the surprised expression on my face) the merchant laughed:

"Don't worry, there isn't a catch. It really is a scroll of teleportation to Farstead. I bought it long ago for myself, as a backup in case of a bandit attack. I've been riding around with it for two years now and never had the need to use it. I'm even beginning to regret investing so much money into it. I'm selling it almost at the asking price - the mage sold it to me for nine hundred and fifty gold, so my mark-up is quite small."

"Fifty gold a small mark-up? Are you trying to ruin me?" I recovered from the initial shock and started to bargain furiously. Those who knew me before prison would have never believed that a quiet and modest programmer of security systems, always buying things for the price asked by the merchants, would fight so hard for each copper. And I would, as well! My Trade stat says I must. "Take off forty gold and I'll take it straight away."

"Ah, a grown man who still believes in fairy tales about discount!" The NPC wouldn't give in. Of course it wouldn't since it was programmed to rip off players as much as possible - the maximum cost of the item plus a half. Players are obliged and must spend money in Barliona, rather than take it out into the real world. "The most I'm prepared to reduce it by is five gold. Just think about it, I kept the scroll safe all this time - in the rain keeping it dryer than myself. Did I suffer all these hardships just to make a profit of some measly ten gold? Forty five and not a copper less!"

It took me five minutes to bring the price of the scroll to nine hundred and seventy gold. The crowd that formed around us started to hand out advice on how to get the wily merchant to stop being so tight. And when it was the merchant's turn, they'd advise him not to make a deal with such a greedy buyer. Such good people lived in Beatwick, so sympathetic and neighborly. I'd be quite happy never to have set my eyes on them.

After I paid the needed total and increased my Trade by a whole level, bringing it now to 7, I was about to leave, but remembered the strange Spider Eye. I had to identify it anyway and that wasn't something I could do by myself. Perhaps the merchant would manage it.

"Dear Sir, I also have this thing here, would you mind having a look? Is this in any way useful?" I asked, taking out the eye, horrible and unpleasant to the touch, and handing it to the merchant who suddenly became as still as a statue. Dumbfounded, he looked at the item in my hand and a couple of seconds later a message flashed in front of me:

Item identified: The Eye of the Dark Widow. Attention! The owner of the item has access to a quest. Do you wish to look at the description?

I became almost a mirror of the merchant's frozen stance. A quest obtained from an item could mean only one thing: I had in my possession a way to another Legend of Barliona.

I swallowed with effort and read the quest description:

The Eye of the Dark Widow. Description: a hundred thousand years ago, before humans appeared in Barliona, the world was ruled by cruel

and capricious Tarantula Lords, who subdued all other races with their power. After a cataclysm the Tarantula Lords vanished, and all the races tried to wipe the thousands of years of Tarantula yoke from their memory, letting them be entirely forgotten. But in the depths of the Free Lands there still exists a cult worshipping these Lords, and its Patriarch dreams of bringing back the Tarantulas and submerging the world in fear and pain. Stop them or it will be too late. Go to the Emperor for further instructions. Quest type: Legendary. Level requirements: 100+. Group requirements: 20+ participants. Reward: hidden

Twenty level hundred players, who will need to make their way deep into the Free Lands and bring down some Patriarch... For all the esteem in which I hold my dear self, organizing a raid like this is beyond me - at least at this point in time. But that's no reason to throw away such an object! I turned the Eye over in my hand for a little while and put it back in the bag. That's right, I might make some use of it yet.

"Five thousand now and another forty in a week's time," the words of the trader, who seemed to regain his faculties, completely stunned me. Usually such things are only in use among the players and are little more than an inventory item for NPCs. But here was forty-five thousand gold on offer! And that's despite my red band and the fact that an NPC would automatically try to rip me off as much as possible. I don't think so. First I would have to find out more about the Eye and who the Tarantula Lords were and only then would I make a decision.

"No, thank you. I am not going to sell the Eye right now."

"Ninety thousand gold. Tomorrow," by the looks of it the trader decided to floor me with this one. What was it about this thing? I went to the manual and made a search for the item's name. Nothing. At all. A search in the forums also brought zero results. Could it be the same as with a quest chain, where you wouldn't be allowed into the hidden help area until you accepted the quest? Most probably. But I cannot accept the quest now. A hundred levels are, after all, a hundred levels. It would be laughable to even approach the Eye with my current fourteen levels.

"No, thank you. I will not sell the Eye even for two hundred thousand," judging by the long face of the trader his third offer was probably going to be in this area. When I get to Anhurs and create my own Clan, it should become clearer what to do with the Eye. It cannot disappear from the bag since it's not a Legendary item, so there it can stay.

I left the disappointed merchant, who immediately started to pack up shop to the frustration of the locals, and headed back to the forest. The counter measuring my forty eight hours spent outside the village was reset, so I again had two days to rescue the wolf cubs and kick some goblin ass.

The wolves were still sitting in the place where I left them - behind the shrubs before the wooden gates of the mine. If that's how they've been guarding the entrance before, how did a lone goblin manage to make his way outside? There wasn't another exit, as far as I remember, and it wasn't possible to climb out of the pit. Well, who knows, maybe even wolves need to sleep...

Having taken the necessary items out of the bag, I commenced my metamorphosis. At first I went radically green. I painted my arms, face, legs and in general anything that may show from under the skirt and tunic. The wolves stared at this outrage full of incomprehension. From an ordinary human being the Shaman was turning into a green paint covered God-knows-what. One thing was comforting: there were no witnesses – it's not like the wolves were going to tell anyone of my loss of dignity. The leather tunic left enough space for me to stuff plenty of grass in the relevant places, giving me a truly feminine appearance. When I put on the skirt and the wig, the pack leader couldn't help snorting. Yeah, I'll make a note to kick the leader's grey hairy behind once we get rid of all the goblins.

The main thing was for my disguise to work or all my efforts would have been in vain. Before heading off to conquer the pointy-eared minions, I went to the nearby stream and looked at my reflection. It was really something! I did a great job of making myself look truly ugly: green, scary and black haired. A real orc. But something was still lacking. I wrinkled my brow, as the image remained incomplete. Yes, I was green, in a skirt, with a Mallet in my hand, but some small detail was missing. The goblins wouldn't fall for me as I am, I was damn certain. A quiet growl made me turn around. Grey Death, if I correctly understood that was the name of the she-wolf, brought me a small bone in her teeth. That it! The orc-woman in the picture had a bone sticking out of her nose. I tore off a couple of hairs from the wig and used them to tie the bone in place. Now the look was complete. If I didn't manage to seduce anyone looking like this, I understand nothing of goblin notions of beauty. One thing made me nervous – the she-wolf kept snorting, as if she was laughing at me. That's fine, keep laughing, I'll find a way to get my own back.

I gathered my wits about me, selected one of the archers on the closest tower and stepped out of the bushes. Now was the moment of truth. The hidden pack of wolves, ready to attack the goblins, stayed in the grass. Some time went by, but the little buggers didn't look like they were going to do anything. Did they just completely fail to spot me or something? All right then, let's give them a hand. I filled my lungs with air and whistled, carefully watching the status of the goblin. If he became aggressive straight away, my idea had fallen through. All that careful paint application would've been for nothing.

A couple of seconds went by, but the goblins were not turning red. I no longer had any doubts that they saw me: both archers nearly jumped over the railing, trying to get a better look at the beauty that had come to pay them a visit. Suddenly the goblin that I kept selected gained a buff in the form of a heart: 'Adoration'. He threw down the bow and started to climb down from the tower, leaping over steps. The other one wasn't far behind. Did it work then? I started to take slow steps towards the forest and the protection of the wolf attack force. The love-struck goblins opened the gates and sped in my direction. Yup, those guys were ready - completely losing their heads as they ran towards me, blowing me kisses on the way. How disgusting. One of the lover boys jumped to a shrub behind which a wolf was sitting and tore off a few branches. Were they going to bring me flowers as well? Cool, I think I'd like that... Blagh! What's got into me! I have to take the goblins deeper into the forest, where their screams wouldn't be heard. I hurried away from the mine. Immediately the goblin that I selected acquired a second buff: 'Fervour', again in the form of a heart. Oops. So that's dating orc-style then, eh? Great. I ran off about two hundred meters from the mine and turned towards the goblins, who were rushing to get their hands on the orc beauty. Damn! I didn't think things through when I put my ambush right on the edge of the forest. The wolves were shifting in the shadows either side of us and hurrying to take their new places for the attack, but weren't quite going to make it. Goblins were going to get to me first. Bugger it! I can't summon any spirits, because I'll get out of character and this duo would wipe me out in the blink of an eye. Even if their stats are focused on Agility, I was no match for their 30 levels at my level 14. Killing me would be a walk in the park. Gripping my Mallet, I decided to use that to fend them off until the pack got here. I only needed half a minute or so.

The goblin flew up to me, arms outstretched, and tried to catch me in his embrace, but got hit by the Mallet straight on the nose. He staggered back and cried out and acquired a third heart-shaped buff: 'Flirting'. A couple of moments later all three buffs merged into one big heart: 'Love'. So there you have it. At least someone loves me in this game. Turning around to his rival, the goblin shouted:

"Gawe to heel, you spawn of a sklix. Zis wommun iz mine!"

"Fir wommun laik zis I keen dips yoor mugs in da dungs! I wunt her too!" shouted the second. I had no time to be surprised before I saw a message:

Attention! A member of the Kartoss Dark Empire has fallen in love with you! To make it possible for the lovers to understand each other the game administration grants you the opportunity to understand and speak the language of dark goblins. Have a pleasant game!

You have learned a new language: 'Dark Goblin'

Achievement earned!

'Romeo and Juliet' level 1 (19 seductions of the members of the Dark Empire until the next level)

Achievement reward: the chance that you can get a member of the Dark Empire to fall in love with you is increased by 1%

You can look at the list of achievements in the character settings

Bloody hell! I've always dreamt of gaining such an important and almost unattainable achievement. Now the main thing was not to let anyone know that I had it. Generally, learning the language of the Dark Empire is not that hard - you just have to go to the library and spend a couple of months there, studying texts and speaking with a Guardian. After a certain amount of time the Guardian would offer you a book and teach you one of the hundred languages of our continent. Any one you'd like - from the widespread orcish to the rare language of the kobolds. But I had no idea that you could gain a language through such a 'gift'.

The goblins started to squabble about which of them was the better match for me. They had already switched from words to fists when my wolf attack force arrived. The fight was short, but unusual. The wolves tore into the goblins, but the latter didn't even try to put up a fight. With huge, tear-filled eyes they looked at me as her who betrayed all their hopes... Err... I mean him, rather! To hell with all this! Now I'm the one getting confused.

Experience gained: +400 Experience; points remaining until next level: 351

From each goblin I got two gold and a pair of worn trousers. They had neither weapons nor potions. Well, never mind. The main thing was that we've found a harmless enough way of defeating the goblins. And if

I had to sway some hips and batter some eyelashes - once again I'd say that if there were no witnesses, it never happened. These thoughts were going through my head as I went for the next group of 'Romeos'...

The wolves were clearly up to something. Until I hit the goblin with the Mallet, not one of those mongrels attacked the pair that was hurrying after me. What was the point of leaving them in an ambush? Just so they can snigger and watch me be chased by a crowd of admirers? In any case, it was finished now - all the four towers were free, the gates were open and only the ten or so workers, the warrior and the commander remained. I was wary of the last two. The warrior would have a boosted Strength stat, but the boss was an unknown. He might even turn out to be a wizard. I had to be careful.

Thanks to the 'Romeos' I raised myself up to level fifteen, but decided against allocating the free stat points. The higher a particular stat was, the harder it was to level it up in a normal way. No, I can wait it out and not spend them until I absolutely have to.

By the way, since we're talking about stats, I decided to get to the bottom of what bonuses Endurance gave me. It was good that it reduced the level of pain I felt, but by the looks of it Endurance also had to reduce the amount of damage I sustained. However, not a single message that came up said anything about damage being reduced in any way on account of Endurance. Did it have to be activated in some way then? What did the help section say?

Endurance determines a player's ability to ignore any damage from an opponent for (Endurance /10) %. This is calculated and deducted from any incoming damage automatically, before the analysis of blocking, dodge or damage reduction from defense.

Now I understood why I didn't see Endurance in the messages. A message 'sustained XXX damage' shows the harm caused already after it's been reduced on account of Endurance. In my case that was by 1.1%. Not much, of course, but sometimes even such margin may allow you to stay alive.

I gathered the wolves into one attack formation and headed towards the mine. Enough goblins remained there to give us a fair amount of trouble.

"The Mastermun came! The Mastermun came!" all ten goblins threw their picks to the ground, fell on their knees and started to kowtow to me all as one. Did they really take me for their master? What the heck am I going to do with them? I selected one of the goblins and looked at his properties. Goblin. Just a goblin, totally lacking the 'dark' adjective. I took a better look at the closest one and saw a collar on him. Slaves! There were a dozen slaves here gathering the ore.

"Aarrrgghhh!" shouted the warrior guarding the tent and ran at me. "You no wommun! You dress-crossing spy! Enemies in the camp!"

Level thirty. A close combat fighter, being a warrior and all, was running towards me, waving his yatagan around. Think again, wise guy! I can run too. However, unlike an archer, I can summon Spirits as well. The wolves again froze like statues, reluctant to be the first to join the fight. I can live with that - I'll down this one myself and they can look out for the boss joining the fray. Usually one of those comes part and parcel with a long and hard fight.

I brought down the warrior quite quickly: ten Lightning Spirits and I was done. The wolves did the right thing to keep away from him - he was running around like crazy, waving his yatagans left and right. He could have easily hit someone.

Then there was only the tent and the NPC workers, who weren't even thinking of getting up from the ground. Strange: there was so much noise, but no-one came out from the tent. It's not like the boss is asleep, is it? Well, time to wake him up then.

I came up to the tent and started banging on the roof, ready to jump away if I needed to. Silence. Gathering up my courage, I lifted the flap and looked inside. There was no-one there. This simply can't be! This is the final location where the boss should be found! I looked around the tent and noticed some strange movement in a small pile of blankets. Aha! He hid himself!

I threw off the blankets and stared at a small, pot-bellied goblin, covered in gold chains and rings and wearing a really expensive-looking suit. Seeing that he was discovered, the goblin sat down, crossed his arms on top of his stomach and started speaking in broken common:

"You get gold, I you not see."

"My understands and speaks your tongue," I

replied in Goblin. It was strange and I had to say it word by word, but it was still much better than that messed-up common.

"Oooh! A tall guest, as a beauty disguised is speaking our language in! Or our tall guest really a beauty is?" the emboldened goblin had the 'Adoration' buff fading in and out next to him. Just what I need - this one getting all lovestruck with me too. I dragged the wig off my head and untied the bone. There. I could even breathe more easily now. The goblin was noticeably saddened. Naturally: when Miss World turns into an ugly toad in the blink of an eye, it's a real tragedy!

Miss World. I even sighed. Each year a beauty contest is held in Barliona. One necessary condition is that the participant's appearance must correspond to their real appearance. For three years in a row the title of Miss Malabar was given to paladin Anastaria. She was a very beautiful girl. Endless poems have been dedicated to her and many players travelled to Anhurs, the Empire's capital, just for a chance to catch a glimpse of her. I came across her only once or rather just saw her about a hundred meters away. I don't know what stat she had leveled up in, but it completely knocks you off your feet. Brrr. At the same time she is the deputy of Hellfire from the Phoenix clan and the second most high-level player in the Empire, as well as the author of nearly all the boss manuals. She is someone who looks at the results of your gameplay, and not at bells and whistles like money or presents. She isn't interested in them... I pushed away my dreams into the background and focused on the goblin. By this time a piece of roast meat had found its way into his hands and he was gobbling it down with involved concentration, as if his being attacked and taken prisoner never happened.

"Ten gold prepared am to pay you I," he finally deigned to speak to me after he finished chewing the meat. "To work off the loss of my warriors must. For Magister ore gathering we are behind. Mine ore have you to."

Quest available...

I didn't even look at what quest was available to me. I quickly stepped over to the cheeky undersized boss and hit him with the Mallet between the eyes. A couple of times just to be sure. The goblin slumped to the ground, but was still alive - his Life Bar was barely dented, but he acquired a 2-hour buff 'Stunned'. That's better. Now I had to look around the tent and see what we had here or my inner Hoarding Hamster would never forgive me. What the...?

Quest available: 'Head of the Green Raiders'
Description: You have captured the head of the Kartoss Dark Empire infiltrators. Take him to the nearest town and hand him over to the person in charge. Quest type: Rare. Reward: +400 to Reputation with the Malabar Empire, +500 Experience, +30 Silver coins, a Rare item from the town stores. Penalty for failing/refusing the quest:

-400 to Reputation with the Malabar Empire

Oh! Of course I'll accept it. Now I knew what to do with this guy. Also, he mentioned a rather interesting position: a Magister. The Dark Empire had the same division of ranks as Malabar. If Malabar had an Emperor, four Advisors and twenty Heralds, Kartoss had the Dark Lord, four Masters and twenty Magisters. Heralds and Magisters could teleport to any point they wished within the bounds of their respective Empires - without limits. However, they were seen by the players as often as the Emperor himself. Which means hardly ever. So, this little pot-bellied creature was given an assignment by none other than a Magister. Great! This meant that he would make a very valuable prisoner. It was an opportunity to get an additional bonus from Malabar. I absolutely had to deliver him and it was just as well that a portal to Farstead was already in my bag. Two beings could walk through it easily enough.

After tearing up a blanket, I tied up the boss, in case he suddenly woke up. Two hours is plenty of time, but it's best to play it safe. And now to the looting and pillaging.

A small chest immediately caught my eye. It was finely carved, with intricate symbols on its sides. It also had one small but really unpleasant feature - a broken key was sticking out of the keyhole. Damn. The lid was locked - it looked like the goblin had no time to open it. He was in too much of a hurry when I started to bang on top of the tent. Annoyed, I kicked the immobilized goblin. Just because. Why did he have to be in such a hurry? Didn't he know that I was dropping by for a visit? What should I do now? I couldn't leave the chest behind, my Greed Toad would strangle me, but taking it with me was out of the question. It wasn't loot, but part of the scenery: if you took it out of the tent, it would simply disappear, along with all its contents. I had to stop thinking and start acting. Now then... I wondered what's more impressive - a cannonball that could blast through anything or a wall through which nothing could break? Or, rather, the Mallet or a closed lid? No better time to find out. I put the chest on the side and started to hit it. 'Might makes right' - I learned that one while still a child. I could see no other 'might' at my disposal, so a minute later the lid fell to the floor with a subdued bang and I stared at the loot that fell out of it. Not bad. Not bad at all! Looks like I struck lucky! There was a small pile of gold. Wow! Three thousand gold, which were immediately reduced by 30%. Five scrolls of teleportation, to Kartoss, by the looks of it. I'll save them for later: when I increase my level they'd come in handy for teleporting to the Dark Empire. Or I could sell them at an auction - at about a hundred thousand each. I took two gold rings off the goblin with a +10 to Agility and a neck-chain with +12 to Stamina. That was some boon! If ordinary rings with a +5 stat bonus cost upwards of 100 gold, a ring with +10 could cost around five thousand! I'd leave the chain for myself though. Shame as it was to admit it, it was better than my own, even if I wouldn't be able to wear it until I gain 15 more levels. It could only be used by someone with level 30. On the second thought, I'd sell it as well. I urgently had to start leveling up my Jewelcraft. I had the recipes, but, as it turned out, I was seriously short of time. The small chest also yielded something that made me more happy than anything else - a map of our continent. In general, maps had this interesting feature in Barliona - they could scale up, as needed. For example, if I had to look at the continent as a whole, the map would take one scale and if I wanted to look just at Malabar, it would become a different scale. It would have another scale for Farstead and another for Beatwick. This only worked, however, if the needed area was actually on the map. If it wasn't there, the map would show nothing, so details either had to be bought or you had to add them to the map yourself if you had the Cartographer profession. I quickly glanced at the map that I got off the goblin. It had twenty percent of discovered terrain in Kartoss, one percent in Malabar and one percent in the Free Lands. I rubbed my face in astonishment, not believing what I saw. Twenty percent of the Kartoss Empire map could mean only one thing - I could look forward to a long and happy life! I could rip so much money from the players for a copy of this map that even thirty percent, which was deducted from me by the Corporation, would seem like small change. As it stands, players usually venture into Kartoss without any maps, as those are extremely hard to get. Yes, my friendship with the wolves sure brought me luck!

The tent contained nothing else - that is, nothing else that was there for the taking. There were, of course, cushions, blankets, a small chest and many small objects. There was the tent itself, as well. But none of this could be taken. I could put any of this in the bag for a couple of seconds, until the items disappeared. As soon as I send the goblin to Farstead, the tent itself will disappear as if it never existed. It's a pity and a shame, but it's all right. Everyone had gotten used to this by now.

I put the wig back on, slung the goblin across my shoulder and came out of the tent. The wolves were circling the cages with the wolf cubs, unable to open them with their paws. The cheered up little wolves squealed with joy, jumping around the cages in expectation of reuniting with their parents. The ordinary goblins never bothered to get up from the ground. Right, I had to decide what to do with them. I couldn't just leave them here.

I threw the boss down on the ground and undid the wire that held the cages together. That's it - Step 2 is finished.

'Freeing the Wolf Cubs' quest completed. Experience gained: +550 Experience, points remaining until next level: 1.

Step 3 of the 'Last Hope' quest chain will become available in six days' time. You will get this quest automatically.

Wow! This quest could be connected with something. Six days... The time when the Vagren comes out... Is the 'Last Hope' connected to the

Beatwick Vagren? What does the manual say? It's as silent as the grave. Damn. It's a real pain when you can't look at normal forums, not moderated by the Corporation representatives...

I had some hope of being able to carry out at least half of the Headman's quest. I went through the ten previously killed wolves. As soon as I touched their bodies, they immediately disappeared, leaving behind a tail. Ten bodies - ten tails. Now I was only lacking the tail of the Grey Death to finish the quest. I looked at the she-wolf's tail thoughtfully. I couldn't help wondering if they really were that clever - as soon as she saw that I was holding the wolf tails in my hands and stealing glances at her, she turned her back to me and a moment later was running as fast as she could from the mine. The wolf cubs ran after her. They were followed by the ordinary wolves, with only the pack leader staying behind. He came up to the goblins, who were lying down on the faces, snorted and ran after the pack. That's it. Now I had to decide what to do with the ten literally floored goblins.

"Now - you get up! No time for lying about!" I shouted in Goblin. The green workers immediately jumped up and formed a neat line - in the order of height.

"So, let's get to the bottom of this. Who's in charge here?"

"You are, mastermun," said one goblin and all ten of them again fell to their knees.

"I know that. Who's in charge among the rest of you? Who do I speak to?"

"That me, mastermun, me you talk to," replied the same goblin.

"Great. Then I have a question. What are you doing here?"

"We mining ore, mastermun."

"I see, I asked the question wrongly. Why were you mining ore?"

"Our old mastermun ordered us to," the goblin nodded towards my prisoner.

"And where do you put the gathered ore?"

"We near the tent put it. Today our former boss sent ore off. No mind, we gather more. New mastermun will happy be. Will new mastermun take us?"

Attention! You may hire a work team of resource-gathering goblins. Conditions: you must provide the goblins with daily food and daily working wage - 1 silver coin. Level of goblins is determined by player character level. Level of all resource-gathering professions is determined by player character level.

Wow! Ten virtually free bodies to provide me with resources that I so sorely need. The only drawback was that this was a team focused on gathering, not production. I did, however, get it for nothing. In Anhurs you can hire various work teams - for gathering, production or research. But their cost was extortionate and the workers frequently died, since you had to feed them and otherwise look after them. If you forgot to feed them for a day - you were left without a work team.

My hunter never had a work team of his own, because I did not log into the game every day, but since I have such a major stint of time online, I had to make use of the opportunity.

"I'll take you on. From now on, I'm your new boss."

Achievement earned!

Supervisor level 1 (hiring 4 work teams until the next level)

Achievement reward: the work team's working speed is increased by 5%

You can look at the list of achievements in the character settings

"Have you already eaten today?" seeing the vigorously nodding goblin mugs, I refined the question: "How many days' food supply do you have?"

"Five days, mastermun. Former mastermun a big vat cooked for us, we not eat it all yet," hearing this came as a big relief. I planned to teleport to Farstead right away to turn in the boss, but leaving without first resolving the food situation of my new workers wasn't an option.

"Then this is your job for the week. You mine the ore and don't mind the wolves, they won't touch you. Put the ore here," I pointed to a small hollow in the ground. "In two days Shaman Mahan will come and will say a password 'Blah-Boom'. You obey him like you do me, understood?" the goblins quickly nodded and I continued: "Why are you loitering here? Off to work with you!"

In a split second they were gone – they grabbed their picks, spreading throughout the mine, and I went around it gathering everything dropped by the 'Romeos' when they ran off after their 'Juliet'. After me, that is. I walked some distance away, but still managed to catch the goblins whispering amongst themselves:

"New mastermun, she a real beauty! All green and in a skirt, her bust bigger than my head! Pity no bone in nose, but that fine - it grow in time."

CHAPTER THREE
FARSTEAD

"*'M GATHERING A PARTY FOR THE RORTUS DUNGEON! Need healers and a tank!"*
"*WTS 40 Wolf Pelts! Just 20 gold each!"*
"*WTB a lvl 20 Warrior sword with a bonus to STR!"*

Farstead welcomed me with familiar town buzz. In this respect it was no different from all the other standard towns in Barliona, from which only Anhurs really stood out. Similar-looking two-story stone houses, gray walls, from which here and there hung the shingles of merchants or various profession trainers. There was a cobbled street, an overturned cart, half-drowned in a haystack (probably a favorite playground for the local kids), and crowds of people, both players and NPCs, hurrying in every direction. Although there weren't exactly hoards of players around, they were making a great din. If you were to believe the manuals, the Krong province was meant for players between level 20 and 40, so looking for good offers on items or groups would be a waste of time here. Savvy players under level 50 level up by themselves or in special clan locations and only visit a town for the Bank, the Dating House, for traders or profession trainers. Those now shouting about forming groups for Dungeons or buying low-level gear are... Let's put it this way, such players are usually called 'noobs'. That sums it up. There's little joy in ending up in the same group with a beginner tank or healer: "Oh, I didn't manage to select you as a target and so couldn't heal you in time. Why didn't you heal yourself with bandages?", "Oooh, look at that cute Rat, let's not kill it", "Aaahhh! I'm being attacked! I'm leaving the group!", "Do you kids want daddy to show you how to use them pointy things?"... A couple of times I was careless enough to end up in a group with such players and had very little desire to repeat that experience. They never read any manuals or forums, but are more bigheaded and arrogant than the elves.

The portal threw me out practically in the middle to the main town square. Why was it the main one? Because it contained the local government headquarters and a Barliona Bank branch.

Generally speaking, the Bank of Barliona is really something else. As if playing a joke on real banks, the Barliona version resembles a small three-meter-high gazebo surrounded by small trees. There are no thick walls or armies of guards. There is no need for them, because when entering the gazebo each player ends up in a separate dimension, a personal room of sorts. In each room there is a small table with a gremlin sitting behind it, always wearing black brassards, and constantly writing something. You could give him gold to be deposited and he is the one to retrieve it on withdrawal and hand it over to its owner. The gremlin receives requests for credit or for expansion of your personal room - its initial modest size meant that it wasn't ideal for storing all your resources. The only item storage limitation the Banks had was that you couldn't store more than ten items of the same class in them. This meant that you couldn't save up more than ten Legendary or ten Epic items and so on. The Bank had no intention of turning into a warehouse. Clans kept all the accumulated riches inside their own castles, kept secure by guards and by protective spells. There were even special clans dedicated to the production of 'wards' and clans that focused on breaking through these 'wards'. Same as anywhere, really. I had little to save for the rainy day other than the Warrior Orc figurines. I was going to the Bank for a different reason - I had to withdraw my Hunter items. Extra money and gear, even if focused on Agility, would come in handy. Before I got there some words stood out from the general buzz and caught my ear.

"Hey, you know what I read on the Phoenix forum yesterday? They are prepared to pay a hundred grand in gold for information about the Jeweler who created the Karmadont Chess Pieces!" Overhearing the conversation between two dwarf players made me throw my prisoner to the ground, pretend that I was stretching my stiff shoulders and generally look like I was simply passing by and not paying any attention to anyone around me. In actual fact I turned into one big ear.

"What were you doing over there?"

"Well..."

"Ah-ha! You're thinking about applying to join, aren't you?" laughed one of the dwarves. "Don't you know that they don't take anyone under level sixty as a matter of principle?"

"Yes, I know. It's just they've got interesting stuff going on - every now and then they upload videos of Dungeon tactics and even if these are mostly old Dungeons, they are top quality walkthroughs! This way I can learn from their experience. And also Anastaria posted new holograms..."

"So what about the Jeweler and the hundred grand?"

"Ah, yes! It's posted on the main page of their website: 'Attention! We are prepared to buy information about the Jeweler who created the Karmadont Chess Pieces. Payment for the information - a hundred thousand gold.' This is followed by a message: 'Jeweler! We are offering you a place in our ranks and the title of a Master.' Just imagine - a Master!"

"So what?"

Shaking his head as if to say 'what a noob!', the first dwarf gave a resigned sigh and went on:

"In Phoenix 'Master' is the third top rank in the

clan! It means full access to the vault, the right to order about Recruits, Raiders and Mercenaries. They only have eight Masters and those have been in the clan from the day it was created, but now they are making such an offer to some unknown Jeweler!"

"Yeah, they're a pretty serious bunch. Well, whatever. Did you hear what Roxie came up with yesterday? She and her friends..."

What followed was of little interest. I stopped stretching, slung the goblin across my shoulders and headed off to pay the town authorities a visit. So, by the looks of it, Phoenix, the best guild in the Empire, is offering the Jeweler, that is me, to enter its ranks as a Master. And this is all because of some chess pieces. At the Pryke mine the Regional Governor let it slip that the pieces are a key to somewhere, but could this 'somewhere' be worth more than the rank of a Master? I really must make a closer study of the chess piece properties and it wouldn't hurt to sift through the forum on this topic either.

The idea of joining Phoenix is quite attractive. Not only was it the best clan on the continent, but Anastaria is a member as well. Phoenix was one of the oldest clans in the game. When the clan's raid group received its twentieth 'First Kill', it began to represent our Empire on the annual contest of the top clans. Phoenix took part in seven contests and twice became the best clan in Barliona. Although in the last four years their position had weakened and they were unable to get higher than the third place. The Emperor decided that a month before the next tournament, which was set to take place in nine month's time, an internal imperial contest should be held to decide which was the best clan in Malabar. Phoenix would once again have to fight for this title, but I could bet that it would take the top place with little difficulty. My evil-minded internal 'Greed Toad' started to fuss and kick me around: I also have a 'First Kill', as well as plans to create a clan of my own, so I also should have the right to take part in the tournament. To make it worse, the Hoarding Hamster gave it his full support - probably because he remembered all the nice prizes that were given to the winner of the last tournament.

Damn, why am I stuffing my thoughts with rubbish again? I have to go and hand in the goblin, drop by the Bank and visit the profession trainers. I also need to buy a return teleportation scroll - that timer didn't go anywhere. Speaking of the timer: '43 hours 25 minutes.' That's fine. I have enough time.

"Halt in the name of the Emperor!" Two mustached guards blocked the entrance to the administration building, pointing their halberds in my direction. At least I remembered that I was green all over and cleaned myself up before the jump. Better not show up in front of other players looking like that. It could lead to a serious misunderstanding.

"Halting," was my simple response. It was dangerous to argue or quarrel with guards. They could easily throw you in jail for twenty-four hours. 'Do you have any reputation with the province? No. This means you're an unreliable social element. You can sit in the cell and do some thinking, until we find out for sure, so to speak.'

"I caught an infiltrator and have come to hand him in. Let your superiors figure out why there's a dark goblin hanging around in Krong."

The guards came closer and warily examined my face. Did I miss some when taking the paint off? I thought such things were fairly simple in Barliona.

"How can you prove that this is an infiltrator or that you are the one that caught him, instead of stealing him from the real brave heroes? Why didn't you ride into the town properly - through the gates on a horse, but got here by teleporting?"

Picky bastards! Just because I have a red band on my head doesn't mean that I commit a crime every five minutes, between killing players and NPCs. Ok, breathing deeply and staying calm. I have to hand in the quest and no hurdle in the form of two jobsworth Imitators is going to stop me.

"Because it's an infiltrator! Just look at him! What else could a dark goblin be inside the Malabar Empire? It's not like he's an honest merchant! That I didn't steal him you can see for yourselves, since I'm not carrying the mark. Yes I do have the headband, but there is no mark saying I've committed a crime. As for not riding into the town on a horse - well, I don't have one. To top it off, I live in Beatwick, which is two days travel from here. Teleporting is faster, even if more expensive. Does that answer all you questions? If yes, please let me through - I need to hand over the infiltrator to the person in charge here."

The guards had no further questions and I

walked into the administration building unhindered. What's good about Barliona is that you can get to see an official at the level of a town mayor in a couple of seconds. You just come and have a chat. No conditions and no long waits. If two players come at the same time, each ends up with his own copy of the official, without holding up the others. From the level of the Governor things get more complicated. And if getting to see him is not impossible, getting through to Heralds and Advisors is much more difficult. Getting an audience with the Emperor is practically impossible. As Eric said, two hundred thousand gold is the normal price for a ticket to see the Emperor.

"How can I help you?" the Farstead Mayor looked up from his papers, giving me an expectant stare. I threw the goblin on the carpeted floor, flexed my shoulders to get rid of the virtual stiffness and said:

"I caught this munchkin near Beatwick, a village right on the border. An infiltrator, by the looks of it. I decided not to kill him and brought him to you instead. That's it, I think."

"Take him away for questioning," the Mayor told the guards, who appeared when he rang a small bell. "As for you, young man, please wait for the results of the questioning in the adjacent room. What if it's just a merchant and you have disrupted his trade," in such a simple manner the Mayor left me in little doubt as to exactly how much trust he had in me. Damn, I'll have to waste my precious limited time stuck in here. But... not much for it, since I was the one that brought him in, I'll have to take the responsibility. After settling down in a small but cozy room, I decided to get some sleep. I would have to sleep at least once in the two days that I could spend outside Beatwick, so why not get some rest right here and now? I barely closed my eyes when a guard shook me awake:

"Mr. Mayor wants to see you."

I looked at my timer: '38 hours 22 minutes.' That was some nap! Five hours gone in a flash, although it feels like I dozed off just five minutes ago!

"Please allow me to express my gratitude on behalf of the Malabar Empire and present you with a small reward for your services," said the Mayor in a completely different tone and handed me a scroll.

Quest 'Head of the Green Raiders' is completed

Reward: +400 Reputation with the Malabar Empire. +500 Experience; points remaining until next level: 1101

Level gained!

Free stat points: 10

Item acquired: Irrepressible Leather Pauldron. Durability: 60. Physical damage resistance: 30. +4 Stamina, +4 Intellect. Item class: Rare

"Now have a seat, there is something I have to tell you," the Mayor said in a much more informal tone, falling silent and lifting his folded hands to his lips, as if in a prayer, but without closing his eyes. You got the impression that he didn't know how to start.

"Today you delivered a very interesting prisoner to us. I'd even say exceptionally interesting. He has already been sent to Anhurs, where he will be questioned by one of the Advisors or Heralds. I was asked to relay the fact that Kartoss representatives have already contacted our Heralds and offered ransom for the goblin. Negotiations on his price are being carried out as we speak. According to our laws ten percent of the ransom for the prisoner belongs to you. It will be transferred to your account. Now about what happened. The appearance of a squad of dark goblins is a very unusual event in our neighborhood. This is not the only squad either. The prisoner said that ten of them have been put together and sent to the Krong province to gather resources that are so badly needed in Kartoss. What Kartoss needs them for is something the Heralds will be finding out. The search for the remaining eight squads is being carried out by eight heroes that have just been hired for the purpose. However, something else is worrying the Advisors. All of the squads have to be communicating with each other in some way. There simply must be someone who is coordinating the activity of the goblins in these lands and setting them various tasks. At the moment we have no way of finding this sentient. The Malabar Empire is asking your help - please find him. I understand that you cannot leave Beatwick for too long, but we suspect that all the threads in fact lead there. Our prisoner is flatly refusing to tell us the identity of the coordinator or what else they might be doing here and even the telepathic mages cannot break through the defense he has on him. We will see what the chat with an Advisor will yield. In any case, you are the one that brought this prisoner, so we will entrust the search for the coordinator to you. If in two month's time your search brings no results, the assignment will be given to one of the heroes hired to look for the goblins. We have to be sure that the coordinator will be found and it would be foolish to rely entirely on a free citizen of sixteen levels. You have two months."

Quest available: 'Search for the Dark Coordinator'
Description: The Dark Empire of Kartoss has been actively sending its squads into the Krong province. It is believed that the activity of the ten Kartoss squads is being coordinated by one sentient. Find him. Time given for completing the quest - 60 days. Quest type: Unique. Reward: +4000 to Reputation with the Malabar Empire, +4000 Experience, +10000 Gold coins, a Scaling item from the Emperor's stores. Penalty for failing the quest: +40 to Reputation with the Malabar Empire, +400 Experience, +100 Silver

"I will find out who is coordinating the activity of the squads," I almost stuttered as I accepted the quest. Could a simple goblin trigger the system to give me a unique quest? I can understand it with the Eye - the chance of such an item dropping during the first completion of a Dungeon is very high. Barliona is extremely vast, so quests like that drop quite often. A clan like Phoenix completes them fairly regularly. I'm certain of that. However, getting a unique quest from a Mayor is just nonsense! Could my stars have simply aligned in such a lucky way?

"Excellent. Then until we meet again. When you find out the identity of the squad coordinator just say: 'I call upon a Herald. I require your assistance." One of them would turn up right away. Now, if you please excuse me, I have business to attend to. The guard will show you out."

I left the administration building feeling dazed. That was some stroke of luck! To get a quest that gives bonuses even if you fail it is a dream for any would-be slacker. Right. I need to calm down or get all these emotions under control. What do I have to do in Farstead? Why did I come here in the first place? I have to find out if there is a Shaman trainer here. I need to drop by a Cartographer and buy maps of Malabar and the town. I also need to find profession trainers, buy a scroll of teleportation to Beatwick and to the town. Should I buy a portal scroll to Anhurs too, perhaps? If it's less than two thousand gold, I'll get it for sure.

But first - to the Bank.

"How can I be of service?" the drawling and somewhat squeaky voice belonged to a small gremlin, dressed in a checkered suit and sporting two enormous goblin-like ears.

"I would like to access my account and withdraw items belonging to Mahan the Hunter."

"Identification was successful. The items of Mahan the Hunter are in your personal room and you may withdraw them," the gremlin said a few seconds later. "Regarding accessing your account, we would like to offer you a new system for the storage of cash funds. Now as soon as you get the money, it could go to your account immediately, bypassing the need to visit the Bank. Any needed amount, limited only by the size of your deposit, would always be in your purse. The cost of the service is two thousand gold a year and also five percent of the total of any transaction with the account. Would you like to sign up for our new offer?"

Wow! A new banking feature in Barliona! The idea of introducing such a deposit was quite ingenious, since now PK-players would only be able to get their hands on Legendary Items, with money remaining out of their reach. But two grand a year and five percent from each transaction, on top of the minus thirty percent from the red headband... This is just way too much money for me. But then again, it would mean greater security...

"All right, sign me up," ignoring my inner Greed Toad, which was protesting vigorously and stomping around my head with a sign 'We want our money back!', I decided to set up the new account. Keeping my money safe was a number one priority, as I had little desire to inadvertently enrich random robbers.

"It's done," the gremlin handed me a new purse, which immediately found its place on my belt. "Your current funds on account amount to sixteen thousand and forty five gold, thirty two silver and forty five copper coins. You have been given the purse for this account. There are also two invitations in your name, here they are," the gremlin gave me two golden coupons: my four hundred thousand of potential gold pieces. All that remained was to find a buyer and it's in the bag. "Is there anything else you want?" seeing me shake my head, the gremlin went on: "Thank you for using the Bank of Barliona. Your personal room awaits you," he pointed towards an open door.

A personal room in the Bank... It's a bit of a joke really. There's a table, a chair (not even a chair, a stool) and an empty cupboard for items and all of this was contained in three square meters. There was barely any place to turn. I took out the Orc Warrior figurines and arranged them on the table. What was so valuable about them? They looked like ordinary green chess pieces. And yet people were prepared to pay crazy money for them and offer sky-high positions. This was crazy. I took one of the orc figurines and looked at its properties. What did we have?

"Grichin the Unbreakable. Around three thousand years ago the orc tribes..."

I already knew this text. The head of the Pryke mine told me the story when he examined the figurines. The description text could not fit on one virtual page, so I scrolled it down, right to the end. Ah! What's this?

$$C^2 = A^2 + B^2$$

An ordinary and uncomplicated line of characters. No explanations. Nothing. Just a quadratic equation. But why on earth was it there? I started to go through each figurine in turn.

$$||X|| = \sqrt{X_1^2 + X_2^2 + \cdots + X_n^2}$$

1, 1, 2, 3, 5, 8, 13, 21....
Seven digits after the dot
*
*
=
[Value entry field]

Entry field. As soon as I pressed it a virtual keyboard appeared in front of me, for typing in the needed value. I entered an empty line. Nothing happened. I put in each sign from the figurines separately. There was no result. I then spent almost an hour on entering different combinations. Zero. Judging by the text, you had to work out some value with precision of seven digits after the dot, but I saw no logic at all in these lines.

Having spent all that time on attempts to come up with a value, starting from an empty line and ending with typing in random numbers, I gave up. There was no result. Damn, this is really messing with my head! That's it! I need a break. I would walk around, drop by the merchants, visit the Cartographer and chill out for a bit. Perhaps some clever thought would hit me after that. One thing was clear - I would not be leaving the figurines in the Bank. What if I get a sudden insight into how to solve this puzzle and the figurines are stashed away out of reach. I think not. I put the Hunter's items and the chess pieces in my bag and left the Bank. What could those signs mean?

"Good sirs, is there a Shaman trainer and a Cartographer in your town?" I asked for directions from the first patrol that I came across, as they were cruising the town streets at a steady pace. Even despite my red band, which would produce a negative reaction with the NPCs, the guards were obliged to answer the questions asked of them.

"We do have a Cartographer. To get to him you need to walk to the end of the street, until that overturned cart, then turn right and then keep going straight until a fountain with a unicorn. From the fountain you turn left and three houses later on the right you will see a sign with a map. That's where the cartographer lives," said the guard. His chesty yet quiet voice strongly reminded me of the orc from the mine, which brought to my memory the desire to find out why he was sent to Pryke and stripped of the title of a trainer. "We don't have any Shaman trainers, just one former one by the name of Almis. If you want to learn something about Shamans, you can go to him. Almis lives right by the town wall. To find him you need to go straight..." the guard started to give me a rather complicated set of directions to Almis, so I caught only half of what he was saying. First I needed to buy a map of the town that would show me where I was and then simply ask a guard to point out the location, mark it and steadily make my way there.

"Any more questions?"

"No, thank you. You were of great help."

"We serve the Emperor!" barked the guards and unhurriedly continued on their beat.

"Dearie, can you help out a weak and helpless woman?" I almost got as far as the Cartographer when an old lady standing in a house entrance called me over. She was leaning on a walking stick and holding a sealed envelope, which she was stretching towards me. A delivery quest! At last I'm becoming an ordinary player, who is being asked to do various assignments! And where you get assignments, you get Experience, reputation and money. Of course I will help the elderly woman, the Cartographer and Almis aren't going anywhere.

"I'm at your service, dear lady. What was it that you wanted?"

"I wanted to send a letter to my friend Mabel. Both of us have become too old to walk over for a chat, so we've decided to send each other letters. Would you deliver it? It isn't far, just around the corner. It's a house painted with a flower pattern," she waved her hand assumingly towards the said house.

"Of course I'll do it, give me the letter and I'll deliver it in no time."

"I'll be honest with you, my good lad, I have no money, so I can't pay you anything for your good deed. I can only put in a good word for you later."

"Who cares about the money if it's that close," I said cheerfully, though inside I was very disappointed. Just my luck to come across a free quest, of which there are plenty in Barliona. Such quests are aimed at socialization of the players when they have nothing better to do. Just a few grains of Experience, no money or reputation. Few people waste their time on them. Fine, if I said I'd do it, backing out of it wouldn't look nice. There wouldn't be any consequences, of course, but I would feel bad about ditching the old lady, even if she was an NPC.

Quest accepted: 'Deliver a letter'
Description: Deliver a letter to Mabel, who lives in a flower-painted house. Quest type: Common. Reward: 10 Experience. Penalty for not completing the quest: None

I celebrated starting to get quests too soon. How could I forget about the socializers? And I got all excited about raking in all that cash and Experience. Yeah, right, in my dreams. Mabel turned out to be a wrinkled old woman, leaning on a stick, just like the one that sent me. It was as if they were sisters - they even resembled each other somewhat. Probably the developers didn't want to spend too much time on their appearance and used the same template, sticking them into different houses and forgetting all about them. This isn't the capital, where each NPC is thought-through to the extent of being able to tell the history of their ancestors several generations back at the drop of a hat. Here on the periphery, where there aren't that many players, they didn't have to bother all that hard.

"Oh, thank you sonny, I've given up hope of getting a letter from Patricia. Before we used to write to each other every day, but these days few people want to help us out. Everyone wants to see some cash for the help, but help is best given freely, is it not? No-one's really mindful of old age..."

Quest 'Deliver a letter' completed. Reward: 10 Experience, points remaining until next level: 1091 Experience

I nodded in a resigned fashion, giving little heed to Mabel's moral instruction. A socializer quest, not much you can do with it. Aside from getting no money out of it, you're bound to have to listen to moral stories about the injustice of the world. The old woman finally fell silent, I turned around and tried to quietly disappear, but that was all wishful thinking.

"Dearie, can you help out a weak and helpless woman? I jotted down a note for Patricia here, but have no-one except you to deliver it. Would you do a kindness for Granny?" Mabel, was ready to hand me a sealed envelope. When on earth did she have the time? All she seemed to be doing was stand there giving me a lecture, but now had an envelope ready all of a sudden. "I'll be honest with you, my good lad, I have no money, so I can't pay you anything for your good deed. I can only put in a good word for you later." This one's at it too - 'No money, can't pay, but you must do the work well and without a complaint and we'll just put in a good word for you.'

"Of course, dear lady. I will deliver your letter to Patricia, don't you worry. Good day to you."

Quest accepted: 'Deliver a letter'
Description: Deliver a letter to Patricia, who lives in a brown house. Quest type: Common. Reward: 10 Experience. Penalty for not completing the quest: None

Patricia stood in the door of her house, as if awaiting my return.

"So, is Mabel still with us?"

"She's alive and well and is sending a letter back to you, here you go," I said, handing the old lady the envelope.

"That's good to know. We're living in troubled times, you see. Everyone's out to wrong old and frail people, they threaten to..." this one also hopped on the moral lecture bandwagon. I really do have a good deal of respect for old people. Before I ended up in Barliona, I often visited my old parents and would usually give up my seat to an older person in public transport. However, hearing moralistic lectures several times a day, especially from NPCs in a Game - was too much.

Quest 'Deliver a letter' completed. Reward: 10 Experience, points remaining until next level: 1081 Experience

"Dearie, can you help out a weak and helpless woman? I jotted down a note for Mabel here, but there's no-one except for you to deliver it. Would you do a kindness for Granny," the old lady's words, who was giving me the envelope with an innocent smile, nearly gave me a coughing fit. A cyclical quest! Well, I'll be! Count on me to get this 'lucky'! I could spend the rest of the day running between the two old women, who would keep bashing me with lectures on morality and ethics and asking me to deliver the next letter. I almost decided to decline, but was hit with a crazy idea. And why not?

"Can you tell me why you can't give her the letter yourself?"

"I told you, I'm too old and have no strength to walk over there. And if you delivered the letter, everything would be just swell," she once again tried to give me the envelope.

"Then hang on tight," I warned the old lady, came up to her, took the letter, crouched, gripped her by the legs and stood up.

"Aw!" Patricia's voice had notes of panic in it. She gripped my hair with one hand and started vigorously waving the other one around. "What are you doing, you maniac?! Dear me! Ah! Oh!" the old woman started to wail and fret.

I confidently headed towards the flower-painted house, where Mabel lived. A cyclical delivery quest, you say? Well, well. We'll see just how advanced an Imitator was installed in these old ladies when they find themselves sitting opposite each other. Will they keep trying to pass messages through me or will they start speaking directly? They can give those moral lectures to each other then. One thing worried me somewhat - the wailing exclamations of the old woman we loud enough for the whole town to hear and could have got me in trouble with the guards.

"My goodness, Patricia, you've got yourself some stallion there!" exclaimed Mabel when we arrived at her doorstep. I put the now quiet old lady down and was surprised once again by how similar they looked. The developers really decided not to work too hard on a free cyclical quest, took one prototype and just changed the color of its clothes.

"Here you go, please sign for a successful delivery," I said, smiling, seeing the befuddled faces of both grannies. "Now you can talk enough to last you a whole week, I'll come by in the evening and carry Patricia back home."

"Why are we standing on the doorstep?" fussed Mabel. "If you've come for a visit, do come in for a cup of tea. You also come in - since you've brought Patricia here, you can look after us for a bit."

Quest accepted: 'Serving old lady friends'
Description: Look after two lady friends who had just met up. Quest type: Uncommon. Reward: 80 Experience. Penalty for failing or refusing the quest: 3 hours of community service

'What!? Where the heck did those three hours of community service come from? You can go to hell with quests like that!' I thought angrily and got ready to leave, but then saw a group of guards who were casting interested glances in our direction. A chill went down my spine. Looks like they did come in response to the old woman's cries after all, but decided not to interfere and see first how it all ended. If I refused right now, I'd be immediately tied up and spend those three hours doing community service: washing walls, cleaning horses or sweeping the square. What possessed me to carry this granny here?

"Of course, dear ladies, I will look after you, since I helped you meet up," I muttered, following the old ladies into the house.

Mabel's house turned out to be very cozy and full of light. The white and seemingly weightless curtains were hung on the windows and big pots with flowers stood on small tables. As the old lady passed one of them, she swiped one of the leaves with her finger, carefully looking at the result - she probably wipes dust (which doesn't exist in Barliona) off her flowers on daily basis.

"You go to the kitchen, dearie, and make us some tea. You'll find cookies and sugar in the cupboard; when you make it, bring it here," said the hostess, after settling down in a comfy armchair. "We'll have a girl-to-girl chat while you're at it."

"Tea is a good thing, of course, but I don't know how to make it, I never learned," I made a last-ditch attempt to get out of the quest.

"Have to teach you everything these days - how will these youngsters survive without us, I wonder? It's like you can never retire," grumbled Patricia, and then waved me away. "Go and don't come back without the tea."

"And don't forget the cookies," Mable reminded

me, as I examined the message that appeared before my eyes.

New Rare Cooking recipe learned: Aromatic Black Tea. Total recipes: 3

I quickly opened my cookbook to have a look at what it was I just learned:

Aromatic Black Tea.
   - ❖ Description: Excellent black tea from the leaves of the highland tea tree, which give off an unforgettable aroma. Crafting stat bonus: + (Crafting) to the maximum Energy value. Whoever drinks this tea will feel extraordinary vitality. Duration: 12 hours. On use: Restores 20% of Hit Points and Mana. Minimum level: 10.
   - ❖ Crafting requirements: minimum Cooking level 5.
   - ❖ Ingredients: simple water, leaves of the highland tea tree.
   - ❖ Instruments: Cooking kit.

Great! I got a nice little bonus practically free! Sure, I'll make the tea for the old ladies, and then see what the result of doing that with Crafting could be!

I spent some time preparing the tea, found a tray and placed on it two cups full of hot tea, steaming with fragrant aroma. Now I had to find some cookies, which the grannies implacably demanded. Their ceaseless chatter could be heard even from behind a closed door. What a boisterous pair! I wondered how their tongues weren't hurting from talking all the time... After going through practically every cupboard I was about to go to Mable to ask for the exact coordinates of the cookies, but found them in one of the farthest shelves. They were hidden behind an almost full bottle, which was labeled 'Cherry liqueur'. I glanced around thievishly and poured some liqueur into both cups of tea. They really shouldn't have shanghaied me. I don't remember wrongs, but I don't suffer from amnesia either. The liqueur shouldn't do them any harm, but just in case I selected the cup and had a look at its properties. Better safe than sorry.

Aromatic Black Tea with Liqueur. +4 to the maximum value of Energy, +50 Attractiveness to the maker (does not stack with similar effects). The drinker of such tea becomes slightly tipsy and feels an exceptional surge of energy. Duration: 12 hours. On use: Restores 20% of Hit Points and Mana. Minimum level: 10

Plus fifty to Attractiveness? It sounds familiar, but I don't remember what it affects. I went to the guide to look it up.

Attractiveness - a character stat that has a value between 0 and 100 and which determines the attitude of NPCs towards the player. It is impossible to choose to level up in this stat - it can only be increased by temporary buffs, a change of clothes, communicating with NPCs or other available means. Unlike Reputation, which affects the entire faction, Attractiveness affects each NPC separately, including an NPC belonging to a faction with which you have a negative reputation. When Attractiveness reaches 80 and above, NPCs of the opposite sex could offer the player a visit to the Dating House. You can look up your current level of Attractiveness of your character to an NPC in that NPC's properties.

That it! How could I forget?! This is the thing for which players create beautiful-looking characters, dress in bright clothes and wear jewelry. The higher the Attractiveness, the higher the probability of being given unique quests. I took the tray and entered the room with endlessly chattering old ladies and smiled - when I looked up my level of Attractiveness in Mable's properties: it was a solid three. It was a surprise that the old lady let me into her house at all if she finds me so unpleasant.

Without looking in my direction and barely pausing from their talk, the old ladies quickly drank their tea, taking no notice of its temperature. I knew that I couldn't leave until I was dismissed, so I sat on the sofa and briefly closed my eyes. A five-hour nap is a good thing, but it's no substitute for proper sleep. The old ladies started off on another lively discussion and without noticing it, I fell asleep for the second time that day. I was woken up by a song:

And it's no, nay, never,
No nay never no more,
Will I play the wild rover
No never no more.

Embracing each other, the old ladies swayed to the melody and diligently sang out the lyrics, looking at the world with tipsy eyes. Great, now they'll accuse me of making grannies into drunkards. At some point the hazy gazes of Mabel and Patricia fell on me and they stopped singing.

"Just tell me Mabel, how could a young man, who makes such delicious tea, end up in prison, eh?"

"You don't say, Patricia! I'm at a loss with it myself. He seems to have it all: hands, feet and a head, but he still ended up a murderous thug. All the youth is like this today - they want all it quick and easy."

"I think that's because he doesn't have a proper woman behind him! If he had a wife, she'd stop him going down the slippery slope!"

"Too true! I happen to have an unmarried lady neighbor. She'd put him on the straight and narrow. Even our blacksmith is afraid of her. She's scary, he says... What does he know of beauty in women?"

"You don't say. Always walks past my house with thin stick-like waifs. There's hardly anything there to look at. And your neighbor's a different story - a pleasure to see how she can carry three sacks of flour on her shoulder."

At this point I completely woke up and stared at

the old ladies. What the heck is going on? Drunken NPCs are planning to marry me off? And to some female version of Hercules too? Baffled, I looked from Patricia to Mabel and back. I'm really in it now! First I carried the old lady here and then got them so drunk on liqueur that they intend to get me married. I was afraid to think of what would happen next.

"But where would this pretty boy find the money for our sweet dove? He doesn't have a penny to his name, just look at him. I reckon we need to help him, what do you think?"

"Helping is good. But would he manage it? How many seekers have we already sent? None came back, the woodwothe did them all in, including my own sweetheart," Mabel wiped a tear.

"He'll make it, just look at the wild glances he's giving us. It's like he was himself a woodwothe!"

"True, that. Dearie," Mabel turned to me now, "we decided to help you. You're kind and understanding, arranged this meeting for us, and all. A good lad! But that's not enough for you to win over our sweet lass. You need to prepare yourself. She has to see you as a handsome lad and not some roving riff raff. We know of a hidden treasure. A long time ago a rich merchant Swiftbel buried it and put a woodwothe to guard it. If you can get the better of the wothe, the treasure will be yours and you can ask our sweet lass for her hand in marriage. What do you say?"

Quest accepted: 'Don't wake the wothe in its snooze'

Description: Deep in the forest, ten kilometers to the south of the town (the location is marked on the map) there lives a woodwothe. Find it and take Swiftbel's treasure that it is guarding. Quest type: Rare. Reward: Swiftbel's treasure. Penalty for failing or refusing the quest: none

The quest description didn't say a word about marriage or a time limit, so I agreed to take it. Me passing up a rare treasure-finding quest? Not gonna happen!

"That's very good then. Now carry me home, I've been here for ages now," said a pleased Patricia and stretched her arms towards me.

Quest 'Serving old friends' completed
Reward: 80 Experience, points remaining until next level: 1001 Experience

I said good bye to Mabel and, having carefully delivered Patricia home, who was now looking pleased and casting a masterful gaze at the surroundings, I was on my way to get the maps.

The Cartographer was a representative of a species common in Barliona: gnome, greedybuggeritis vulgaris. For two gold he offered me to buy 'the most exactest ever' map, put together by a 'daring and lucky' explorer. The snag of it was that I knew full well that good maps cost upwards of two hundred gold, but fell for the Cartographer's words like a little kid. After handing me the map and taking my money, the gnome did all he could to see me out, saying he was busy, that he needed to visit his grandmother and generally had a headache, but I did manage to unfold and take a look at what I bought. Oh boy! A map like this I could draw myself even without the Cartographer profession! It had arrows, some incomprehensible unlabelled signs and drawings of supposedly interesting locations that took up half the map. With predictable trepidation I turned the page and looked at the plan of the town. Whoever drew this map should be banned for life from ever repeating the feat. The streets were simple straight lines forming a grid and here and there had labels like 'Bangk', 'Meine square' and 'Toomple'... I looked at the gnome and was met by the gaze of big, honest eyes, radiating incomprehension.

"Is something wrong? I didn't have time to look at the map myself, but I was assured that it is the very best. Don't you agree?" this greedy salesman asked this with such overplayed naiveté that I gave up. After all, that's the way he's been scripted: to trick the players as much as possible, thereby getting the most money out of them. What was the point of getting angry?

I left the gnome only twenty minutes later, after I acquired the full set of maps of the Malabar Empire and its main towns, including Farstead. I also trained in the Cartographer profession, and was now able to correct the maps myself. It is a very useful skill that brings in a lot of money and levels up just through drawing pictures. All these goodies cost me seven hundred gold. I didn't even manage to level up in Trade, because the gnome flatly refused to give me a discount.

Never mind, the maps were worth it. I asked the nearest patrol for the exact location of Almis and headed over there to pay him a visit. Let's see what a former Shaman trainer looks like.

The door of Alamis's house was opened by a plump maid whose snow-white lace apron made a contrast to her dark skin. After giving me an appraising look, as if examining the contents of my personal bag and the amount of money in my possession, she deigned to utter:

"Come in, Mr. Almis has been expecting you since the morning."

I was expected? Or was Almis expecting someone else and the maid simply mistook me for the intended guest? In any case, I won't leave here until I've found out everything about my former boss. I sat in a comfortable armchair and began to examine the room when an old man dressed in a plush dressing gown and bunny-eared slippers joined me in the armchair opposite. I seem to be running into a lot of old folks today. Judging by his sure movements and lack of glasses or a walking stick, the old man was hardly older than seventy. I saw that he even had all his teeth when Almis - I was sure that I was in the presence of none other than the former Shaman trainer – gave me a wide smile. I stood up and bowed to the former trainer - it's nothing to me and he might like it.

"My greetings to you too, younger brother. Have a seat, I've gotten used to everyone sitting in my presence now," Almis paused for a minute, looking me over head to foot, and then continued: "You're quite a sight, to say the least! It's been a while since we had a Shaman show up around here who had every chance of becoming a Harbinger. According to Prontho, it is Kornik that you need, as he's the only one that can cut a diamond like this and get the main principles of Shamanism into that thick head. And with the recommendation that was given to you by the Supreme Spirit of Air, you simply must be something else even without training. By the way, I was warned that you would visit me today, but I'll admit that I expected to see you much earlier. Did the story of Swiftbel's treasures capture your imagination so much as to get you so delayed?"

"So you know about Swiftbel?" I asked in surprise, staring at Almis's shining smile. He's looking at me like I was a little child, I swear.

"If course, but you needn't worry yourself on that account. Running around the forest looking for some treasure is of little interest at my age. When you get your hands on it, drop by and tell me how you managed to get the better of the woodwothe."

"And who is Prontho?" I asked the name of the unknown being that gave me the recommendation. I didn't think I had the time to get to know anyone well enough for them to give me such a detailed description...

"You know him. He is a High Shaman, the orc who is currently the head of the Pryke mine. My former teacher."

"But why was he stripped of the ability to teach? Why was he sent to the mine? Who is Kornik? Why is it him that I have to go to for training?" I fired my questions at him one after the other. While Almis seemed to be in a mood to give answers, I had to make the best of it.

"Is this all that you wanted to find out today," Almis raised an eyebrow in question, "or did you have a couple more questions? Don't hurry, have a think, what if you missed something? If so, write it all down on a piece of paper then read it over a few times to check in case you forgot something. And as soon as you've done that, you can proceed to tear up the paper and throw it away. You are a Shaman and not some chattering fishwife to behave in such a stupid manner!" at the end Almis even stood up a little and raised his voice and it dawned on me that he was being sarcastic rather than telling me what to do.

"The Supreme Spirit brought news that your Totem is a Dragon," said Almis now in a calm voice, as he leaned back in his armchair. "I propose an exchange. I answer any three of your questions and you show me your Dragon. Dragons are such interesting creatures."

"I don't know how to show my Totem. I'm just an Initiate Shaman. I have to get to a trainer to learn how to summon my Totem," I tried to get out of showing Draco. There's no reason to show him to just anyone, but Almis abruptly interrupted me:

"A trainer will not be teaching you to work with the Totem. He will tell you where to look for its physical incarnation. You would have to learn how to communicate with the Totem yourself!"

"So how do I summon him?" I uttered in bewilderment, more for myself than for Almis, and then one bright thought entered my head. Why am I so slow? I just have to look in the manual and the forum, where everything is written out just for such dimwits like myself. I was about to enter 'Totem' into the search when Almis said:

"Choose a place where you would like to see your Totem and then call him in your thoughts. To put him away, ask the Totem to disappear. Do it."

Choose a place and call him? Seems simple enough. I looked at the small empty table that stood between the two armchairs and thought it was a good place for Draco. I then closed my eyes, brought the image of the Totem before me and said: "Hi, come to me, let's play for a bit." For a couple of seconds nothing happened and I was about to repeat my call, when a projection of a playfully swirling little Dragon appeared above the table.

"To pway? I wike to pway. Where's ballie?" I heard a child's voice which seemed to come from everywhere. Judging by Almis's enthusiastic (though not surprised) expression, he either didn't hear anything or the fact that Totems could speak was nothing unusual to him. "Will thewe be peases today? I wiked them wast time."

"How sweet," Almis whispered in amazement, stood up from his chair and started to pace by the table, watching Draco. Then he turned to me and said, "I'm taking him. You'll still never manage to incarnate him - no-one has seen dragons for hundreds of years.

Come to me, my little one," Almis stretched his hand towards the projection, clearly intending to take Draco away. Such impudence left me dumbstruck for a few seconds, but I quickly came to myself and jumped up to scream about the violation of my rights. I wouldn't just let someone take my Dragon! Suddenly the room was filled with a terrible roar of the Dragon, which drowned out all other sounds. I was landed with a bunch of debuffs with a sign 'Not applicable to the owner': 'Stun', 'Daze', 'Petrify' and so on. The duration of the debuffs varied from a few seconds to a couple of minutes, but this wasn't the main thing. The main thing was that a stream of fire spouted from the Dragon into Almis and the former Shaman trainer ceased to exist in Barliona. Only a pile of ash remained in his place, which was dejectedly lying there on the scorched floor. The Little Dragon started to chirp indignantly, circling around and casting angry glances in every direction, while the stunned maid stood there agape, too scared to even breathe.

“Listen, run away quick, I will call you later and we'll play then,” I asked Draco in my thoughts, helplessly closing my eyes not to see the black blotch on the floor. Barliona is a truly horrible game: I had already felt real panic, pain and pleasure. Now came the time to find out what is felt by people when all their hopes and plans are destroyed. Just now, with the help of my Totem, I destroyed an NPC, thus violating the main condition of my parole. Any minute now the guards would appear and I will go back to the mines for the remainder of my prison term. My head began to swim, my feet gave way and I fell into the armchair.

"Murder!" as if reading my thoughts, the buxom maid gave out a wild scream as soon as Draco disappeared. "Master's been killed! Guards! Grab the killer!"

The guards that popped up out of nowhere quickly surrounded me, their halberds pointed at me from every direction. The head of the guards waved his hand and on the projection that appeared everyone saw how Almis stretched his hand towards the projection of the little Dragon, I shouted in indignation, jumped up, as if giving an attack command, the Dragon opened his mouth and the wave of fire left a big soot mark where Almis just stood.

"Mahan, you are accused of the murder of Almis, the former Shaman trainer, with a Dragon as the murder weapon. You have the right..."

I closed my eyes and hung my head as I listened to the guard. The clan, the Chess Pieces, the Herald's quest, the Emperor, Prontho, Swiftbel's treasure... It all now looked so unreal and impossible that a lump had appeared in my throat. Why, oh why? Why did he try to get his hands on Draco?

"Good day, gentlemen, what are you doing in my home?" the sound of the voice made me open my eyes and stare dumbfounded at an open door to the next room. Almis, alive and well, was looking questioningly at the guards. If Almis in that silly dressing gown and slippers had made you smile, Almis the High Shaman as he stood at the door commanded respect.

He had a Shaman's hat with branching stag

horns, that were almost grazing the door frame, a large cape, billowing behind him as if in the wind, and a staff with a curved, loop-like top, inside which swirled a blue-grey cloud, illumined by silent flashes of lightning. On Almis's shoulder perched an amber-eyed hawk, which periodically filled the room with a piercing cry, which put a two-second paralyzing debuff on those present. An embodied Totem! And Almis himself was clearly a High Shaman in full battle gear! To be honest, he looked terrifying enough to make a shiver run down your neck, so when the guards lowered their halberds as they stared at Almis, I unconsciously backed off, was tripped by the armchair, fell, and, realizing that it was too late to run, tried to dissolve in the damned piece of furniture, to avoid becoming an accidental target for any smiting.

"We are apprehending the criminal that killed you," taking no notice of Almis's appearance reported the guard, totally unperturbed by the absurdity of his statement.

"Ah, that's it, is it? I agree, criminals must be apprehended, but I do not see any in this room. Can you remind me once again, what is this young man accused of?"

"Your murder!" I was starting to like this commander of the guards. He stuck to his guns, despite the fact that even his subordinates had started to glance at each other in incomprehension. Good on him. I'm also rather curious as to whom the little Dragon burned if Almis was alive. Everyone saw the projection.

"My murder?" Almis ostentatiously raised his eyebrows, "Mary," he looked at the maid, who stared at him with huge frightened eyes and kept trying to back off, despite her back already being against the wall. When she heard herself being addressed, she gave a high-pitched exclamation, started shuffling her feet even more, sliding against the floor and trying to push through the wall with all her weight, "Please make some tea for me and for my guest. And calm down, I'm not a ghost."

"As for you, gentlemen," Almis turned towards the guards, "Allow me to lay any doubts to rest - I am alive and well and have no intention of dying or allowing myself to be killed," after that he entered the room, which was immediately filled with freshness and the smell of thunder. Almis looked at the black spot that was left after 'him', shook his head reproachfully and mumbled something like 'Catherine will eat me alive', and then went on: "I have not lived for two hundred years to be incinerated by some projection. Mary, the tea!" Almis raised his voice when he saw that the maid was still trying to break through the wall with her body.

The guards weren't giving up, so Almis had to allow himself to be touched to prove that he wasn't a ghost. When they left the house, Almis sat back in the armchair as if nothing had happened and scratched his nose, as if trying to decide on how to start the conversation. He was about to say something, when the maid came in and, casting strange glances at the High Shaman, put the tray on the table, and then immediately run back a few paces. It seems she was having a terrible day: first me with my Dragon and then Almis, who died and then revived like a Phoenix. Later she will probably go and buy many strong drinks and try to forget this day like a bad dream.

"Mary," Almis said to the maid, again making her jump, "Everything is all right. No need to be so distressed. If you have doubts that I'm alive, you can also come up and give me a poke, I promise...," Almis had no chance to say what he promised, as the maid flew up to him and started to poke him in his shoulder and chest with her fingers. She finally gave a clear sigh of relief and said:

"Mr. Almis, you're alive? I was so afraid that you were... Well..." she was lost for words for a short while, looking at Almis and at me in turn, and then suddenly turned towards me and started to wail:

"What on earth is going on? He came with the Dragon, scared me half to death, ruined the carpet, will probably make the cups all filthy too, and then...".

"Mary, I think you still have a lot of things to do in the kitchen," Almis said gently, but categorically, which made Mary fall silent, throw me an angry glance and leave the room.

"Take no notice," Almis explained when he saw me gaze in surprise at the departing maid. "Mary has temporarily replaced my housekeeper, Catherine, who went into the town today and left in her place this walking incongruity. And although this isn't Mary's first time working here, she still hasn't gotten used to certain peculiarities." After making a brief pause to pour both of us some tea, Almis started to drink it with a visible pleasure that was almost contagious. I was full of questions, but if the host decided that now was the time for a tea ceremony, interrupting him would be very rude. I took up my cup and followed Almis's example. It was ordinary tea, which very slightly restored some Hit Points and Mana, adding no buffs or debuffs. I was even disappointed – ordinary old ladies had a much more delicious and useful tea than a High Shaman. We spent five minutes in tranquil silence. I tried to appreciate the tea, but failed miserably. The vast majority of players log into Barliona with their sensory filters turned on, so many objects lacked any taste, because it was unnecessary. I had a feeling that the High Shaman's tea was a striking example of this rule: it had no taste, color or smell. Finally Almis put his cup down and looked at me.

"Patience is Shaman's main strength. Without it commanding the Spirits is impossible: they are all like little children, capricious, willful and restless. If a Shaman is impulsive, he will achieve nothing. Let me provide you a brief explanation of what happened today. First. I found out about Swiftbel's treasure fairly easily - you were being watched by the Spirits that I sent from the moment you left the Mayor. As soon as a Shaman appeared in Farstead, even if it was a foolish and an inexperienced one, I was immediately told of this. I became interested in watching you: who you were, what would you do and how you would show yourself. By the way, if it's not too much trouble, after our talk I will ask you to make the tea the honorable ladies taught you to make. What we were drinking just now could only be called tea at a very long stretch. Second. Prontho said that you possess a unique Totem, a Dragon, so I had to check whether your link with him was a strong one. Our world has many, let me put it this way, not very nice Shamans, who could be very capable of performing an alienation of your Totem, if it does not suit your Spirit. This is why I created a projection of my Spirit and sent it to chat with you. The projection turned out to be rather crude - I only noticed its appearance after I sent it out to you. Bunny-eared slippers... So embarrassing. But the Spirit did his job – if it was possible to alienate the Dragon, you would have lost him. I think it would have been better to experience disappointment now than when the Dragon grew and you got used to him. But it was fine in the end, so accept my sincere admiration for such a beautiful Totem. I know that you have very many questions, but I will answer only three. Think about them carefully before asking."

"Why was Prontho sent to Pryke?" I fired off right away. That was essentially the reason why I came to Almis.

"He did not obey the will of the Shaman Council. Next question," replied Almis, unperturbed.

Oops. A fail. When will I learn to think and listen? I have to stop being so impulsive, it got me in enough trouble already. So how do I ask in a correct way? I started to ask questions of myself and reply to them in Almis's manner. I really do have to think before asking. So, what did Prontho break? Rules. Which rules did Prontho break? Those imposed by the Shaman Council. Why did the Shaman Council decide that Prontho broke the rules? E-ehh... Mmm... Well, it's not a bad a bad question, is it? I was about to ask it, when the answer struck me: because the majority of the Council members voted for it! I'm getting nowhere with this! Almis sat there with a smile, enjoying my attempts to arrange the information that I had and force my brains to work. Does it really look that amusing from outside? Think, head, think! And I'll get you a cap like the one on Almis, horns and all.

'Mages think'... My memory brought up the words of that lady Shaman that I read before my first test. Antsinthepantsa, if I find you I'd give you one big hug. Just hope you keep playing until that time.

"Why did you stop training Shamans?" I finally blurted out. That was the question that was really turning in my mind, but I kept putting it off for later. It didn't seem that important, but something told me that I should dig in that direction.

Almis leaned back and gave me a thoughtful look.

"A good question. I will answer it later. What is your last question?"

Dammit! I had hopes that I would be able to phrase my third question based on the answer he would give me now. But if that's the case, then here you go:

"What can be done to enable Prontho to teach Shamans once again? If that's what he wants, of course," I added quietly, but Almis heard me. Well, doesn't matter- if getting the reasons for Prontho's punishment out of Almis was impossible, of which I was now sure, perhaps I may discover the reason for my former boss's exile by approaching the problem from the opposite direction.

Almis sat in the armchair for about a minute, swaying slightly back and forth, thinking something over intently, by the looks of it. Did I really guess right and ask the correct questions? Or is he now thinking how to tie my questions to what he intended to tell me from the start? I sighed. It was quite hard to understand NPCs. They were practically people and in many ways they even acted the same, copying human behavior with startling accuracy. Imitators, that says it all.

"You have me rather stumped, I'm afraid. Now I will have to think what to tell you and what to leave for Kornik. He won't be too pleased with me if I told you everything that I know about Prontho here and now. While I'm thinking, please make me some tea. But without the liqueur," added Almis, just in case.

"It's simply astonishing what an unforgettable and unmatched taste a properly prepared drink can have," Almis said some time later, as he enjoyed the aromatic tea that I had prepared. Mary watched me like a hawk the entire time I was making it, probably thinking that I had plans to usurp her place. She even tried to shoo me out of the kitchen, until I told her that Almis asked me to be the one to make the tea, following which she grumbled that she didn't hold with all these random strangers stomping around the kitchen, but did furnish me with the necessary tools and ingredients.

"Let's get back to your questions. I put off my Shaman trainer powers twelve years ago - right after Prontho was excluded from the Council. I just couldn't take the outrage that was taking place," Almis sighed, as if recalling some unpleasant moments of his life. "I had an apprentice, a very gifted apprentice, who had every chance to become a Harbinger. He earned the title of a Great Shaman just a year after beginning his training and had to go through just one trial to gain the 'High' title. But something inside him broke and at one tragic moment Geranika, that is his name, turned against his brothers. His strength was like that of a High Shaman and his malice like that of the Dark Lord of Kartoss. I was unable to stop him: although I did have the chance to do that right at the start, I just didn't have the heart to do it... And then it was too late, because my former apprentice gained such immense power that even a Harbinger may not have managed to bring him down. When Geranika started to destroy Shamans to be the only one, as he put it, to command the Spirits and the world, my mentor demanded the forming of the Great Shaman Circle. That was the only thing that was powerful enough to stop Geranika. There was a terrible price to be paid for its creation - full stripping of Shamanistic abilities from all five members of the circle, but there was no other way. The head of the council, Geranika's older brother, turned down the proposal, calling Prontho an upstart, an unweaned cub and panic spreader, who could not see past is own nose. Then the orc broke the rules and challenged the head of the Council. According to our rules, if the challenger loses the duel, he is exiled from the Council and is stripped of the right to teach others. The High Shaman Prontho lost, Geranika disappeared and it has been twelve years since anyone heard of him. After this incident something broke inside me and was no longer able to teach: I am beset by fear that my new apprentice could follow in Geranika's footsteps. This is why I watched over you earlier - I had to see whether I should let you into my house or not. As for your third question... Prontho's status could be restored in only one case: if it is proved that the duel between him and Shiam, the head of the Council, took place in violation of the law. Kornik insisted that he felt the presence of an alien Spirit during the fight, but he was unable to get a single word out of Prontho. Will you take it upon yourself to find out what really happened?"

Quest accepted: 'Restoration of Justice'
Description: Following a duel that took place twelve years ago for the title of the head of the Shaman Council, High Shaman Prontho lost and was permanently stripped of his title and the permission to teach others. There is a suspicion that the duel took place in breach of the rules. Find out the truth about this duel from Kornik, Prontho and other witnesses. Quest type: Class-based unique: Reward: the return of the title of High Shaman to Prontho, a unique reward from the head of the Shaman Council, +(Variable) to the

Reputation with the Shaman Council, +(Variable) to the Reputation with the Supreme Spirits of Higher and Lower Worlds. Penalty for failing or refusing the quest: none

"I will find out what happened twelve years ago, and will definitely discover the truth," I assured Almis as soon as I read the quest description. Today seems to be my lucky day for quests! A Unique one, a Rare one and a Class Unique one! Now I just have to weather out the three months of confinement in Beatwick and I can head out to uncover the truth. I stayed at Almis's another twenty or thirty minutes, talking about entirely irrelevant topics, after which I thanked him for the information and headed off to look for Cooking and Smithing Trainers. I had to learn how to make ingots for myself, a necessary skill for leveling up in Jewelcraft.

Towards the end of the day the town came to resemble an anthill: you could hardly get through the streets for all the players milling about. Where did they all come from at such a far end of the empire? They should have stayed back in Anhurs instead of getting in my face here. Most of them were running around on foot, but a couple of times I saw players on horses and once even spotted a riding griffin speeding through the sky. What did a level 100+ player forget in a location like this? Or is this one of those heroes hired by the Herald? Griffins or 'flying cows', as they were otherwise called, were the most popular means of travel for players who reached level 100 and who just didn't know what to do with their money. Their big pile of money. The simplest 'flying cow' cost a million gold, but gave so many advantages that some players took out loans from the Banks of Barliona or in even in the real world to buy a Griffin in virtual reality. In my opinion, they were crazy self-indulgent rich kids. If I could get my hands on a hundred of these birdies and then sell them, all my problems would disappear.

"A crocodile! Get him!" a shout came from an NPC, which immediately drowned out the buzz from the players. Yeah, sure thing, NPC is announcing stuff, so everyone must listen. I turned around and looked at the source of such a wild scream. I think I'm beginning to like playing a Shaman. When I was running around as a Hunter, I either didn't take any notice of such details or simply never came across them. A real genuine kobold was walking Farstead streets. Or, rather, a player who chose a kobold as his character. A player who consciously decided to challenge Barliona. These were called by an old-fashioned word that came from ancient games: a hardcore player. Few understood the meaning of these words, but it was used for all those who dared to become a kobold, a goblin or a naga. At the same time, with his level thirty he had already proved that one could play a kobold just as well as any other race. I opened the manual and looked up the properties of the race. Yeaah.

Racial penalty to Intellect: -75%. Ratio of the necessary stat points: 1:3.
Racial penalty to Strength: -50%. Ratio of the

necessary stat points: 1:2.

Racial penalty to Stamina: -50%. Ratio of the necessary stat points: 1:2.

Racial bonus to Agility: +150%. Ratio of the necessary stat points: 4:1.

Racial bonus to Rage: +50%. Ratio of the necessary stat points: 2:1.

Racial ability: Resistance to poisons.

Racial ability: Ability to see in the dark.

Racial ability: (+Level*5) resistance to physical damage due to thick skin.

Racial ability: Ability to breathe under water.

Racial skill: Slowing poison.

Racial restriction: Reputation gain rate is halved.

Racial restriction: Attractiveness gain rate is halved.

Racial restriction: Experience gain rate is halved.

Racial restriction: Stats gained from equipment bonuses are halved.

This isn't just crazy, this is downright suicidal! You might somehow get used to or compensate for the stat penalties, by leveling up as, for example, a Hunter instead of a Mage or a Shaman - the bonuses to Agility and Rage seem to point that way. But with such penalties to Reputation, Attractiveness and gear playing should be simply impossible. How did he manage to get as high as level thirty? Did he do it just thanks to Agility? Reptilis Y'allgotohellis. Even his name choice seems to be making fun of normal players. It was strange that he was completely ignoring the screams of the crowd, including the NPC-children running away from him in all directions. He simply walked purposefully in one direction: judging by his trajectory, towards the tavern. In general, this was quite an extraordinary event for Farstead. And no wonder - there's a crocodile in town. Terrible stuff!

"I'll show you!" An enormous NPC smith, aimed a blow at the kobold with his large club. Reptilis clenched his fists, and without saying a word continued on his way at the same unhurried pace. He really was a hardcore player!

My first impulse was to stop the man, but I quickly thought better of it. Who was I, with my red headband, to interfere with an NPC playing out his scripting? Did I really need this? It's not like I've joined the paladins of late. I have too many problems of my own to go and get landed with someone else's. Moreover, Reptilis is probably quite aware of how NPCs see him. To get to level thirty playing such a crocodile is no walk in the park.

Boom! The club landed on the kobold's head - or rather on the place where the head had just been - and loudly hit the ground. With an imperceptible movement Reptilis slid sideways and lifted his tail, from under which a green cloud appeared. The smith froze like a statue. Briefly holding his gaze on me as he glanced around, Reptilis headed for the tavern at the same slow pace, paying little heed to anyone else. Looks like kobolds have a rather useful air-fouling ability. Could it be transferred to someone else, I wonder?

CHAPTER FOUR
SWIFTBEL'S TREASURE

I SAT DOWN ON ONE OF THE BENCHES, which were scattered in large numbers in the centre of Farstead, and decided to do a full revision of all my quests. I had to decide which of them to do now and which I could postpone until I got out of Beatwick. So, what did I have:

- ❖ 'The Path of the Shaman: Step 2. Find Shaman trainer Kornik.' Class-based.
- ❖ 'Searching for your Totem.' Class-based.
- ❖ 'The Hunt for Grey Death.' Common.
- ❖ 'Night terror of the village.' Rare.
- ❖ 'The Last Hope. Step 3.' The quest isn't there yet, but it should appear soon. Rare.

❖ 'The Eye of the Dark Widow.' This quest wasn't there either, but it should appear at level 100. Legendary.

❖ 'Search for the Dark Coordinator.' Unique.

❖ 'Don't wake the wothe in its snoose.' Rare.

❖ 'Restoration of Justice.' Class-based unique.

Nine quests and only one of them a common one. Not a bad collection for a sixteen-level player. The first two quests, like the last, can definitely wait - until I am released from Beatwick. Number three to five are based in Beatwick - when I return tomorrow, I will decide what to do with the wolves and the Vagren. The Eye can be put on ice until the happy ever after: either until I reach level 100 or I sell it at the auction house. The search for the coordinator has to be started in Beatwick - I only wish I had some clue as to who it could be. If he's coordinating various tasks, he either has to keep travelling between different bases or receive a lot of visitors. I should ask Tisha or the guards how often there are guests in the village and where they end up calling. That leaves the old ladies' quest, which I would be dealing with today. But business first.

The enormous mage tower, where I went to get the portal scrolls, loomed over the entire town. Inexplicably, in each town, even Anhurs, the mage tower was always the northernmost structure. Only the wall or the gates would be north of it. No-one knows why that is, and if they do – they are keeping quiet about it. Perhaps there is some quest tied to that, who knows with those developers?

The tower met me with its standard double entrance. This was another feature of Barliona - personal development through the Game. Through the main entrance you could enter the tower, climb five hundred steps and in the room right at the very top meet the local mage. It so happens, that each town has one resident mage. Within the bounds of the Empire they follow a certain ranking, but within a town there is only one, who is the local High Mage. Now then. The main entrance takes you to the mage directly, but the second one enables you to get a discount off him. When you use the second entrance, the system picks a theme at random and gives you a number of questions to answer. The first mistake stops the trial. Before the first question, the person who took the risk of choosing the second door is given a negative discount value, minus two, I think, and afterwards each correctly answered question increases this value by one. Thus, in order to reach zero and pay the same price as the player entering the normal door, you must answer at least two questions. Then the work on the discount begins. As a Hunter I tried my skill with this only a couple of times. I ended up with questions on literature and art. In both cases I was knocked out on the second question. The nastiest part was that if you failed to buy anything from the mage after the trial, you could kiss good bye to normal prices. The extra charge amounted to 200% and was demanded by every mage in Barliona.

So if you decided to try your luck - be prepared to buy transportation scrolls at an extortionate price. In the real world players set up special resources, where everyone posts the questions that they got, but the developers aren't paid for sitting on their hands either and constantly update the database. They say the corporation has a whole department focused on this alone. Never mind, good luck to them in their difficult work.

I almost stepped through the main door, when something inside me protested. Here we go again. Why on earth do I think that I would be able to get farther than two questions? Of course, I'm not exactly low on gold at the moment, but I'm not that eager to just throw away five hundred gold either. Damn. I have to go for it! Even if I don't make it, it will set a precedent that the inner voice should not be trusted.

You have entered the Door of Choice. The question theme has been assigned: Mathematics. Please confirm that you are ready to start answering questions

Mathematics! I nearly jumped for joy, but tried to control myself. That was some stroke of luck! With my special interest in non-standard problems! My inner voice was right! With bated breath, I pressed the virtual button and awaited the first question. Generally in Barliona any confirmation is given by pressing virtual buttons. There is no voice control for things that influence the player or their character directly. In the first years after the game was launched there were a few unpleasant investigations when players imitated voices of other players and gained access to their characters.

Question 1. Name two numbers, consisting only of digit '1', the sum and the product of which are equal. Time provided: 4 minutes

This was simple. I knew the answer to this one from way back before my imprisonment: 11 and 1.1. But, if my memory serves me right, I spent quite a bit of time solving this problem. Usually the first question is easy, to get the player in the working mood. Strange. I filled in the text field and pressed the button. I couldn't help feeling good about the three additional minutes that transferred to the following questions.

Answer accepted. Current discount bonus: -1

Question 2. 1000 gold was paid for a teleportation scroll and the remaining amount to be paid for it is equal to the amount that should have been paid for it if what was paid for it was equal to what is yet to be paid for it. How much does the scroll cost? Time provided: 7 minutes

Maaan... You'd do your head in, before you make any sense of that sentence. This has to be translated into human language: 1000 gold has been paid for the scroll and X more remains to be paid, and if X had been paid, X would have still remained outstanding. From this perspective this wasn't that hard a question.

1000+X = X+X. Therefore X=1000 and the teleportation scroll costs 2000 gold. I was really hoping that this wasn't a hint for later. I answered two questions and reached zero. I now had five minutes rolling over to the next round.

Answer accepted. Current discount bonus: 0

Question 3. We have a ten-digit natural number. We know that its leftmost digit is exactly equal to the number of zeroes in the number written out, the digit following it is equal to the number of ones and so on until the rightmost number, which is equal to the number of nines. Time provided: 9 minutes

Now this is more interesting. It's hard to name the number right away, so we'll go down the path of logical deduction. Let's suppose that the number contains only zeroes. Then the first digit should be a 9 - nine 0s and a 9. If we have a 9, then there should be a 1 in the last place. Then we have eight 0s instead of nine. We remove the 9 and put in an 8. We already have a 1, so we'll have seven 0s instead of eight. Now that we have a 1, we'll put it in the second place. But now we have two '1's. And we get a 2 and two less 0s. Damn, I'm getting confused. Starting again. I should write out all the alternatives on virtual paper. I opened the notebook and started to write down different steps.

We have - all 0s: 9000000001. Now there's eight instead of nine 0s. 8000000010. Then, we have a 1, and the number looks like this: 7100000100. Now we have two '1's, so in comes a 2. And we have fewer 0s again. Now the number is 6210001000. Checking. Six 0s. Two 1s. One 2 and one 6. It all checks out. I looked at the timer. There was 4.5 minutes left. Moving on.

Answer accepted. Current discount bonus: 1
Question 4
J + S = O; M * A = D; M + M ≠ 2M
(O / F) + (M + M) - J = ?
Time provided: 8 minutes

My first answer was no stroke of genius: (O/F)+(M+M) - J = WTF. Not in the slightest. M+M ≠ 2M. This was a bunch of nonsense, not mathematics. If each letter corresponds to a particular number, this formula cannot be correct. Therefore M could stand for two different values at once. This fundamentally contradicts what I know about formulas.

I immediately decided against numbering the letters of the alphabet and using that as the letter number value. The first formula was contrary to this logic, since Y has to be the greatest value. For a couple of minutes I couldn't even see from what direction I should approach this problem. The answer was buried here somewhere, but it would take a lot to dig it up. I looked at the timer. 4 minutes. Dammit! I'll be stuck here solving this rubbish until next winter.

Stop! Winters? Seasonal numbers? How about...

(10 / 2) + (3 + 5) — 1 = 12. So the answer is 'D'! A clever trick they thought of with M + M ≠ 2M! It really

isn't equal!

Answer accepted. Current discount bonus: 2
Question 5
Continue the sequence: HHHeLiBO...
Time provided: 5 minutes

Winter. Gold. The square of the hypotenuse. I spent the first two minutes trying to understand the logic and continue the sequence and then two minutes on trying to see if I could come up with any associations. Nothing. When the timer showed only a few seconds left, I typed in a bunch of symbols at random into the answer box. They do, after all, say that if you give a monkey a typewriter and infinite time it would eventually come out with the complete works of Shakespeare.

Answer accepted. Current discount bonus: 2
Your answer is incorrect. Thank you for taking part in the interactive questionnaire. Please note that goods bought at a discount cannot be sold to other players. Have a pleasant game!

Not this time. It also became clear why no-one was selling the results of their mental labor. There are probably many know-it-alls, who'd answer all the questions that I got in just a couple of minutes and get a discount so large that the Mage would have to hand over his goods almost for free. So they put a stop to such easy riches.

"Good day to you, traveler," I was met by a venerable-looking old man, wearing a long snow-white robe. "You have passed through the trial four times - a worthy result. In honor of this I will be providing you my services with a direct discount," the mage glanced at my red band, "and a small extra charge. I don't know what crime you've committed, but the band shows that you have not yet atoned for it in full. What is it that you wish to acquire?"

I left the High Mage the most pleased Shaman in Barliona. First, I bought five scrolls of teleportation to Beatwick and Farstead, with the transportation radius of the distance between the two. These scrolls cost me four hundred gold each. Now I can explore the surrounding lands without worrying about how to get back. I found out the cost of the teleportation scroll to Anhurs. And cried. Ten thousand gold with the discount. I think not. I'll use my feet when it comes to it. I also bought two scrolls with the Bone Trap spell designed for a 100-level creature. It cost me five hundred gold per scroll. I decided to try and take the Vagren alive. It might be expensive, but the reward for catching a creature of that level should be substantial. If black goblins started running around this region, chances are that the Vagren is linked to Kartoss too and I wouldn't mind getting an extra bonus from the Mayor.

"Good day and welcome! How can I help you?" Next came the Jewelcraft trainer. It was time I got serious about getting to know the new capabilities of my main profession.

"I would like to be trained in Jewelcraft," here I noticed the trainer's face losing some of its enthusiasm. He probably took me for a newbie wanting to study a rare profession from scratch.

"Please touch the book," he uttered in a distracted tone. Touch the book? Why? Damn, why didn't I take an interest in professions as a Hunter? That way I'd know what to expect now. But if I must, I must. I put my hand on an open book with empty pages, which immediately filled up with a bunch of symbols.

"Not bad, not bad," the trainer muttered in a completely changed voice, which now had notes of interest in it, after he glanced over the emerging scribbles. I had no idea what language it was written in and I understood nothing in the symbols and numbers that appeared in the book. "I see you have had clear success in producing Unique and Rare items. You are particularly proficient with rings. Would you like to choose a specialization for yourself? Picking one costs two hundred gold."

A specialization? I don't get it. What specialization? I immediately looked in the manual. I knew nothing of specializations within a profession.

Search: 'Jewelcraft and specializations.' The text that appeared brought me out of the dark realm of ignorance. Upon reaching level 10 in Jewelcraft, you could pick your first specialization: rings, neck chains, earrings, precious stones and custom jewelry. The first level of the specialization gives a 10% increase to the speed of item design, to durability and to the chance of crafting a Rare Item. The next level of specialization unlocks when the skill reaches level 50, the third at level 150, fourth at 250 and fifth and last at level 500. You keep playing and learning, but will still die ignorant, eh? My Hunter did not have a single specialization and I had no idea about all these special features. I quickly looked at the bonuses provided by my other professions.

Mining influenced Stamina and Strength. At level 10 it gave these stats a 5% boost, and at level 50, 150, 250 and 500 each time added another 5% to the current base level of the stat. That's a pretty handy specialization: I should run to a Mining trainer right away and get Hardiness.

In Cooking you had specializations based on the type of food prepared and its subsequent stat bonuses. None changed my main stats. A pity.

Cartography came with Influence on World Perception, scrolls of some kind and extra Intellect! At every five levels in the profession Intellect increased by 5%. I'll start leveling up in Cartography right away! I went into the settings and set myself a reminder every evening that I had to draw the map of the places where I had been that day. This was another leveling-up opportunity, which only depended on my diligence. There was no way I'll be missing out on it.

Trade did not have any specializations.

"Yes, I would like to choose my specialization," I replied, handing over the money to the expectant trainer. A nice fact: although I spent quite a lot of time looking around the manual, the NPC didn't seem to notice it at all. All Imitators have it in their settings to monitor the behavior of the players and not interfere with them reading the manuals. "I would like to pick the ring specialization," of all the specializations rings seemed to me the most neutral specialty.

"Are you sure? Keep in mind, that you would not be able to change your specialization later. Only the Emperor would be able to remove it."

"No, I am not sure," - What was I saying? "I would like to specialize in precious stones." Right. Time to do as Antsinthepantsa said on the forum: I am completely switching off my brain as a process and starting to work only on the level of intuition. Rings are more profitable, effective and worthwhile, but I wanted gemstones.

"Are you sure?"

"Yes, absolutely."

You have chosen the 'Gem Cutter' specialization. The speed of cutting gemstones and the chance of creating a Rare gem has increased by 10%

"Congratulations. Now let's settle the matter of your training. I can offer you five scrolls which you do not have. They cost two hundred gold each. Would you be taking them?"

Leveling up in Jewelcraft will cost me a pretty penny, by the looks of it. A thousand gold was gone in a flash. Never mind, we'll put it down as an investment in the future. I bought all the scrolls that the trainer had and immediately learned three of them.

Copper Gem Ring.
- ❖ Description: Copper Gem Ring. Durability: 40. 3 random Stats from the main list: (Strength, Agility, Intellect, Stamina, Rage). Crafting stat bonus: + (Crafting level) random Stat from the main list: (Strength, Agility, Intellect, Stamina, Rage). Minimum level: 12.
- ❖ Crafting requirements: minimum Jewelcraft level 12.
- ❖ Ingredients: 2 Copper Ingots, Ordinary Cut Malachite.
- ❖ Instruments: Jeweler's tools. Casting mould.

Gemstone: Ordinary Cut Malachite.
- ❖ Description: initial cutting of Malachite, though crude, still makes it look attractive. 1 random Stat from the main list: (Strength, Agility, Intellect, Stamina, Rage). Crafting stat bonus: + (Crafting level) random Stat from the main list: (Strength, Agility, Intellect, Stamina, Rage). Minimum level: 10.
- ❖ Crafting requirements: minimum Jewelcraft level 12.
- ❖ Ingredients: 1 piece of Malachite.
- ❖ Instruments: Jeweler's tools.

Malachite Jewelry Box.

❖ Description: A neat and sturdy box or jewelry. Can carry 5 items. Crafting stat bonus: The Box can carry an additional (Crafting) number of items. Item class: Uncommon. Minimum level: 10.

❖ Crafting requirements: minimum Jewelcraft level 12.

❖ Ingredients: 2 pieces of Malachite.

❖ Instruments: Jeweler's tools.

I put two more recipes for cutting of Lapis in my bag. They required level 16-17 in Jewelcraft, and were of little use to me yet. The copper gem ring was a disappointment: despite the stats added by the socketed stone, the ring would only give a +3 bonus by default. I would get a better result simply by combining a wire ring with cut Malachite. But the Common Cut Malachite and the Jewelry Box made my day. Each Malachite cut with Crafting gave +5 to a stat, against the +4 from the Stone Fang and Stone Diamond. Again, a very pleasant bonus. And if the Jewelry Box takes up only one slot in the inventory, it's practically priceless - I would put all the chess pieces there and free up a lot of space. The only downside was that it would be hard to sell it. It could only be used by Jewelers - for everyone else it would be no more than part of the scenery. And buying something that you can make yourself... Is stupid and wrong; I was sure that all Jewelers could make such Jewelry Boxes for themselves. It's decided then - when I get back to

Beatwick, I would be making one of these for myself.

"One more thing. I want to make you aware of one restriction straight away. Until you gain the second level in the specialization, you cannot craft items where the sum of the bonuses raises the stats by more than twelve. I am warning you because I can see that you have a rare stat like Crafting. It isn't every day that a Jeweler has a visit from a free citizen with such a specialty."

"Thank you, honorable sir, for the teaching and the warning," I tried to be polite, but inside I was outraged. I already made plans, picturing in my imagination extensive sales of items with +50 stat bonuses and mentally swimming in gold, but they turned out to be doomed from the start! It was all training and leveling up instead. This was a direct hit on my pocket - until level fifty in Jewelcraft the stat bonus of my items would not exceed 12. What a snag...

The Mining trainer was an almost square-shaped dwarf, who taught me the Hardiness specialization for three hundred gold. He even presented me with a patch for my cloak: 'Swinger'. No stat bonuses, just Attractiveness increased by 1. Considering my standard value in that, this was a very relevant addition.

At the Cooking trainer's I managed to learn only five recipes: Roast Wolf Meat, Deer Meat, Hare Meat, Fox Meat and Boar Meat, which restored between 30 and 120 Hit Points. There was nothing else available until level 5.

The last trainer I decided to visit before leaving

Farstead was the Smithing Trainer. I did all I could to avoid this profession at the mine, but it still caught up with me. I found the trainer, an enormous orc, sitting by the smithy, from which some player was being carried out. I didn't get it - did that player collapse? If the character had to be carried out, it meant that the player had lost control over him. That was possible only in one case - complete Energy loss.

"He overdid it a bit," said the orc, seeing my interest, "This blockhead was told several times - take a break! But oh no! He's all strong and tough! Now he won't be able to set foot in the smithy for a week - he just won't have the strength. Why are some free citizens so brainless? It's not like anyone will do the thinking for him. What did you want?" The last question was to me.

"I would like to be trained. To end up like that guy," I nodded in the direction of the player, who was being put down by the wall of the smithy. He would regain his Energy in an hour, so nothing really terrible would happen to him. However, the fact that an overworked player would be landed with a week-long 'Weakness' debuff, as the manual helpfully pointed out, was news to me. With a debuff like that you could not work on any profession - whether production or gathering-based. That would be a serious hit on the finances of the careless player. So I won't be removing my Energy loss warning, it can stay where it is.

"Training is simple enough if you have the money. Ten gold for the training and another five for the instruments, said the orc, periodically glancing at my headband. Damn! What stopped me training in Smithing at Pryke?

"Here you go," I gave the orc the money. "My resolve is firm and I would spare no expense."

"Hrm," snorted the orc, accepting the gold. "Maybe there's some hope for you yet, if that's the way you see it."

You gained the 'Smithing' profession. Current level: 1

You received an object: Smith's Tools (Attention! Does not take up inventory bag space)

I opened the page with the Smithing skill and began to study it.

Smelting ingots.
- ❖ Description: This ability allows you to smelt 5 pieces of ore into 1 ingot. The speed of smelting is determined by the player's Agility and level in Smithing. Crafting stat bonus: when smelting ore you have a (Crafting) percent chance of discovering a Precious Stone, corresponding to the level of ore.
- ❖ Ingredients: Copper ingot (from level 1 in Smithing): 5 pieces of Copper Ore; Tin Ingot (from level 10 in Smithing): 5 pieces of Tin Ore; Bronze Ingot (from level 40 in Smithing): 4 pieces of Copper Ore and 1 piece of Tin Ore; Silver Ingot

(from level 60 in Smithing): 5 pieces of Silver Ore; Iron Ingot (from level 80 in Smithing): 5 pieces of Iron Ore. Recipes for ingots of level 100+ are bought separately.

❖ Instruments: Smith's Tools.

My heart missed a beat when I read about the Crafting bonus and I immediately went to the manual. The chance of a Sapphire Vein appearing - one thousandth of a percent. Sapphires are mainly obtained by sifting through Elementhrium Ore, from where the drop chance is already half a percent. If I level up my Smithing to 260, I would be able to smelt Elementhrium Ingots, even at my current level of Crafting, I would have a 4% chance of getting a Sapphire. I looked up other rare stones. Emerald: the chance of a vein appearing - two tenth of a percent, drop rate when sifting - two percent. Diamond - one ten thousandth and one thousandth respectively. My palms were sweating from excitement. You needed level four hundred and sixty in Smithing to smelt Phantom Iron, from which you could get a Diamond, but Diamonds were worth enough to cover any leveling-up expenses. I started to pace nervously by the Smithy - now the main thing was to make sure that no-one found out that Crafting and Smithing could combine so nicely. I was sure that the leading clans knew about this feature, but were in no hurry to share this information with competitors. Doing so made little economic sense. Even the manuals and the forum only said that Crafting was a stat that influenced production professions. That's it. The search didn't turn up any other results for 'Crafting', as if all other information on this was removed on purpose. Come to think of it, that made sense - considering the money that circulated in Barliona, bribing or even getting hired as a moderator of the forum or the manual was pretty easy. This meant that I had to keep very quiet about my Crafting and begin to...

My train of thought was interrupted by a quiet cough from the orc.

"Why are you running around here, kicking up all the dust? Did you come here to learn or do laps? If it's the latter, take a hike, we don't want any loiterers here!"

"I beg your pardon, sir. I'm at fault here," you had to be respectful to NPCs, a rule I established while I still had my Hunter. "I was just so glad that I could become a real smith now that I got lost in daydreams for a minute."

"You will never become a real Smith if ingots is all you end up doing. And right now you don't know how to make anything else. Being a Smith is a calling," the orc said solemnly. I had a strange feeling that our conversation was beginning to resemble an introduction to a quest. I had to keep the orc talking - what if there was some bonus at the end of it?

"I bow my head before your wisdom, honorable teacher. Can you tell me how to become a real smith?" after being addressed in this manner the NPC would hand me a quest for sure, assuming he had any to give.

Of course, this also depended on the reputation, but in that case the NPC had to reply that he did not trust me sufficiently yet and couldn't share such a secret with just any stranger.

"Don't you get it? You have to work, you dolt!" the orc pointedly turned around and went into the smithy. Nice 'quest' - right to the point.

Just before leaving Farstead I dropped by the Alchemist's shop. There I sold the things set aside after sorting and also bought a few instant potions for restoring +300 Hit Points and +300 Mana. Now I could confidently set out in search of treasure. After checking my purse I whistled - that's some shopping spree I went on today! I had just ten thousand six hundred and eighty-four gold left. No matter, Swiftbel will reimburse me!

I began to suspect that getting my hands on Swiftbel's treasure might come with slight difficulties when I was just a couple of kilometers from the spot marked on the map. My path was blocked by an enormous bog, which the map entirely omitted. I settled down by a branching tree that grew right by its edge. I had very little desire to be snooping around a bog in the middle of the night - who knows what creatures might be lurking in this place. Losing twelve hours to a respawn on account of my own stupidity... I think not. I still had twenty-six hours left until I had to return to Beatwick and a short rest wouldn't make much difference. I will find a way to get across this obstacle in the morning - with a fresh start in the sunlight. I opened the map and began adding to it the ground covered during the day. Cartography was a great thing. Even with my non-existent drawing 'talent' you could still draw good precise maps. The main thing was to remember, preferably in detail, the entire route you'd travelled. Then the quill in my hand would itself sketch in the necessary marks - in all the scales at once. I closed the map and, immediately gaining level 2 in Cartography, took out two pieces of Malachite and looked up what I had to do to craft a Malachite Jewelry Box. It didn't require any specific instruments; everything I needed was in my bag. Not much point in wasting the evening being idle.

Working with Malachite turned out to be interesting and engrossing. It's probably great to be a sculptor! There are plenty of stones lying around: you just take a chisel, a hammer and off you go. Your own hands are your only limit. If they are clumsy, no number of Sculpting trainers would fix that. Any sculpture would turn into a Quasimodo. After I cut out the lid and put it into its proper place, I leaned back on the tree and examined my creation. It was simple and fairly plain, even a bit crude in places, but for me the Jewelry Box wasn't just another crafted item, but something I put my heart into making. Eh... it's been quite a while since I crafted anything! This is way more interesting than mindless mob killing.

Item created: Malachite Jewelry Box. Free Jewelry slots: 9. Item class: Uncommon. Minimum level: 10
Skill increase:

+30% to primary profession of Jewelcraft. Total: 91%

I placed the Orc Warrior figurines in the Jewelry Box, put my things back in the bag and went to sleep. All that was left to do now was wait for the morning and get to the place marked on the map.

Damage taken. Hit Points reduced by 1: 1 (Bite). Total Hit Points: 729 of 730

I woke up from a sharp prick and immediately jumped to my feet. What happened? Although whatever it was bit me for only 1 Hit Point, it hurt a hell of a lot.

Damage taken. Hit Points reduced by 1: 1 (Bite). Total Hit Points: 728 of 730

I instinctively slapped myself on the place where I was just bitten. What the heck is going on?

Experience gained: +1; points remaining until next level 1000

Experience? I think I've completely lost track of what's going on. Maybe I should try to wake up? I looked at the hand with which I slapped at something. No way! How could I forget about these good old bloodsuckers? Mosquitoes! Totally ordinary mosquitoes, which are never in short supply throughout the expanses of the game. Unlike their real cousins, virtual mosquitoes are noiseless, which means it is practically impossible to track their movements. What's even worse, if one doesn't wear special clothing they take off one Hit Point at a time even from a player completely covered in plate armor. And, judging by the locations of the bites, they went through the armor as if it wasn't there. Of course, one or two bites presented little danger to the players, but when a whole swarm turned up, you would struggle to survive without area-of-effect spells. They'd eat you to death.

I looked around. Under the light of Barliona's second moon, which just rose in the sky, I spotted an enormous moving cloud of these insects. Barliona mosquitoes were two or three times bigger than the largest specimens in the real world, so spotting them was easy enough. In just a few moments I was entirely surrounded by this flickering cloud.

Maaan. If I only had something with mass-effect, I'd get a couple of thousand experience points right away. As it stood, I was looking at being sent for respawn. I got a better grip on my Mallet and looked at the cloud.

Damage taken. Hit Points reduced by 1: 1 (Bite). Total Hit Points: 727 of 730
Damage taken...
Damage taken...

It began. I was furiously flailing around with the Mallet, getting around 5-10 Experience points with each swing. But it seemed that the mosquitoes were just multiplying on the spot, while my Hit Points were melting away.

Energy level: 30. Stop, you angry Shaman!

Dammit... Just what I need! I summoned another Healing Spirit on myself and it started to dawn on me that I wasn't getting out of this fight alive. Judging by the timer for my return to Beatwick, I've been fiercely waving that Mallet around for two hours, but there seemed to be no end to the mosquitoes. I was set to run out of Mana in about two minutes - and that's despite my fairly fast level of regeneration! I was letting too many bites get through. These bloodsuckers are going to eat me alive, as sure as rain. The battle wasn't without its upsides, of course. I reached level 23 in Endurance, which continued to increase steadily. Intellect went up to 57, Strength to 23 and Agility to 14. Even Stamina went up by four points, ending up at 34. Experience gain was a given: in two hours I gained two whole levels, bringing my free stat points to twenty. That's all very well, of course, but I still wasn't that keen on being sent for a respawn. Not keen at all. But if I continued to swing my Mallet, my Energy would fall to 0 and for two hours I would be at the complete disposal of the mosquitoes. The Shaman-shaped dinner would be served.

I had to think of something and quick. The mosquitoes wouldn't disappear until I disappeared. The sun, which should be here in a couple of hours, has little effect on them. They can fly quite fast, so I wouldn't be able to run away. Nor swim away, if it came to it. Stop! Swim away! They can't go under water! So what if the bog is full of strange green sludge instead of water - I can live with sitting in it for a couple of hours. As far as I remember, that's the timer the mosquitoes have for changing their target.

Waving my Mallet around and still receiving Experience point by point, I hurried to the edge of the bog and made a running jump into the sludge. I knew I probably should have checked the depth first, but I was completely out of time. The level of Energy had passed 20 and was quickly making its way to 10. If it reached that mark, for the next two hours I'll be a statue. So I had to take the risk.

I was lucky. The place where I submerged myself, head and all, wasn't actually that deep - just up to my chest. I took a lungful of air, more on account of habit from reality, and dove completely under the sludge. Immediately there appeared a window telling me that I had enough air for three minutes. After that I would either have to come up for ten seconds or drown. But the air was full of mosquitoes, which would very gladly renew the timer for finding a new target. But then again... That's if they would manage to get to me in those ten seconds.

Moving slowly as I overcame the resistance of the mire, I headed towards Swiftbel's treasure and away from the mosquitoes. When just a few seconds remained until I ran out of air, I carefully came up and looked around. I managed to walk only about fifty meters, so I could see the swarming cloud of insects very well. But they could not see me! And this was great! I counted the ten seconds necessary for restoring my breath and was about to dive back in, when I saw a message:

Achievement earned!
Diver level 1 (27 minutes spent under water until the next level)
Achievement reward: Time that can be spent under water increased by 1%. Current time: 3 minutes 1.8 seconds
You can look at the list of achievements in the character settings

Diver is a somewhat better achievement than the 'Romeo and Juliet' one I got a couple of days back. If I remember correctly, there were treasure-finding contests held among Divers. I would have to look that up when I get to Anhurs.

I surfaced to restore my air bar three times, until the mosquitoes were nowhere to be seen. My Mana was almost restored and Energy was no longer drawing nervous glances from me every few seconds. Things were looking up!

Damage taken. Hit Points reduced by 2: 2 (Bite). Total Hit Points: 768 of 770
You will lose 2 Hit Points every 5 seconds for 30 seconds or until the time you remove the Leech

I had run out of any emotions by this point. I summoned a Lightning Spirit on the leech that attached to me and looked around. The closest island wasn't far - about a hundred meters away. If I were to swim it, I'd get there in a minute and catch my breath afterwards. It would also not be a bad idea to...

Damage taken... You are losing 2 Hit Points every 5 seconds...

There weren't nearly as many leeches as mosquitoes, but they had a very unpleasant trait: I had no idea where they were biting me to target them and hit them. Even with my sense of pain turned on to full, I didn't feel them bite, so I could only be guided by the messages on the damage sustained. I then had to stop and remove the evil bloodsuckers.

It took me half an hour to get through the hundred meters to the little island. At one point it even occurred to me to leave the leeches that latched on to me where they were so I could get to the islet as quick as possible, but after ten meters of this experiment my Hit Points diminished by twenty percent. So I had to stop, summon a Healing Spirit on myself and then get the bloodsuckers off me.

The little island met me with surprising calm and green grass. Almost completely drained, with just twenty points of Energy, I fell on the grass. The hundred-meter swim also gave a decent increase to my stats: +2 to Stamina, +3 to Intellect, +3 to Endurance and a new - 19th - character level. This treasure hunt was turning into quite a boost! In just a couple of hours of my search I leveled up by as much as it took me a month of work at the mines.

The place marked on the map wasn't that far away now - I could even see that islet about three or four hundred meters ahead. I had to get there to collect the treasure, but I wasn't rushing there headlong. My inner voice insisted that I must not take the direct route there, and I was in complete agreement with it. The watery surface that separated me from the islet with an unassuming tree in the middle was just a little too smooth and calm.

I settled down on the grass for a think. I wasn't even thinking, but waiting for something. The island where I ended up wasn't that large - about thirty meters in diameter and almost completely round. There was something strange about it. Suddenly there was a barely audible splash of water. A shadow flashed nearby and immediately vanished, but I had enough time to select it. An Alligator, level 20. Another obstacle before the treasure, by the looks of it. That does it! I'm fed up with being the whipping boy. Level 20, you say? Great! Where did I put my Tambourine and Mallet?

The Shaman has three hands...

There came a subdued growl and the alligator immediately appeared on the surface. It swung its head around and, finding its bearings, headed in my direction. Come on over - here I am. One Lightning Spirit took off half of the crocodile's Hit Points, so I waited until it climbed onto the islet and summoned the second spirit. A piece of meat and an Alligator skin made for decent loot. I picked up the meat and threw it in the water. I'll lure these gators out one by one.

'One by one' didn't happen. As soon as the meat fell into the bog, the entire surrounding area started to move and alligators came out from all directions. Oops... I didn't really count on this when chucking the meat in the water. But... Let's see what I'm capable of as a Shaman. Amount of Mana: one thousand nine hundred and eighty; each Crocodile needs two Lightning Spirits and each Spirit costs seventy six points of Mana. Therefore, I should have little problem summoning twenty six Lightning Spirits in a row. After that I would rely on my regeneration.

In total, there were forty alligators. I ran around the island constantly summoning Lightning Spirits, but it was so full of crocodiles that there was barely any place to turn. A couple of times it was very close and I had to use a healing potion, but on the whole the fight didn't present much of a problem. My Mana regenerated fairly quickly, the crocodiles were slow, despite their large numbers, the Tambourine worked like a dream and the Spirits turned up immediately after the summons. When the last crocodile dropped out of the game for the next three days (the time it took for normal mobs to respawn), I reached level 21, gained +3 to Intellect, +2 to Endurance and an open path to the island.

I collected the loot and, after a short swim, reached my goal. Now all I had to do was climb the hill to get to the tree and meet up with the woodwothe.

A quiet splash made me freeze. I thought I downed all the local reptiles - what else could be splashing around here? Slowly, making no sudden moves, I turned around. I just knew that there was something odd about the island on which I was fighting the alligators. As it happened, it wasn't an island at all. It was an enormous turtle, which stretched out its wrinkled head as it moved in my direction. Like a tank. Only about forty meters remained between us when the turtle swiftly moved its head, caught something in the water and started to chew. A bar labeled 'Fullness' appeared above it, 5% of which turned green. So it wants to snack on me, does it? I selected the Turtle and looked at its Life Bar. Well I'll be... Level 100, one hundred and fifty thousand Hit Points. It would take me about a week to down it with my spirits...

The Turtle made another quick move, grabbed its next victim from the bog and chewed on it industriously. It's pretty nimble for its size. The level of 'Fullness' rose to 10% and then, just as unhurriedly, it moved towards me. Strange, I thought that no-one lived in the bog except for the crocodiles. What is it catching?

Think. I need to think and fast. I wouldn't be able to kill it. Nor would I be able to run away. Can I feed it? What with? Alligator meat! I have forty pieces of it right here! Around ten meters remained between me and the turtle, so I quickly threw all the meat I got from crocodiles out of the bag and ran some distance up the hill. Please, please let it work...

The turtle crawled out of the bog, stopped by my pile, which looked rather silly compared to its enormous size, sniffed the meat, like a dog, and started to eat it. Twenty percent of 'Fullness'. Forty. Seventy. Ninety. Ninety nine. That's it, there was no more meat.

The hungry hulk lifted its head, looked at me and again, slowly began to move in my direction. Damn my luck! I turned around and ran as fast as I could to the opposite side of the island. It may not be large, just fifty meters in diameter, but while this mammoth crawls over to me I'll think of something.

It was a great idea, but it was not to be. As soon as I turned and took a few steps, the Turtle shot out its head at the speed of an arrow, clenched me in its jaws and slowly began to chew. The pain was hellish. It was like being crushed between two grinding stones - my Hit Points were in a free-fall, I was screaming, but the pain wasn't going anywhere.

Suddenly it all stopped. I fell to the ground, fitfully trying to breathe in. A minute went by before I could recover enough to look around. My Hit Points were at 25. The durability of all my items was reduced by 70% and the enormous hulk of the sleeping Turtle was lying next to me, with its 'Fullness' bar at 100%. After I summoned four Healing Spirits in a row on myself, I was able to get up on my still unsteady feet.

My Endurance had gone up to thirty by now and I was meant to be feeling 6% less pain. Somehow I didn't notice this reduction at all while I was being chewed up by the Turtle. If anything, it felt more like it had increased by 100%. I even shuddered at the memory. And all this for some treasure? Where the heck was it then? I'm here, the island marked on the map is here, so where's the chest with the treasure?

I waited for my Mana to completely recharge and headed for the tree standing in the middle of the island. If that chest was anywhere that would be the place.

"Halt, traveler! You have gone through the fire, now you must go through water," a hairy formless something appeared between myself and the tree. So that's what a woodwothe looks like. And you're the one behind all of this? You are the bastard responsible for the mosquitoes, the leeches and the crocodiles? The little turtle sleeping peacefully nearby also gets a special mention. You're the one that's done all this? Level thirty, two and a half thousand Hit Points, defense - unknown, but that no longer matters. I'm angry and irritated and the wothe had the luck to be in my way.

"My first question..." the woodwothe began, but I brazenly interrupted it. I've had it with all their riddles!

The Shaman has three hands...

That's for the mosquitoes. They could have eaten me alive!

"Stop, Shaman! What are you doing?" the woodwothe began to wail, dropping its question.

... and behind his back a wing...

That's for the leeches. It was bad enough that it forced me to dive into the green sludge, but it decided to sprinkle some leeches on top. What if I had a phobia?

"This is against the rules!" Yeah, yeah, scream all you like. Boil over in indignation. I could use those extra couple of seconds.

... from the heat upon his breath...

How about them crocodiles? They may not have given me all that much trouble, but that's only because I switched on my brain and thought better of jumping in the water. I dread to think what would have happened if I failed to listen to my inner voice.

"Let's strike a deal!" Ah, so the woodwothe likes to bargain, eh?"

... shining candle-fire springs.

And that's for the 'ninja turtle'. One Spirit won't do for that one, I think three would be just about right.

"Mercy! I'll offer you a ransom for my life," the wothe's voice was getting hoarse now. And little wonder - it only had ten Hit Points left. I'd be able to finish it off with my Mallet, if need be. It had no business springing itself on an angry Shaman. It's a sure way to get itself swatted. Wanted me to answer riddles, eh? A couple of Lightning Spirits and all the riddles solve themselves.

"Do you swear that you wouldn't do me any harm in either thought or deed?" I asked the wothe, kneeling down. The strangest thing, I still had forty points of Energy left, but I felt the entire weight of the world on my shoulders. "Well?" I growled, seeing the wothe go quiet. It won't do to go into shut-down without finishing it off. "If the answer's 'no', your fate is your own choice. The Shaman has three..."

"I swear!" shouted the hairy something and, a moment before losing consciousness, I felt the heaviness leave me. But I didn't care anymore. I was tired and had to rest...

I came to myself, judging by the timer, only ten hours later. The peacefully sleeping mountain that was the Turtle, disappeared. It probably doesn't like sleeping in the open air. I turned around and under the lone tree saw the round hairy something, which put me to sleep for so long. It had no feet or head or eyes. It was a practically round fur-ball.

"Awake now?" like a balloon the wothe was gently floating above the ground.

"Awake." I confirmed sullenly. "What did you hit me with?"

"The spell of forgetfulness. I didn't think that you would attack straight away. I thought you'd first try to solve the riddle, give yours brains a good run-around, but that's not the way things ended up. I turned out to be unprepared. What did you come here for? There's nothing here except me and the mosquitoes."

"Well, I haven't dropped in for tea, exactly. I was told that Swiftbel buried his treasure here. That's what I came for. No point it going to waste."

"Aahhhh! You're a seeker! I nearly thought you

were some villain up to no good. I guess the sisters sent you here. What on earth did you do to them to get sent to a sure death?"

"Death?"

"Of course. You don't think I'll just hand the treasure over to you? I haven't been guarding it all these years to give it up to random strangers. And don't look at me like that. You should have killed me right away, when you had the chance. Now I prepared myself. You can, try, of course, but in that case my oath not to do you any harm will become void."

"I see. So there's no chance for me to make it out of here alive?"

"What the heck do I need you for? You can go as you please. You may even stay here, you're not in my way. You wouldn't find the treasure anyway, nor would you get the better of me."

"Hang on. You said that you were prepared to bargain for your life. Did you not?" I waited for the wothe to give a snort of agreement and then continued, "Then I would trade your life for the treasure."

"You think you're so damn clever? It won't work. Swiftbel put me under a ward. I cannot hand over the treasure even on the pain of death. I can only give it to him or to his friend. As far as the bargain goes, in place of death I grant you the opportunity to speak to me. I would even answer your questions. Not all of them, of course, but some.

"Well, I am the friend," if the ransom idea didn't work, I will try to get it out of the wothe by other means.

"You can't be the friend. Swiftbel hid the

treasure forty years ago, when you weren't even a twinkle in your parent's eyes," you could feel it smile, pleased at its own joke. Does this mean that the treasure was hidden even before Barliona was launched? This is a sign that this is a quest prepared in advance, rather than being a randomly generated one based on the player's actions. That's good to know. Such quests bring 'tastier' rewards. All that's left now is to get my hands on these 'tasties'. Perhaps I should take the risk and try fighting it again? I just have to summon five Lightning Spirits... Will there be time?

"Besides, I remember Swiftbel's friend very well," continued the wothe. "You don't look anything like him."

Didn't work. Fine, we'll try a different approach.

"Tell me honestly, haven't you got tired of sitting here? After all, you're a wothe of the wood, not the bog. To be stuck for forty years all alone, guarding the treasure that you've never even seen... Isn't all this rather silly?"

"What do you mean - not seen the treasure? I look at it every day," asked the wothe in surprise, but something in its voice seemed off. I had to dig deeper.

"And what do you see? A closed chest? Are you even sure there's treasure in it? Maybe the only treasure is the chest itself! Did you even once look inside? I can bet that you haven't."

"But... Swiftbel said that..." said the wothe, now sounding not so certain. It was time to move in for the 'kill'. I just wanted a glimpse at what I came here for - if it's worth it, I may even attack the wothe for it.

"You believed a merchant? It's practically in his job description: deceive everyone to get more profit. How did he persuade you to guard the treasure?"

"He didn't. It was his friend, whom I just couldn't refuse. Few could have refused that one," the wothe hesitated a few moments and then asked: "Are you sure there is no treasure there?"

"Of course! Do people visit you often? If the treasure was real, the bog would have been overrun by other free citizens. Do you see many of those?"

"You're the first. Usually some common folk turned up. One time Mabel sent her husband, she probably got tired of living with him."

"By the way, how do you know the old ladies? They don't seem to be the type to make friends with a woodwothe," I just couldn't see how this local wonder became acquainted with template-NPC old ladies from Farstead. They're so ordinary that were even made from the same prototype. Or is there something more behind their resemblance? Could the conditions of the quest really state that Mabel and Patricia must send players to the wothe for certain death? You could say that they formed a criminal association with the local evil entity! It just doesn't seem like them at all.

"I know this through Swiftbel. They are his sisters."

So that's how the old women knew about the treasure! And I almost began to think badly of them.

"You're really getting me confused here," the wothe finally decided. "What if I really am guarding an empty chest? That would be scandalous! I'll become the laughing stock of the wothian assembly!"

"Then let's have a look at what's in the chest. Maybe there isn't much sense of being stuck here anymore. It's not like I want to waste my time on an empty chest - they can find another fool for that."

Skill increase:
+20% to Charisma. Total: 60%

The wothe disappeared for a few seconds and then re-appeared, saying in a pleased tone:

"How could I doubt a man like Swiftbel? Way to go with egging me on! The treasure does exist, how could it not? Its value is such that crowds of knights would risk their heads just for a chance to get it."

"What is it, then?" I wasn't counting on this when I was trying to get the wothe to peek inside the chest. I thought it would get the chest out, open the lid and we'll both look inside. Now it seems I was the one that got fooled.

"It's a treasure! As to what it is, that's none of your business," the wothe made a show of floating around me and then drifted off to the tree. "If you're done, I'll get some sleep now. Got tired faffing around with you here. If you decide to attack, don't bother waking me."

Now it's mocking me. Going for a nap! Damn, can't even think of anything to ask it. Although...

"By the way, why a bog? Could the treasure not have been hidden closer at hand? It seems stupid to drag a great chest all the way into the wilderness."

"Swiftbel didn't drag it, as it happens. His friend brought the chest on him," replied the wothe, yawning.

On him?

"What do you mean 'on him'? Swiftbel's friend is a horse?"

"Why does it have to be a horse..." the wothe floated up to me again. "Swiftbel's friend is no horse. He's a dragon! Just an ordinary dragon. For him flying over the bog is child's play."

A dragon? From where? Few of these have been seen in the entire history of Barliona! For instance, I've never heard of a player who has or read any mention of this on the forums. And here you have some merchant flying around on a dragon!

"How did Swiftbel end up with a dragon for a friend?" I asked, genuinely surprised.

"This I don't know. Perhaps the sisters could give you a clue, they were very close with Swiftbel," the wothe yawned once again. "Come on, decide already. I want to sleep and you just can't make up your mind whether to attack me or not. The sooner we settle this, the sooner I'll get some sleep."

Changes to the 'Searching for your Totem' quest. You managed to find out that Barliona's dragons are real and not a myth. Merchant Swiftbel had one of them as a friend. Find out from the merchant's sisters how he got a friend like that. If you fail to find this out, speak to the Shaman trainer

"Hold on. Does this mean that you have to hand the chest over either to Swiftbel or to a dragon? Either one or the other?"

"All the dragons are one family. I could give the treasure to any of them. But not one of them has been seen in forty years."

"Would you give it to him?" almost too anxious to breathe, I asked the woodwothe, and then said in my head:

"Draco, hello. Would you like to play?"

"To pway? I wike to pway. Do you pwomise that we pway? We didn't pway wast time."

"We will, for sure. Come now."

"To whom, 'him'?" chuckled the wothe, "It's not like you have a friend who's a Dra..." it didn't manage to finish, as a projection of a little dragon appeared next to me.

The world froze. It was like someone flicked a switch and turned off all the bog sounds at once.

"Hewwo. I came to your call," the high-pitched child's voice put an end to the silence that surrounded us.

"My Lord!" I could be wrong, but judging by the wothe's look, it fell to its knees. If it had any.

"Who's this? What's he doin'?" Draco looked at it in surprise.

"He's just fooling around. Just imagine - before we could play hide and seek, we need to get hold of a chest. The wothe - that thing lying over there - has one, but doesn't want to give it up. It says it would only give it if a Dragon asks it. So, do you want to play hide-and-seek?"

"Hide and feek! I wike hide and feek!" Draco even started spinning around me in anticipation of the fun. "Am I Dwagon?"

"Yes, a Dragon."

"Gif me the chest," Draco looked at the wothe. And then added, "Pweese."

"Yes, Lord," immediately a small - about knee-high - chest appeared next to the wothe. So that's what all the fuss is about! Could it contain a Legendary or an Epic item? That would be great!

"And now we pway. Wothe, you with us?"

"If you command, my Lord," the wothe showed no sign of getting up from the ground.

"I command it. Pway with us. I'm 'it'..."

The hide-and-seek took us about two hours. The island turned out to have an abundance of hiding places - so much for me thinking of the tree as the only place to hide. Small hollows, stones, and even a burrow where the wothe lived - all could be used for hiding. I never touched the chest and Draco didn't ask why we weren't using it. He even tried it out as a hiding place, but the see-through tail always let me know that my Totem was behind the chest. At last Draco started to yawn and asked if he could go now. I had to promise that soon I would call him once again and we would continue the game.

You have summoned your Totem: Because

**your Totem is still disembodied, the next
summoning can only happen in 7 days' time**

Ehh... And I was all set on continuing to play
with Draco later today. But never mind. In seven days'
time I'd be sure to summon him again.

"So you have a Dragon as a Totem," said the
wothe when Draco disappeared. "It's been a long time
since I've seen one of them. I even forgot what it feels
like - when a Dragon is looking at you."

"That's right. So can I take the treasure then?" I
glanced at the chest that was still standing by the tree.

"Yes, you can. My service had come to an end.
I'll go back to the woods and seek out a dryad. Or a
couple..." the wothe fell silent and, before disappearing,
uttered: "The little turtle will wake up in a minute. I'm
not controlling it any more. Good luck to you."

In a minute? The teleportation scroll takes thirty
seconds to activate. I had no idea how long it would
take for the Turtle to get to the island (what if it decides
to nibble on me some more), but I'd venture a guess
that it's not long at all. This means...

I ran to the chest and lifted the lid. So, where's
my Legendary or Epic Item?

**Leara's Ball Gown. Description: "The world-
famous beauty Leara took great pride in her
wardrobe. The star of the collection was a special
dress, the likes of which has not been seen in
Barliona. A girl wearing this dress would become
the owner of a truly unique object and would gladly**

fall into the arms of him who presented her this gift." Durability: unbreakable. If the item is presented to a female NPC: +100 to Attractiveness with that NPC. Item class: Unique, nothing like it exists in Barliona. Level requirements: none

'Don't wake the wothe in its snoose' Quest completed

I automatically threw the dress into my bag, took out a scroll of teleportation to Beatwick and activated it. While the portal was being formed, I had time to think that it's been a long while since anyone had fooled me so beautifully.

CHAPTER FIVE
THE HUNT FOR THE VAGREN

T HE NEXT DAY I BOUGHT SOME FOOD from the trader and headed out for my work team. I have to supply them with rations for the next couple of days and should take some ore off them as well. By now they should have something to show for all that pick-swinging. Then I would drop by the Smithy and will start to level up in Smithing, what if a gem...

"Hey Mahan," my thoughts were interrupted by a low and self-assured voice. "What are you doing here?"

I looked around and saw no-one. What the...? Am I starting to hallucinate now?

"Look up," said a breathtakingly beautiful female voice. I looked up and saw two griffins, silently flapping their wings above my head. Well I'll be... It took a lot of willpower to stay upright, as my legs became like rubber and I sincerely hoped that I didn't actually start to drool. Anastaria! And Hellfire with her! Both leaders of the Phoenix clan in person!

"I'm in exile here," I somehow managed to get a grip on the awe that overwhelmed me and respond. "People, if it's not too much trouble, would you mind coming down? Looking up at you like this is doing my neck in."

"Hel, this boy's cheeky," chuckled Anastaria.

"Or maybe he has no idea who we are. Let's land," Hellfire barely moved his hand and his griffin began to descend.

I stood there, trying to suppress the shakes. Two top players of our continent within Barliona. Hellfire had a 340-level dwarf warrior and Anastaria, a 330-level human paladin. What on earth did they want with a 20-level player? They shouldn't even take any notice of someone like me...

"Don't fret, we're not PK-ers," the paladin beauty's voice was simply divine! "If I understand correctly, you are one of the five prisoners that were the first to complete the Mushu Dungeon, correct?" with some effort, I forced myself to nod, following which Anastaria continued: "I'm Anastaria, this here is Hellfire. We represent the Phoenix clan, have you heard of it?"

I took several deep breaths, gathered my thoughts and was finally able to come out with something other than groaning:

"I know full well what Phoenix is and who Hellfire and Anastaria are: the two most leveled-up players from our continent, leaders of the most successful clan, winners of the intercontinental clan tournaments and holders of a mindboggling number of First Kills. If you took me for a complete noob, without any real interest in the game, you were mistaken."

"Great! Then we can go straight to business," Hellfire stopped examining the scenery and turned to me. "You didn't answer my question. What are you doing here? What does this 'exile' mean? Since when do 'red riding hoods' get exiled?"

I briefly told them the main points of the law, which required the first six months of the sentence to be served either at a mine or in a settlement."

"So you've managed to earn Respect with the guards in less than six months?" Anastaria's somewhat distracted demeanor changed to visible interest. "How did you manage that?"

Damn... Should I tell them about Jewelcraft or not? If yes, they would probably ask me to show them and then simply to hand over the chess pieces. Then I would never solve the riddle contained within them.

"I stood up for another prisoner, who was set up at the mine. Then I killed the culprit. I was thrown for respawn and the commission for prisoner affairs ruled that I should be given three character levels and Friendly status with the guards. And then it was simple: Rats. I'm a Shaman, who can summon Spirits, and rat tails provided a decent reputation increase. So that's how I got out in three months. You could say I just got damn lucky."

"You got lucky with the Dungeon too?" now

Hellfire joined our conversation.

"To be honest, yes. Eric, one of our five-strong group, saw a dot in a mountain. He played Barliona before prison as a tank, so we believed him. That dot turned out to be a cave entrance. We completed the Malachite gathering quest and went through the Dungeon. It was aimed right at our level, so it wasn't too difficult."

"But Eric, as you call him, Leite and Clutzer said it was actually pretty hard," judging by the way Hellfire was watching me, he was expecting some sort of a reaction. It was strange, but the more time I spent in Anastaria's company, the more I wanted to curl up in a ball under her feet. She's just an ordinary girl, even if unbelievably beautiful, with such wonderful hair that you want to... Right, pull yourself together, you sop!

"'Hard' is when you've had a hundred wipes and are out of ideas on how to keep going. When a Dungeon is completed at the first attempt - it's not that hard," where was I getting all this confidence from? "And how did you find out about Leite, Clutzer and Eric?"

"They've gone through a trial and became our Recruits. They're part of Phoenix now. When you get to Anhurs, drop by our clan's representative office. You're expected there already. When you complete the trial, you'll join us as well," Hellfire did not have a shred of doubt that I would be unable to turn down his offer, and my pride reared its head. So what's this then - Eric, Leite and Clutzer are already in Phoenix? Have all our plans for creating our own clan gone to the dogs now? Well, you can all go bugger yourselves! I won't join, and that's that! Damn, this really has got to me. I was really hoping that I could play the remainder of my sentence with others like me - former prisoners. But it didn't turn out that way at all...

"Right, we're done with small talk, now to business. We are looking for a squad of dark goblins. They're roaming around somewhere in this region. Have you seen anything?"

"Can't you see from the air who's where?" I was genuinely surprised.

"That's the problem - there's a ziggurat standing in this area, with a forty-kilometer radius of effect."

A ziggurat? This was serious! I went to the manual to refresh my memory with the description of this wonder from Kartoss.

Ziggurat - is a unique Kartoss device for suppressing the maps and airborne forces of the enemy. A Ziggurat conceals a certain area of the map and is located in a random spot of the covered area. It is impossible to conduct a search from the air in an area affected by a ziggurat: all Kartoss buildings and units gain the 'Invisibility' buff.

"Have you fallen asleep?"

"Eh? No, just thinking. A ziggurat in this province? Guys, are you sure you're not confusing something? All right, there may be a squad of dark goblins, even ten quads with ten goblins in each. They are all level twenty-thirty. A ziggurat is something a lot more serious! Only a Magister can set one up! Why would there be a Dark Magister of Kartoss in the Krong province?"

"You really aren't a noob," smiled Anastaria. "When you join the clan, I'll take you into my squad. Although... stop! Hel, get him!"

A gust rushed through the area. Hellfire, who was standing a couple of meters away, was suddenly sitting on me - I was pinned to the ground and practically immobilized.

"Stacey, what happened?" though Hellfire didn't understand anything, he carried out Anastaria's command without question. Like an experienced raider - first do, then ask why. It's the only way it works in the Dungeons.

"Our little Shaman here is getting just a little too curious. Are we looking at competition here? Even if he's too much of a small fish to be a competitor. Hel, think about it: we didn't say how many goblin squads there were. We didn't say what level they were. We didn't say how many goblins there were in each squad. But Mahan told us all these things just like that, while the Herald shared this information with us as highly confidential. You don't find it all a bit strange?"

"You think the Number Twos hired him?" Hellfire's voice became steely. He bent my head so I saw his grey eyes. "Mahan? Is there something you want to tell us? Or will we have to be persuading you? You think I don't know what the red band on your head means?"

"Just let me go, I'll tell you all I know," I growled. Hellfire looked questioningly at Anastaria, waited for her nod and got off me. Phew! Right, the time had come to spill the beans. I got up, flexed my neck that was roughed up by Hellfire and began my tale:

"It so happens that I was the one who discovered the first squad of dark goblins. I found it and destroyed it, taking its leader prisoner," I recounted that entire fight, including the 'Romeo and Juliet' achievement. I kept quiet about the Wolves, since they weren't really connected to the goblins.

"That's how I got hold of a work team. They are mining the ore not far from here. That's it, I think."

Hellfire and Anastaria even laughed when I told them about how I lured out the goblins, but as soon as I mentioned the work team, they immediately fell silent.

"So those ten were yours?" Hellfire finally muttered, after the tale of my adventures had come to an end.

"Were?"

"You see, we've already been roaming this territory in search of goblins for two days," Anastaria's tone was strangely apologetic. "We only found out about the ziggurat today, when we were adding our route to the maps. Anyway, we saw your goblins from the air, took them for a dark goblin squad and because our quest said 'destroy' we didn't even bother landing. You know what a meteor shower is, right? Well, I'm afraid you don't have a work group anymore."

"What???"

"Right, chill it." Intervened Hellfire. "You should put up signs when you hire work groups. You can take any complaints to the clan, they'll be reviewed there."

"Hel, there's no need to be this way. He's a small-fry, where would he get the money? You could say he had a great stroke of luck, and we just stripped him of ten grand in gold."

"Ehh, Stacey! One day your kindness would bring our clan to ruin! Here you go!" Hellfire threw me seven thousand gold into the trade window. "The cost of a beginner level work group ranges between ten and a hundred gold. The annual profit that they could generate for you wouldn't exceed ten thousand gold, so you can't have any claims against the clan from the financial side. On behalf of the Phoenix clan please accept my apologies for this misunderstanding. I hope that your gaming experience has not suffered. Stacey, let's keep flying, we have another square to cover."

"Mahan, if you see the goblins, let me know," Anastaria handed me a communication amulet. "Call me right away."

The griffins soared into the sky, leaving me in a state of complete befuddlement. Seven thousand gold is good, of course, but now I would have to mine the ore myself. I wonder if they took the gathered ore or just left it lying on the ground. If they didn't actually land, it should still be there. I have to go and check. I'll do some swinging with my pick as well - take my anger out on a Tin Vein at least. Why does Phoenix think that all the players owe them? And, most importantly, how could Eric, Leite and Clutzer flake out on me like that?

The mine was transformed after the meteorite attack. There were huge holes and piles of stones and not a trace of my workers. The place where the ore was collected was also worse for wear, or rather, it had simply disappeared under a pile of enormous rocks. Even if my former workers did gather anything, it was impossible to get at it now. Damn! I took out my pick and unleashed my fury on the vein. Although why get angry? Some high-level players flew by, made it clear who was boss around here, paid some money and flew off. Same as everywhere else.

"Oi, you there," a rough voice interrupted my involved, Tin Vein-facilitated anger management session. I'd taken off around 40% of its durability in about half an hour. Not bad for a vein of this level. My hand still remembered how these things were done. "Wotcha mucking about with here?"

Taught by experience, I looked up. There was another standard griffin and a great bird of flame. I knew well enough who it was that managed to get his hands on the only phoenix in the game. The Dark Legion clan, or, 'Number Twos', as everyone called them behind their backs. The phoenix was carrying none other than Plinto, the head of the clan, a three hundred and thirty-level player. A rogue. Hellfire offered him a crazy amount of money to buy out the phoenix, but Plinto laughed at his requests. He said that this was showing Phoenix's proper place - under Plinto's ... Basically, there was a non-stop war between these two clans. Phoenix's strength was in their mastery, while the Dark Legion's was in sheer numbers. When a crowd of a hundred 100-level players are trying to catch a 200-level player, the outcome of the battle is very hard to predict. The Dark Legion had tens of thousands of members - Plinto accepted everyone. This included those rejected by Phoenix and those eager to take part in capturing a castle. Almost all high-level PKers were members of this clan, but the Dark Legion always remained in the second place. Right now I had two main players from this clan floating above me. I seem to be having quite a day for running into people.

"I'm mining ore," I had little desire to be rude to Plinto, who was famous for his short temper. He could send me for respawn in the blink of an eye.

"Have you seen any goblins?"

I could barely restrain myself from saying that I was looking at a couple right now.

"Yes, there were ten of them in this mine. Then Hellfire and Anastaria from Phoenix flew by and destroyed them. You can see the result: total chaos and ruin." They really shouldn't have killed off my workers. It wasn't much, but it was still revenge.

"They're here?! Dronn, call in reinforcements!"

"Plinto, we can't. Remember the conditions of the quest? Only two clan representatives on this territory. Any more would mean a fail. We've already found two groups out of nine. Those bastards got at least one. Who the heck knows how many duos are still flying about in the Free Lands?"

"Then get mercenaries! I need twenty level-200 mercenaries. They have to slow Phoenix down. We could use an extra twelve hours. We'll be first!" Plinto looked at me: "Where did you see them last?"

"Not far from there, they flew off that way," I

waved in the direction the killers of my work team had departed.

"Quick, let's follow them! Here, take this for the info," Plinto opened a trade window and threw me seven hundred gold. "If you see them again, give me a call," a communication amulet landed on me after the money. There was a slight breeze and both players were quickly out of sight.

Let's see. What's going on here? What kind of a quest would be limited to only two clan members? And we're talking about the most powerful clans too. I remembered the Mayor's words: "The search for the remaining eight squads is being carried out by eight heroes that had been hired by the Heralds." So this means that four more must be flying around here somewhere. Plus the ziggurat. Plus the coordinator. Right, stop. This has nothing to do with me. I got a better grip on the pick and continued to smash the Tin Vein. My task is simple - live a quiet life and don't bother anyone. I had little desire to get involved in clan disputes.

Attention! The 'Last Hope' quest chain has been blocked due to the destruction of Grey Death and her pack. Pack respawn time: 4 months

I blinked in surprise at the message that popped up. The wolves have been killed... I had high hopes of getting a nice bonus at the end of this rare quest chain... But then these high-level players flew in and destroyed everything... I threw myself at the Tin Vein in powerless rage. Why am I so unlucky of late?

Experience gained: +10 Experience; points remaining until next level: 8145
Skill increase:
+40% to Mining. Total: 101%. Mining increased to 13
+2% to Stamina. Total: 60%
+2% to Strength. Total: 67%

I looked at the results of my work: Seven pieces of Tin Ore. Maybe I really should forget everything and just keep leveling up in the mining profession? You don't have to think or make any decisions. Just swing the pick without a care in the world. I picked up the ore and walked over to the next vein. I had twenty hours before I had to return to Beatwick, veins respawn on daily basis, and there was plenty of food. I'll just stay here and work.

By the end of the day I'd smashed six more veins and raised my Mining profession to level 14, made small gains in Experience, Stamina and Strength, and also got forty pieces of Tin Ore. Working in the advancing twilight was awkward, so I trudged off to the village. When you knew the way, it took just two hours of unhurried walking. Right next door, you could say.

In about thirty minutes I came out of the forest and saw a site of battle. Not as much of battle as the immediate death of the wolf pack. The bodies of the wolves, the leader and Grey Death were strewn about twenty meters away from an enormous black crater.

Strange that the wolves didn't disappear as soon as they were killed. Dead mobs do not despawn only in one case – if they are still part of a quest. Like the wolves whose tails I collected the other day. Ah! Should I take the tail off Grey Death as well? That way I'd at least complete the Village Headman's assignment...

The tail of the she-wolf practically fell into my hands of its own accord, after which the entire pack faded away. That's it. They've served their purpose.

Quest 'The Hunt for Grey Death' completed. Speak to the Beatwick Headman

I continued on my way, but then a small speck caught my eye. I came closer. It was a piece of paper, held down by a rock. Who would be littering the expanses of Barliona with something that doesn't exactly cost a pittance? I kicked away the rock, picked up the paper and read the text, written in neat handwriting:

"Hello again, Mahan. I decided not to bring up Jewelcraft in Anastaria's presence, but this topic is of great interest to me. In his report Eric pointed out that you have three levels in Crafting. He mentioned your rings separately, as well as how you brought down Rats with your Spirits. I know full well how Crafting is gained and how you level up in it. In my clan only twenty people have this stat, and only four of them have it at a higher level than you.

Now, to business. I weighed up all the pros and

cons, and am now quite sure that you are none other than the Jeweler who crafted the Orc Warriors from the Karmadont Chess Set. We'll talk about them separately, it's not like you actually need them. But now is not the time for that conversation. Anastaria's birthday is a month away and she is crazy about chess. According to the rules, Dwarf Warriors are the next part of the set to be crafted. These are what I need. Everyone knows about the orcs (there are hundreds of fakes on the Anhurs market now), but no-one has the dwarves. Go to the Bank, use password 'Hellfire-Lapis Lazuli-dwarves', and you'll receive the materials needed to make them. Because of the limitations imposed by the assignment Anastaria and I are doing, and your compulsory presence in Beatwck, I cannot recruit you into the clan at this time, but you should know that you will become a Master in Phoenix as soon as our search is finished. In a couple of weeks I will drop by for the results, wait for me in Beatwick.

P.S. Sorry about the wolves. Judging by the fact that they have not despawned, these were quest-related mobs. Since you're the only player I met in this location, these were probably your wolves. I will leave the letter for you here – you're sure to come across the wolves tomorrow if not today.

P.P.S. Don't let me down. If Anastaria fails to get her present, I will be very upset...

Hellfire, head of the Phoenix clan."

So, looks like Eric and Co. have sold me out completely. I'd been very naïve and revealed all my cards to them with the Crafting skill, but those gits went and changed all their plans the moment they were offered a place in a leading clan. And really, who the heck am I? Just some prisoner, whom they've known for just a couple of weeks. What have I got to offer them in the game? Nothing. But in Phoenix they would be protected from ninety percent of other players. Except for the Dark Legion, no-one wants to get on Phoenix's bad side. Good call, guys, covered your asses well and good! And Hellfire, he's a piece of work... Decided to make a present. Via an offer you can't refuse. Killed my wolves too! Who the hell does he think he is?

If any player crossed my path at that moment, I would have attacked him without a second thought. If you're surrounded only by schmucks, it's easier to serve the rest of the sentence at the mine - just mining the ore every day and making rings, without a worry about the future.

By the time I was approaching Beatwick, my conscience got the better of me. To hell with Hellfire, I don't care about him, but Anastaria... She never did anything bad to me and even protected me after a fashion from the dwarf. And I sent Plinto in her direction. Just doesn't seem right. Taking out her one-way communication amulet, I squeezed it and called up Anastaria.

"Yes," sounded the paladin's divine voice. "Who is this?"

"Hi, Anastaria. This is Mahan, we met this morning..."

"Mahan! Where are you now? What quest are

you on?" Anastaria's anxious voice interrupted me.

"What do you mean, 'where'? I'm walking up to my place of exile. Beatwick. What happened?"

"All right, we'll get to that. What do you need me for? Did you come across another goblin squad?" I may have been imagining this, but was Anastaria either catching her breath or trying to quickly come to a decision?

"It might as well have been goblins. At the mine where you killed my work team I ran across Plinto. He's also looking for the goblin squads. To top it off, I overheard his conversation with his deputy. They found three squads and there are four more players flying around this area. That's it from me, I think. I wanted to warn you about Plinto and pass on the information about the goblins."

"Thanks for the Plinto warning, but the goblin info's already out of date. The algorithm for finding the squads was elementary - it was either mines or logger's cabins. Hel and I found four squads, which means that two more were found by the other groups. Two hours ago, when we destroyed the last squad, a Herald appeared, accepted the completed assignment and told us that not a single clan member was to be found on the territory of the Krong province in the next couple of months, on the pain of failing the scenario. The Herald promised to be on a particular look-out for any free players or groups that may hinder a certain player from completing his part of the scenario. You know, you don't have to be a genius to figure out who that player is. It's you! You are the one who found the first squad, so it was you who was given an assignment with a set time limit. Hel has flown into a rage and I simply don't understand anything. What's going on?"

"You flew away?"

"Yes, the Herald sent us to Anhurs. Mahan, can you tell me your quest? Can I help in any way? Please understand, this scenario is very important for our clan. If you need anything, just say - whether it's money, gear or scrolls. Anything you ask for would be sent straight to the Bank with your name on it. Don't hurry, have a think about it."

"There isn't that much thinking to be done. I need a full set of level 21 gear, with bonuses to Intellect. Getting equipped around here is a big pain." I wasn't going to pass up on a gear freebie. "I have no need of money, but scrolls... Anything with AoE damage would be great. As for the quest - I told you everything at our meeting. There is nothing more to add. I have no idea why no-one from your clan is permitted to show up here. May I ask a question, by the way?"

"Sure. The gear will be sent today. As for scrolls, I think we can put something together for your level. Would a hundred do?"

"Yeah, that's plenty. So, Have Eric, Leite and Clutzer really been accepted into Phoenix?" I still had trouble believing that they ditched me. They just couldn't have, whatever Hellfire may say.

"Yes, but not all. A few days ago we were approached by several beginner-level players who had First Kill. This really piqued my interest, so I personally oversaw their testing."

"Testing? What's that?"

"Identification of their abilities. Eric turned out to be an excellent tank and he's already been sent for a leveling boost. Clutzer's a decent DD. But Leite didn't pass the trial. He makes a pretty average DD and we decided not to take him. Now we're looking for Karachun to assess his abilities."

"So how come you let Leite go? After all, we all got a scaling item for taking the second place in Malachite gathering. Letting a player with such pauldrons go is somewhat careless," I noted in surprise.

"An item doesn't make the person. If you have clumsy hands, no amount of gear will help. We gave Leite a chance, but he didn't take it."

"Fine, another question. What is a Phoenix Master?" I asked nonchalantly. You can relax, Oh Gorgeous One. This just made for another point against joining Phoenix. So I am supposed to think that Eric and Clutzer are now in the clan and even came out with a full report... Yeah, right, they just ran in and typed it all up, especially about the non-existent second place and Leite's pauldrons. So, it looks like Karachun was the one you spoke to... But he doesn't know about the fifth place or Leite's sword.

For a while there was a silence and I even started to think that we lost connection when Anastaria spoke again:

"So that's how it is! Now I know how you got Crafting. Did you already solve the riddle? You wouldn't share the formula with me, would you?"

Oops. I'm treading on very thin ice here. Anastaria knows about Crafting? How? After all, Karachun only saw the rings and heard that I was able to change stats...

"I don't quite get what you're on about," damn, what a clumsy evasion. Totally childish.

"All right, it doesn't matter. Just in case, remember - my analytical department is one of the most powerful in the game. We don't just sit there making strategies for going through Dungeons, we know how to use our heads too. If you need any help - just say. As for the Master... All together there are several ranks in Phoenix. Right at the top there are two people - the clan leaders. Hellfire and myself. The second tier down there are Treasurers, two, in our case, and five Castle Owners. The third rank in our hierarchy is held by the Masters. We currently have eight of those. Masters are the most valuable players for the clan. They are even paid a salary from the clan treasury. For example, one of the Masters is a player with level 20 in Crafting. As far as I know, this is the maximum level of Crafting in Barliona. On the fourth tier are the Specialists. We greatly value people who bring money into the clan and so create very favorable conditions for them to develop. The clan accepts any players with over 200 levels in any profession, irrespective of the results they get during testing. Fifth are Raiders. As you can see, they rank lower than Specialists. Sixth are Fighters. These are our potential Raiders. And seventh are Recruits. These are simply hired players who've expressed a desire to join the clan.

Eric and Clutzer were immediately given the rank of Fighters, bypassing the Recruit stage. Their test results were just too good. As for their low level – with time that can change easily enough. Did I answer your question, future Phoenix Master?"

"Yes, thank you. And we'll have to see about that Master thing. Catch you later."

So, for the next two months I won't be seeing any members of the leading clans. That is, while I am looking for the Dark Coordinator? That's just as well. I'll have time to think of how to formulate my polite refusal to join Phoenix. Judging by what Anastaria just told me, I will be practically rolling in it in her clan. If you add to this my desire to quietly pass my time until the end of my sentence, this was the ideal scenario. I would gradually level up my professions and may even join Phoenix on a few raids. I would be invited to receptions with the Emperor and there would be crowds of players offering me untold riches just to put in a good word for them. I would have it made. But I was very much put on guard by the inconsistencies in the words of Anastaria and Hellfire. If Eric had sold me out completely, in his report he should have said that we took fifth place in the gathering of Malachite and that Leite got a sword of some kind. If Anastaria personally met these players, it hasn't been all that long for her to forget the details. Something wasn't right here. My inner voice was very firm in insisting that I must not join Phoenix. And that joining any clan at all was out of the question – I had to make my own. Why – I had no idea, but I'm a Shaman, and this means that

I have to trust my feelings…

Four days flew by in what felt like an instant. When I handed in the wolf quest to the village Headman, I gained access to his other assignments. 'There are no quests in Beatwick' - yeah, right! You can fetch the water, gather wood from the forest or sweep the street. Just in the first day of doing quests I raised my reputation with the Krong province by 500. After that I went to the blacksmith and arranged to loiter around his place for four hours a day.

The smith turned out to be an altogether strange NPC. He was silent and huge and all his replies to my questions were monosyllabic and came through gritted teeth. At least he wasn't kicking me out of the smithy.

Leveling up in professions ended up being very productive. I raised my Smithing to 8, first casting Copper and then Tin ingots. When I was smelting Copper Ore the stars aligned correctly and a piece of Malachite dropped for me. You had to see the Smith's eyes at that point! He stood there for a couple of minutes, muttered something inarticulate and went out to get some fresh air. I planned to focus on Smithing for another week or so and then switch to Jewelcraft.

Nor had I forgotten about the Dark Coordinator.

"Hi, Tisha," I sought out the Headman's daughter after leaving the smithy.

"Hi, Mahan," replied the pretty girl, fixing her hair. After Anastaria, who represented the real world, all NPC beauties seemed to pale in comparison. "I see that you're making progress in our village. My father's happier than ever: now the water arrives on time and the wood too. And the matter with the wolves has been settled. They really have caused too many problems for our flocks, as the father says. Did you want something?"

"Yes. I have a question. Listen, I would like to visit some neighboring villages, maybe they have some jobs as well. You don't happen to know who travels a lot between villages and whom I can ask where it's best to start?"

"The Merchant. He visits all the villages once every three weeks. He was here just a couple of days ago, so we won't see him for a while. Then, who else... Ah! Slate, our smith. He goes between the villages quite often. We don't have that many smiths in our area, so he travels around mending everything, As far as I know, he should be venturing out again soon. I think that's it. We don't have anyone else travelling between the villages."

"I see. Can you tell me if you get visitors from other villages very often? Maybe I can ask them how things are over there."

"No, we don't get many visitors. There's the Merchant and also some free citizens, but we haven't had any of those for over six months now. We have no inn, so there isn't much for visitors to do here."

"Thank you, you simply saved me. I will ask Slate which village would be the best to visit. Though he's a bit of a silent type - you can't get a word out of him."

"Well, he's still wary of you, that's all. He's used

to working alone and now you invited yourself to his smithy. So he doesn't know how to handle this. Our smith is a good and kind man, really. Even likes poetry."

"Poetry, you say? Do you know how long he's been living in Beatwick?"

"About as long as we have - a couple of years."

I left Tisha in possession of two suspects: the Merchant and the Smith. And the version with the Merchant, who was trying to offer me crazy money for the Eye, looked a lot more likely. I just couldn't see the smith as a goblin coordinator. This meant that I had to check out the Merchant. Something to do when he returns in three weeks' time.

After four days of working side by side Slate still hadn't warmed up to me. He still shot me sullen side-glances from under his eyebrows and was untalkative, responding only in short phrases. I really had to do something about this. It's high time we became friends.

"Slate, Tisha told me that you travel around villages, fixing things. Is that right? Can you please teach me the art of repair? I know how to craft, but have no clue about mending things. For example, most of the stuff I'm wearing is already on its last legs, but I have no way of fixing it."

"Repair, you say? That's not hard to teach." Ah! Finally we have progress! So many words at once. "But to repair, you first have to know what it is you'll be repairing. You can't learn everything. You can repair items made of metal, leather or cloth. But you can train in only one of these. Which do you need?"

"Shamans mainly wear leather items. I can put on mail or plate items, but I'll be moving around like a tortoise. Slowly and steadily." Just in case I asked:

"Is it possible to change a specialization? For example, if I get tired of mending leather items, could I train to repair items made of metal?"

"Yes, you can. Any repair trainer can re-train you. So, what did you choose?"

"Yes, I'd like to learn to repair leather items."

You have acquired the 'Repair' profession. Current level: 1

You received an object: Repair Kit (Attention! Does not take up inventory bag space)

You have chosen the 'Leather Repair' specialization. You can now repair leather items up to (10*Repair) level

Nice one! I thought repair would be part of smithing, but it turned out that it had been given an entire profession of its own! It even had specializations!

"So, how do I use all this?"

"It's fairly simple," it was beginning to look like I finally found some common ground with Slate. "You put the item on the table, take out the needle and thread from the Repair Kit and start sewing up the torn areas. This way its durability will be gradually restored."

"Thank you. I'll try it out right away." I picked out the necessary instruments, took off my rather battered jacket and started to repair it.

"And you know, Mahan... I'm sorry for the first welcome I gave you," I nearly ran the needle through one of my fingers on hearing such words from the smith. "I didn't realize you were a normal guy. I thought we were sent a cutthroat and was afraid you might get up to some bad business. But things turned out rather different. Anyway, don't hold it against me..."

In due course the day had arrived. Or night, to be exact. The night of the revenge for my respawn. The night of the Vagren hunt.

The actual method of capture wasn't particularly ingenious. I would come out to the middle of Elizabeth's courtyard, summon the two Bone Traps around me, and then sit between them and wait for the 'ol' red-eye'. I didn't doubt for a second that he would show up. After all, this is a quest mob, so we were meant to find each other. Today I asked Little Tim not to be released from his enclosure, saying that I had to take a walk in the moonlight. I am a Shaman, after all.

"Elizabeth, where are you going at this hour?" I was very surprised to see the mistress of the house going out so late in the evening.

"Ah... It's you... I...." Even in the twilight I could see that Elizabeth was blushing like a young girl. You had the impression that my landlady was heading out for a date. At her age too! And I even knew where she was heading - probably to the local Headman. Eh, Elizabeth!

"I'm going out for some fresh air," she managed to regain her composure, glanced at the fence gate and asked, "Will you be taking long with your walk? After all, it's quite chilly - you might be more comfortable in the house." A soon as I completed the Wolf quest, Elizabeth offered me to move from my current cramped abode to a normal room in the main house. But I refused, at least for the time being. Until I've caught the Vagren I didn't want to disturb the household with my stamping around at night.

"Well, I better go," only now did I notice a small bundle in the woman's hands. Why would she need that on a date? Or was she going to a completely different place? But where?

The night in Beatwick was coming into its own. As before, it was pitch-black and its silence was tinged with the sound of the forest, but now it featured a Shaman squatting between two traps. Elizabeth never came back, although it was past midnight now. I looked at Tiny Tim. The dog showed no sign of agitation and was calmly pacing around the enclosure. It would be such a laugh if the Vagren decided not to show today and I would have wasted nearly a thousand gold on traps! That would be a pity... I don't think I got the night wrong. But there was no-one here... Nothing. I'll pop over to Farstead tomorrow and buy a couple more traps. Wouldn't be a bad idea to drop by the old ladies and ask how Swiftbel came to know the dragons. And then to the Bank - the parcel with the gear should have arrived from Anastaria. I had long since outgrown what Kart made for me, but, being so far away from the auction house and normal merchants, it was practically impossible to buy a decent replacement. And I should also collect the Lapis that Hellfire promised me. As it happens, after four days of thinking it over I decided to have a chat with him. I was prepared to work for the clan, but not as a member. Joining a clan was to be avoided at all costs or I would miss out on some very important bonus. I spent a couple of hours looking through the manual for things that you could lose out on by joining a clan, but found nothing. On the contrary, the recurring message was that with joining a clan you gained access to the main aspects of the game in Barliona and the player acquired the full set of features... Perhaps this was just my paranoia playing up? Who knows... I also took stock of the fact that Hellfire was talking to me from a position of power. For him that was normal. After all, he's the highest-level player in Malabar, and was simply incapable of speaking in any other way. Phoenix already had the bonuses from the First Completion of the Mushu Dungeon and as for the chess pieces that Phoenix so covets... I wouldn't hand them over until I solved their riddle. After that we could talk. Again, if I am unable to solve it in two months, I would have to ask Anastaria to give me a hand. It would mean that it was too much for my brains to crack it alone. But this was all for later, I had different task in hand now.

As if it was waiting for me to stop making various grand plans, a shadow fell a couple of meters away from me. I heard Tiny Tim's muffled squealing and realized that the hour that I was so eagerly awaiting finally came. The Vagren was here.

A humanoid dog was standing a couple of meters away from me, right opposite one of the traps.

Just what the doctor ordered! If it went for me now, it would step straight into the trap. And in the morning we'll see who's been nimble enough to be running around Beatwick and causing all the mischief. One thing didn't seem right - the Vagren was without the mist and I could see his properties without much trouble:

Vagren. Gender: Female. Level 95

So, it was Elizabeth, after all. Eh, my dear hostess... What would happen to your children if I hand you over to the priest? What would happen to Clouter? Damn! I even felt sorry for her. Was there perhaps a different way of solving this?

Several minutes went by. The Vagren still stood opposite me, hopping from one foot to the other and seemed to have no intention of attacking. Did she need some encouragement? That can happen!

"Why are you just standing there? Who are you waiting for? Do you need a special invitation? Go on, jump. I'm ready."

The Vagren started at my words, but stayed where she was. Curiouser and curiouser, as Alice put it. Why is she hesitating? And, more importantly, why aren't the Vagren's eyes red? Why is it not aggressive?

The sound of a falling object made my hair stand on end. What the heck was that? I was protected from the Vagren, so I boldly tuned around to see who just joined our little party.

There was a cloud of mist and two glowing red

eyes.

"Ehh.... Hi?" I couldn't say anything more stupid at this moment. The Vagren gave a subdued growl and lunged at me. Or not at me - I never had the chance to find out because she got stuck in the trap like a butterfly. That's one down. Now I had to catch the misty something and it's in the bag. Well, attack already!

There was an attack. And a wipe. Mine.

I saw for myself how a Bone Trap worked. As soon as the red-eyed beast went for me a green film formed around it. This was the freezing part. At the same moment bones began to appear, which surrounded the beast from every side and confined it into a prison of sorts. That's that - now I had two suspects for all this shady business on my hands. In the morning we'll see who is what around here.

Pleased, I was about to leave, when the bone trap was smashed to smithereens and the angry irritated beast slid out of it. A moment later it was right next to me.

You have been poisoned and immobilized. You are losing 300 hit points every 5 seconds; duration - 2 minutes. Total Hit Points: 490 of 790 You have been poisoned and immobilized...

The re-eyed beast stood next to me and was probably watching me die with great pleasure.

There was a flicker and I ended up by the entrance of the local cemetery. The bright sunshine made the message that appeared look somewhat pale:

Attention!
In connection with your death, your level of Experience has been reduced by 30%. Current Experience: 360; points remaining until next level 8040

Right, let's look at what we have. A female Vagren, probably Elizabeth, is currently in my Bone Trap. Some kind of a beast, made of mist, claws and poison, has sent me for respawn for the second time in a row - right after it demolished a trap intended for a 100-level creature. What are the options?

I came to myself and ran towards Beatwick. The twelve hours it takes to respawn mean that now everyone would be walking around the trap and wondering what on earth it was doing in the middle of the courtyard. I was the only one who could look inside it.

"Tarry a moment, my son," I ran just a few steps, when I was stopped by the priest. "I heard that you have caught the night terror of this village of ours. I already went to have a look. I admit that your plan was good. Let us go, you can hand over this troublemaker to me. I could not see inside the trap, try as I might."

Update of the 'Night Terror of the Village' quest. The priest of god Vlast believes that the Bone Trap contains the Nigh Terror of the Village

Oops. So now it looks like the priest would come with me, see Elizabeth and call her the Night Terror of the village. I would complete the quest and my landlady would be punished and sent to Farstead. Sure thing - Clouter and Mariana are all grown up and can look after themselves just fine. In any case, they are NPCs and there are no street children in Barliona, so they'll be fine. I once again considered the advantages I would get by completing this quest: +500 Experience, +400 to Reputation, a Rare Item from the Headman...

"You are mistaken, holy father. The Night Terror is a misty beast with red eyes. I saw it yesterday and that's what was caught by the broken trap. Last night I put up another trap by mistake and accidentally caught my landlady. But this is definitely not the night monster, because for that beast the trap was merely a brief annoyance." I'm not handing over Elizabeth. Just don't want to.

"What landlady?" The priest was surprised. "Elizabeth? She's been running around the courtyard all morning fretting and moaning. So don't feed me stories about the Night Terror. It's clear enough that there can be nothing else in the trap. There was no-one else that could have been caught in it. Let's go - you can show me. I'm just really eager to hand it over to the law-enforcers."

This stopped me in my tracks. How could Elizabeth have been running around the court fretting and so forth in the morning? She's the Vagren! That is, she was meant to be sitting inside my trap. But... If Elizabeth is free, who did I catch?

"So, shall we go and look?"

"All right. I'm also rather curious who I may have caught by mistake," I said, trying to give myself a potential future loophole by implying this was an accident, and we headed for Beatwick.

"There he is!" Elizabeth met me in the courtyard, nearly finished with tidying up. "Made a mess and ran away, did we? And I have to clean up after you? We should have let Tiny Tim out – he wouldn't have allowed for such outrage to take place here. What is this monstrosity?" My landlady pointed to the trap standing in the middle of the courtyard.

"Hold on, Elizabeth," the priest defended me. "Mahan caught an evil-doer. Don't open it yet, I will put a defense around the trap. I'm certain the beast would try to escape."

The priest made a few deft movements and the trap was surrounded by a green cocoon. My jaw almost hit the floor when I looked at its properties:

Movable Prison. Allows you to detain NPCs of level 250 and below for 24 hours and players of level 250 and below for 1 hour

And it's not like the priest used any scrolls! He did it all by himself! Who is he? Out of habit I looked at the priest's properties:

Priest of god Vlast. Level 1*N

It was a standard description. Such obscuring of

the level is in place for all NPCs, with whom reputation is lower than Esteemed. So what N could be in this particular specimen, was anyone's guess. But it was definitely at least 100. According to the manual, the Movable Prison could be made by mages of 120+ levels. I should have a chat with the priest about where he got an ability like that.

"What happened, my son?" The priest looked at me in surprise. "Do get on and open the trap. I put a thorough defense around it. No-one would be able to get out!"

I selected my trap, went to the settings and chose deactivation. He's wrong about no-one being able to get out of it. Someone like Hellfire and Anastaria wouldn't even notice it.

The trap fell apart and there were sighs of surprise from everyone present.

"What on earth are you doing now? Not only did you fill my yard with junk, but put Tisha in a trap as well! That's it! My patience has reached its limit! This very day I will go to the Headman and he can find a different place for you to live. I don't want to see your face here anymore..."

Elizabeth started to give me a proper dressing down, but I didn't care. I looked at Tisha with wide surprised eyes, as she smiled shyly at those present and tried not to look at me.

"Looks like we have our villain," the entire courtyard fell silent from the priest's simple words. Even Tiny Tim who was running around the enclosure, froze, trying not to make any noise. Everyone looked at me and at Tisha in surprise.

"My goodness..." was all Elizabeth could utter, covering her mouth in horror. "How could this be?"

Tisha finally looked at me with her green eyes, full of hope and pleading. 'Don't give me away', those eyes seemed to say. 'I beg you'. We stared at each other for a little while and suddenly a message appeared in front of my eyes:

Attention! If you give up the Vagren to the priest of Vlast, the 'Night Terror of the Village' quest will be completed. If you refuse to give the Vagren up, the 'Night Terror of the Village' quest would be altered and your reputation with the representatives of god Vlast would fall by 1000 points

Do you wish to name Vagren Tiliasha as the Night Terror of the Village?

"You are mistaken, holy father," I said once again. "Yesterday Tisha was taking a walk nearby, I invited her over. And the rest is simple: we quarreled, I put up the trap in anger and ran off to the forest, to take out my rage on the wolves. But I did not come across any more wolves and it seems that Tisha fell into my trap. Tisha, please forgive me, I was a fool," I looked at the Vagren, hoping that she was smart enough to confirm my words.

"I will think about it," said Tisha, fixing up her hair, 'We have a lot to talk about. I don't want a repeat of what happened yesterday. Agreed?"

"Agreed. We do have a lot to discuss."

The quest 'Night Terror of the Village' has been altered. Go to the village Headman for further instructions. Your reputation with the priests of Vlast has fallen by 1000 points. Current level: Mistrust

"What are you staring at?" Elizabeth was the first to regain her composure and started to order her workers around. "Can't you see that this was a stupid lover's quarrel? Off to work with you!"

The priest shot me a glance which was meant to dispel any doubt that I just made the biggest mistake of my life, removed his movable prison and went back to his temple. Yes, what I just did may have been stupid, but Tisha was no mist monster.

"Let's go to my place," Tisha came up to me and again looked me straight in the eyes. "I think there is much I have to tell you about what's really going on in Beatwick..."

"Tisha?" the Headman looked up at up in surprise when we entered the house.

"Daddy, something happened... Mahan caught me in a trap yesterday," I saw the Headman's eyes narrow. "In my main form."

"He knows?" the Headman's commanding face turned into a frozen mask.

"Now – yes. And he refused to hand me over to the priest too. I think the time has come to tell him all the truth. What if he can help us?"

The Headman took a few minutes to think over his daughter's words and then said:

"Can you make us some tea please? This can take a while. And you sit down," the Headman was addressing me now. "I did not want to get you involved, but it seems fate would have it otherwise."

Like heck this was fate. That's how it's been programmed in your settings, I thought darkly. I didn't sell out your daughter - so I get a change to the quest. Tisha brought the tea, sat in an armchair and looked questioningly at her father, who seemed to be hesitating to start the conversation. Fine, if everyone is so hesitant, I'll start.

"Let me tell you what I know. So, a week ago the priest of Vlast gave me an assignment to find a certain 'Night Terror of the Village'. I prepared myself, went on a hunt and saw two unusual creatures last night. Unusual for me, that is. A Vagren and some incomprehensible mist-covered beast. I managed to catch the Vagren, but I had no such success with the mist beast. In the end it turned out to be Tisha in the guise of the Vagren. For some reason the priest is convinced that the Vagren and the Night Terror are one and the same and was terribly offended when I wouldn't hand Tisha over to him. But I didn't do it because I saw the real monster with my own eyes. That's all I've got. Your turn," I looked at the Headman in question.

"My family has always been unusual," said the Headman, having digested my words. "It's just a fact of life that all of us are Vagrens. This is neither good or bad. It just happens to be the case. In our previous life, as we call out life before Beatwick, I held a very high position, but at one point everything changed. My colleagues and acquaintances turned away from us and set head-hunters after us. This was all because of my eldest son. He did not want to accept our way of life and crossed over to the enemy. When I was offered to move to Beatwick and make a new start I fully embraced this opportunity. You have to take care to protect your family. But trouble had followed us even here."

"This is all because of the mist monster," added Tisha. The Headman gave her a stern look and continued.

"Yes, this is all because of the mist monster. Two years ago we moved here. At first everything was going really well – we were given a good welcome by the local people and established good relations with the Priest, who knew what we were right away. Trouble started a few months after my appointment. Animals started to disappear from the flocks. Every seven days either a cow or a sheep went missing from the village. And one time claw marks appeared on the gates. I thought up the story about a werebeast and our family went hunting...."

Tisha gave a fitful sigh, as if recalling unpleasant moments from the past.

"That was the only time when we saw the beast up close. It didn't hide, feeling itself in control of the situation. It tried to attack us several times and each time we fought it off, inflicting considerable damage. In the end the beast started to run away from us and we managed to corner it. But even when cornered, we were unable to destroy it. It turned out to be too smart. Choosing the weakest among us, it attacked Tisha. And then I made an unforgivable mistake. Instead of attacking the monster, I threw myself in front of my daughter. The beast left me something to remind me of this for the rest of my life," the Headman unbuttoned his shirt and I saw a terrible scar on his shoulder. "I have one exactly like this on my thigh. The monster started to hide from us and I was unable to walk for half a year. I had to receive visitors in my home. From that time our house turned into the local administration office. The previous house was demolished, the place where it once stood is now taken up by the square. Each night my sons have been going out on the hunt, but they haven't seen the beast since that time. Tisha is the first to see the monster this close in the last two years."

The Headman paused, finishing his tea, and then continued:

"But this is not all. It turned out that the beast isn't resting in the six days after it eats an animal. It raids the neighboring villages, appearing once a week in each of them. I made the decision that my family would destroy this monster. This is why my sons are hardly ever seen in Beatwick. They are travelling between the villages, hoping to catch or destroy the Night Terror', as the Priest calls it. He has a reason to think that we're behind this: he once saw my son kneeling over a freshly killed sheep. We haven't managed to prove that we are the ones hunting the killer. Nor does the Priest have any evidence that we are the Night Terror. We are maintaining neutrality, but the initial trust is no longer there. Until our Priest is presented with the real monster, he would not believe me or anyone else that we are innocent. For two years now the beast has evaded us and we need help. Don't worry about the reward - it will be considerable. Would you help us?"

Change to the 'Night Terror of the Village' quest. The Headman's family turned out to be Vagrens, who have spent two years hunting the mist monster. Find and destroy it. Quest type: Rare. Reward: +400 to Reputation with the Krong Province, +500 Experience, +10 Gold coins, a Rare item from Headman's Stores. Penalty for failing/refusing the quest: None
Do you wish to accept the changed quest?

"I will help you destroy the monster," it would be just wrong to refuse a quest that lacks any downsides.

"All right. Tisha, see Mahan off," the Headman leaned on the back of the chair, looking satisfied. "I realize that you can't travel to other villages, so you can take a break for a week. In six days we'll meet again and will go on a joint hunt for the mist monster. He's as good as done for."

After returning home I took out a teleportation scroll to Farstead and activated it. While it formed, I took stock of the results of my second run-in with the mist beast. The thing was two-nil in the lead. It might also be reasonable to ask: who, aside from Tisha in her Vagren guise, is Tiny Tim afraid of? Is the mist monster a Vagren as well? The Headman's eldest son, for example... I needed help, but had little desire to approach Anastaria. I'll wait a week and get to the bottom of this myself. The Merchant should be arriving soon enough too and I had to do some very thorough work on him. I had little doubt at this point that he was the Coordinator. Now I just had to prove it to the others.

CHAPTER SIX
KORNIK

A S SOON AS I STEPPED OUT OF THE PORTAL, a
message appeared in front of me:

**Quest update for 'The Path of the Shaman.
Step 2' and 'Searching for your Totem'. Shaman
Trainer Kornik has come to Farstead to meet you
and is currently Almis's guest. Visit him. Quest
type: Class-based**

No way! I was missing normal Shaman skills so
much that I even started to think about buying a portal
to Anhurs, finding Kornik and getting him to teach me.
I didn't worry about returning - I would be
automatically teleported back in two day's time. If I
could return three times - why not make use of one of
them. Nothing terrible would happen. However, if

Kornik came to Farstead himself, I couldn't fail to visit him. But I would do this after the bank and the old ladies. I had no idea where the trainer might send me and how long my visit would take.

"How can I be of service?" the changeless gremlin was sitting at his table scribbling something.

"I was sent some items and I would also like to receive the delivery under the password 'Hellfire-Lapis Lazuli-dwarves.'

"Please wait," gremlin's eyes clouded over and re-focused a few moments later, "Thank you. Your items await you in your Personal Room. Please note that just over twelve thousand gold has been transferred to your account. You can look up the exact amount in the transfer description. Sender - the Mayor of Farstead."

"Thank you for the information," I happily thanked the gremlin and headed for my Personal Room. So they did sell the goblin that I caught! Twelve thousand gold was a very pleasant surprise.

A big pile of gear was lying in the middle of the room. I picked up the first thing at random and looked at its properties:

Master Rick's Leather Pauldron. Durability: 600. Physical damage resistance: 80, Magical damage resistance: 40, +24 Stamina, +32 Intellect. Item class: Rare set. Number of items in the set: 8. Level requirements: 20. Crafted by: Rick Deadeye
    Set of 2 items: +50 Intellect
    Set of 4 items: +200 Defense from all damage

types

Set of 8 items: +300 Intellect

My inner Hoarding Hamster collapsed with paroxysms of love for Anastaria. Right now he was not just prepared to hand over the Orc Warriors to her, but promise to craft all the remaining chess pieces in the next couple of hours. The eight-item set with stats like these could be worth around fifty thousand gold! While the Greed Toad was trying to revive the Hamster, I started to don the new gear.

Putting aside the Crafting gloves, I couldn't help feeling pleased when I looked at my stats: Yeahhh... Stamina: 238. Intellect: 757. Defense against all types of damage: 280. Physical damage resistance: 840. And there was me thinking I was such a cheater with my rings. That was before I got acquainted with Master Rick! How could level 20 items, even rare ones, have such stats? There were several letters lying on the table. I opened the first of them and it all became clear as I read it:

"Good day Mahan. I am sending you several items, as promised. I'm sorry I couldn't find a cloak at such short notice. Rick doesn't know how to make them and the rest of our Tailors didn't have anything for level 21. I gave instructions to buy a cloak of your level with appropriate stats from common NPC-traders, but this would take time. We'll send it soon. I'm not sending any rings or neck-chains - you're a Jeweler yourself and would be able to create something much better than

what I may have to offer. You can see that the items you were sent are somewhat unusual. They were created by our Master, Rick Deadeye, who has 12 levels in Crafting. You should have some idea how much such a set would cost at an auction. And I'm not even going to get into the scrolls. As you can see, the Phoenix clan is very interested in having you join our ranks: we wouldn't have sent you some cheap rubbish that you can buy from any Merchant.

And now we get to the important part. We need to talk. Please contact me as soon as you can. I have already kicked myself several times for giving you a one-way communication amulet. To fix this I'm sending you a normal two-way amulet, so I can contact you at any time. Now then. Your trick question about Leite's item was impressive and unexpected and I wasn't ready for it. Yes, they have not been accepted into our clan. We recruited Karachun to get hold of the Mushu Dungeon First Kill. The remaining three refused to join and are camping in a safe zone in Anhurs, having resolved to wait for your decision on joining. As Eric said: "If Mahan joins, we'll follow him and if not, I hope you don't hold it against us if we give it a pass. Promises have to be kept. If we ditch him now, where is the guarantee that we wouldn't ditch Phoenix too? This isn't want you're looking for." It was a worthy reply, I even began to respect the dwarf. Hellfire was unwise to exaggerate about their presence in the clan. I had to confirm his words, which meant deceiving you. Hel thought you would rush in and join us to be with your friends. But everything actually worked out for the best. If you joined the clan, we would have failed the quest from the Herald. In essence it's quite simple - we must give you a chance to carry out a certain mission. I am sure that you have many questions and I am prepared to answer them. Once again - contact me. You can't write everything in a letter.

The main reason why the clan needs you is your third level in Crafting and the Karmadont chess pieces. You can, of course, try to deny that you're the one who made them, but try to weigh up all the pros and cons for yourself. From what I saw, you have a head on your shoulders. Figuring out the bit with the Crafting was elementary - Karachun told us about the rings and their stat bonuses, we compared that against the recipes and got our answer. That wasn't hard. The only thing that Rick was curious about was how you managed to change stats, since you need character level of 150 and 100 levels in any profession before you can access the design mode. It goes without saying that this is unlocked via a quest chain, which needs several people to complete - it's physically impossible to solo. Our analysts are still racking their brains how this is possible and are even putting Karachun's words into doubt. But Eric, whom I contacted specifically on this account, has confirmed that you were able to change the properties of the rings you crafted. All my analysts are in a state of shock and can only shrug at this. This is the third reason why we want you in the clan.

As you can see, I'm showing you all my cards. Your move, Jeweler.

Kind regards, Anastaria, head of the Phoenix

clan."

It was a good thing that the Personal Room had a chair, so I just sat down instead of dropping on the floor. Right, time out. I'll leave the thinking for later. Now I will read the other letters and then make some decisions. If my head is still working by the end of it. I opened the third letter and read on:

"Hello Mahan. Listen, some weird shit is going on. Our three-strong fighting force had gathered together in Anhurs two days after leaving the mine. Then, out of the blue, we were contacted by Phoenix representatives, asking us to join the clan. It was an attractive offer, of course, but we made a firm decision to wait for you. We weren't that keen on ditching anyone. Today I had a visit from Anastaria, the leader of the Phoenix clan herself. She asked about Malachite mining, the items we were given and the place that we had taken. I don't consider any of this a secret and gave her honest answers to all of this, about the fifth place and what each of us got. She showed a lot of interest in you, in the rings and in how you changed their stats. This I also told her, although now I think that perhaps I shouldn't have. So, in general, know that the Phoenix people were asking about you. We'll be waiting for you at the 'Jolly Gnoom' in just over two months. We cannot come to join you - PK-ers have become a real pain. As soon as you leave the city, they pop up right away. If you can, please send us the money that we got from the Dungeon - we're running a bit low at the moment.

Eric.

Once I leave Beatwick, the drinks are on me. So what if you can't get drunk in Barliona - the drinks are still on me! Eric and the guys didn't ditch me after all! And I was all set to get upset... Now, what do we have in the third letter?

"Hello Mahan.
Sending you the Lapis Lazuli. I hope that you're able to work it by now. Fifty pieces of Lapis should last you a good while. Anastaria's birthday is four weeks away. Don't let me down.
Hellfire, head of the Phoenix clan."

The first thing I did before deliberating on the letters was go to the gremlin and send Eric ten thousand gold and the gloves that dropped in the Dungeon. That's it. I just sent and forgot about them. They were becoming a tempting annoyance in my bag. I also wrote him that I was all right and would be heading out to Anhurs in two months' time - though it might take me about a week to get there. After this I sat down in the Personal Room and finally let it hit me. My hands were shaking and not a single sensible thought entered my head, except for: "What to do?"

Very soon an epic plan ripened in my mind: Kornik came to Farstead. If he was here, he could explain to me why my feelings seem to be glitching. Why is my head pointing me towards Phoenix, but my heart away from it?

Once that decision had been reached, it was much easier to start doing things and I started to put everything away into my bag: a hundred scrolls of Wall of Flame dealing 1000 points of damage and the pile of Lapis Lazuli from Hellfire. Then there was only the two-way communication amulet left. I looked at it despondently but still put it around my neck. The deal with it was simple enough - either I take it and use it or I return it, together with all the items. After one good look at those I was entirely disinclined to return them. At least for now. I really didn't want to feel like a complete sell-out, so after giving it a good think, I wrote a reply:

"Good day, Anastaria.
Thanks a bunch for the items and the scrolls. As soon as I outgrow them, I will repair them and return them to you as good as new. As you correctly pointed out, I understand full well what such a set can cost. Perhaps for you this is not so much, but for me it's simply enormous. Even if I do join Phoenix, I do not wish to be in the position of a poor relation who gets clothed from the lord's charity. I am not used to being a dead weight.
Shaman Mahan."

I read over the letter one last time. I didn't appear to make any promises, but didn't agree to anything either. Until I sort out the mess inside me, I'll keep making such excuses. I sent the reply and was hit by a crazy thought. I started a new letter:

"Hello Hellfire. I got the Lapis and will try to work it. Here's the thing: I told Anastaria about the Number Twos that I ran across in the Krong Province. One of them I recognized as Plinto, on account of his Phoenix. I have a request. Can you send me the nicks and appearance holograms of the top twenty players from Phoenix and the Number Twos. It would be useful to know who to trust and who to avoid at all costs."

If Hellfire replied, I would know exactly what to do with his chess request for Anastaria. He wants the Dwarves, eh? Well, bite me!

"Dearie, can you help out a weak and helpless woman?"

Patricia was still standing in the door of her house, stretching an envelope towards players running past. Some players stopped, their gaze growing cloudy as they looked up the quest in the manual, and were off again a few minutes later. No-one wanted to get involved in a socializer quest.

"Greetings to you, dear lady," I came up to the old woman and bowed. "I finished your assignment and now possess the treasure of Swiftbel, your brother. I have a few questions for you - would you mind answering them?"

"Well, dearie, you do some work for me first and ask them questions after," Patricia's abrupt reply completely threw me. "Shouting it all out loud. Brother! Swiftbel! Treasure! You're walking around like some Red Riding Hood who just brought pies to grandma. I won't be telling you anything! And don't even think about carrying me to Mabel, like last time. Practically all the neighbors were laughing at me after that. No, no. I won't tolerate such an outrage a second time - I'll summon the guards right away."

And there you have it. I happen to have a quest connected to you, granny. And you've decided to get all stubborn. I looked at my Attractiveness with Patricia in the settings: 1. At least it was 2 last time. Stop! Last time I completed a quest, that's why Attractiveness went up. And later I made that tea for the old ladies.

"Then let me deliver that letter for you, it's on my way anyhow."

"Right you are too. I've not sent the letter yet! Everyone wants to get enriched at the expense of the old and frail," Patricia was back to her old tune about the unfair life of an NPC in Barliona, but I was only half-listening. If I wasn't mistaken, in the next few hours my feet were going to get pretty worn out...

I was right. My Attractiveness with Mabel was also set at one. After reading me a lecture on how people shouldn't quarrel, must look after the young and respect the old, she handed me the reply. I returned to Patricia and discovered that my Attractiveness rose to two. So I kept walking between the old ladies, having to listen not only to their lectures, but to what other players thought of me:

"Such a dolt. It's a flippin' socializer! Ditch it."

"Let's go to an instance. Nothing to catch here!"

"Dude, what the heck are you doing? Trying to find out who gets tired first, you or the old bags?"

Well, well. Players rushing around Farstead

weren't exactly tolerant. They had to watch a touched-in-the-head Shaman running between old lady NPCs, delivering a letter, getting a new one and going straight back. What a moron, right?

During my fortieth round the old ladies started to repeat themselves. That is they once again started to say that everyone tries to enrich themselves at the expense of the old and frail. Finally, the moment had arrived. I may have lost five hours outside Beatwick, but on another return to Patricia I knew that I would get:

Attractiveness with Patricia: 100

"I bet you've got quite worn out by now, sonny." said the old lady in a completely different tone, as soon as I gave her Mabel's reply. "You've been running between us half the day almost - probably done twenty miles by now. We've even run out of ideas for what to write, had to send empty letters and all. But you kept delivering them, without even looking inside. Take me to Mabel, we need to have a chat."

Finally. I carefully gripped Patricia and delivered her to Mabel like some precious cargo. Precious indeed! My Totem depended on it.

"Eh, Patricia, you've always had a weak spot for stubborn fools," Mabel stood by the house, watching her sister being transported. "This just isn't fair! Why did he come to you and not me? Maybe I want a ride as well."

"Mabel, if you're envious, there's no need to

shout about it," Patricia gestured me where to put her down.

"Dear ladies, I've come here on business," I unburdened myself of the pleased-looking old lady and decided to cut to the chase.

"So fidgety, this one," said Mabel, throwing up her arms. "Always hurrying somewhere. You think we should have tested him a bit longer?"

"No sister dear, we've given him quite a runaround as it is. He didn't even breathe a word of complaint, and you're calling him fidgety. What is it that you came for then?"

"No, no, no!" Mabel interrupted again before I could open my mouth. "What are we, some wandering tramps to be loitering by the threshold? Come on in, we'll have a proper chat inside."

Mabel's house was just the same - still as white and full of light as it was last time.

"Do make us some tea, Mabel. Mahan makes great tea, but it gives you a whopping headache afterwards. We better do it ourselves this time," Patricia, as rules of hospitality dictated, settled into an armchair and started to order her sister about.

"Right you are - how can we chat without a cup of tea first?" the hostess started to fret and headed off to the kitchen.

"So tell us how you managed to vanquish the woodwothe," tea taken care of, the old ladies now gave me their full attention. I considered denying there was any wothe there to speak of, but thought better of it - getting on the bad side of the old ladies wasn't worth the risk. I briefly described my adventures, not forgetting to mention the dragon.

"So it looks like Aarenoxitolikus got dragged into this after all," Mabel said thoughtfully. "I would have never thought that you had a Dragon for a Totem. Can you show him?"

"I can't. I'm not a real Shaman yet - I haven't completed the necessary training, so I can't summon Draco for a couple more days. And how did Swiftbel meet Aarino... Aarenoxitolikus?" - that's some tongue-twister of a name.

"Just call him Dragon. Brother found out where they live from an ancient scroll. And then did what you did. He just went and paid them a visit, the fidget. There he made friends with Aarenoxitolikus and they spent the next twenty years together."

"And where is this scroll now?" I was trying not to breathe in case I put off the old ladies.

"I will make my own way back," Patricia got up and adjusted her dress, leaving my question unanswered. "Thanks for freeing the wothe, Mahan. Our brother did wrong when he put it to guard the treasure. It was languishing and lonely there. As for the scroll, finding the way to it is not easy. Not easy at all. But we've told you what it is already. Whether you heard us or not, that's your business. Go now. And don't visit us again - we'll pretend we don't know you and won't give you any more assignments."

I was about to object, when an invisible force gripped me and shoved me out of the house. The loud bang of the closing door was accompanied by the message:

Update of the 'Searching for your Totem' quest. Swiftbel found an ancient scroll which describes the path into the land of Dragons. Where the scroll is right now is a mystery that you must solve. The merchant's sisters gave you the necessary clues. If you fail to discover them, speak to the Shaman trainer

I looked angrily at the door that concealed the old ladies. What clues did they just give me exactly? I went over the entire conversation in my head and didn't discover a single lead. But approaching a Shaman Trainer would come as the very last resort, when I admit that I was unable to find the Totem myself. Missing out on a pet that might have rare stats and abilities was out of the question. It's a standard thing in Barliona: if you do something yourself - you'll get a slice of the big pie. If you ask for help - you'll only get a biscuit. Tasty, but small. And it's the big pie I'm after...

"Where on earth have you been?" If I was now looking at Almis's full-time maid, he definitely had a preference for plump ladies. "Mr. Almis and his guest have been expecting you for a good while now. They've already had their third cup of tea and still there was no sign of you! Disgraceful!"

"Catherine, bring him right through to the sitting room. And no need to grumble - Shamans are not late, they always come at the time they consider appropriate," came the voice of the former trainer and the maid immediately fell silent. Flashing her eyes and making it clear that she will be watching me very closely, she took me to the room where two men were waiting for me. Or, rather, one man and a sentient who was completely wrapped up in a grey cloak. Judging by his height it was either a gnome or a dwarf who had been very ill for a long time.

"Kornik?"

"We have no time for idle chatter," a deeply elderly voice came from under the hood. "Almis, you know what you have to do. Warn the others."

"Yes, teacher. I understand."

"As for you, young apprentice, we have to get going. Great change is coming to Barliona and you have to be ready for it," Kornik took me by the hand and immediately Almis's place vanished. As did all of Farstead. Stunned, I gazed at the great mountains propping up the sky. The golden glow that surrounded Kornik and myself kept out the snow, which was racing around us in a blizzard. Was Kornik really a Harbinger? I opened up the map to see the description of the province where we ended up. Yeah... We were right on the fringe of the Free Lands, not far from the ocean that separated Barliona's continents. The map helpfully showed me fog in all available scales, with just a contour of the border between the land and the ocean. I didn't have this region on my map. Never mind - I would pencil it in in the evening, though I had no idea how this could be of use to me other than leveling up in Cartography. Not only was it the very edge of the world, it was also very hard to get to: Kartoss was lying right between us and the Malabar Empire.

Kornik loudly breathed in the frosty air, which was allowed through by the aura, pulled back his hood and looked at me with the enormous - once brown, but now faded - eyes of an elderly goblin.

"I had no time to wait for you in Anhurs. Terrible events are coming and we must prepare for them. First, you need to get your Totem. Now we will pay the Dragons a visit. There you will swear an oath of allegiance to the High Lord. Then..."

"I'm sorry, teacher. But I must get my totem by myself." When on earth did I get this impudent? "Thank you for your offer of help to speed up the process, but I must find my own way to the High Lord," if I understood correctly, that was the title of the head of Dragons.

For a few moments Kornik drilled me with a penetrating stare.

"All right. If you can provide a good reason why you must find the Dragons on your own without my help, I will agree. But your reason must be indisputable."

"I cannot give you a reason. This... This is something within me - I feel that this is the way I must do things and if I accept your help it would mean a greatly inferior result," I decided not to beat about the bush and tell Kornik the whole truth. As ridiculous as it might be. Even if he's an NPC, he's a clever NPC with access to the information that I need. If I don't get help with sorting out my feelings, one day I'll go mad from the inner contradictions between logic and emotions.

This isn't easy for someone who'd been guided by his head his entire life. And a pretty shabby head at that, I thought, remembering how I ended up in prison.

"That is the most cast-iron reason that a Shaman can give," there was now a hint of satisfaction in Kornik's voice. "It looks like our training process will be considerably speeded up if you're able to follow your instincts. So let's not waste any time. Have a seat," leading by example, Kornik sat down right there on the snow. "To begin with, tell me what you know about Shamans."

Is this another Prontho? The orc also asked me this question before sending me off to the Trial. I gave a pretty stupid answer at the time and was reluctant to make a fool of myself again. I opened the manual page on Shamans to refresh my memory about the steps and was about to gladly recount them to Kornik, when another bout of inner contradiction stopped me in my tracks. This isn't what the goblin wants to hear now, he is clearly asking about something else.

"What do I know about Shamans?" I closed my eyes and tried to listen to my feelings, and then said slowly: "Shamans... Shamans speak to Spirits... A Shaman's spirit must be firm, steadfast, gentle and pliant..." my eyes closed and, completely immersed in my inner world, I even stopped noticing the biting wind. These words were said by Prontho and the Great Air Spirit, so I must be able to say them too.

"All this is true, apprentice, but these are someone else's words," Kornik's voice reached me through the web of my thoughts. "Don't use someone else's words, find your own."

Antsinthepantsa's post popped up in my head: "Thinking is for mages, Shamans feel..." And that's when a light bulb lit up inside my head. I knew the answer I had to give Kornik.

"You can't describe what a Shaman is. How can you describe the wind, the rainbow or pain? You can only feel it. Someone who doesn't accept the Shaman's essence would never understand what a Shaman is, while anyone who had attained this understanding wouldn't be able to find the words to describe this to the others. For me being a Shaman means to be guided by my feelings, for Prontho it's the sense of duty and for you, teacher, it's probably something else. For each of us being a Shaman is finding our own path and following it to the very end. What do I know about Shamans? Nothing and, at the same time, everything. I don't know the Shaman I would turn into after my training, I would have to get to know him all over again, and I still have questions for myself as I am now. But I know one thing - if you're a Shaman, you are unique. I'm speaking of real Shamans here - not just those who managed to get a Totem, but lack the ability to gain the title of a Great Shaman."

Character class update: Class 'Initiate Shaman' has been replaced by 'Elemental Shaman'. Seek your trainer for learning to work with Elemental Spirits

Attention! You have earned the rank of Elemental Shaman without obtaining your Totem.

If you are unable to obtain your Totem in the next two months, your rank would be brought down to Initiate Shaman

"The Supreme Spirit was right. He does have a chance," muttered Kornik. For some moments there was a silence disturbed only by the howling of the wind.

"I have to teach you many things, my apprentice," continued the goblin a short while later, when I came to myself and opened my eyes. Sitting down in a lotus pose I prepared myself to listen to the Harbinger. I still had about thirty hours until I had to be back in Beatwick, so there was plenty of time left for training.

"We'll start with the summoning of the Spirits. Right now you are an Elemental Shaman who doesn't have a Totem of his own, but who can still summon Elemental Spirits. In total, there are four types of Spirits: Fire, Water, Air and Earth. In turn, each type of Spirit comes in four classes: mass and individual damage and the same for healing. Yes, don't be surprised - even Fire Spirits have the ability to heal."

Right, I see. I will now have access to sixteen Spirits, but will be able to add only eight summonings to the active zone. So something will have to be sacrificed. This isn't much of a worry at the beginner levels, but starting from level 100 I would have to build my active zone according to the opponent. It is foolish to summon a Fire Spirit on a Salamander or an Air Spirit on an Air Elemental.

"Each type of Spirit," Kornik continued,

"accessible to you has its rank. The more often you use a certain type of Spirit, the stronger Spirits of this type become. You have to choose the direction in which to develop, because you can strengthen only one type out of four. The strengthening would apply to all the Spirits you can currently summon or would be able to summon later: from Younger to the Supreme."

This is clear enough too. This marks the start of the work needed to level up a skill. You have to choose one school, or how the Shamans call them, type, and work with the Spirits of this type. The more often you summon, the stronger the summoned Spirit becomes. It's a pity that I bypassed working with the Younger Spirits or I would already have a specialization.

"You have to understand that Spirit summoning is not free. You have to give them something in return. Either some of your Life or a gift. Simple Spirits require bread. Don't forget that if you want to reduce the amount of Life you give to the Spirits, you have to perform a sacrifice once a week. The sacrifice is made on an Altar, which each Shaman possesses. You will receive yours later."

Something else that was bothering me has been laid to rest now. From the time I became an Initiate Shaman, I was wondering how to perform a sacrifice. The manuals didn't say a word about that. I once even left tea for the Spirits at Elizabeth's house, but it remained where it was. It turns out you needed an Altar.

"And now for the last thing that you must know about Shamans. To remove any doubt that you are an

Elemental Shaman, you must have a cloak. Here," a piece of cloth decorated with feathers appeared out of nowhere in Kornik's hands. I carefully took the item and unfolded it, trying not to damage the feathers. Will I really have to wear this? It's good to be a Harbinger, like Kornik - no external attributes or stupid cloaks. I sighed and put on the cloak, looking at its properties. The miner's cloak I had from Pryke should have been replaced long ago and since Anastaria didn't send me one, I'll use what I've been given:

Kornik's Shaman Cloak. Durability: unbreakable. Description: Increases the rank of the summoned Spirit by 2. The penalty for summoning all Spirits is decreased by 10%. + 15 to Intellect, +5 to Stamina. Item class: Rare, only usable by Shamans. Level restrictions: 20+

"Now the time has come to teach you. Henceforth you are an Elemental Shaman."

Kornik lifted his hands, shouted something and snow (which still didn't penetrate the sphere) began to swirl around me and a series of messages began to flash before my eyes:

You have learned how to summon the Air Spirit of Healing. Spirit type: Air. Description: You appeal to the world of Spirits, summoning a Spirit, which gives part of its essence to the injured person. The strength of the summoned Spirit and the amount of the essence given is determined by

Intellect and Spirit rank. Kamlanie time: 2 seconds. Cost of summoning: (Character level)/2 Summoner's Hit Points, Cost of Healing: (Character level)*4 Mana. Restores (Intellect*3) Hit Points. Cannot heal earth entities: Dwarves, Kobolds, Gnomes, ... Bestows additional healing on air entities: Air Elementals, ...

You have learned how to summon the Spirit of Air Strike. Spirit type: Air. Description: You appeal to the world of Spirits, summoning the Spirit on your opponent to take part of his life force with it. The strength of the summoned Spirit and the amount of life force taken from the opponent is determined by Intellect and Spirit rank. Kamlanie time: 5 seconds. Cost of summoning: (Character level)/ 2 Hit Points of the summoner. Cost of attack: (Character level)*4 Mana. Damage: (Intellect*3) Points. Range: 40 meters. Cannot attack air entities: Air Elementals, ... Deals additional damage to earth entities: Dwarves, Kobolds, Gnomes, ...

The Spirits of the air healing wave and air wall provided AoE healing and damage. Quite good, but in each of the learned summonings both damage and healing were three times less powerful than with a single target. This provided an advantage only if there were more than three opponents or injured parties. Otherwise you had to work with each target separately. I learned similar summonings for Water, Fire and Earth. They were practically the same, the only difference being in the names.

A few things stuck in my memory right away: you could not heal humans and thaurun with Fire Spirits, orcs and trolls with Water Spirits and elves and pixies with Earth Spirits. It was the same with damage - each type had its limitations.

"You have to choose the type of Spirit that you will be advancing, apprentice," I heard Kornik's voice after going through the entire list of spells. "A Shaman must make his choice at the start and follow it his entire life. No matter how wrong that choice might have been," did I hear a note of sadness in Kornik's voice?

This made me quite thoughtful. On one hand the choice seemed obvious: Fire. Damage from all four types was the same, but psychologically it's fire that everyone fears. I don't know the visual side of the summoning, but calling a Fire Spirit should at least send some sparks flying. One thing that stopped me was you couldn't use it to heal humans. Leveling up a Spirit type that doesn't grant you the ability to heal yourself is pretty stupid. Which should it be then? Earth, Air or Water? Should I toss a coin, perhaps?

"Did you make your choice?" Kornik hurried me. So impatient! I'm having a think here and he's distracting me.

"Yes, teacher. Water. I choose the water type."

"Explain your choice."

"I could refer to my feelings again, but this time I was guided by simple calculation. Fire and Air are immediately ruled out, because I, as well as my friends, are humans, gnomes and dwarves. If I can't summon strengthened Spirits on us, what do I need them for? Then we have Water and Earth left. I thought of choosing Earth, but saw that it comes with a limitation for elves. I may not have any elf friends, but I do have a few acquaintances. Then only Water remains. I don't know any trolls or orcs, aside from Prontho, who can be healed by an ordinary Spirit."

When I mentioned Prontho, the goblin's face wrinkled up in a smile.

"Yes, that stubborn fool can be healed by simple bandages, all right. He'd survive anything. So be it, then. From now on and henceforth your personal type of Spirit is Water!"

Personal Spirit type determined: Water. Water Spirit summoning rank: 1

I added the fire and water spells to the active zone, filling up all the available slots. Now I could face anything!

"Teacher, since we've mentioned Prontho, I would like to know what happened on that ill-fated day when he challenged Shiam. And where is Geranika now? And, the most important question - what is going on with me? Why do I keep taking one decision with my head, but a different one with my heart? When I let myself be guided by my head the result is complete nonsense."

"Is this all that you wish to know," Kornik raised an eyebrow questioningly, "or do you have a couple more questions? Don't hurry, have a think, what if you missed something?"

Maan, Kornik seriously reminds me of Almis right now. What is it with NPC-Shamans? Are they all programmed to answer a question with a question?

"No, this isn't all. I would also like to know why you flew all the way to Farstead to see me. What threat is Barliona facing? Why the hurry with the training and obtaining the Totem? What is it that Almis has to do? This covers it now, I think."

Goblin's laughter echoed through the mountains.

"According to all the rules you should have felt embarrassed enough to ask my pardon for your impertinence, bow your head and await my permission to ask questions. But it seems you haven't heard about these things called rules," Kornik looked at me shrewdly. "And that is good. Before I answer your questions, I would like you to summon a Spirit. We can talk anywhere, but training you without being noticed by Geranika we can do only here. Heal yourself!"

Heal? No problem. There doesn't seem to be anything difficult about that. I selected myself and started to summon a Healing Spirit. How can this be a test? Just some fooling around, that's all.

Damage taken. Hit Points reduced by 2036: 2316 (Fire Spirit summoning) - 280 (Fire resistance). Total Hit Points: 384 of 2420

The Fire Spirit did come with a visual component, and quite an impressive one at that! For a couple of moments I resembled a Bengal Light, with sparks flying off me in every direction. At least it didn't hurt: looks like your own Spirits couldn't cause you pain. But what the heck?! I wanted to be healed! It took considerable willpower to stop myself from summoning another healing Spirit. One was quite enough.

"So festive and pretty," came the sardonic voice of the goblin, "but the result is not quite what you should get from a healing spell, is it? I think you should stop torturing yourself and try using a target," a practice dummy of the type used by players to perfect sequences of blows or spells appeared a few meters away from me. "Do continue."

I selected the 30-level dummy and decided to summon an attacking Water Spirit on it. Even if I was wrong, I would simply heal the dummy.

I was wrong.

Attention!
In connection with your death, your level of Experience has been reduced by 30%...

The AoE Spirits deal three times less damage than a single-target Spirit, but this was more than sufficient. I had too much Intellect and too few Hit Points remaining after my first unsuccessful attempt. The respawn point was located just next to the spot where Kornik took me. The dummy was almost completely covered in snow now, a sign that the blizzard lasted all the twelve hours I was gone.

"I was starting to think you decided to stick

around the Grey Lands forever," came the grumbling voice of the old goblin. I turned around and saw that the teacher was sitting on an inexplicably acquired carpet and sipping a hot drink. Still surrounded by a golden aura, he looked me over with a grin and added: "I have a proposal for you. I will teach you the right way to use the Spirits, but you will be permitted to ask me only one question. If you manage to get to grips with the Spirits by yourself, I'll answer all your previous questions. Make your choice."

Who says I must choose anything? I have the manual and the forum! Time to stop acting like a dope and start reading. So, the summoning of Spirits...

The hour I spent on sifting through the available materials bore no results. The official documentation didn't say a word about how to use the Spirits. Or, rather, the information was there, but it wasn't what I was looking for. Everyone referred to some sort of a Spirit-choosing mode, but made no mention of how to enter it. As far as I could see, wasn't this exactly what was involved in putting the Spirits into the active zone?

Stop! Where's the Spirit selection? Before, when I had just two summonings, I didn't bother cluttering my brain with such nonsense. But now the number of available Spirits has noticeably increased, so perhaps I should specify the slot of the active zone from which the summoning should take place.

Let's try this. I selected the snow-covered dummy and, putting some distance between us just in case, I mentally selected the Spirit and began the summoning. So, what did we have?

I didn't sustain any damage, which was great, but the fact that instead of damage the dummy had a healing Spirit land on it didn't seem quite right. At least it was a water and not a fire spirit. So it looks like first you have to choose the type of Spirit and then the summoning category: damage or healing. Let's try this.

I selected the dummy again, chose a Water Spirit, repeated the Spirit selection and started to summon. Yes! Water spray flew in all directions from the dummy, almost immediately turning into icicles. It's quite freezing here, by the looks of it. Ending up outside the golden sphere was certainly not a good idea. But right now that was inconsequential - I did it! I managed to figure out the Spirit summoning by myself! I looked at the goblin somewhat mockingly and repeated the summons: dummy, Water Spirit, Water Spirit. Summon!

"Hehe," the goblin gave a little laugh when the dummy became surrounded by a puddle of water where bodiless Spirits were dashing around, periodically causing damage. That's right. These were Water Spirits, but the AoE version. So my method wasn't working. I had further thinking to do.

After a couple of hours of experiments it sunk in that I wasn't going to learn how to summon the needed Spirit by myself. Didn't have the brains for it.

"You're not here to tell me you've given up already?" asked Kornik slyly.

"I need a hint. At least tell me the direction in which I should be working," I mumbled sheepishly.

"In that case you'll get only two questions.

Agreed?"

"Agreed," two is more than one, in any case, and I couldn't figure out what the problem was by myself. Neither my head nor my intuition seemed of any use. Moreover, even the old familiar Spirits of Lightning and Healing would no longer be summoned on demand. Something was refusing to work in my shamanistic magic since I jumped to being an Elemental Shaman.

"Then here's a hint for you. You were right when you were working on who it was you were summoning. Now think how you go about doing it."

How do I summon? I take the Tambourine, hit it with the Mallet, accompanied by 'The Shaman has three hands' and that's it, the Spirit is summoned. But then Shamans that I had seen in the past arose before my eyes. They kept hitting the tambourine and constantly singing something. Could that be it? Do I have to stay continuously in a state of summoning?

The Shaman has three hands
And behind his back a wing.
From the heat upon his breath
Shining candle-fire springs...

Yeah... Ten seconds - and the world changed. Or rather it was my game interface that changed. Almost a quarter of my field of vision was covered by eight transparent Spirits. They were constantly turning, as if showing themselves off from every side. Four Spirits had a counter under them, probably the rank of the spirit. A rather sheepish-looking '1' was shimmering there right now. My Water Spirits were still weak, very weak. I stopped my summoning to examine the updated interface. Ten seconds went by and the interface with the Spirits vanished.

So that's what the mode for working with the Spirits is like, eh? I selected a dummy, called up the mode once again and then focused on one of the Water Spirits and unleashed it at the target.

Bam! The dummy shook and water sprayed in all directions, clearing the snow in its wake. I repeated the Spirit summons and the dummy played the role of a fountain once again. Did I finally get it? I spent around ten minutes playing around with Spirit summoning, healing myself, the dummy, even Kornik, who, disgruntled, mumbled something like: "So big, but no brains at all." When I stopped the kamlanie, I exited the mode for working with Spirits. On one hand this was convenient - I had the needed Spirits always before me, in plain sight, and their summoning speed increased with this convenient interface. At the same time it looks like the class is unpopular exactly due to this aspect of Shamanistic abilities. In the time it takes you to enter the right mode and summon a Spirit, you can be outmaneuvered a hundred times and sent off to respawn at a leisurely pace.

"You've earned two questions. Think carefully before asking them," Kornik's voice brought me back to reality.

"My questions are the same. I still want to know what happened on that ill-fated day when Prontho dueled with Shiam and why I make different decisions with my heart and with my head?" and before Kornik could open his mouth I added, "But I have a massive request for you. I would like to get a full answer and not something like: "There was a duel, and you can feel the right way.' I know this anyway. Teacher, if we have so little time, please leave the riddles for later and answer the question directly. After Beatwick I will come to Anhurs, drop by for a visit and we'll play riddles all you like. We really don't have time for that at the moment."

Your reputation with the Shaman Council has increased by 10 points. You are 990 points away from the status of Friendly

"Hehe," the goblin smirked, "I really did intend to give you an answer like that. Word for word. I'll have to think of a different answer now, hehe."

"And how about simply giving a proper full answer?"

"But giving a straight answer just isn't interesting. Not flying to the Dragons and finding the scroll by yourself was your own choice. And don't look at me with such surprise. Do you really think Almis and I weren't watching you when you were running between the honorable ladies? I can give a full answer to one question and a vague answer to the other. Choose which is most important to you."

"Then tell me about Prontho - I'll sort out my own problems, but I mustn't lose the thread of the events of many years ago. This is more important."

"You've made your choice. Then listen, apprentice, about what is happening to you. You are a Shaman. What makes Shamans different is that they can feel certain things within the surrounding world. For example, a Shaman always knows if anyone is staring at him or feels if there's a fight or an ambush nearby. These are only the external manifestations of what the Spirits are able to tell them. But sometimes unusual Shamans appear. These are not only able to feel external phenomena, but internal ones as well. Some call it intuition, others premonition. But the essence of it remains the same - it is the ability to foresee the future. Such sentients exist among Mages, Warriors, Hunters and Shamans. Within each class there can appear a free citizen who doesn't just perceive, but also senses. Why you're able to do this is a question for you. I don't know who you were in your previous life. I hope that you would be able to understand this by yourself."

Kornik paused, giving me a chance to think over his words. It turns out that the ability to feel is not specific to Shamans, but to certain players. Players with the ability to be prescient. People who use their intuition in the real world...

I suddenly recalled the time when I was a 'free artist' in Barliona. I was around twenty when I started studying hacking and information security. What else can a former student of the philological department for ancient languages do? There were no prospects for development and there wasn't much of a career in being an ancient culture enthusiast. So I chose computer security. This was followed by two years of stubborn and monotonous reading of books, attending training courses, sitting tests and meeting up with similarly crazy people as myself, until one day the Corporation announced a contest for hacking Barliona. At the time the game still didn't have that many players, despite active propaganda by the Government. There were plenty of virtual worlds around, some of them of even superior quality. Players had choice. And then the contest was announced: whoever managed to gain possession of another player's account would be given a reward of thirty thousand gold, which at the time already corresponded to real money. The contest lasted two weeks, without any limit placed on the number of winners.

Barliona descended into chaos.

Hackers from around the world got down to business and for about a week Barliona was inaccessible. Servers were down, accounts were hacked and characters deleted. There were howls of rage from players on the forums, thousands of cases were filed with the courts, but the Corporation steadily weathered all these woes. A certain policy had been adopted and followed through, whatever the immediate results. The chaos lasted a week and then suddenly stopped. Completely stopped. The injured parties were compensated and given commemorative gifts and everything seemed to settle down until another contest was announced six months later. It had the same purpose as the first: anyone able to break into the game and gain access to another player's information would be given a reward - a much bigger sum this time: a million gold.

Barliona held out for a week, until our three-strong strike force joined the fray. Yes, there were three of us. Me, my friend (the one who developed the security system used by Marina for her Imitator) and our mentor. The one who taught us everything we knew.

"A real hacker doesn't just know his stuff better than anyone," he liked to repeat. "A real hacker has intuition. If you can't sense that you need to click in this particular place right now and then go and launch a script in that particular location, you will never be able to call yourself a hacker. You may be an advanced programmer, a security expert, or even a break-in guru, but you will never be a hacker."

We spent three days trying to break into Barliona. The updated Imitator completely blocked all our attempts to get through the defense. Two days before the end of the contest, we gathered as usual at my friend's place and planned our next move. Everyone was out of ideas and we were close to giving up. That's when it all happened.

I stared vacantly at the stream of data coming from my capsule and, comparing it with an analogous data stream of another player, I began to randomly change the parameters of the intercepting device that we inserted between the capsule and the game server. Even now, seven years later, I would not be able to explain what it was that I did. I was typing something in, making some changes... At that moment it felt like the right thing to do. My friend wanted to speak to me, but my teacher stopped him, saying that I shouldn't be distracted.

Twenty hours later, tired and hungry, I slumped down on the floor and fell asleep. I did it. I managed to program a model of another player's data in my own capsule. The result was far from ideal, since replicating this action required a precisely configured capsule table of the target player, but it didn't matter. What did was that I managed to enter Barliona as another player's character. When I woke up only my friend remained in the flat. Our teacher left us in a hurry, having volunteered to inform the world that the desired result had been reached. It turned out that he left us for good.

When the Corporation examined my method, which our (now former) mentor claimed as a brain child of his own, it immediately offered him a job. The promised prize was paid out and the contest ended. Gaming capsules were upgraded within a month, with the Corporation providing a free replacement, so the break-in couldn't be replicated. And a couple of months later we got a letter from our mentor in which he noted with regret that in his entire life he had never had such inept students. He regretted that he ever took us on and was hanging on to the prize as compensation for the time he wasted on us. If we weren't happy with this we could always take up our grievances with him in the Game.

My friend deleted his character that very day and, as far as I know, doesn't set foot in the Game as a matter of principle. He says that he's happy enough in the real world. I kept away for three years, after turning into a 'free artist'. I did all I could to make trouble for Barliona from outside. I never found any major holes, but it was enough to make a living. I always ended up finding undocumented quirks of the Game thanks to a feeling that there was something wrong in a particular function. Then one day, after a breakup with a girlfriend, I rolled up a character and then it was too late to stop...

It looks like in some way the Game allows you - if not to develop then to enhance - intuition that we have in reality. And not just for me, but for other players too. Those who cannot really explain why you shouldn't take that flight or board that train. They simply know this deep down and that's that.

"If you are done meditating, I shall continue," Kornik didn't go anywhere while I was on my jog down the memory lane. "You wanted to know what happened between Prontho and Shiam. Then listen."

I had a great difficulty concentrating on what the goblin was saying. Memories are a great thing, but you have to live in the present.

"Twelve years ago Almis's apprentice lost his mind and crossed over to the Kartoss side. Geranika asked the Dark Lord to make him his protégé, losing forever any chance of coming back to Malabar. To prove the extent of his resolve Geranika sacrificed the Spirits of forty Shamans - ranging from Great to High in rank - to the Dark Lord. In return the Lord of Kartoss granted him such power that even I was unable to get the better of him and was forced to flee in shame. Right now Geranika is almost equal in strength to the Emperor or the Dark Lord. But there was still a chance to strip him of his might. Until the Supreme Spirits confirm a Shaman's power, he could be deprived of this power. And the Supreme ones are very unhasty entities... We had a whole month. Prontho proposed to set up a Shaman Circle. Shiam was against it. He couldn't believe that his brother defected to the dark side and didn't want to destroy him with his own hands. A conflict arose between him and Prontho, following which the orc issued a challenge to the head of the Council. This went against all our rules and laws. The actual combat between the High Shamans was brief and rapid. But something didn't seem right to me. I felt the presence of an alien Spirit on the battlefield. Not a Spirit, even... I cannot say exactly what it was, but it definitely couldn't have been summoned by either Prontho or Shiam. The head of the Council was strong, but he couldn't push Prontho out of the circle. I trained that green die-hard myself, so I know his strength very well. Prontho was stronger, but he lost. The orc refused to answer my questions, only repeating that since he lost such was his fate. Bloody fatalist. Perhaps you will have better luck in getting something out of this blockhead, who knows..."

Update of the 'Restoration of Justice' quest. The Deputy Head of the Shaman Council, Kornik, is convinced that a foreign entity was present at the duel, but doesn't have any proof. You must find out

the whole truth about Prontho's duel

"And where is Geranika now?" I uttered involuntary.

"That would be a third question, but I will answer it. Right now he is hunting me, without ever setting foot outside the Dark Lord's castle. He may have formally remained a Great Shaman, but in strength he greatly surpasses a Harbinger. And not just a Harbinger - even an Advisor would not come out victorious from a duel with him. And now, apprentice, it is time for you to go back. You must not do anything foolish. You can go back to your beloved mine after it's all finished."

"What is finished?"

"The question limit is reached, even exceeded. You'll find out everything yourself soon enough. We will meet next when the Supreme Spirit of the Higher World deems you ready for the trial of initiation into the rank of a Great Shaman. And also," Kornik looked up into my eyes, "when the time comes to choose, make the choice with your heart and not your head. Here is your altar."

Item acquired: Altar for sacrificing to the Spirits. Does not take up inventory bag space

The world blinked and I found myself in front of the Beatwick gates. The snoring of the guards, whose breath was a clear sign of their fervent devotion to Vlast, the pounding of the hammer in the smithy and the three Neanderthal-like haymakers became so familiar in the past few weeks that I really began to feel this was home. I winked at a kid running past me and headed off to Elizabeth's house. I had no idea what Kornik meant by 'make the choice', so I decided not to burden my brains with such things. If he thinks that I'd find everything out soon enough, then so be it.

CHAPTER SEVEN
THE ORC WARRIORS

T HE DAY AFTER KORNIK RETURNED ME to Beatwick I went to the mine to be alone and think over the hints the old ladies were meant to have given me. As I was banging away at the Tin Vein, I recalled our conversation word for word. Both with Mabel and with Patricia, beginning with 'Dearie, can you help out a weak and helpless woman?' and ending with 'won't give you any more assignments.'

A couple of hours later I managed to set aside several sentences, which allowed me to mark out at least a rough path forward, which seemed to run contrary to the general logic of the conversation:

'You're walking around like some Red Riding Hood who just brought pies to grandma'.

'You've been running between us half the day

almost - probably done twenty miles by now';

'...you've always had a weak spot for stubborn fools';

'But you kept delivering them, without even looking inside';

'...some wandering tramps to be loitering by the threshold'.

The old ladies didn't say anything else out of the ordinary. The socialization twaddle that was rammed into my brain each time I delivered a letter wasn't worth bothering with. It was hard to believe that any directions could be coded into it - deciphering it would be just too difficult in that case. So it looked like I'd have to try to make sense of these five sentences.

It could be immediately surmised that the scroll was within a twenty-kilometer radius of Farstead. One thing wasn't clear: the direction in which these twenty kilometers should be counted. Should I just walk around the circumference? There must have been a reason they mentioned stubborn fools. But I shuddered to think how much time it might take to do that. I had to narrow my search.

Could this be linked to Red Riding Hood? What did she do? She was bringing pies to her grandmother. Where did the grandmother live? As far as I remember, in a forest, or beyond a forest where the Grey Wolf lived. After finishing another vein and throwing the ore into the bag, I opened the map and looked up which side of Farstead had a forest. Damn. There was a forest. A lot of it: practically a thirty-degree sector immediately outside the town. The teleportation scroll to Beatwick wouldn't work in that area - I would have to go back to Farstead and get to the village from there. Or find what I needed very quickly and return to the town.

So, it seems that the scroll is located twenty kilometers from Farstead in a forest. You have to be stubborn to find it. Because the forest is big and the scroll is small. 'Without even looking inside' and 'some wandering tramps' didn't fit the logic of the search so far, but I felt that they would come in useful as well. When I make it to the right place, I'll figure it out. Another vein flickered and disappeared, leaving five pieces of Tin Ore behind. I smiled. Today I increased my Mining to level 18 - two more levels and I could look for other types of mines. What if there are Marble or Iron veins around here? All quite useful for leveling up. But that's for tomorrow. Today I had to finish off the remaining three veins and get back home.

"Mahan, you're using the wrong spoon," Clouter shot me a glance and then stared back at his plate. After the incident with Tiny Tim we didn't talk at all. Clouter did all he could to avoid me. Our paths only crossed during the compulsory dinner, to which Elizabeth started to invite me after I completed the wolf quest. At the dinner the lad, who was known to the entire village as an irrepressible talker, turned into a mute, only dropping a rare phrase on what an uncouth and uneducated person I was. In some sense I agreed with him. Elizabeth always served a dinner consisting of at least three courses, which were followed by a dessert. 'She's not a rich woman...' - yeah right!

Whatever the truth may be, each person at the table was faced with three forks and two spoons. At my first dinner, when I started to eat fish with an ordinary fork with four long prongs, everyone stared at me in great surprise. I began to feel uncomfortable.

"Mahan," Clouter told me off for my unacceptable table manners for the first time, "You eat fish with this fork," he pointed to one with four shorter prongs. Somewhat surprised, I changed the forks. What's the difference? Both have four prongs, only with slightly different lengths. It seems I just don't get certain things...

"Avtondil, it is impolite to reproof adults at the table," Elizabeth corrected her son.

"But mum! He was using the wrong fork! Why was I forced to learn what each of them was for, but no-one's correcting him," he nodded in my direction. "Tiny Tim still squeals a little when he sees Mahan."

"Mahan is a guest and you are my son! That's the end of it. Each time you correct him will land you cleaning the pigsty."

"That isn't fair!!! What if he starts eating with his hands? Can't I say anything then either?"

"Avtondil!"

"I'll do it, you'll see," he replied stubbornly. "It's better to be with pigs than eat with someone like this." Clouter threw his napkin on the table, "I'm going. The pigsty awaits."

"Oh dear," sighed the landlady, when Clouter left. "I'm sorry Mahan. Clouter is trying to be a grown up. After all, he's the only man in the family. But he's still small and doesn't understand some things."

From that day on Clouter always corrected me, despite the punishment. I was either sitting wrong, or using the wrong fork or passing the knife incorrectly - and so on. The daily dinner turned into a struggle with my own nerves - not to lose my temper with the little NPC. He had a strange program in him, very strange.

"Clouter, I need your help," today I decided to break the vicious circle of my uncultured behavior. Elizabeth and her daughter gave me some very surprised looks and Clouter sat there staring at his plate, same as always. "You are right, it's just unacceptable to be this uncivilized. Thank you for constantly correcting me, but I want to do more. Can you teach me all the subtle wisdom of forks, knives and the correct way to be at the table? It just so happens that no-one taught me this. Will you do it, or shall I ask Mariana?"

"Why won't I do it? Mariana doesn't know anything," he fired off. "She herself eats the salad with a fish fork instead of a salad one."

"We have a deal then? We'll start tomorrow first thing in the morning. An hour a day and I'll learn it all in a week. Once we succeed - the present's on me."

"What is it?" Clouter lifted his head and stared at me with interest.

"It'll be a surprise. If you teach me all this table wisdom in a week, it'll be a good one."

"It's a deal. I will drop by tomorrow and wake you up. Mum, I'm off to the pigsty. Have to say good-bye to the piggies. I'm not going to be visiting them anymore. That place just doesn't smell very nice," a gust seemed to rush through the room and the lad disappeared. A smart kid.

From then on I had a rather busy time of it. The mornings were given to Clouter. He would run to my summer house, shake me awake and then dump a small mountain of various cutlery straight in the bed and start teaching me what to do with it all. As I listened to the lad, I grew more and more surprised. Where would an eight-year-old village kid learn all this?

After the lesson I went to the mine. Hellfire, Plinto and other heroes hired by the Heralds have cleaned out the surrounding area pretty well and I didn't come across any more goblins. Aside from the Tin mine, there were also Copper, Marble and Iron mines in the neighborhood of Beatwick. Although I couldn't tackle Iron Veins yet, I took the opportunity to level up my skills through Marble Veins every day. It wasn't all that useful, however, since Marble wasn't used in Jewelcraft and I didn't have the Sculptor profession. So I ended up saving up the Marble for sale.

The second part of my day was dedicated to leveling up in Jewelcraft. I had a good supply of ingots and Malachite, so I made rings and cut stones. It was monotonous and repetitive, but I had to occupy myself with something...

"You're quite deft at this stuff," said the Smith in his bass voice, after I finished forming another Bronze Ring. "But I just don't understand why you need so many rings and gems. Are you going to pickle them or something?"

"I will sell them to free citizens when I go to Farstead or to the Merchant when he passes by here again. I have no need of the rings myself, but I must get better at my profession," I threw the rings in the bag, left the smithy and sat on a wooden block by the door. Tonight Tisha and I will be hunting the Night Monster, so I had to get some rest.

This week turned out to be quite productive. I raised my Mining to 25. Eleven more levels and I would be able to go to the Iron mine. Mining wouldn't get any higher because I only managed to increase my Jewelcraft to 19. Smithing did not go up that much, just to 14, but I got sixteen pieces of Malachite as I was making the ingots. With my gradually diminishing supplies this was handy. However, the one thing that leveled up the most during this week was Cartography. Each day the damned ziggurat that operated in the area erased my map and all I had drawn there the previous day. I had to draw it in again, but for a Cartographer a repeat drawing was same as a new one. This resulted in level 29 in almost four days...

In the evening, there was a meeting of the monster hunter strike-force at the Headman's house. There was me, Tisha, the Headman and the two Vagrens from the painting - Tisha's brothers whom I met in person for the first time.

"If I'm not mistaken, the monster is rather fond of Mahan. That's no laughing matter, Tisha," said the Headman. "Mahan, you task is simple. You have to lure the Monster out to open ground, the square would be best for that. These two," he nodded towards his sons, "will be waiting for it on the roof. When you get the monster there - dive under the porch straight away. You'll hide out there while Lloyd and Treyl will be catching him. The main thing is to spot it - then we won't let it get away. Now go, we'll meet exactly at midnight."

After I came back home, I cooked some food to give at least a little boost to my stats, came out of the summer house and sat on a bench. Just a couple more hours remained until night time and my cue to go to the centre of the village and make myself very visible on the main square. We figured that the mist beast would come after me itself. I set up a warning message to stop me oversleeping, leaned against the wall and closed my eyes. With such a busy timetable there was barely any time left to rest.

The quiet squeaking of the front door made me tense up. Pretending I was still asleep, I half-opened my eyes and watched how Elizabeth carefully closed the door and went to the gate, constantly looking back at me, and then, quiet as a shadow, slipped into the approaching night. My landlady's hands held the same bundle as a week ago. Where could she be going? There was still plenty of time - two whole hours - so I decided to follow this lady for a bit. Even if she was going on a date, something wasn't right here. I had a gut feeling that my landlady was connected to the monster's appearance. And if I had a feeling, it needed checking out.

I let Elizabeth put about fifty meters between us and silently followed her. I was afraid to come closer, since I lacked any stealthy tracking skills, unlike Hunters or Rogues, so I moved like an elephant on tiptoe.

Elizabeth's behavior was becoming 'curiouser and curiouser'. She kept to the side of the street, staying in the shade of the houses. Constantly glancing back, as if afraid of being discovered, the woman moved purposefully towards the village square. Could she be visiting the Headman after all? If that's true, this guy had it all sorted - just sent off his daughter and sons to hunt the monster, himself staying at home to receive a lady friend!

I stopped and watched from afar how Elizabeth came up to the square, looked around and instead of going to the Headman's house, turned into the neighboring street. What the...?

Moving as fast as I could without making any noise I sped after my landlady. My suspicions that she was connected with the monster now transformed into certainty.

After a couple of minutes Elizabeth came up to the stockade and stopped. Glancing back just in case, she pressed something and two logs of the fence lifted, as if they were threaded through by a pole. Bowing her head, the woman left the village, pressed something again and the logs returned to their places. That's just nuts! The fence has a secret door and my landlady is using it. Where could she be going?

Although I saw well enough where Elizabeth pressed the lever, I couldn't figure out how to use it. Or, rather, there wasn't any lever there. Realizing that if I tarried much longer I would lose sight of her, I disregarded stealth and jumped over the stockade. I grabbed the top ledge, lifted myself and dropped on the other side. It was just as well that they decided not to sharpen the top of the stockade in Beatwick - these were just simple logs. Otherwise I would have been in for an unpleasant experience. I dropped to the ground like a sack (-25 Hit Points, but this was currently irrelevant) and just had time to see the blurry silhouette of my target heading in the direction of the temple.

Damn! Could she be visiting the Priest instead of the Headman? Vlast didn't seem to be too hung up on chastity. And here's me suspecting the poor woman of all kinds of vile things. But my inner worm of doubt completely chewed through my certitude of Elizabeth's innocence, stating: trust everyone, but always cut the cards. When I see her go into the temple I can relax and go back to Beatwick.

The woman went around the temple and headed to the cemetery. I carefully approached the cemetery fence and looked inside. Elizabeth settled down on a small patch in the centre of the cemetery which was free of graves, took out some candles from her bundle, placed them in a particular configuration, then lit them and sat at the centre of the figure that they made. In a couple of moments I heard her voice, which was mumbling some sort of an incantation in anything but the common tongue.

And what are we doing here? I looked at my internal clock: it was an hour to midnight. Soon I'll have to run to the square to lure out the monster and I'm still here spying on Elizabeth. Although I was very interested in what it was she was doing. Especially why it happened to be during the night when the mist beast came out.

Elizabeth continued to mumble the incantation and I felt someone's hot breath on my neck. Slowly, trying not to make any sudden moves, I turned to face my predicament.

I was greeted by two red eyes and the mist that covered the beast head to toe.

"I'm happy to see you too," I wrinkled my brow when the thing snorted right in my face. The furnace-hot breath of the beast, which was mixed with some unpleasant sharp smell, made me veer away. "How's it going? Let's negotiate - I have a proposal. There must be something that you want and I'm prepared to help you get that something," I wasn't even a little afraid. I thought I was heading in the right direction. I had to get this thing talking, and the next bit could be figured out later.

The beast snorted again, engulfing me in another wave of hot air, and in one blurred movement was right next to me. It was so close I could touch it, something I had exactly zero intention of doing. I was no longer scared of dying, but I wanted to live all the same. I stood still as a statue, hoping that the beast may not recognize me, when two clawed paws shot out of the mist and grabbed me by the neck. Immediately the 'No Air' status bar appeared, measuring the two minutes I could survive without the said substance. I resisted, but to no avail: I couldn't kick the misty bastard, its arms were too long, nor could I unbend the paws clenching my neck. The level difference was too big. Was I really looking at yet another respawn? Tisha sure would be happy when I turn up with a confession to make... Instead of waiting for the monster in the square, I went looking for it myself.

But I did find out how it turned up in Beatwick: the secret entrance known to Elizabeth. And it looks like she happens to be a common demonologist, who summons this terror on the village once a week. But why would she do that? And what kind of a beast is this?

The air bar flickered one last time and my Hit Points started to fall with frightening speed. Never mind. A plan had already ripened in my mind on how to stop the beast appearing in a week's time and expose Elizabeth for who she is. Before, if she was the Vagren, I would have given some thought about what would happen to her children, but if she's the one summoning this horror on the village, there isn't much else to be done - she had to be handed over to the authorities.

Attention!
In connection with your death, your level of Experience has been reduced by 30%...

"I see you're becoming a familiar face around here, my son." The priest of Vlast was standing by the temple when I respawned there. "Did you decide to mend your ways and hand in the Vagrens? Yes, I know everything about the Headman and his family. Even if they have come over to the side of light, any priest would immediately recognize them in their human guise."

"The Vagren is innocent. There's something else at work here."

"And what is it?" the priest looked at me with interest.

"We'll know in a week's time; I thought up of a way to catch this little monster. But I need your help. Can you make me a scroll with the Movable Prison spell?"

"Eh. I don't know how to make scrolls - I don't have the Cartographer skill."

"What does Cartographer have to do with it?" I was very surprised by the Priest's words. Is there something I don't know about my profession?

"Yes, you see, one of the Cartographer specializations is 'Scroll Scribe'. Only they are able to transfer their spells or recipes onto scrolls."

Wow! I'll have two of those! I just happen to have some original recipes that I produced! If I manage to transfer them onto scrolls and put them up at the auction, I could earn good money. There are plenty of collectors of various recipes in Barliona.

"All right, I'll think of something myself. Thank you for the advice."

"Don't mention it. What do you have in mind?"

"I have a certain suspicion. I'll check it out in a week's time."

"I will await your news," the priest turned

around and stared into the distance.

I heaved a deep sigh, anticipating my conversation with the Headman and Tisha, and headed off to Beatwick. I made a decision not to tell anyone about Elizabeth until next week.

"Mahan! Where were you?!" Tisha flew out of the house and run up to me. We waited and waited for you last night, but you never came! Just vanished without a trace! What happened? We had an agreement!"

"Just a moment, Tisha, calm down," I heard the Headman's quiet voice behind me. I turned around and saw him giving last-minute instructions to his sons, who were already on their horses and about to head out to the next village. "Mahan is a free citizen and they are not so easy to destroy. When their Life is reduced almost to zero, they travel to the Grey Lands. Then twelve hours go by and they return to the nearest graveyard. A very interesting trait that only free citizens possess. If I remember correctly, the cemetery is exactly the place you've just come from. Right?"

I gave a resigned nod.

"So the beast got you before you could lead it to the square, eh?" I started and was almost ready to give the Headman a big hug. He asked the question himself and was ready with the answer - an answer that happened to get me off the hook. I love NPCs like that.

"Yes, I wasn't fast enough. We should start right on the square next time. The thing is just too fast."

"Then in a week's time we'll meet right on the square. This time we'll get it for sure. It's really into you for some reason."

I exchanged a couple of phrases with Tisha and went home. Although now I could hardly call this abode a home. Elizabeth was ordering the workmen about as if nothing happened - sending some to chop the wood and others to fetch the water.

"I see you like taking night-time walks," she remarked, turning to me. "You should go to the gates and scare off the children that keep scratching them. We end up having to fix them every week."

"I will, for sure. Is the kids' next trip to the gates scheduled in a week's time?" I was watching the woman's reaction very carefully. "I'll just go and have a look at who it is that's scratching those gates. Then I'll drag them off to the Headman for sure."

Did I imagine it or did Elizabeth tense up? That's fine - it's good to keep you on your toes. I have a week to think of a way to deal with you, dear landlady. Or, rather, I already know what to do - all I need is to hop over to Farstead and back. I wouldn't even be too stingy with my gold for something like that.

I took out my last portal scroll. Time had come to get to grips with my Totem...

Farstead met me with drenching rain. It didn't get in the way (the droplets flowed down a transparent sphere around each player), but it didn't do much for visibility or NPC spirits. The majority of shops were closed when it rained, the prices in the tavern doubled and the town itself acquired the status of a 'conditional safe zone'. During the rain it was permitted to kill other players in the town if you managed to avoid getting seen by the guards and waited out the eight hours in some hiding place afterwards.

This is why bigger towns had a so-called 'safe-zone'. It was a zone where it never rained, where players knew they had nothing to be afraid of. But the prices in this zone were several times higher than in the normal zone a few streets down. As I understood it, Eric and Co. holed up in such a zone, so their money was disappearing at an alarming rate. Never mind, they should last a couple of months or so.

Ignoring the gremlin, who habitually inquired how he could be of service, I entered the Personal Room. There were two letters there. The letter from Hellfire was not unexpected, but the other, from a player under the nick of Nurris, was a surprise. I had no idea who this was or what he wanted from me. Well, we'll see, I guess. I opened the letter from the head of Phoenix first:

"Hello Mahan. As you asked, I'm sending you the holograms of the top twenty players of the Phoenix and the Dark Legion clans. Good luck."

I just don't get it. What happened to all the questions about when he'll be getting the chess pieces, the rate of my progress and so on and so forth? And more to the point - a whole week had gone by and Anastaria hadn't contacted me once. Why? Baffled by all these questions I picked up the second letter:

"Hello Mahan.
We are not acquainted, but I know you through

someone else. Mike told me that you know how he ended up in prison. Yes, I am that very reason. He also explained the incredible way a prisoner marked 'no parole' managed to make it into the main gameworld. He would have had to spend five more years raising his reputation by himself. But your help messed up the law-enforcers' plans. They had to choose: either break the rules or let Mike go. By the way, if you haven't guessed it, I'm talking about Kart. He said that you'll understand what this means. Now then. As soon as he left the mine, I paid his bail and got him out of the game - thankfully the sum wasn't that big. Now he's in rehab. Ten years in the game is no joke.

Now, about you. Mike has already told me all about you, begging for money to get you out as well. You can't bail someone from a mine, only after the prisoner himself makes it into the main gameworld. I looked at your case. I don't have a hundred million to spare, so I'm sorry. But I did find one million. I owe Mike too much. I have access to prisoners' cases, so I know the size of your compensation and the cost of removing the red headband. The money has already been paid and the payment is currently being verified. I think your headband should disappear in about a week.

P.S. Mike will not be coming back to the game. He spent too long outside real life. Good bye. I believe I repaid his debt in full."

My hands were shaking from the emotions that overwhelmed me. The red headband will soon disappear! This means that I could no longer be killed without any fear of punishment and I would get the standard level of Attractiveness with NPCs: 20 points. Kart, Kart... Thank you so much for not forgetting me. When I get out I will try to find you through Nurris.

I once again took out the chess pieces to try and solve this damned riddle. It wasn't giving me any peace, but I made no headway at all in solving it. It was all too abstract.

So, we have:

$$C^2 = A^2 + B^2$$

$$||X|| = \sqrt{X_1^2 + X_2^2 + \cdots + X_n^2}$$

1, 1, 2, 3, 5, 8, 13, 21....
[Value entry field]
Seven digits after the dot
*
*
=

The first formula was the Pythagoras theorem, the second - the formula of volume or Euclidean space and the third - the Fibonacci sequence. What connected them all? Nothing. I tried inserting different values, but there was no result. Where shall I use the seven digits after the dot? Why can't I think of anything? Where the heck is my intuition, damn it!

I spent several hours staring at the text input field, entering different possible answers from time to time, then shoved everything back into the bag and headed off to the High Mage. I had to buy a couple more scrolls to Beatwick and Farstead and also another Bone Trap, but for level 170 this time. I dreaded to even imagine how much it would cost.

Things did not turn out to be that bad. They turned out simply terrible. Today was clearly not my day. I chose the door with the questions again and got one of my least favorite themes: Cultural studies. If I managed to get the first answer right, just about, at the second one I folded. The scroll of teleportation to Farstead and back cost me a thousand two hundred each way. Crazy stuff! With an aching heart I handed over three and a half thousand for the Bone Trap. It's been a while since I'd spent quite so much, but there was no helping it. I knew what I was getting into.

I dropped by the Smithing Trainer and learned the 'Smelter' specialty. Now I had a five percent chance of getting as many as two ingots from five pieces of ore. Nothing big, but still a bonus. Then I visited the Cartographer to learn the 'Scroll Scribe' specialty and immediately obtained a bonus from it: my Intellect increased by five percent. I looked at the description and couldn't help feeling pleased: I could make scrolls with recipes or spells of up to level fifty inclusive. Did someone ask for a spell scroll? I made a scroll with 'Summoning a Water Spirit - Water Dart'. Great! On one hand I'll be leveling up in Cartography and on the other these would come in useful when I ran out of Mana. I sat on a bench and created twenty scrolls of healing and damage. Who knows when I get caught by that rainy day...

That's it. I had nothing left to do in Farstead.
Time to solve the puzzle handed me by the old ladies.

"Mahan, wait up," I heard a voice with some
strange clicking in it. "My wants to you talkings.
Buggerations! The koboldish has switched on again.
Just a moment!" There was a thump and a normal
voice continued. "I need a hand with something. Will
you help me?"

I finally caught sight of the owner of the unusual
voice. A little way off stood Reptilis Y'allgotohellis the
kobold, spreading his green paws as if to show the
unfairness of this world. He was already level forty.
He's been leveling up fast! A real hardcore player.

I took a careful look at the kobold. He had very
decent gear, clearly of an unusual level. He also had a
stud on this tail (probably to hit opponents with) and
some sort of a stringed instrument that resembled a
guitar across his back. Is he a bard as well? It was a
world gone mad.

"I need help to complete a quest. I'll pay five
thousand gold. Will you come with me?"

"Five big ones in gold? Do you need to kill
someone?" I smiled.

"I can do the killing myself. I'm an Assassin."

"Then what do you need me for?" Wow, he's not
just a hardcore player, but someone with a rare class
too.

"I have a quest and it states that two players
must get to a point twenty kilometers from here. We
have to stomp that way," Reptilis nodded towards the
forest. Exactly in the direction I was going to head off

myself. Had he gone through the old ladies as well?

"On foot?" I pretended that I was categorically unkeen on a long walk.

"Why on foot? I have a ride there, so we'll get to the place in an hour for sure."

"All right, what's this quest then? Who gave it to you?"

"Yeah right. I'll just go and spill the beans to ya right here and now. You haven't even agreed to anything yet and already started with the questions."

"All right, let's go. I don't mind doing this. I don't have much to do in the next two days anyway."

"Group up?" A group invite from player Reptilis appeared before my eyes.

"Grouping up," I accepted the invite. If this green wonder really does have a means of transport, our paths converge for sure.

"Wow, how did you manage to hike up your Intellect so much by level twenty one? I use to be a mage before and didn't have it that high until level forty."

"Not much to it, really. The answer is very simple: gear. Good gear that gives a lot of Intellect. Why did you stop playing a mage? Got fed up with it?"

"Not exactly fed up, but something along those lines," Reptilis flashed an evil grin. "One day I will catch whoever it was that landed me on this path and give him a good piece of my mind. I'll shove the scumbag's words all the way down his throat, so he remembers them long and well."

"Wow," I couldn't help smiling. "Watch out! An

angry croc is heading this way."

"Very funny. Gonna die from laughter any minute." Reptilis stopped, turned, and looked up at me, "You better move your ass. You should be earning your pay instead of cackling here. Take no note of the fact that I'm a kobold. Right now I'm your employer."

"All right! Whatever you say! I'll imagine you as a stunning big-chested elven maiden, with obligatory blonde hair, long ears and soft white skin."

"Go bugger yourself..."

Your group has disbanded

"Hold on," where does this pretty boy think he's going? I need him as a horse, when all's said and done. "I'm sorry. Just not having a great time of it right now, so I let rip at you. Group up again."

Reptilis stopped, thought something over for a couple of seconds, but did, in the end, send me another invite.

"Let's agree from the start. Not a word about my height or crocodile-related innuendos. Otherwise no money for you."

"Agreed."

An agreement has been reached. You will receive five thousand gold from player Reptilis Y'allgotohellis if you accompany him to the spot marked on his map. While carrying out the agreement you must not drop any hints to Reptilis about his low height or resemblance to a crocodile

"Then let's go. My beauty is outside the town. The guards have too much of a dislike for her."

Not far from the gates, chewing on some life-form sticking out of its mouth in the form of a hoof, stood the THING. A wyvern. I knew these mounts very well and have myself hunted for their eggs for selling at the auction later.

"Here she is," said the kobold, satisfied, having noted my reaction. "She's still young, but she'll deliver two people where they need to go."

"That's some interesting horse you've got there," I recovered and climbed on the wyvern's back. Reptilis got into a special saddle near the neck, while all I could do was perch on the back and pray that I wouldn't fall off on the way.

"Just a bit. Ready? Then let's go."

Contrary to my fears, the wyvern's movement was steady and sure-footed, as if it understood that it was carrying as precious a cargo as myself.

"Reptilis, why are you playing a kobold? If you don't want to talk about it - sure thing, but we have over an hour of travel ahead and it would be nice to chat. I haven't talked to ordinary players for over four months now."

"Then first tell me how you ended up in prison. I'd like to know who I'm travelling with as well."

"Ah, it's all very simple in my case. Have you heard of such a person as 'the Terror of the Waste Collectors'? That's me."

"You're the one who fouled up the lake?" smiled

Reptilis. A least I thought he smiled, since I couldn't see from behind.

"Well... Just a bit, as you say."

"They say you really gave it to that Imitator. But I just don't get why do this all of a sudden? What the heck did you need it for?"

"I made a dumb bet with a girl. Stupidly fell for her dare. And then someone made a mistake. Either it was me when I was typing in the address or her when she sent it to me. We agreed to work on a test system to see if I could break it. I broke it all right, but in the process sent the real Imitator for an extended holiday. They stuck me in the can for eight years for that. But I raised my reputation with the guards and left the mine. That's it from me. What about you?"

"My story's simpler. I was the leader of one of the mercenary clans and in one raid we were in charge of guarding a new Dungeon - to allow Phoenix to go through it first, but they rather exquisitely played us for fools and my clan fell apart. People were pinched by various clans and I decided to prove to everyone, and above all myself, what I'm capable of as a player."

"But what does some scumbag have to do with any of this?"

"That was the Phoenix representative that played us. He was the one taunting me that I was nothing as a player, while he played naked for three years and reached level 150+. So I decided to reach the maximum level. The highest level kobold right now is at 225, so I have some way to go. That's fine though! At first it was hard, but now I'm even glad to be playing a kobold. No-one expects dirty tricks from a little croc."

"I should point out that you just called yourself that," I smiled. "So what's your quest? And why in such total backwater all of a sudden? After all, there are mainly starting players around here. Low levels, simple Dungeons and beginner resources. While you, judging by the wyvern, have invested a fair amount of money into the game."

"Oh, here it gets even more interesting. What I haven't managed to attain in the real world, I am getting to achieve in the game. Have you heard of a player called Anastaria?" It was just as well that Reptilis was sitting with his back to me, so he didn't see how the name made me start. Could it really be all fixed up?

"Yeah, I have, I think. They say she's the most beautiful and incredible girl, a goddess..." damn, I was beginning to drool again.

"So you've heard, eh? And judging by your reaction even seen."

"Why do you say that?"

"Well, you don't need to tell me if you don't want to - that's your business. It's just she's under a very interesting curse. Phoenix, of which she's a member, once completed some unique quest connected with killing sirens who were being reborn. Now then. The head of the sirens cursed Anastaria, casting on her a unique debuff. From then onwards Anastaria has been emitting a poison, which is invisible and unidentifiable by any amulets. Those entering into the zone of action of this poison fall head and heels in love with the lady paladin. As a reward the Emperor taught Anastaria to use this poison, controlling its intensity, so now she can emit it at will. That's the long and short of it. When players affected by the poison talk about Anastaria, they involuntarily start to drool, get a runny nose, and in general turn into complete lovestruck idiots. I don't know about an antidote, haven't looked for it."

"Cool beans, but I don't really get the connection between the head of Phoenix and a forty-level kobold."

"Ah, so you do know her... It's very simple. We met after my victory in the Anhurs arena. Chatted about the past and she turned out to be an ordinary girl who was interesting to talk to. Quite clever as well."

"Yeah right. You haven't fallen under the effect of the poison yourself, have you?"

"The poison doesn't affect kobolds. At all. It was interesting to watch the misty eyes of the entire tavern when Anastaria decided to test my racial immunity. The players were all but praying to her at that point. They say many ran to the Dating House straight after that."

"It's a nice story, but it's a bit hard to believe. Whatever the visualization, this is still only a game and virtual reality. Why would normal players start drooling?"

"That's pretty simple too. This is about the capsules. Remember going through the full test before the initial immersion? So, the system determines the smells that awaken the greatest desire in you. Simple chemistry, nothing more. Moreover, Anastaria's poison cannot affect players aged under twenty one. Those who are not allowed in the Dating House."

"And what happened then? So you met Anastaria and saw the ineffectiveness of her poison in your case. Why did you leave Anhurs for the middle of nowhere?"

"I'm here on a quest from the Assassins' Guild. I had to sneak into one NPC's house and procure a piece of paper. I stole the paper, but then discovered something interesting. A certain unique quest connected with Dragons. Anastaria is not just some girl. She's a great lover of all things unique in the game. And she shows great favor to someone who has unique items. It's a weakness of hers. As far as I could find out, no-one has a Dragon. So I went searching for one. If I get lucky, I'll have a reason to make a pass at Stacey."

"You even know her real name? I see you're a serious admirer."

"Who doesn't? Oh, we're here."

We covered the twenty kilometers in what seemed like a flash. I looked at my return timer. Yes, it really has already been an hour. The time flew by very quickly as we talked. We stopped on a small clearing, about fifty meters in diameter, with a house in the middle. Not a house even - a hut. My heart began to race and I was sure - this is where I had to go. I could feel it with every fiber of my soul. It looks like Reptilis and I had a quest for the same item - the scroll. Was there only one of it or would we get a copy each?

"Wait," I stopped the kobold who was about to enter the house. "There's more here than meets the eye. Try to think of how the phrases 'But you kept delivering them, without even looking inside' and 'wandering tramps to be loitering by the threshold' could be applied to the current situation."

"Strange. I thought Beauty did a good job running through all those trees - when did you manage to hit your head?"

"If we go through the door now, we'll fail the quest. I also have a quest connected with getting the scroll."

"What scroll? A Dragonkin lives here who will tell us here to find Dragons," Reptilis shrugged and continued, "Say what you like, but I'm going in. I have no desire to hang around here doing nothing."

"Last question. Give me the exact wording of your quest," I was trying to bring the kobold to his senses. We mustn't enter the house or there would be a big 'boom'. How could I explain it to the crocodile?

"In the area marked on the map seek out the Dragonkin who would tell you how to find the way to the Dragons. A compulsory condition for completing the quest - take another player with you. What the player was needed for I had to go offline to find out. The Dragonkin would demand..."

"He would demand for one of you to be sent to the Grey Lands and the other to receive the information," Reptilis was interrupted by the Dragonkin coming out of the door on four paws. They're pretty scary-looking, I noted. A muzzle reeking with malice, teeth bared, like in the ancient Chinese pictures, a tail and four paws. A strange mix of a horse and a Dragon.

"So you brought me here as fodder?" I turned around to Reptilis, or rather the empty space where he just stood.

"The time is running," said the Dragonkin. "The winner will get the prize. Fight!"

Your group has disbanded
Damage taken: 400, 1240 (weapon damage) - 840 (armour). Total Hit Points: 2020 of 2420.
You have been poisoned! Your Hit Points will decrease by 220 every 5 seconds for 2 hours: 500 (poison damage) - 280 (poison resistance). Total Hit Points: 1800 of 2420.
You have been stunned for 5 seconds!

Reptilis de-stealthed right behind me and started to systematically and purposefully send me off for respawn - with the ensuing consequence of me failing to get the Totem. Seeing that I had no time to enter into the Spirit summoning mode, as soon as the stun expired I grabbed the scrolls and began to use them one after another. Healing to myself - damage to Reptilis. Healing to myself - damage to Reptilis. I didn't have many scrolls, but probably enough for one fight. If it wasn't for Anastaria's armor, this lizard would have simply downed me with darts and some other sharp pointies in the first few seconds. What a bastard! He knew where he was taking me and chose a low level player. I'll kill the scumbag!

Two minutes later I ran out of the scrolls and Reptilis's Life bar was still half full - the Spirits missed or were blocked by the armor too often. Or, more likely, it was stupid to summon Water Spirits on a semiaquatic. He must have resistances.

"So you think your threads make you a good player?" I heard the lizard's voice for the first time in minutes. We stood opposite each other, breathing heavily, each trying to outstare his opponent. I don't know why Reptilis's breath was heavy, but I've been taking a real beating. Even raised my Endurance by one in this time.

"If you little piece of shit, turned your brains on even for a second, you would've seen a 1 under my name. Do I need to spell it out for you or will you finally start using the body part you shove your food into? Do you think an ordinary player, who knows nothing about the game, would be able to get a 'First Kill' by level twenty? So your level 40 for me is child's play. Say your prayers, you flippin' lizard. I'll write a message to the admins as well, saying you tricked me out of five big ones in gold. We had an agreement. You are guaranteed to be dragged through the courts in the real world. Kiss 'good bye' to your Anastaria."

"Fudge off. I'll drop your gold in the Bank after I send you for respawn."

Attention! You have the NPC and player profanity filter turned on. To turn it off go to the character settings (only for players aged 21 and above)

To hell with it - I'll turn it off later. I have other

fish to fry right now.

The Shaman has three hands...

Go hang, you green goon: the Spirit mode is up and running. For starters I need to remove the poison, which consistently kept taking off 220 Hit Points every five seconds. Having summoned a Healing Spirit, I was looking forward to the relief of being fully healed, only to suddenly discover that the poison didn't go anywhere. On top of that, Reptilis flew into combat again. Quickly chucking all the fire spells out of the active zone and summoning a damage Spirit on the kobold, I tried to think of what to do with the poison. I knew that Shamans were able to remove it in some way, but why didn't Kornik teach me this? Could I figure it out myself?

I sent four damage Spirits at once at Reptilis, forcing him to stealth, and started to summon another Spirit, concentrating on an empty slot in the active zone. Work already!

You are summoning a Spirit from a free slot of the active zone. Do you wish to add available Spirits to the slot?

No, I don't. Damn, it didn't work.

Do you wish to add an additional Spirit to the free slot?

Yes, that's exactly what I'm looking for.

The following additional spirits are available to an Elemental Shaman: Spirit of Control, Spirit of Cleansing, Spirit of Strengthening and Spirit of Intermittent Damage. Do you wish to add Spirits to the active zone?

Yes! Right now! All the water ones, please!

A healing Spirit on myself and a cleansing Spirit on top of that. Yes! The poison debuff disappeared. Now we'll have a proper fight! So, where are you, you puny croc?

The effect of the Spirit of Control turned out to be very interesting. Reptilis continued to fling some nasty stuff at me, but he did it so slowly that I could dodge the incoming pieces of metal. The Spirit of Control had a 5-second duration, but it was enough for me to summon a Spirit of Water Shock on Reptilis, which caused intermittent damage. Small though that was, it allowed me to put about 10 meters between us and launch a couple more Damage Spirits at the kobold. Fire ones, this time. Slowly, but surely the reptile's Hit Points began to melt away. Reptilis used restoration potions a couple of times, almost completely healing himself, but my Mana reserves were almost endless. Whoever said that Shamans were a weak class in PvP?

"Mahan, stop!" A couple of minutes into the fight Reptilis had only 10% of his Hit Points left.

"What's that? Decided to talk, have we, once you

realized that you can't win by force? And where were you before, handsome? Not a chance: this is too good an opportunity to kill someone without being sent to the mines! You shouldn't have attacked me, you green bastard."

"What do you want with information on Dragons anyhow?" Reptilis was no longer attacking, but just stood there and, wincing, took the hits from my Spirits.

"I have a quest. And what do you need it for? To get to Anastaria?"

"That's not the main reason," sighed Reptilis. "I told you how I became a kobold. Yes, I like this character now, but I haven't forgotten that once I had a clan and that I want revenge. Brutal revenge on the bastard who tricked me out of the money - one of the influential Phoenix players. He constantly hangs out with the Emperor. I want to make him duel me in front of the palace and for that I have to get a Dragon. Only that would get me into the palace. The moron from Phoenix highly values his place in the shadow of the Emperor, who, in turn, hates duelers and generally violence in any form. Whatever the results of the duel, both of us would be permanently banned from the palace. I may not give a flying fig about this, but for him it would be a far harder blow than a change of character. And now only you stand between me and my revenge, since you're not letting me have the Dragon. What can be so important about your quest?!"

Reptilis was almost screaming now. Yeah, some situation we have here... I understood the guy very well: changing a high level mage for this joke of a character, finding a way to get your own back and then running across a Shaman who just wouldn't die. That's some trip-up.

Although...

"Hold on. If I understood correctly - you're seeking the way to the Dragons only as a means of getting into the palace. Would only a Dragon do?"

"No, any unique item would work. But where would I get it?" Reptilis was gradually regaining his composure.

"Do you have fifty thousand gold?"

"What?"

"Look," I took out the dress and opened up its properties for viewing. "Do you think the Emperor might like a thing like this? Fifty thousand gold and the dress is yours. What do you say?"

"I don't have that much money right now," Reptilis grew thoughtful. "I can give you thirty now and will send the twenty, as agreed, to the Bank in a week's time."

"It's a deal. But you do understand that I will still have to kill you now? I need to get to the Dragons. Really need it. And it's also no good leaving unfinished business. If I started to bring you down, I have to finish you off good and proper."

"Go for it," Reptilis smiled, having fully regained his composure and apparently already making plans for the future. "If you sell me the dress, I'm fine with it."

"By the way, a duel is a shabby move. I can propose an alternative..." I quickly described what kind of revenge could work at the Emperor's reception. "This way is much more interesting and saves you getting banned from the palace."

"That's some twisted mind you've got there," grinned Reptilis, drawing up another agreement and making our deal official. The damned thirty percent evaporated to the Corporation and twenty one thousand gold landed in my pocket.

A curious fact: I didn't feel a hint of greed when letting go of the dress. Even my inner Toad took its loss calmly. I could have sold it for three or four hundred thousand in Anhurs, but I felt I was doing the right thing.

"What will happen to the wyvern?" I nodded towards the 'horsie'.

"It'll be fine. It will stand there for a couple of minutes and disappear - I have the reigns. All right, you can finish me off now. I owe you twenty five thousand more. I won't forget. And thanks for the advice. Those Phoenix douchebags really got to me with their snarks - it's just a total shi...-pi-i-i-i-i-i-i-i."

Ding!

"What did you say?" I asked, holding my breath.

"Now don't pretend you're just out of kindergarten and never heard swearing before."

"Who cares about swearing? Can you please repeat your last sentence? Word for word."

"I said: Those Phoenix douchebags really got to me with their snarks ".

"In full."

"It's just a total shi...-pi-i-i-i-i-i-i-i."

I went to the settings and removed the profanity filter. Later on it would be quite interesting to see what words the developers bestowed on the NPCs in Barliona. But that didn't really concern me right now.

"All right, I'll be seeing ya. Perhaps we'll meet again," ten damage Spirits flew at Reptilis and a message appeared before me:

Achievement earned!
Killer level 1 (19 player kills until the next level)
Achievement reward: Damage dealt to other players increased by 1%
You can look at the list of achievements in the character settings

I waved away the questionable Achievement and took out the chess pieces. The Dragonkin wasn't going anywhere and I just had to check if my guess was right. Could everything really be that simple? For the second time that day I looked at the properties of the Orc Warriors:

$$C^2 = A^2 + B^2$$

$$||X|| = \sqrt{X_1^2 + X_2^2 + \cdots + X_n^2}$$

1, 1, 2, 3, 5, 8, 13, 21....

Pythagoras' theorem. Euclidean space. The Fibonacci sequence.

Formulas which completely lack any connecting

logic. But if I was right...

Pythagoras. Euclid. Fibonacci.

Pythagoras. **E**uclid. **Fi**bonacci.

Pi! E! Phi!

It is true that few would be familiar with these three constants, but I was one of those nerdy people who try to explore a studied subject as thoroughly as possible. After deciding to be a programmer, I ended up memorizing the main mathematical constants to their first ten decimal places:

3.1415926536; 2.7182818285; 1.6180339887.

I opened my in-built calculator, worked out the number I needed (13.8175802), and entered it into the text box. Well? Did I get it or was it more of the same old?

The world froze. The Dragonkin, who was still standing in the door, fell on all four of his knees and bowed his head. A whirlwind appeared a couple of meters away from me, from which eight two-meter-high orcs walked out one after another. With yatagans. I've spent so much time examining the figurines that I could easily put a name to each of the orcs. Grichin, Grover, Vankhor... All the eight great Warrior Orcs stood before me and waited for something.

I selected the closest orc and looked at his properties. He was level three hundred and fifty. I swallowed as I imagined these warriors putting themselves at my service and respectfully bowed my head to them, honoring their great deeds.

Suddenly the orcs began to speak one after another:

- *That day the sky was covered with darkness and massive hailstones rained down,*
- *When the Great Creator of things realized that his hour had come...*
- *Only he could not die and so to his rest he departed;*
- *Then he sealed the doors to himself for ever, disturbed by no-one to be.*
- *Within a cave he hid all he knew, possessed and created.*
- *Only the one who finds the way to him shall be blessed*
- *Through the tandem of gods. Hero Karmadont found the way.*
- *Raised of a servant, Emperor he became midst the echoes of the Shining Mountains.*

Holy cow! What does this mean? What Shining Mountains? Do they mean Elma - the mountain range stretching from the deepest south of the content right to the extreme north? In the morning its peaks sparkle like flashlights - it's so damn mind-blowingly enormous!

"The Dwarves know more," added Grover. After this the orcs went back into the whirlwind and sound returned to the world. Hey! What about a quest? Or an achievement?

I felt cheated. Was Phoenix really prepared to make me a Master just for these lines? I automatically looked at the properties of the figurines. They only contained the lines about their feats now. There was no additional text, let alone any text input field. Just your regular unique chess pieces, what they should have been from the start. The main thing was making sure that Anastaria didn't find out that I was in possession of several lines pointing towards some point on the map of Barliona. A point that contains the virtual creator of this world.

CHAPTER EIGHT
THE TOTEM

"K EY!"

I'm a man of steady nerves, but when the Dragonkin's malicious muzzle repeated the same phrase for the fortieth time, you developed an irresistible itch to put your boot in it.

As soon as the portal with the Orc Warriors disappeared, the Dragonkin got up from his knees and, as if nothing happened, placed himself in the doorway of the hut.

"I need the scroll that will take me to the Dragons," I approached the four-legged NPC.

"Key!" the Dragonkin rumbled for the first time.

"What key?"

"Key!"

"I found the clearing and met all the conditions.

I demand to be given the scroll!"

"Key!"

I spent a frustrating half an hour trying to knock it into the head of this pseudolizard that the quest's requirements have been met, but it stubbornly refused to hand over the Dragon scroll. It just kept parroting one word: "Key". I had no clue what the key was or why it had to be given to the Dragonkin. Did Reptilis keep something from me? After all, it was his quest that got us here. Or was it something unknown to him as well?

I sat before the door and drilled the Dragonkin with a stare. I couldn't jump this hurdle, so I had to think.

"What about..."

"Key!"

"I've had it with you! Here's your key!" I put my hand in the bag and took out the first thing at random. It was the Eye of the Dark Widow, but who gives a damn anymore?!

"Not this key! Key!"

Well, that was progress. New words and all that. So it looks like this NPC has been programmed with an algorithm for identifying a particular key. I took out the Malachite Jewelry Box, removed the Orc Warriors from it, replacing them with a piece of Tin Ore, and tried to hand it to the Dragonkin. Let's see how he reacts to this one.

"The key is in the Jewelry Box," I lied to the Dragonkin, completely unabashed.

"Open it!"

"You open it! I'm not your servant! The key is in

the Box, the Box is in your hands, this means that the key is in your hands."

A second later the Dragonkin was staring at the thing he was just given. Here you go! It could only be opened by Jewelers, for everyone else the Jewelry Box was just piece of the scenery. The Dragonkin heaved a deep sigh, pressed the Box from both sides and it cracked like an overripe nut, with the ore dropping out of it.

"This is not the key. Key!"

Reading the forum and the manual got me nowhere. I had no idea where Reptilis dug up this quest and so found myself in a jam. I knew and felt that my quest would also lead me to this exact clearing, but the crossing over of two different quests had some unexpected consequences. Reptilis's quest got picked up first, moving my one aside. There was only one NPC, both of us came to him at the same time and started fighting in line with Reptilis's quest as well. A pity I sent him for respawn - could have done with punching his green mug one more time right now. Unfinished quests get reset every four months - time that I didn't have. If I fail to get the Totem, my rank would be demoted in two months.

Looks like I'm out of options...

"Speaking!"

"Hi, Anastaria. This is Mahan. Do you have a minute? I need your help."

"If it's not urgent, can it wait twenty minutes? I'm a little busy right now."

"All right. Call me when you're free."

I really didn't want to get involved with Phoenix, but it looked like there was no other way for me to get to the Dragons.

"Hello again," twenty minutes later I answered an incoming call from the amulet.

"Good day," a male voice greeted me the other end. What on earth? Where's the lady paladin? "My name is Rick Deadeye, you should have received the gear I made, along with this amulet at the Bank. How did you find it? Is it to your liking? I tried to give it a neutral appearance, though the initial recipe had a flamboyant look. Imagine this: orange with bright green. I thought you would've refused to wear something like that."

"Where is Anastaria?" I barely managed to interrupt the verbal torrent that hit me.

"Unfortunately she had to leave the game for a while. She asked me to contact you, saying that you needed help. What can I do for you?"

"Rick, I don't really know..."

"If you are uncertain of my status, let me assure you that I can take all decisions right up to declaring war on another clan. I hope your request is not of this kind. I have little stomach for war."

"Tell me Rick, what is your level of Eloquence? Or Chattiness? Whatever's the right name for it."

"Oh, have you already met such players? My congratulations! This is a very rare stat. Even more rare than Crafting. But we're not talking about me right now. How can the Phoenix clan be of help to you?"

I didn't have a lot of choice, so I sketched out my

situation to him, as far as Reptilis's quest was concerned. Mine was broken anyhow.

"The Dragonkin is standing in the doors of the house and demanding you give him a key: is that right?"

"Yes."

"And he has no intention of handing you the information about the Dragons, does he?"

"How... ?" I asked, dumbfounded. How did he know? Didn't Reptilis say that this was a unique quest?

"No need to get so worked up. These Dragonkin are scattered throughout Malabar in memory of Dragons that had existed long ago. The key is the scepter of the NPC from which you managed to steal this scroll with the quest. Yes-yes, I did say 'steal' - that's the only way to get this quest. At one time our entire clan was looking for a way to find the Dragons, but it was a futile effort. There are no Dragons in Barliona. We even contacted the game administration to verify such an absurd ending to the Dragonkin quests: just an ordinary hologram of a flying Dragon. But in any case, you have my congratulations: very few in Barliona get to touch the history of Dragons. Is this all?"

"Yes, thank you for your help."

"Then I'm off. Good bye!"

Well, I'll be! Some pickle Reptilis landed me in, that under-kicked croc! Four months of waiting for the quest to reset! Good bye Elemental Shaman! Why is everything so crappy?

"Key!" The last words I must have said aloud,

because the Dragonkin was at it again.

"I have no key. You can relax and go home now. Show's over"

The Dragonkin, like some obedient pony, turned around and entered the house. What to do? Go back? My spirits were so low that I wanted to howl. Why didn't I listen to Kornik and fly with him for the Totem? Decided I was smarter than everyone else, did I? After imagining the goblin's mocking eyes when I went back to him with my head hanging low, my spirits seemed to hit rock bottom.

Knowing that there was nothing left for me to do except return to Beatwick, I decided to make Anastaria's present. I had to make the Chess Set anyway, so why not do it right here? I had all the tools with me, as well as the holograms, and I didn't have to take any notice of the Dragonkin. Perhaps I'll raise my spirits at least a little this way. That settled, I sat down right on the grass and took out the holograms sent by Hellfire - the representatives of Phoenix and the Dark Legion and leading players of our continent. When the last image was copied to memory, I switched to the design mode. I was feeling so damn awful...

I immediately discarded four images of players from each clan, which for some reason were grey in my mind. If they were grey, it meant I didn't need them. I began to carve the figurines from the ones that remained. Anastaria was, of course, the Queen. As soon as I pictured her in a mantle, with a crown, an up-turned proud chin and a haughty gaze, the image of the lady paladin started to flow, dissolved and then appeared in the form of the figurine I was aiming for, surrounded with a bright glow. The first was done. The image of Hellfire just refused to be formed into a King. The crown just didn't suit him and I put him aside and moved on to other figurines. Knights, Bishops, all the eight pawns and one Rook came together right away. Only two images and two pieces remained - a King and a Rook. Strange. For some reason I thought that Hellfire should be the King, but an unassuming and inconspicuous gnome was wryly looking at me from the picture, as if asking: 'Try me!' All right. If he's asking, we'll have to go with it. I looked at the player's name: Ehkiller the Invisible. The name didn't mean anything to me, but there were no other options left, so I had to try him. If he fits, I hope Hellfire won't kill me.

He fit. As soon as I imagined Ehkiller with a crown and a cape, his image began to flow and took the shape of the King I was looking for. Strange - why him? Why not Hellfire - who without further ado turned into a Rook? I'll put it down to artistic license.

Things weren't exactly straight-forward with Number Twos either. Plinto simply wouldn't become the King, try as I might. Going by previous experience I tried to make him a Rook, but that didn't fit him as well. That's just crazy. Knight, Bishop, Queen - were all wrong. Only the pawns remained. Even in the design mode, where the consciousness was completely separated from the body, I swallowed. If Plinto finds out that I made him into a pawn, Number Twos will put me on their black list with everything that entailed. I hope that Anastaria will have a chuckle at the hint and won't inform that unbalanced person of the fact. The place of the King was taken by another player whose name was also not particularly known. And the Queen turned out to be the player that I saw with Plinto. I wasn't sure I knew what I was doing anymore.

When all the sixteen figurines took their places I exited the design mode, took Lapis and Malachite out of the bag, but right before re-immersing myself saw the Dragonkin right next to me. What could he want now?

Cutting the stones didn't present much of a problem. They had the same shape, so after forming one stone in my mind, I reproduced it in eight pieces of Lapis and eight pieces of Malachite. Just before combining the projections of the figurines with the stones I decided to add a few slight improvements. I tried to give all the Phoenix figurines proud and brave demeanor, but in the majority of cases the figurines acquired an air of arrogance, as if the rest of the world owed them. Only Rick, who spoke with me today, retained a human face. I made Number Twos look more fierce and angry. If they are to be green, let them resemble orcs. The result was quite interesting - only the King and the Queen failed to undergo this metamorphosis. The features of the other figurines became distorted with such fury, that it looked as if they were the ones who owed Phoenix and had to pay it back this very second, but were all tapped out. So be it, then. Another instance of artistic license.

After tweaking their appearance, I combined the figurine projections with the stones and opened my eyes. Done. When I get to Farstead, I'll send the figurines to Hellfire. If he asked for them so insistently, I had to grant his wish. 'Happy Birthday', Anastaria, you'll have to find a chessboard for them yourself. Damn, I couldn't help feeling pleased after making something with my hands. And then I was completely overwhelmed by a sudden rush of pleasure:

Item created: Cursed Chess Pieces of Balance
Description: This has no precedent in Malabar's history: the first ever binding of an object to a particular player. From this point on a close bond shall exist between the players of the Phoenix and the Dark Legion clans. Every three weeks, the players represented as Kings in the Chess Set must play against each other until a winner is declared. If one of the Kings is offline, he is to be replaced by the Queen, Bishop, Knight, Rook or Pawn. Duration of the game: two hours. If no winner is declared in the course of the game, it shall be considered void. The item is uniquely identified with its creator: Mahan

Depending on the results of the game played with the Cursed Chess Pieces, all the players represented on the board shall receive:
Three-week buffs in case of a win: +10% to all the main stats
Three-week debuffs in case of a loss: -10% to all the main stats
Three-week debuffs if the game was voided: -20% to all the main stats

Item class: Unique, cannot be destroyed. The binding to the players is now complete. All the bound players have been informed about the creation of the Cursed Chess Pieces of Balance

Attention! This item cannot be repeated. There is no recipe

You created a unique item. Your reputation with all previously encountered factions has increased by 200

Skill increase:

+1 to Crafting. Total: 4

+3 to Jewelcraft. Total: 22

You have received the title 'The Cursed Artificer'

I swallowed after reading the message. I'm screwed. If before I had some chance of avoiding punishment for depicting Hellfire as a Rook and Plinto as a Pawn, having created a chess set like that, I doomed the clans to eternal strife. They'll never forgive me this, even if I was a member of one of these clans. Who asked me to craft anything in such a mood? And what's that?

Item acquired: The Key to Dragons. Description: Ancient as the world itself, Dragons always honored beauty and uniqueness. After leaving this world, the Dragons instructed the guards that only those worthy should be granted passage to them. You have met their condition for obtaining the Key to the Dragons by creating a

unique item in front of the Guard. Congratulations!

There was a flash and a small iron key appeared in my hand.

"Key!" rumbled the Dragonkin who stood next to me, pointing to my hand.

"Here you go," I handed over the piece of ironware.

Item acquired: Scroll of teleportation to Dragons. On use: transports you to the place where Dragons live

After receiving the key and handing over the scroll, the Dragonkin gave a pleased snort and trudged off to the house, completely forgetting I was there. That was that: now I'll activate the scroll and receive the Totem. I can't wait any longer.

The clap of the opening portal made me start. I turned to the sound and saw a smiling man dressed all in white. It was a Herald.

"Good day, Mahan. I hope I will not detain you too long. Let's get straight to business. Let me congratulate you on creating such an interesting artifact. You have become the fourth free citizen of Barliona and the first on our continent to create a binding item. The Emperor sent me to you to exchange the created figurines and bring them to the palace. The chess match will be overseen by him personally. The participants will be compulsorily transported for the game."

"Exchange? For what?" I picked up my ears. The Emperor's goodwill is worth a lot in Barliona.

"These are the words not of a boy, but a man. I was very much afraid that you would have to be persuaded by being told of the dangers of keeping the Chess Pieces in your possession. What is the Emperor offering? First - unimpeded access to the external gardens of his palace. Second - his personal ring. And, of course, his personal regard for such an interesting master."

I did well in managing to stay on my feet, although the Hamster fell on his back and was not showing any signs of life. And it wasn't even the access to the palace garden or the ring that got me so excited. These things were also hard to get, but not entirely impossible. I was more blown away by the 'personal regard' of the Emperor. This could mean only one thing - reputation. Keeping in mind that I have the wonderful ability to increase my reputation by five units daily, in a couple of years my character could level up his reputation with the Emperor. And this means free entry to the palace! That was the silver lining of me creating these Chess Pieces.

"I agree. Here you go," I handed over the figurines to the Herald.

Your reputation with the Shaman Council has increased by 100 points. You are 900 points away from the status of Friendly. The reputation with the Malabar Emperor cannot be increased on account of the 'First Kill' Achievement

Item acquired: The Ring of the Emperor. Description: The person presenting this ring is acting on my instructions and for the good of Malabar. Number of uses: 1

"Thank you and until we meet again. According to the rules, you, as the creator of the Chess Pieces, are obliged to be present at the first game, which is set to take place in three days' time. Your presence will be hidden, so as not to break the concentration of the clan Kings. Good bye! One of us will drop by to get you three days from now."

The Herald opened a portal and disappeared and I was left staring stupidly at the indulgence in my hands. He's really more of a 'Richelieu' than an Emperor. Now whatever I did, even if I killed someone, I would not be sent back to the mines. I have a one-time 'get out of jail card'. Great, I'll have to use it wisely.

"Hello," I responded to the sudden throbbing of the communication amulet.

"Mahan, is this some kind of a sick joke? What are you doing, you dumbass?" I would've never thought that such a beautiful girl could scream like that.

"And good day to you too, Anastaria. Aren't you supposed to be offline?"

"What offline? What have you created? What the hell are these 'Cursed Chess Pieces'? Have you completely lost it in that Beatwick backwater?"

"Anastaria, let me explain..."

"You have two hours to get the chess pieces to me. I have to figure them out. If I don't get the chess pieces - I will officially declare you the enemy of the Phoenix clan. Understood?"

"I don't have the figurines. The Herald took them - at the request of the Emperor."

"The Emperor?"

"Yeah. A Herald ported in, rewarded me with the permission to enter the external palace garden and a hundred reputation with the Emperor, took the Chess Pieces off me and left. And you can stop screaming at me - Hellfire asked for the pieces as a present for you. Happy birthday! Upcoming birthday, anyhow."

"How dare you?!"

"Stacey, in all honesty, I've had enough of this! Let's speak frankly - what do you want? When I was asking for your help, you didn't even deign to speak to me and handed me over to Rick. And now you call me up and scream your head off. Some great analyst you are, the brain of Phoenix and all that. Let's stop beating about the bush."

"Mahan! You... you..."

"Yes, me! How long can you keep pulling at the cat's tail? What do you want?"

"The Orc Warrior figurines. I know that you have them."

"And what will I get in return?"

"The position of the Master in Phoenix."

"Not interested. Experience shows that I can manage pretty well on my own too. I will create my own clan."

"What do you want?"

"Wrong question. What can you offer? If I got it

right, since the creation of the Orc Warriors up until this moment, no-one managed to create the Dwarves. Therefore, either the pieces have to be created by the same player or the creator must be in possession of the previous figurines. I'm sure that Rick is trying to learn Jewelcraft as fast as he can, but getting exactly nowhere with it. Correct me if I am mistaken."

For a while there was a silence on the other end of the amulet.

"Can you give me a guarantee that I will get the remaining chess pieces if you create them?"

"If we come to an agreement, then yes. A month from the time of their creation the figurines will be yours."

Yup, I'm off and someone's cut the brakes! I was keeping my fingers crossed that I would manage to solve the puzzle contained in the new figurines within a month.

"The Phoenix clan will take your clan under its protection. You will receive a million gold for the pieces made of each stone type. Access for ten players from your clan to our clan's warehouse, where each can choose five items for themselves. Accelerated leveling of ten players from your clan to level 100 under the tutelage of our raiders. Would such an offer suit you?"

"Quite. Drawing up an agreement?"

"Yes, I'll draft the text now and drop it to your mailbox. You can read it at the Bank. Mahan..."

"What?"

"When are you planning to create your clan?"

"As soon as I get to Anhurs. There is no

registration office in Farstead."

"Tell me, is the position of your deputy free?" asked Anastaria thoughtfully.

"I don't understand..."

"We'll talk later. Don't disappear, Unique Shaman."

What a day! Did I really manage to catch the eye of the great Anastaria? Why did she ask me about the post of deputy? Could she want...?

I habitually glanced at my return timer and whistled: I had just eight hours left. Wow! Just how long was I out for with those Cursed Chess Pieces? At this rate I may not have enough time for the Dragons. I immediately ruled out the idea of jumping to Farstead and then to Beatwick for restarting the countdown. I simply didn't feel like spending that much. I only have one portal to Farstead and one to Beatwick left. Should I go to the High Mage and buy new ones? I don't know... At the same time I felt that I'd manage it, if I just stopped dragging my feet.

I was ready to see almost anything as I stepped through the activated portal: mountains, steppes or deep forests. But the place where I ended up in no way resembled a classical abode of Dragons: golden sand, gentle warm sunshine, palms and clear-blue sea. Breathtaking beauty! What if I just stay here, and leave Phoenix and Number Twos to search all over for me?

"My greetings to the first free citizen of Barliona to make it to this island," a low voice rumbled across the beach. "My name is Ayaretolikus, I am the keeper of the memory of Dragons."

"Greetings. My name is Mahan, the Shaman. I bow before you, oh keeper, but can you tell me who and where you are? One feels uncomfortable speaking to thin air," looks like I've become rather bold after my last chat with Anastaria.

"I am several kilometers within the island. Follow the road, it will take you right to me."

Before heading off to meet the guardian I checked the map to see the location of this island.

Attention! The use of maps is not permitted in this location

And that's that. Where on earth have I ended up? One thing was clear - this was an island. But an island where - the World Ocean, an inland sea or a great lake? There was a myriad possibilities.

Realizing that I may fail to get my Totem before returning to Beatwick, I ran as fast as I could towards the guardian. This was no time for leisurely walks.

"Guardian?" I ran up to the large glowing sphere, about two meters in diameter, which was effortlessly hanging a couple of meters above ground. It was an epic spectacle. Only one thing was disappointing - I was hoping to see a live Dragon instead of this ball lightning.

The surface of the sphere vibrated and it seemed like the entire island could hear its voice:

"I once again welcome the first free citizen of Barliona to my island. I, the Guardian of the Dragon Knowledge, ask you, traveler, why have you come here?"

This was somewhat grandiose, but it would do.

"Oh, Guardian of Dragon Knowledge," I decided to emulate the sphere's tone, "I have come here to incarnate my Totem."

"Totem? You have a Dragon as a Totem?"

"Yes, Guardian. Fate has dealt me a Dragon, but he is still very small and inexperienced."

"No need to explain, I shall open a portal to the world of Dragons for you."

"World?"

"Yes, Dragons had departed from this world forever. They dwell beyond Barliona, watching us from outside."

"I thank you for your aid, Guardian."

"Then go. No sense in wasting time. There's never enough of it."

There was a clap and a portal opened next to the sphere. As I walked towards it, I couldn't help wondering about a certain detail: Kornik suggested we go to the Dragons directly. Was he able to jump between worlds, then? I have to ask him when I get the chance. The portal surrounded me with a shimmering glow and once this dissipated I realized that I've never seen mountains before in my life. What I use to call mountains were mere hills. I was looking at real Mountains now, with a capital letter, so to speak. There were sheer cliffs rising high into the sky, the neighboring snow-covered peaks, lost in the clouds, and piercing wind. The scenery impressed.

"Would you believe it? He made it," Kornik was

sitting next to the spot where the portal left me, sporting an unpacked picnic basket and a protective dome.

"Teacher," I bowed, "you said that the next time we would see each other is when I had to take the exam for a Great Shaman. Is it already time?"

"No, not at all," laughed Kornik. "I just made a bet with Aarenoxitolikus that you would be able to make it here within a month. Just imagine, that green reptile decided that my apprentice would need two years to get here on his own."

"So what did you win? And, teacher, please cover me with a dome as well, it's rather cold here."

"A dome? Do it yourself. Or do you think I will be running after you to change diapers every time? You have to start learning things on your own. And I won a barrel of excellent wine. Only Dragons know how to make wine. All the other stuff's a shoddy imitation. When you become the Great Shaman, come by - I'll let you try some."

"Teacher, you didn't tell me how to make a dome. How do I know which of the Spirits can do it?"

"No-one had shown you how to summon a slowing or a purifying Spirit either, but you learned it just fine. You'll figure this one out too. Are you a Shaman or what?"

That stubborn goblin! Just provided the main points, leaving me to figure out the rest. Running around as a Hunter was much better - the trainers spoon-fed you every detail: how to hold the bow, how to throw a trap or how to measure the correct distance.

But here - you'll figure it out yourself, it's no big deal. Or was it something specific to this trainer? The old loon.

Realizing that I wouldn't last long without a dome, I entered the Spirit summoning mode and started to improvise. Despite my daily self-healing and the fight with Reptilis my Water Spirit rank rose only to 2. I didn't even notice when it happened.

So, what do I have for Water: Spirit of Water Strike, Spirit of Water Wave, Spirit of Water Healing , Spirit of Water Healing Wave, Spirit of Strengthening, Spirit of Intermittent Damage, Spirit of Control and Spirit of Cleansing.

All useful and important, but I needed one more Spirit. I didn't know his correct name, but it must have been something like Spirit of Water Shield. Where was I to place it? I had no free slots. It seems that the time had come for me to do some spiritual optimization. A play on words right there.

Spirit of Strengthening. Increases all the main stats by two percent for a minute and is totally useless in combat, as my fight with Reptilis had shown. There is no time to summon it. You have to either attack or heal. But what if I combined the Spirit of Strengthening with Healing Spirits? This would burn through a lot of Mana, but then I'll get a useful buff as I heal. Knowing full well that reading the manual and the forums would be of no use, I still checked them just to be sure - with predictable results. Again, I had to rely only on my intuition...

First of all, let's try to select the Healing Spirit

and summon the Spirit of Strengthening on it. Nothing. The Spirits didn't understand what they had to do. Then how about summoning both Spirits on me at the same time? Still nothing. First came one and then the other. Then let's try...

I was so caught up in the thrill of it all that for a while I switched off, forgetting about the cold. During yet another attempt to combine the Spirits, I understood what had to be done. It was simple object-oriented programming. There is the 'Healing Spirit' class with its properties and 'Strengthening Spirit' class, with its properties. The task was to create a new combined class, inheriting the main features of the preceding classes. But where to get a design kit to combine the two? Should I ask Kornik? That green mug would have a right laugh, saying that his apprentice is a complete doofus and teaching him is a waste of time.

Why do Shamans need a Totem? Is it just for playing with or for riding? Well, Mr. Manual, don't let me down now at least:

Totem: A natural object used as the Shaman's emblem. Totems help Shamans to understand themselves. They act as a means of connection to the inner world and reflect the essences which make up the personality of the temporal, physical Shamanistic 'I'. Totems help to understand why Shamans are the way they are. They point out the strong and weak sides of the character, strengthen its merits and lessen its shortcomings.

Totem properties: Cannot be changed. Can be

used as a mount (after incarnation) or as a Spirit design device. Totems are sentient and must be developed. Every fifty levels the Totem acquires an additional ability, dependant on the Totem type. If a Totem does not suit the Shaman, it can be removed.

Riiight. Everything became clear and simple, especially after reading the first paragraph. That's some dog's breakfast they've cooked up here. Why? To show how cool it is to be a Shaman? Brr... But I got the main bit. A Totem is a Spirit design device. If that's true, then...

"Hi. I need your help. Will you come?"
"Awe we going to pway?"
"No, we won't play. I have to get to grips with the Spirits."
"Awwight. I come."

A projection of a transparent little Dragon appeared next to me. Was I seeing things or had he grown a little? I thought he was smaller.

"Hewwo. How can I hewp?"

"I don't know myself yet. You see, there are two Spirits. One for strengthening and the other for healing. I have to combine them to make a new Spirit, but don't know how. Do you know how to do this?"

"Make a new Spiwit fwom two? Of cowse I know. Be wight back," the Little Dragon disappeared for a few seconds and then came back holding a crystal of some kind in his paws. As soon as Draco appeared a heavy thundering voice sounded: "The Totem Soul. The Shaman must keep it as the apple of his eye. If the Totem Soul is destroyed, the Totem will disappear forever and the Shaman will lose his strength."

Draco, still holding the crystal, shook his head and continued in his childish voice:

"Call the Spiwit you need here and then anoffer and then you get new Spiwit. Wet's twy, I'm cuwious."

A Totem Soul? It's the first time I ever heard about this. The manual and the forums make no mention of it at all. Damn, why is the internal help so truncated? If I could only get into the main net: that's where all the information about Barliona can be found. But here...

I heaved a bitter sigh, brought up the Spirit summoning mode, selected the crystal in Draco's paws and summoned a strengthening and a healing Spirit on it in turn. As soon as the Spirits settled in the crystal, a window with the description of the new Spirit appeared before me. The Water Spirit of Healing Strengthening. Next to the description there were two active bars with sliders: 'healing' and 'strengthening'. After playing around with it I felt somewhat disappointed. It turned out that the Spirits of healing and strengthening summoned separately give off a hundred percent of their force, while a combined Spirit is not equal in strength to the two Spirits making it up. Not only did the summoning time of the Healing Spirit increased, but the effectiveness of the healing and strengthening equaled to only seventy percent of the original. The sliders made it possible to increase one of the parameters to ninety percent, but in that case the other one fell to thirty percent. Such strengthening would be of little use. It also looked like the interdependence between the parameters was non-linear.

I changed the Healing Spirit to the Spirit I ended up with and carried out a similar operation with mass healing. I thought that this combination would be more useful. Now I'll play around with attacking Spirits.

I selected the crystal and summoned to it the Spirits of Water Strike, Intermittent Damage and Control. A triple kidney-shot at the opponent!

The maximum number of the combined Spirits cannot exceed the rank of the Spirits

Damn! Looks like it was too early to celebrate... But, to be fair, it made sense - you had to level up the rank of the Spirits in order to play with combining them. I put together the water strike with intermittent damage, optimizing the active zone. Two free slots appeared, where the Spirit of water shield could be summoned, which, in turn, could be combined with healing and drop a shield around the healed target, blocking some type of damage. Phew! Now let's roll.

I concentrated on the empty slot and started to summon a Spirit.

The rank of Elemental Shaman has access to the following additional Spirits: The Spirit of the Shield. Do you wish to add the Spirit to the active

zone?

Finally! After acquiring the new Water Spirit, I combined it with healing and once again shifted it to the active zone. I won't be freezing now!

I summoned the Spirit of Healing Shield and gave a smiling Kornik a pleased look. Although no, he wasn't smiling, but laughing with impunity. I don't get it - what's so funny?

A minute later it became clear what made my teacher laugh so much. The water shield had a certain property: it was made of water. And it was cold in these mountains. Very cold. When I found myself inside an ice sphere, my shoulders slumped. Kornik is such a bastard! He knows that my focus is Water, but didn't stop me. Although, I'm not much better. I got so carried away that didn't think of how Water would react to cold. The shield should really be made of air, like Kornik's. But I don't specialize in Air. Blast!

After waiting a short while for the shield to dissipate (another question for Kornik: why did his shield last a long time, while mine only lasted a minute?), I started to free myself from my icy prison with my Mallet. Like some chick breaking out of an egg. Why wasn't the dome breaking?

"You awe doing it wwong," I completely forgot about Draco. He continued to circle me, observing what was happening with great interest.

"What's the right way, then?"

"You soodn't hit just anywewe. Find a thpot and hit thewe."

"Will you help me?"

"Yup, found it. Hit wight here," Draco nosed a place in the ice capsule. If that's it - here goes.

"Move away a little, eh? There's gonna be a big 'boom' now!"

I took as big a swing as the confined space of the ice sarcophagus allowed me and hit the spot that Draco pointed out. Then came the fireworks. The ice barrier flew apart in all directions, as if it had been exploded, the icy wind was back, but the golden glow that surrounded me and Draco stood in its path. Where was this strange music coming from?

"Wow... It worrrked grrr... Grrrreat... Rrrr..., pllaying, crrrows," when I stepped back from the bright light, I looked at little Draco circling nearby. Although there was no more 'little Draco'. A young two-meter Dragon was cruising through the air around me. "Isn't it grrreat?" he said, happily, "I can prrrrounounce letter 'Rrrr'. It's brrriliant!"

I faked a smile and patted the Dragon on the back. I don't get it - did I just incarnate him? How on earth?

'Searching for your Totem' quest completed
Quest 'The Path of the Shaman. Step 2' completed

And that's it? Could all my tribulations with the scroll have been simply aimed at successfully getting out of the ice capsule with my Dragon? What happened to the unique bonuses? Where is the gaining of unsurpassed might? Where are all these things, I ask? And where are the Dragons, if it came to it?

"I greet you, my son," while Draco continued to 'grrrowl' at anything and everything as he learned to speak properly, an enormous green Dragon landed on the ground next to me. I should probably mention that I only now noticed that my Dragon was black as night. I'd got used to him being transparent, so it didn't register right away.

"I greet you, father," I bowed before the Dragon. I wasn't really getting the deal with the father-son stuff, but played along just in case.

"My name is Aarenoxitolikus, that green reptile that Kornik mentioned. You may call me Renox."

"Don't you go spoiling my apprentice," I heard the goblin's voice. "Quit it with all the role-playing: 'son', 'father'... He's a Shaman, not a Dragon."

"Dragon? How can I be a Dragon? I'm a human."

"You are a Dragon!" Renox's roar echoed through the mountains.

"He's a Shaman!" Kornik shook the mountains with a matching roar.

"Hey therrrre Dad!" Draco just completely floored me. "Can you rrreally believe it? I'm alive again! And I've regained my memorrry!"

"People, can someone explain to me what the heck is going on here?" I probably looked stupid, but I really didn't understand a thing.

"Kornik, you start. I'll correct you, if need be," thundered Renox.

"A Shaman must have a Totem. Without it he's

nothing. There are a myriad of ways to get a Totem. You can ask for one from your teacher or find it by yourself. Or you can do something unusual and pull the Totem out of the Grey Lands. Essentially, everything's as it's meant to be."

"Mahan, I am astonished by how you managed to understand the combination of Spirits with a teacher like this. Kornik, please lay aside your principles at least once and explain everything properly."

"Don't interfere with my educational process. I teach the way I want to teach. Do I meddle with your Dragons, trying to teach them how to fly? So you stay out of this too."

"Do you at least know what happened here?" I asked Draco, who was continuing to 'grrrowl' at the stones. Kornik and Renox had descended into a deep ideological debate on the meaning of existence. It was useless trying to interrupt them and I had only two hours left until my return.

"Nothing special. I was a Drrragon, but a hundrrred years ago I died while fighting the ice giants of this worrrrld. I was only thrree hundrrred yearrrs old, just out of an egg, you may say, and in the first battle was careless enough to get hit by a rock. I wanted to help my family. My father had spent a long time looking for a way to reincarnate me, until he found out that I could be incarnated as a Totem. Even if it's for a short time, it's still better than total oblivion. He appealed to the Shamans and they summoned me to this world as a Totem. In the last hundred years no-one got a Dragon as a Totem and even if they did, I would have ended up as an ordinary naive and foolish little cub. Even now, when we return to your world - oh, I'm no longer growling my 'r's! - I would again turn into a small baby. To get my memory back over there I would have to be raised to level 200."

"And why did your memory come back to you here?"

"I was born anew. From an egg. And born together with a brother too."

"With who?"

"Surprise! With your dome you made an ice egg and with his breath Father turned it into a real one. Do you think you would've failed to smash an ordinary ice barrier with your Mallet? So from a Dragon Egg there hatched two Dragons. One who was reborn and the other... The other is you, brother."

"This one's at it too," it turned out that Kornik and Renox had been standing nearby and listening to Draco's tale, having stopped their debate. "Stop muddling his brain or it'll boil over soon. Don't listen to them, they won't teach you anything good. Life is much more complicated than just being a Dragon. Looks like you'll have to be told what really happened here. A hundred years ago at the request of this green lizard, the Shaman Council reincarnated a dead Dragon in a Totem."

"Like you can talk about being 'green'," dropped in Renox, without a hint of offence.

"No derailing. Now then. So we did incarnate him, but we couldn't find any worthy candidates to receive this Totem. We tried out a few volunteers, but all died in the Dragon fire. Even Geranika wouldn't risk it. And then you turn up with a Dragon for a Totem. When Prontho found out he barely restrained himself from abandoning his mine to spread the word among other Shamans. He did restrain himself, his sense of duty was stronger, but he sent me a message. And I started to watch you. Right, I'm veering from the business at hand now. Dragons. Even if you simply incarnated the Dragon, he would have remained a non-sentient. Well, when I say 'non-sentient'... In time he would have grown smarter and learned to carry out your commands, but it would have still been a long way from a real Dragon. That would have happened if you took the standard path and accepted my help. But you chose the way of the Shaman. And in the end we have what we have. In this world your Totem regains his memory and can speak with his family - but no more than fifty percent of the time, because the rest of the time he must spend with you. It is also possible to return his memory to the Dragon in our world, but for that you need to bring him to level 200. When you go back he will only be level 1 and you would only be able to summon him for two hours a day. For now this is all he can do. As his level increases, so will the time he can spend in your world. So that's how it is."

"And about that bit where I became a Dragon...?"

"You hadn't become anything! You were a Shaman and that's what you have remained. So what if on your return to our world you'll be a total wreck for a couple of days and develop immunity to poisons? All of them. And a couple of other things, which you'll have to deal with yourself. You still have much growing to do until that time comes. It's nothing to concern yourself with right now."

Strange, if I've acquired these abilities, why hasn't the system informed me about them?

"And how do Dragons level up? I ask because I'd like to know how to return your memory." I looked at Draco.

"Summon me often and set me to hunt various critters. But if I get sent to the Grey Lands, I'll lose ten levels. Remember this."

Yup, this is just like a common Hunter's pet, but one that allows you to work with Spirits. Not bad.

"Is there anything else I need to know? I'm beginning to run out of time now. I will have to be getting back."

"The rest you'll learn as you go along," said Renox and then turned to a pleased-looking Kornik and rumbled: "You won the second time too. Where did you find an apprentice like this?"

"The second time?" I looked questioningly at Kornik.

"Renox promised a reward worthy of an Emperor to whoever gained his Totem, and said that anyone who made it possible for him to speak with his son, even briefly, would be altogether enriched. We made a bet that you won't even bring up the reward. Got another barrel of wine off him."

"You have my thanks, Shaman. Only a Harbinger is able to take something material out of our world, but there are things of greater value than gold:

information. Look at these two maps. They mark the places with ancient treasure vaults of the Dragons. We have no need of them now, but they could be of use to you. You can take someone with you to the first of these, but to the second you must go alone. And most importantly - I see that you have begun to restore the Karmadont Chess Set. I liked that man, he was a great ruler. Just remember this: whatever logic or hints may tell you, always choose the right way. "

Gameworld maps updated. Your maps have been updated with the marks of two Dragon treasure vaults. The marks have been numbered

The right way? What right way?

"That is all. It is time for you to go back."

"Can I ask a question. How did you and Swiftbel become friends?"

"High Shaman Swiftbel helped Renox to look for a candidate who could get the Dragon as his Totem. A wasted twenty years," Kornik replied for the Dragon.

"But the old ladies, his sisters, said that..."

"For them he will always remain a merchant, a trader and an adventurer. Not everyone needs to know the truth."

"Hold on. Another question."

"Kornik, I'm beginning to understand you. You give him an inch and he'll take a mile", remarked the elder Dragon.

"At our last meeting you said that I should be preparing for something, that there was very little time.

What did you mean?" I ignored the Dragon's words. If I'm being impudent, I may as well go all the way.

Kornik looked thoughtful and then, carefully choosing his words, said:

"Great change is coming to Barliona, but the Emperor is refusing to see it. He's totally blind."

"Change? What change?"

"Enough questions. You will find out for yourself soon enough, if you continue to do what you have been doing. You have to become a Great Shaman. Keep learning!"

Quest accepted: 'The Path of the Shaman: Step 3.' Completion of the trial to become a Great Shaman'. Description: complete the trial to become a Great Shaman. Next trial: in 3 months' time. Quest type: Class-based

The question about what it was I should 'continue to do' was about to leave my lips, when I suddenly found myself right in my bed in Elizabeth's summer house.

You have acquired a passive ability - Dragon Blood: immunity to all poisons.

Attention, a new stat has become available to your character: Spirituality. Spirituality affects the ability to work with Spirits and put together different Spirit combinations and allows you to summon Spirits of other classes; as you level up in this stat, the penalty for combining Spirits is

reduced

Do you accept? Attention, you will not be able to remove an accepted stat!

I think I'll go for it! I should have filled up the last empty slot long ago. Even if this isn't a straight-forward damage-based stat, I rather enjoyed combining the Spirits. Some good stuff came out of that.

A new stat has been unlocked for the character: Spirituality. Current level: 1

I looked around, about to wonder why Kornik took me back to my bed, after leaving me by the village gates last time, when I became submerged in pain. At first it was an insignificant tingling throughout the body, then I acquired a 'Modification' debuff and the pain began to grow. I held out as long my willpower permitted, but then broke and stared to scream and howl. The pain was terrible. When 'Modification' changed to 'Transformation' I was already barely conscious - just lay curled up in bed emitting an occasional howl.

"What happened?" somewhere on the edge of consciousness I heard the worried voice of Elizabeth. "Mahan, what happened?"

A veil of pain completely obscured my consciousness. My hearing probably went, because the surrounding world was submerged in muffled silence. It seemed like an eternity had gone by before the red haze before my eyes flickered and I came to myself. It was as if someone had pressed a button and turned off the pain. My first thought was: 'It's so good to be an ordinary player! There's no pain and you can leave the game any time.'

"Mistress, mistress, he woke up!" I found myself in a well-lit room.

"How do you feel?" I managed to focus my gaze on Elizabeth.

"I'll live," I tried to understand how I was feeling. There was no more pain, all my stats were norm... What?! The level of Endurance had increased to 27! Just how much enduring did I do?

"Oh dear, you really gave us a fright," continued the landlady. "I didn't even know what to do! You were burning like a furnace. The priest came to look, but couldn't do anything. You spent two days in a fever, rolling around in the bed. And today it's like you've been reborn. Would you like some tea?"

I didn't get it - why was she being so nice? I looked at Elizabeth's properties and was a little surprised to see that my level of Attractiveness with her was at 34. Another fifty and she'll start flirting with me. Why, all of a sudden?

"Mahan! Are you alive already? Tomorrow we'll start learning to work with spoons and forks. I only taught you the very basics, there are still so many details to learn - it's right scary! I'll drop by tomorrow morning. And don't forget that you promised me a present." Clouter quickly run into the room before immediately zapping off again. I just seriously don't understand anything.

I had little desire or inclination to lounge around in bed. After getting ready to go, just before leaving the room I glanced in the mirror. My red headband! It was gone! How could I have forgotten? Now it was clear why everyone was so nice to me all of a sudden: I had regained the standard twenty points of Attractiveness.

There came a clap of an opening portal and a Herald entered the room.

"My Lord," Elizabeth, who was still standing by the door bowed in a graceful curtsy. It was so elegant that it could not be spoiled either by her simple dress or her hair gathered in a tight bun. Who was she?

"Mahan, I have come for you. In five minutes the chess match between the Phoenix and the Dark Legion clans will begin. As the creator of the chess pieces, you have been invited as an observer. Come."

Elizabeth stared at me wide-eyed and in her properties Attractiveness rose by 20 points in one go. Now it was fifty four. Women. Whether real or NPC. The more important the company a man keeps, the higher his Attractiveness.

I was ready to go, so I stepped through the Herald's portal straight away. I would finally see the Emperor's palace with my own eyes.

CHAPTER NINE
THE SHAMAN'S MISTAKE

T HE EMPEROR'S PALACE DAZZLED. It was sumptuous, as full of decorations as a Christmas tree and glittering in all the colors of the rainbow. Neatly trimmed hedges, paths of golden sand, grass that made you think you've never seen 'green' before in your life - the developers had made a real effort with this location. The palace of the Malabar Emperor was considered the height of the creative endeavor of designers and artists. Every three months contests were held on how to improve its already perfect look. Though seemingly an impossible task, the creators still found bits to improve, which the designers would make, while players, who had managed to experience such beauty, would enthusiastically recount the wonders of the palace to their friends.

Video recording didn't work inside the palace

and it was impossible to take screenshots - these functions were disabled at the level of the capsules and code. Even media programs about the palace only showed the publicly accessible territories. The palace remained a mystery and a beckoning centre for all the players in Malabar for the entire fifteen years of the game. Similar palaces existed on other continents, but the design and the style of each was different - as was the reputation that you had to obtain to enter the palace. If you wanted to have a look at all of them you had to reach 'Exalted' with all the five Emperors. As far as I knew, there was only a small handful of such players.

"Please follow me," the Herald brought me back to earth from my exulting contemplation of the palace's wonders. "According to the rules, the creator of Cursed Items cannot be seen by anyone in the Palace. To accomplish this you and everyone around you are placed in different instances. Even if you walk through a player, neither he nor you would feel anything. This is because the Imperial Palace is one of the few places on our continent where violence is forbidden."

This was news. Did this mean that each player enters his own copy of the castle, while other players are presented to him as projections?

"And what about items? For example, what if I take a chair and throw it at another visitor? The chair is local and everyone has access to it."

"You're not the only one so quick-witted," smiled the Herald. "As soon as a visitor touches anything, it gets transferred to his dimension. So it's impossible to hit another guest with it."

"Then how about this. Two guests grab this sword, for example, at the same time." I pointed to an exquisite blade on the wall. "Will there be two copies of it? Or will it go to one particular person?"

"For that we have guards around here. As soon as visitors start experimenting with inflicting damage on each other, they are immediately removed from the palace and are forbidden to ever come back. I should tell you that the Palace has seen a fair number of such guests in its history. Some of them are still writing letters to the Emperor asking for pardon, but His Majesty is firm in his decision. This way please."

We went through the arch of a door and found ourselves in a hall full of guests. There was a buzz, like in a disturbed beehive. Players constantly whispered to each other, and, if I wasn't mistaken, were separated into two camps - into two big groups of people, each about thirty to forty strong. Phoenix and the Dark Legion. Almost everyone who had access to the Emperor's Palace was gathered here, flashing angry glances and making rude gestures, and, in general, doing their best to show their disdain for the other clan. Judging by the fact that no-one took the slightest notice of us, the Herald's words were true - I remained unseen by the others.

"The Emperor is currently giving some parting words to the players - please wait in the hall. When he finishes, I will take you to the game room. You can stay here and look around."

I followed the Herald's advice and headed

straight for the players. I had little interest in the Dark Legion, so went over to the Phoenix crowd, which included Anastaria, Hellfire and Rick - among those I definitely recognized.

"Stacey, tell me again - why did we come here? It's not like I have nothing better to do." When I came right up to a small group consisting of people that I had depicted as chess pieces, I began to make out their conversation.

"Calm down, Hel. If Killer told everyone to show up, he meant everyone. You'd better check out Plinto blowing his top over there. Stupid pawn. When I catch Mahan and tear out his reproductive organ for making these chess pieces, I'll remember to thank him for this particular portrayal. I even felt like clapping, when I saw this."

"Yeah, he sure hit the mark with that. But why of earth am I a Rook? I get it with Plinto: no-one ever really took him seriously, despite the levels, but me... I feel quite offended."

"Don't take any notice. You and Rick are the backbone of our clan. Essentially you and he are keeping the fighting and economic parts of the clan afloat. That's why you are depicted as towers - like an unshakable foundation. I'm rather perplexed by something else. How does Mahan know about Ehkiller and Evolett? It's not like they've ever made themselves stand out."

"And what does the boss say? Has he already contacted the administration?"

"He's as silent as a grave. Said that we won't get

a word out of him until the game has been played."

"Damn. I don't want to get a debuff," Hellfire even looked downcast, "I had plans to take people through a couple of Dungeons. I don't want to strain myself unnecessarily."

"Who cares about the debuff? At least for now. We'll figure out how to deal with it in the run-up to the tournament. Do drop by once this is over. Reconnaissance has reported that anomalies have been detected in six more places aside from Farstead. I sent groups there and will fly there myself tomorrow to investigate."

"Ziggurats too?"

"Looks a lot like it. The map isn't working and there were goblin sightings. Level eighty this time. If we were out of luck in Beatwick, again because of that damned Shaman, in these zones we have to be the first."

"By the way, Stacey, what are you really planning to do with him? Make him a Master?"

"No, he won't go for it. I will buy him. I'll take the Orc Warriors off him now and the other chess pieces later."

"And what if he refuses?"

"Like hell he will! We've come to an arrangement; I'll wait until we're allowed to fly to Farstead and hand over the agreement to him myself. Just a little of the poison and even the craziest agreement would look like the best deal to him."

"Maybe it's best not to play with fire? They aren't worth it. You only have three more cautions left. Why take such a risk? I think there is a more effective method. The red headband will help us out and the pain factor hasn't gone anywhere."

"Let's talk later. I already worked through all the possibilities. The chess pieces will be mine. And that's that."

"Mahan, let's go," I didn't see how the Herald appeared next to me. "The Emperor has finished with his parting words, the game will start as soon as you enter the room. Please come this way."

Damn! There was a lot of interesting stuff I was hearing in the talk between Anastaria and Hellfire and now I was being dragged away from them. One thing was clear - Phoenix won't be getting the figurines, no matter what agreement they try to send me. If Anastaria needs them, I could find a use for them too.

The small office where I found myself was completely packed with different shelves full of books, scrolls and other paperwork. There was dim candlelight, two armchairs, a table with a chessboard carved into it, my chess pieces and a jug of wine. There were also two players sitting opposite each other: Ehkiller and Evolett, each giving a hateful look to his opponent. Several players came up to their Kings wishing them luck, then came the bang of the closing door and both players breathed out, leaning back in their armchairs in relief.

"You're looking well there, brother," said Ehkiller, looking pleased.

"You're not looking too bad yourself, old boy," Evolett replied to him in the same tone. I was ready for anything: swearing, screaming or threats, but I would've never dreamt that the de-facto heads of two clans that hate each other would end up being brothers. Were they were blood brothers or sworn brothers, I wondered? And where's my armchair or will I have to stand for two hours?

"Why do you never visit? Allie's been asking if anything's happened to you." Ehkiller continued. "Has Barliona sucked you in to that extent?"

"Not really. It's just the new election campaign is coming up and the boss is hoping to run for mayor, so we're all hands on deck. You wouldn't believe it, but I haven't set foot in the game in three days. Just haven't had the time. I even lost one work team that way, just couldn't get to them and they wouldn't accept food from anyone else. How's it going on your end?"

"Same old. Allie and I are off on a trip tomorrow - to the sea. It's been a while since we've been. I'm gone for about three weeks, just until our next game, as it happens."

"And who will run the clan while you're gone?"

"Stacey. It's time she grew up."

"Yup, my niece is one smart cookie. Will she cope?"

"Of course she will. She's in charge of her own department of brainiacs, how's a clan any different? She'll do fine. I've been wanting to hand the clan over to her for a while now. I'm beginning to grow tired of the game. Money, power, receptions with the Emperor with unforgettable delicacies... But in real life the half-burnt flapjacks of my wife taste miles better than everything generated by the brain and taste receptors inside the capsule. I'm growing old, Al, old. I'm in my sixth decade now and still playing games. If not for Kartoss, I would have left long ago. Your move."

"E2 to E4. A standard move. Let's decide from the start, do you need a win? Plinto has been tearfully begging me to kick your ass. He's preparing to go on some raid and really doesn't want to get that 10% debuff.

"No, don't need it. It's about time my lot are taken down a notch. They've soared so high they've begun to see ordinary people as losers. Who were they exactly before they joined the clan? No-one remembers anymore. I think I'll let you have the games right up to the tournament."

"You want to win that, eh?"

"Who doesn't? I have no rivals. My apologies, but yours are just a pack of disorganized morons."

"That's fine, no point taking offence - we knew from the start what we were doing when we created the clans."

"True. The only real competition could come from the Azure Dragons clan, headed by Undigit. But he lacks an able organizer. So yes, I intend to win. By the way, I'm about to capture your Plinto. How did the creator ever get the idea of making him into a pawn...?"

"Yes, it's rather amusing. And just look at your figurine - as stuck-up as a goose, nose turned up so high you can see a mile inside. The pieces were made by a good master and came out very well. What do you know about Mahan? By the way, did you find out why the heck these chess pieces even appeared in the Game?"

"Yes. I managed to have a chat with the admins. Such items are being introduced on all the continents right now. The reason is simple - to increase competition between the leading clans and give the rest an opportunity to catch up. As for the creator of the chess pieces, he has my sincere thanks. For example, in Grindos, they created a wooden domino set of non-standard size - with meter-high tablets. Can you imagine the joy of shifting those tiles around? They may puff and pant, but shift them around all the same. We're the ones who have it easy. Sitting here, sipping the wine and having a chat. Now then. The creator of the chess set couldn't have helped it - the admins were looking for a player capable of creating such a thing. When Mahan started to create the chess pieces - at Hellfire's request, as it happens - the Corporation made its choice. He had no chance to create anything else. The chess pieces were forcefully introduced into the game. So it's not his fault."

"Will you take him in?"

"No. And I forbade everyone else from doing so. I want to see what he makes of himself. I don't like the current trends - in the past two years we accepted five players with Crafting and half of them gave up playing, while the other half never gained more than one level in this stat. Let him do his stuff outside Phoenix."

"Have you asked your acquaintance in the administration why we turned up as Kings? We always kept a low profile and then - surprise, surprise! Are you sure there isn't some informant behind this?"

"No, this is more complicated. Your move, by the way. The choice of the figurines was left completely in the hands of the creator, including their appearance. How does he know the real state of things? That's the real question. What are you doing? You'll have a checkmate in three moves!"

"Oh! That's right."

"Some player you are, dammit. Here, take the Queen. Being so well-informed about who is who in our clans is another reason why I want to see how Mahan will evolve on his own. I will watch him from afar and not interfere."

"Is this all you know about him? Do you know that Mahan and the creator of the Karmadont chess pieces are the same person? Is Phoenix's intelligence functioning so badly?"

"Of course I know. But without a full set they are useless. Only when they are all brought together, with the board, will they open the passage to the Creator. One or two pieces by themselves are of little use."

"So he should make the rest."

"You can't force someone to craft something like that. I already gave Hellfire a slap on the wrist for asking Mahan to make the Dwarf figurines as a present for Anastaria's birthday. You can't force someone to create."

"All right. Then I will instruct mine not to touch Mahan either. Let him create in peace. By the way, do you know about the additional six anomalies?"

"Yes, we've already sent groups there. Looks a

lot like the ziggurat that's in the Krong province."

"I still can't understand what it is that the Corporation is cooking up. Putting Kartoss forces in the vicinity of Malabar, with the support of Magisters too... Something big is in the pipeline. But what?"

"Time will tell. At last! Listen, you really need to improve your chess skills. You're playing like a noob! If father was still alive, he'd be very disappointed."

"Don't grumble. You won and that's good enough. Oh, the buff has turned up. You know, it'll be fun playing with this thing on."

"Mahan, please come this way," the Herald appeared right next to me. "The first game has been played and the rules have been met. The other games will take place without your presence. I hope you've had a pleasant time."

"Herald, can I stay for five more minutes?" I begged. Again, something told me: I had to stick around, if only for a couple of minutes.

"If you stay in the palace for three more minutes, you will be denied access to the external palace garden," the Herald's reply was firm. "After three minutes the access to the palace will be lost to you permanently. Even the First Kill would not permit you to return here. Make your choice."

"I will stay here another three minutes. As soon as the time runs out, please do take me back, but I need those three minutes."

"The countdown has begun. You have three minutes. After that you either step onto this portal," the Herald pointed towards the whirlwind that appeared, "or wave good-bye to the palace forever."

"I understand, thank you."

I turned back to the clan Kings. They sat there, slowly drinking their wine in silence. Well, guys, what did you want to tell each other? Two minutes went by before Evolett began:

"I think the Herald will have taken him away by now. He has no business being in the palace with his reputation."

"I agree. So - back to the business at hand. Tomorrow I'm sending Hellfire to Serrest. He has to be taken out of the game for at least twelve hours - the boy's been gaming himself out of line lately. Can you arrange an ambush for him, please?"

"Done. What about Mahan?"

"For now, nothing. We can't go to Krong, the conditions of the quest prevent us."

"And what about the six new points?"

"A lot of time can go by before you develop them and understand what's what. Let Anastaria try, but I don't believe we'll see much success there. I would have to fly to Farstead myself. There I'll find Mahan and have a heart-to-heart chat with him - about the chess pieces and the information about us. No-one informed him - he found out himself somehow."

"By the why don't you want to take him in?"

"The damn condition for the Karmadont Chess Set. You read the scroll yourself..."

"Mahan, your time is up. Make your choice: the portal or banishment," once again the Herald appeared next to me, cutting off the sound of the brothers' conversation.

"The portal," I managed to force out of myself. But it was so difficult to utter those words... The shimmering cloud immediately enveloped me, landing me in Elizabeth's room. What had those two been talking about?

Right after my return to Beatwick I shut myself inside the summer house, completely cut off from the world. The conversation of the two brothers completely threw me. Were they even brothers? Now I wasn't all that sure that what I heard was true and my intuition was silent. I had even more questions now than before this chess match. An analysis of that meeting was in order:

Facts:

1. Two players, who are the actual leaders of Phoenix and the Dark Legion clans, know each other well and carry out certain of each other's requests.

2. The clan leaders knew that the creator of the Cursed Chess Set would be present at their first game and put on a performance for his benefit.

3. As soon as the month that I have remaining to complete my quest runs out, a swarm of high-level players will head for the Krong province. At the same time, a certain number of these players will be very aggressive towards me.

4. There exists a scroll with information about the Karmadont Chess Set.

5. Conclusions: the Chess Set will stay with me until I see that scroll.

What should be placed in doubt:

1. That the players are brothers. Reason: for some unknown purpose these two players have shown me that far from being enemies, they are actually very close relatives. Why did they do this? To show that I can forget about joining either clan since they'll get to me in either one? I don't get it.

2. The arranged nature of the games. Reason: the first game was a show put on for my benefit. It is highly likely that even the scoreboard would remain open during the games. Knowing full well that I would be present at the match and still revealing that Phoenix will be having very bad luck for four months in a row... Smacks a lot of disinformation.

3. Both clan leaders know that I created the Orc Warriors. Reason: a bluff aimed at getting me to finally admit it and hand the figurines over to them.

Yeah... An interesting situation. And yet I'm completely out of ideas. What to do? Damned if I know. Only one thing is clear - I urgently have focus on the important activity of boosting my skills and levels. I have to raise myself up to at least level 40, then I can speak to the clans on a better footing. I have a whole month to level up as much as possible - time I mustn't waste. I will create the present I promised Clouter right now, and then go out into the field tomorrow. Draco also needs to be leveled up. Speaking of which...

"Hi. Come now, we need to talk."
"Coming."

As Draco said when we were in his world, here

he was still small, just over half a meter. Not a problem - I'll get busy with leveling him up from tomorrow. The timer for summoning the Totem immediately popped into view, counting down two hours. It was a level 1 Totem: 20 Hit Points, Strength and Intellect depended on the player, but it couldn't exceed the pet's level by twenty points. No matter, that'll do Draco for now.

"Listen, I keep forgetting to ask: what is your name?"

Draco stopped and stared at me with big naive eyes. Damn! Why am I asking him? He's a child - he'll take any name you give him! But what if a grown-up Draco didn't like it? That would be a pity.

"I see. I asked the question wrong. From today until you reach level 200 you will be called: Draco! We'll figure out what else to call you when you grow up."

"Draco," said the Totem thoughtfully. "Draco... I like it! I'm Draco!"

After clicking 'ok' to the question of whether I agree to this name for my Totem, I came out to the courtyard with the flying kiddo in tow. If I remember correctly, there were many low-level beetles and flies around here, on which I can unleash my pet to hunt and level up.

"A Dragon!" Our 'lessons' were interrupted by an astonished whisper from Elizabeth, who was staring wide-eyed at Draco turning another bug into a little pile of ash. With 20 levels in Intellect, the little dragon could spout fire very well, destroying one beetle or butterfly a couple of levels higher than him in one breath. Thirty minutes of battling the insects in Elizabeth's courtyard raised Draco to level 3. I wondered if he had a system for point allocation, like with the Hunter pets. Or did all his stats go up proportionally at the same time? The manual had nothing to say about that and I didn't even bother looking at the forum. It was quite useless...

"Where did you get him?" Elizabeth regained her composure and respectfully watched Draco flying about.

"This is my Totem," I habitually looked up Elizabeth's properties and was dumbfounded. Attractiveness - seventy points. Another ten and my landlady will start making advances towards me. She is, of course, an attractive NPC, but the depicted character came with a clearly specified age. She's a bit too old for me. Damn, what am I on about? I'll have to be catching her in four days' time!

"But Dragons don't exist... Avtondil, stop!" shouted the landlady, when a gust of ginger hair flew past her and crashed into Draco. My blood froze. If my Totem gives Clouter the same treatment he gave Almis...

"Mum, mum! Look, it's a Dragon! Look at the tail he's got! Oi! No you don't! You'll never catch me!" accompanied by the enthusiastic barking of Tiny Tim, there were now two kids running around the courtyard - a human and a Dragon. The difference in their races was immediately overlooked; the children screamed, shrieked and chased each other, having completely forgotten about us.

"He... won't... do... anything...?" asked Elizabeth, stumbling over every word.

"He shouldn't. He's well behaved," I was about to call Draco back, but was stopped by a message that popped up:

Totem level increased by 1. Current level: 6

A couple of minutes of running around the yard and you get a level? Why, all of a sudden? I suppressed the desire to get my Totem back and simply watched the kids chasing each other around. Then came 'hide-and-seek, 'It' and 'dodgeball', which Elizabeth and I were dragged into. By the end of the second hour since Draco appeared, all of this raised him to level 17. Why? I had no rational explanation for this, so I was simply glad it happened.

"Was this my present?" asked an out-of-breath Clouter, when Draco waved his talon at him and disappeared. That's it: now he's inaccessible for 24 hours. "Can you call him again? I really-really promise to eat all the porridge. I'll run and do it now. Pleeease!"

"I will call him again tomorrow for sure. You can run around all you like then. Now he's tired and has gone to sleep. That's Dragons for you - when they get tired, they go straight to bed. And that wasn't the present. I'll give you the present tomorrow. So run along and eat your porridge – you promised."

"Can I eat the porridge tomorrow?" Clouter looked pitifully at his mother.

"No, you can't. Either the porridge and the Dragon or nothing. That's final!"

"Aww... Life really can be so cruel and unjust.

Such utterly disagreeable constraint on your behalf, mother," sighed Clouter and trudged off to the house. Where did he pick up words like that?

"Don't listen to him. He's read all those words in a book, and still doesn't really know their meaning," said Elizabeth, fixing her hair, when Clouter disappeared in the house. "Is it true about the Dragon? Will he come tomorrow too?"

"Of course. I keep my promises. I haven't forgotten that I promised to look into who's been scratching the gates either."

Elizabeth noticeably started, her eyes grew shifty and, glancing from side to side, she asked:

"Perhaps you shouldn't? Who cares about some kids fooling around? Maybe you should leave off your nocturnal village walks. Not much point."

"I would never go back on my word. And now, excuse me, I need to go and make a present for your son. Promises have to be kept."

The landlady took a breath and was about to stop me, but restrained herself. I could clearly see that she wanted to say something, but decided not to drag the information out of this demonologist. All was clear to me already. She was going through the inner struggle between Attractiveness and her main mission: for now the mission is winning. If she comes and confesses all before the week is out, I'll have think about what's to be done with her.

I sat on the bed, took out the Marble I gathered at the mine and my jeweler's kit and entered the design mode. The idea for the present was simple: since

Clouter loves his Tiny Tim so much, I'll try to carve a dog figurine for him out of Marble. What if it came out well? It'll do me good and will make the lad happy.

Replicating a piece of marble in the design interface, I began to create an image of a dog. Hm. Looks like making an image of a living being from memory isn't all that simple. When I was making the Cursed Chess Pieces, I had the holograms of the players and it was much easier. For a long time Tiny Tim didn't want to come out right. Either the head was wrong or his legs too short. I had no time restriction on being in Beatwick, so I wasn't too worried about how long it might take me to create the dog. Time and again I created and removed the image of Tiny Tim from my memory, until a certain attempt came out perfect. It was him - the meter-high Wolfhound, gentle and fluffy, as the dog was in his virtual life. I combined it with the model of the Marble and opened my eyes to be surprised with a stream of messages:

Damage taken. Hit Points reduced by 24: 304 (Cursed Dog Aura) — 280 (Magic resistance). Total Hit Points: 2396 of 2420
> **Skill increase:**
> **+1 to Jewelcraft. Total: 23**
> **+1 to Crafting. Total: 5**

What the...?!

I lowered my gaze and saw THIS THING. A small Marble statuette of a dog. But this was no normal dog. I was looking at the muzzle of a vicious dog, drooling with bared teeth, with a spiked collar, rabid eyes and flaking skin that had ribs poking out of it in places. The statuette looked hideous. What about its properties?

Cursed Dog. Description: "Hatred and pain turned the gentle house pet into an embodiment of horror. Fear finished off the job and now the Dog hates everything that lives, everything which still contains a speck of kindness. 350 dark magic damage inflicted on all 'light' beings in the radius of ten meters once every five seconds

Attention! This item cannot be repeated. There is no recipe

You created a unique item. Your reputation with all previously encountered factions has fallen by 100. Your reputation with Kartoss has increased by 100

You have received the title 'The Cursed Artificer, Level II': the strength of negative effects has increased by 10%

To hell with all this! I quickly opened the reputations table and saw that my standing with the Malabar Emperor had returned to zero. If not for the daily increase, the reputation with the Shaman Council would have even gone into the negative. Why in the hells did I create THIS THING?

I took out my portable anvil, put the statuette on it and, taking a good swing with the hammer, destroyed my creation. Another characteristic of the creator - no-one besides the person who made it was able to damage the item, let alone destroy it. Hanging on to such a 'wonder' was out of the question. Objects like these had to be destroyed right away, where possible. I had no desire whatsoever to become the second Dark Lord.

You have destroyed a Cursed Object. Your reputation with all encountered factions has increased by 100. Your reputation with Kartoss has fallen by 100

Oof! I breathed a sigh of relief. Then I double-checked that my reputation with the Emperor had also been restored, just in case, and started to think.

So. In some incomprehensible way I created something completely ghastly. Something that I had no intention at all of creating. After destroying it I recouped my losses and even made some gains - leveled up in Crafting and Jewelcraft, but the inability to control what I was making was very worrying. I entered the design mode and called up the image of Tiny Tim. Now, after it had already been created, this happened almost instantly. A normal, gentle fluffy dog. Where was my mistake? I didn't get it. I had to try once again, but this time I would be creating a Rose. Exiting the design mode and taking out another piece of Marble, I began to create a Rose. With a recipe it was quick: One-two and done. What did we have?

Cursed Rose. Description: hatred and anger created this flower...

After restoring my reputation via the same method, I sat on the bed. At least with using a known recipe I didn't gain another rank in 'Cursed Artificer'. Although my Jewelcraft didn't go up either, but that didn't matter. I needed to understand what happened to me. Why could I only make cursed things? Was this because of my title? There was only a small chance of it coming into play during item creation, it wasn't a simple process, however. But now I'm churning out Cursed Items one after the other. What the heck? But, what about...

I took out the Malachite I got in Dolma and began to create for the third time. Something told me that the issue wasn't with me, but with the material I was using to make things. Right, what should I make - a Rose or Tiny Tim? No point wasting materials, the dog it is. Either way I'll get to the bottom of this.

The Happy Hound. Description: love and friendship surround this Wolfhound...
Recipe created: Wolfhound Statuette

The statuette did not have any positive stat bonuses, but I didn't care. The main thing was that I was still able to create normal items. Gradually I began to understand the principle behind the creation of Cursed Objects. I shook out the contents of my bag on the bed and started to go through all the rings I created while I was in Beatwick. This ring is from the Copper I mined in Pryke. A normal ring with positive stat bonuses. But this Bronze ring had some of the local Tin in it. Aside from positive stats it had another interesting feature: -10% to Experience gain. Great. I looked through all the rings and set aside forty-two rings which reduced the gain rate of Experience, Stamina, Energy and other stats. Even their description was appropriate: 'Wrathful Ring of something or other'. So it looks like I couldn't make anything from these materials, since there was always a chance of such 'surprises'. I looked again at the shattered marble remains of the destroyed objects. Phew! So, things weren't all that bad.

I took out another piece of Marble and made use of the 'Essence of Things' ability. I wanted to see what this piece of Marble wanted to be. At first there was silence, which many stones had when they didn't want to be anything other than a stone, but then I was engulfed by a wave of hatred, disgust and revulsion. And all of this came from an ordinary piece of Marble. So it looked like this piece of stone wanted to be a Cursed Object - it mattered little the actual shape it took. But why?

After coming to a decision, I opened the Spirit summoning mode, cleared one slot and started to summon Spirits. Right now I needed a Spirit which would allow me to contact Kornik. He was the only one who could explain to me what to do with all this.

I waved away messages telling me I had access to various types of Spirits and stubbornly summoned one Spirit after another. No, not that one. It's a different one I need. It grew dark outside, but I continued to summon, looking for the Spirit I was after. Am I a

Shaman or what?

Do you wish to add the Spirit of Air Communication to the free slot?

Finally! I almost despaired and wanted to stop the summons, but my inborn sticktoitiveness would not allow me to quit this hopeless business.

Attention! The summoning of the Air Communication Spirit cannot be interrupted. Because this type of Spirit is beyond your rank, each minute your Hit Points will be reduced by 5% +2 to Spirituality. Total: 3

That 5% wasn't much of a worry. I cannot die in any case, even if I tried to summon Kornik for eternity. So here we go: I have to find out what's going on here.

Kamlanie continued for exactly a minute, up until the point the first 5% of Life dropped into oblivion. The pain was so great that I gave an involuntary shout, interrupting the sending of the Spirit. Hm. Getting in touch with Kornik was going to be no simple matter. Not at all how I imagined it. After catching my breath and restoring my Hit Points, I returned to my exercise in masochism.

From my sixth attempt I was able to fully concentrate and ignore jolts of pain, as well as register an increase in my Endurance. Five minutes, ten, twenty had gone by, but Kornik remained out of reach. Did he fly off to the Dragons again?

"WHO?" a desperate scream of pain, anger and suffering sounded in my head. Contact!

"Teacher, this is Mahan. I have a question..."

"RUN, YOU FOOL! RUN! N-N-O-O-O!" Kornik's choking scream struck me like a bolt from the blue.

"Teacher?!"

"Greetings, Mahan. I really have heard so much about you," a suave male voice barged into my conversation with the Teacher. "Let me introduce myself, my name is Geranika. Right now Kornik is my guest, so he's not really free to speak. And I will do my best to make sure he is unable to do so for the upcoming eternity."

"Kornik is with you?" I asked, stunned, continuing to concentrate on the summoning, as another pang of pain hit me.

"Of course he is. I always finish what I start. Remember this. Mmmm. I sense pain. What a pleasant feeling. Suffering, hatred, fear... Soon we shall meet and I will show you all the beauty of Kartoss. But right now you deserve to be punished. No-one dares to break into my fortress in such a stupid manner. Good bye Mahan. I believe that after feeling this slight discomfort you will see that it is better to join up with me."

Geranika said something and I was surrounded by another wave of pain. For crying out loud! My Endurance had already reached level 132 and I was supposed to be feeling 26% less pain, but what I was going through now was quite unimaginable! I immediately remembered the 'Little Turtle' chewing me. This pain was on par with that and for some reason my eyes were really burning too! At last I mercifully sank into darkness as I lost consciousness.

"Mahan, wake up," Elizabeth's voice was like a ray of light in endless pitch-black. I didn't feel the pain anymore, so I lifted myself on my elbows and looked around. I don't get it... Why are my landlady's words the only ray of light? Why am I surrounded by darkness? Although no, it wasn't total darkness – the indicators for the buffs and debuffs hadn't gone anywhere, shining brightly in their usual place. Right, I don't think I've had this particular debuff before:

Blindness. Debuff duration: 3 days

Three days in darkness? Great. Could this debuff be taken off somehow?

"Mahan, your eyes!" I heard Elizabeth's surprised voice.

"What about them?"

"You don't have any!" my landlady was trying hard not to let her voice slide into screaming, but there were notes of panic breaking through.

I felt the empty eye sockets with my hands. Crazy stuff! There's no removing a debuff like that. I'll have to spend the entire three days in darkness.

"Don't worry. I'll be back to normal in three days' time. Can you tell me what happened?"

"We were getting ready for bed and then heard your scream. It was so full of pain and agony that we ran straight to you. Then the scream stopped, as if you were smothered by it. I entered the house and saw you on the floor. I called you and you woke up... Ah! You face is all covered in blood..."

I just about managed to calm my landlady down, wash my face and go to bed. Three days in darkness is just too much. I was hoping to spend them productively, but now it looks like I'll be stuck in the room the entire time. Damn! If I ever catch Geranika, I'll give him a piece of my mind. With that thought I drifted off.

The next morning I could think clearly again and tried to analyze recent events. Kornik was Geranika's prisoner. My teacher was out of the picture. A pity, he was one funky goblin, despite all his foibles. Geranika knows about me and has promised that we will meet again. I'm really not liking this. I'm not a great fan of the idea of meeting up with a mentally unstable NPC, who could resort to using force at any moment. Why on earth has he turned up? It's not like I don't have enough problems of my own to be thinking about this creep as well. The other bad news was that the Spirit that I summoned took off a lot of Hit Points and that Geranika used it to blind me. Even if this was temporary, it was far from pleasant. To put it plainly, my attempt to find out why the resources gathered in Beatwick produce cursed items led to my being blinded. A total fail.

After spending half the day in bed, I realized that if I continued like this I would go mad. The darkness with burning pictograms and the hushed silence of the courtyard, where everyone was trying to be quiet so as not to disturb the sick, were not exactly cheering. I had to keep myself busy somehow or I would start to howl out of frustration. I tried to summon Spirits and contact Almis to tell him about Kornik, but that came to nothing. I simply couldn't see the panel with the Spirits. Could my eyes work in the design mode at least? Let's check it out.

Praise be to all the game developers - the design mode came with its own vision. That meant I had a way to keep myself busy. I grabbed a piece of something at random, really hoping it was either Malachite or Lapis Lazuli. As I recreated the object, I was glad to see it was Lapis. It was sent to me by Hellfire, so I could easily make something of it, without worrying I'd turn out another piece of evil junk. Only one question remained - what could I make? The Dwarves? Why not? Someone will have to make them anyhow. Might as well be me.

I decided to use Eric as the prototype. I could have used Hellfire too, especially since his image had already been created, but I didn't like the guy. And if I didn't like him, the probability that I would come out with something horrible was quite high. I needed the Dwarf Warriors.

Eric. The dwarf who didn't betray me in my hour of need, didn't fall for Phoenix's bribes, gathered everyone together and is stubbornly waiting for me to get to Anhurs. Honest, loyal and level-headed. A real dwarf. He popped up in the design mode of his own accord. Now I could modify him.

A sword, a shield, a helm... Argh. That's not it. The great Dwarf Warriors didn't look like that. Why didn't I ask Hellfire for their appearances and the descriptions of their feats? It just wasn't working with standard weapons. I needed help.

"Mahan, I brought you some food - you should eat," Elizabeth brought me back to the blackness outside by touching my shoulder. I quickly glanced at the debuff timer - it's been ten hours! Time sure ran fast in the design mode!

"Yes, thank you. Elizabeth, can I ask you something?"

"You can call me Beth, no need to be so formal. Do ask, of course."

I almost choked, getting a muffled laugh from my landlady. Eliz... Beth had decided we should be on familiar terms... This could only mean one thing - the level of Attractiveness has reached the coveted eighty points. I'd better watch out or she'll start making advances...

"Do you know the stories of the Dwarf Warriors from the Karmadont Chess Set?"

"Of course. Do you want to know them all or one in particular?"

"Any one would do. I need to understand the logic of how they made it into the history books."

"Then I will tell you about Borhg Goldhand. His story is the most exemplary."

I got comfortable and turned into one big ear. Listening to bedtime (or whatever time of day this was) stories is always interesting. Only one thing bothered me - as soon as I get my sight back, I'll have to catch Beth and stop her from summoning her demon. A pity: just when we started to get on so well.

"All of this happened very long ago," my landlady began the tale. "When the dwarves lived in the cramped caves of the Rurat mountain...

*****

'Borhg, sledgehammering damnation, where are you going?!' a stocky, practically square dwarf, his eyebrows in a frown, watched Borhg going down into the depths of the Black Maw chasm. In the many centuries of his people's history no-one had yet succeeded in descending below the level of darkness. To the place where the thrown torches could not drive back the black and show what the gloomy haze concealed. The daredevils who went below this fateful threshold never returned. Those who went down on a rope were lifted back up with eyes full of terror. Dead eyes. And now another young fool had decided to explore the secret of the chasm - without a rope, trusting only in the strength of his hands and the innate agility of the undermountain people.

"Father, I'll be quick! I have to find out what is concealed by the darkness. What kind of a chief would I be if my subjects end up laughing at me my entire life? Our people need knowledge and I will gain it for them!"

"Fool! If you make it back, I'll beat you like a drunken mule, whatever that means." Although he was very worried for his son, the Chief was a proud dwarf. For three thousand years now the dwarves had to reconcile themselves to the fact that their mountains had an incomprehensible area where no-one could go. And now his son and only heir was daring to do what even the bravest dwarven warriors were too afraid to do: descend into the Black Maw.

"Father, if I do not return, tell Talisha that Borhg Sergenius is afraid of nothing in this world," giving a farewell glance to his father, the young dwarf disappeared in the impenetrable dark.

"Argh, hells!" the chief threw his axe down in anger, but immediately picked it up. A dwarf without an axe and a pick is no dwarf at all. This would mean shame for the rest of his life. But that Brann was something else! Got his daughter to egg his son on to go down into the Black Maw. Right to his death. And how did he come to allow this? He thought the youngsters were just playing around and that their fathers' problems didn't bother them, but no, they saw and noticed everything, those sharp-eyes kids! Could this stupid hundred-year-old dispute now lose him his son?

Two hours went by, but the gloomy veil of darkness remained undisturbed. His son did not return. The father flicked away a tear and headed back to the settlement. He was the Chief and it was his duty to look after the people. He had no right to show any weakness or he would face an immediate challenge from his rivals. But why were his feet so treacherously weak and why did tears keep trying to return to his eyes?

"So where is our weakling?" at the entrance to the settlement the Chief was met by Brann's mocking grin. Compared to his peers, Borhg really did look more of a gnome. Almost a head shorter than the others and narrow-shouldered, he ate less and was constantly busy thinking or doing something. He had even started to visit the exiled smiths, trying to fathom their secrets. Borhg was interested in everything, with a sole exception- he was not a warrior. Everything that was connected with weapons, blood or killing fell outside his sphere of interests. "So he's finally decided to go the way of dogfood, eh? Ha ha ha!"

Only his willpower, forged in his many years of ruling, stopped the Chief from attacking Brann. He was right after a fashion - there was no place for weaklings among the dwarves. The fact that Borhg had survived until he was twenty could only be called a miracle and was due to his own will as the chief. Sooner or later he was going to run out of luck, and that black day had finally come...

According to tradition, the wake for his son took place five days after his death. It was not a very big gathering - Borhg didn't have any friends, only close relatives. To everyone's surprise Talisha came, dressed in white, the color of death, as a sign of solidarity.

"Today we have gathered to celebrate Borhg's return to our forefathers. Let us make merry and dance, showing how we mourn the departed," the Chief addressed the gathering. "Borhg was a good dwarf, even a somewhat unusual one, but..."

"Chief!" an out-of-breath guard burst into the hall.

"Why did you leave your post?!" the head of dwarves frowned.

"Chief... Borhg is coming..."

Not believing his own ears, the Chief ran out of the hall and immediately half-covered his eyes. The caves in which the dwarves lived could not be called dark, but there was never enough light there. And now, from the direction of the Black Maw a bright sun was moving towards the settlement, decimating the centuries-old twilight of the caves. When the Chief's eyes got used to the bright light, he saw that the sun wasn't moving of its own accord, but was carried in the hands of a painfully familiar-looking dwarf. Narrow shoulders, short stature... Borhg had returned. Overcome with joy, the father rushed towards his son, but only a few dozen steps away he froze in his place. It was his son, but at the same time it was a stranger. The dwarf's once naive eyes now shone with great wisdom; despite the unsteady step of the tired-looking figure, it was clear that a lord was now walking through the stone caverns; the black hair of a youth had turned into silver locks of an old man and the bright sun in his hands turned out to be an ordinary hammer.

"Father," Borhg's thunder-like voice echoed through the cave, "I found out what lay hidden in the darkness. We should not be afraid of it."

"Son..." the leader didn't know if he should rejoice or not, so great was the change... Was it his son that returned?

"Father, I have changed. We have to change if we want to survive. At the bottom of the chasm there lives... I don't know what to call it - there lives a something, very ancient and wise. It has been watching us for a long time. When a dwarf descends to it, it shows him what would happen to our people if we continue down the path of war and violence. Father, we will die out! We have to change! Those that dwell under the mountains have to become master craftsmen and I will do everything in my power to make this happen."

"Ah, the weakling's back," Brann appeared next to the rejoicing crowd of Borhg's relatives.

"Father, don't," shouted Talisha, but the old dwarf ignored her.

"Douse your torch, you pipsqueak or I'll shove it down your throat. You're disturbing my sleep!"

"How dare you..." the Chief was incensed, but Borhg interrupted him:

"Leave him, father. Those like him are dragging the dwarves back, into the jaws of anger and violence. We can be warriors, but we have to be craftsmen first. He cannot understand this. He is too weak."

"WHAT?!" roared Brann. "You called me a weakling? You?! In the name of our ancestors I challenge you to a duel! Right now! You won't come back to life a second time." Not waiting for the youth to reply, Brann grabbed his axe and hacked at him from above. Or rather, he wanted to hack at him, because at the last instant the shining hammer flew up, blocking the hit, and then came down on the attacker's head, flattening it. A silence filled the caves. The elvish armor, which Brann had bought for a great heap of gold coins and which was considered the strongest armor in Barliona, was flattened with one quick hit from a weak dwarf.

"Before a dwarf can become a warrior, he first

needs to become a Master," Borhg's voice thundered through the caverns. "I became a Master when I forged this Hammer. The wise being helped me and from now on darkness holds no danger for those who want to embark upon the path of the Masters. But any who desire strength alone... It is best for them not to descend there. They would not return. From this day on, I, Borhg Sergenius, will lead the dwarves on the path of master craftsmanship...'

*****

Borhg kept his promise. Just a hundred years later dwarves had turned into unsurpassed masters in Smithing, having far overtaken the elves in this art. All the ancient Great Masters of the undermountain people are represented in the Karmadont Set. Each of them created at least one shining object, all of which, together with Borhg's hammer, formed the Legendary Radiant Set. Eight shining items. A dwarf wearing it could become a paladin, irrespective of his class."

It was a beautiful story! During Elizabeth's tale I felt that I was standing next to the Chief when Borhg descended into the chasm, mourned the dead with the others in the dwarvish manner and squinted at the bright light of the hammer. But straight away I had questions:

"Who was in the chasm? Who was hiding behind the darkness? And where is that set of gear now?"

"I have no answer to that. After the numbers of dwarves grew and they abandoned the Raurat mountain, there was an earthquake. The city under the mountain, almost empty by that time, was completely destroyed, together with the Black Maw. Whoever it was concealing remains a secret of the ancient masters of the undermountain people, a secret that no-one has yet discovered. That was also the time when the Radiant Gear of the dwarves was lost. It was kept in the central building of the settlement and when the roof began to cave in there was no time to take it out. The King under the mountain, a vassal of our Emperor, periodically sends free citizens to search for it, but this has so far been fruitless. I don't know if this would disappoint you or not, but the King only sends dwarves for this. This is not a path that can be taken by members of other races."

Hang in there, Eric. When you get to level 100, you have some difficult searching ahead of you.

"Thank you, Beth. You were of great help. Now I understand everything..."

The next morning had a productive start. First of all I called over Clouter and gave him his present, which made him explode with joy, then summoned Draco and sent them both to play in the courtyard: let the lad level up my Dragon – it's useful for me and a joy for him. At level 17, the Totem could now stay out for three hours, and by the time that had run out I planned to have my Totem returned to me with at least 25 levels in him. After this noisy crew ran off to the yard, I entered the design mode. I now knew what the Dwarf Warriors should look like. Although... It wasn't right to call the Great Masters 'Warriors'. But if that's the way Karmadont saw them, he must have had his reasons.

Eric's image appeared in the darkness of the design mode. I removed his pick, but after some thought brought it back, fixing it on his back and adding a double-handed axe next to it. You can't have a dwarf without one. Now, to create Borhg from this, I had to make Eric more narrow and short and thin out his beard a little. An apron, that's another thing that's missing. And his face is a little covered in soot. And the gloves on his hands. And burn marks on his boots. And...

There were many other 'and's. When I finished correcting Eric, he looked nothing like the dwarf that I knew. I made eight copies of the figure and was about to exit the design mode, when something stopped me. The figurines looked alike, but it would have been wrong to make eight Borhgs. The system may not accept the result and I would fail to make the Dwarf Warriors. I need to give them some distinctive features, something that would make each master recognizable. But what? The answer came of itself. The Radiant Set. Each of the dwarves created an object from that set, so if this one is given the hammer, and this one the braces and this one the shield... When I finished giving out the items, without even knowing if they actually existed or were the fruit of my fevered imagination, I was completely satisfied with the result. Even if the dwarves had similar looks, the different shining objects made them unique. I decided not to worry about how I would represent this light in stone for now. We'll cross that bridge when we come to it.

"Mahan, why aren't you calling Draco? It's been

two days already," Clouter's disappointed voice brought me back to reality. I opened my eyes and looked around. What did he man 'not calling for two days already'? The lad, head hanging low, was standing a couple of steps away from me.

"Do you mean..." I was about to ask, but stopped just in time. I saw Clouter, which could mean only one thing - the 'Blindness' debuff had expired. In other words - my eyes grew back. The two days flew by as if they never happened.

"Oh, you can see already! I really didn't believe you would," fired off Clouter, looking up at me. "So, will you summon Draco? We haven't finished playing from last time."

"Of course. I'll call him now," I replied dully, immersed in my own thoughts. I created the figurines, now I just had to embody them in Lapis. If I remembered right how things went with the orcs, sculpting takes place at the rate of one figurine a day. I will need around eight days dedicated only to the crafting of the figurines. Does this mean I can kiss good-bye to leveling up? I think not - I had to increase my levels. The figurines can wait, they won't go anywhere. I called over Draco and was about to go and have some food, when my gaze fell on the Totem's level. It was 32, and Draco had turned from a half a meter-long serpent into a meter-long Dragon. At this rate he'd reach the necessary level in just a couple of weeks! I selected Draco and opened his properties. Holy cow! His settings! I could change his settings! Barely restraining myself, knowing that I had to go and level up, I sent the kids back to play. Still, my hands were sure itching to look around the properties and settings and see what could be changed, corrected or selected.

Three hours of walking around the woods brought me little joy. There were no wolves or goblins. The region seemed to lack any creatures altogether. It's like they all died out. I spent the rest of the day working a Marble vein, bringing my Mining up to level 33 and increasing Strength and Stamina by one. A little more, just a little, and I could offer to mine Slate's Iron Vein for him. I thought the smith would agree - what difference is it to him who gathers his materials?

Towards the end of the day I paid a visit to Tisha and made arrangements for the evening. We had plans for a rambling excursion to hunt down the mist monster. I decided not to tell them about Beth. First I'll catch her and have a chat with her, and only then decide what to do next.

I decided not to put the trap up near the house. If I caught my landlady right by the front door, she could say that she was just going for a walk, and I, that good-for-nothing, was hindering her in that. Instead, I went straight to the cemetery and set everything up right in front of the entrance. Now any creature of level 150 inclusive is as good as caught.

When darkness descended on Beatwick there came the sound of steps. Lighting her way with a candle, Beth carefully made her way to the cemetery. So then... why her? Why does she need to summon this horror on the village? Is it revenge against the Headman? That's simply daft. Perhaps it's...

"Oh," like a fly caught in the web, Beth was being encased in the bone trap. Suddenly the night was shaken by her scream: "Mahan, don't! Stop! You don't know what you're doing! Relea–" the bone trap had reached her head and Beth's shout was cut off. I waited for a couple of minutes, making sure that the prison was holding my landlady securely and went back to Beatwick. The time had come to tell Tisha that there won't be any beast tonight.

After a dozen steps I stopped. Or, rather, I was stopped. By two red eyes and mist covering the monster from every side. What the... ? Didn't I catch Beth before she summoned you? Where did you come from? The hot breath of the beast could be felt even a meter away. After standing for a few seconds next to me, a moment later it shifted to the cocoon containing Beth. Having circled it, the monster lifted its misty head and the hairs on my back stood up. The beast was laughing. A malevolent, satisfied laugh. It was sentient! It was no demon! It was something else.

"YEESSS!" a triumphant, squeaky voice with metallic notes in it shook the night. It can speak too! What the heck is this? "TWO YEARS! TWO YEARS I COULD NOT DESTROY HER. THE MASTER WAS GROWING VERY DISPLEASED. THANK YOU SHAMAN! YOU HELPED! FOR THAT I WILL SEND YOU TO THE GREY LANDS WITHOUT PAIN. MASTER WILL REJOICE!" I had no time to respond, when the beast jumped to me, there came the flash of its claws and a moment later the world was gone. There was one small comfort - the beast told no lie: there really was no pain this time, at least of the physical kind.

In connection with your death, your level of Experience has been reduced by 30%...

I'll start losing levels at this rate! Bright sunshine lit the bone trap that blocked the entrance to the cemetery. And what will I say to Beth now?

"Quick, there may still be time to stop them!" strange shouts came from the direction of Beatwick.

"Did you see? They turned into goblins! Dark ones!"

"We have to send a messenger to Farstead! How will we survive without the herd?"

"What's with the guards? Still alive?"

"Alive, thank the gods. Where have they taken the herd?"

"What happened with the neighbors? Did you see how they changed? What if they turn into goblins too?"

Right, something happened in the village, by the looks of it something unpleasant. Did goblins attack and chase away the herd? I have to find Tisha and find out. But first, Beth.

"..se me!" the woman finished her shout as soon as the trap fell apart. "Is it day already!?" Beth looked around, rather lost, and then started to scream at me again: "What have you done?!"

"Beth, let me explain..."

"I'm no 'Beth' to you. Forget that name! Happy now, 'demon fighter'?! Thanks to you darkness has come to our village!"

"What are you on about?"

Shouts kept coming from the direction of Beatwick. Beth was silent for a few moments, listening to them, then her eyes narrowed and she looked at me angrily.

"Last night three families from our village turned into dark goblins. Six adults and seven children. Was that your aim when you hunted me? Well, you can be happy now! You got what you wanted!"

"What are you on about? Beth, I don't get you!"

"Don't you dare use that informal tone with me, boy! For two years I protected our village from a dark curse. Only thanks to me are the residents of the village still human. But you went and with a wave of the hand brought it all to naught. Who are you?! Did the Dark One send you?"

"I don't understand what you're talking about."

Elizabeth took several deep breaths, calming down, and then continued in a distracted tone:

"Two years ago, straight after the death of my husband, someone began to put a Curse on the village. At first its weakest residents had succumbed to it. You saw them: they resemble apes, but are still human. When they became incapable of work that required any thinking, they were sent to cut the grass. They aren't capable of doing anything more demanding than that. I thought it strange that three families started to deteriorate at once, so I decided to put a blessing on the village every week. It helped. The villagers and their animals stopped changing, but gradually the land itself began to change. It became cursed. I wrote to everyone I could think of, but no-one replied to my letters. I warned the Headman, but he only promised to look into it and no more. I wanted to go to the town myself, but the ban... But it's not about me now. For two years I stood in the path of darkness, despite the attacks of the mist beast. And today in one go you destroyed everything I worked so carefully to preserve. Three households have vanished from the face of Beatwick and the residents of the others have begun to turn into goblins - all because of you! Do you understand now what you have done?"

"Why didn't you tell me anything? I would've helped you!"

"And, who are you? A sleek favorite of the Herald? How can you help me in protecting the village? Besides, how did I know who it was that the Headman, only good for empty promises of help, sent to my house? There is no-one I can trust! Even my workers I had to hire in Anhurs and bring them all the way here! Without an amulet I cannot discover who it is, but I know that a Dark One resides in Beatwick. It could be anyone! Even you!"

"But, I only..."

"Enough! I forbid you to enter my house! I forbid you to speak to my children! I forbid you to even to as much as look in my direction! I curse the moment I agreed to take you into my house!"

Elizabeth turned around and went to the village and a very interesting message hung before my eyes:

Your reputation with the priestesses of goddess Eluna has fallen by 1000 points. Current level: Mistrust. You are 1000 points away from the status of Neutral

Goddess Eluna... The head of Barliona's pantheon, who are staunch enemies of Kartoss. And now I have Mistrust with her priestesses. I don't think I feel so good...

CHAPTER TEN
JUST WHEN YOU THOUGHT THINGS COULDN'T GET ANY WORSE...

"TISHA, CAN YOU TELL ME WHAT happened here?" After pulling myself together, I returned to the village, where I immediately came across Tisha. She and other villagers were busy trying to fix the gate: at the moment it was completely ripped out and lying in a ditch.

"Mahan, I'm sorry, I really don't have time now," she quickly said as she rushed around. "Hold the pole! Begin attaching it now! One-two!"

Seeing that I wasn't going to get anywhere with the Headman's daughter right now, I went over and helped to fix the fallen gate. Judging by the damage, it had been broken open from the inside. When the gate had been returned to its place and a couple of carpenters were starting to get it back into shape, I tried to speak to Tisha gain.

"What happened here?"

"Oof, that wore me out," after wiping her brow and fixing her hair the girl continued: "No-one knows what happened. This morning members of four households suddenly turned into goblins. They let the entire herd out of the enclosure and drove it towards the exit. The stupid animals went in a straight line and took out the gates in their path. But the gates we can fix. The main problem is that we have no cows now. The entire hundred-strong herd, which we so carefully protected from predators, was spirited away by six adult goblins in five minutes. It's enough to make you lose heart. How?! How could they transform like that? It's impossible!"

"Nothing is impossible in this world," the Headman joined the conversation before I noticed him. "Mahan, I cannot send anyone after it - we are peaceful villagers, not warriors. Help us to get the herd back. The village won't survive without it!"

Quest available: 'Returning the Herd'

Description: Beatwick villagers that turned into goblins have driven away a herd of cows. Catch up with them and bring back the cows. Quest type: Scenario. Reward: Variable, depending on the degree of success. Penalty for failing/refusing the quest: Variable, depending on degree of failure

"I'll help you. I will run after and return the stolen herd right away," my jaw nearly hit the floor when I saw the conditions of the quest. Now you could be sure that the Corporation had launched some sort of a scenario in Beatwick. But why here, right on the outskirts of the Empire? There are practically no players here! And it even came with a variable reward or penalty. It looks like a special Imitator will be tracking the progress of this quest and will make a decision depending on my actions. What a 'lively' neighborhood I'd ended up in.

"Can I have a horse? I would catch up with them faster this way."

"Unfortunately, no. My sons galloped out of the village when it was still night, when we realized that the mist monster had disappeared. So you will have to go on foot - there are no other horses in the village," the Headman shrugged in dismay.

There was no point in dropping by Elizabeth's place to pick up my things. After that incident in Pryke, when I was robbed by other prisoners, I carried everything with me. But when I'm back I will certainly have a talk with Beth. I don't care if she forbade me to visit her - attractiveness didn't go anywhere, only the reputation was reduced. It's time we had an honest heart-to-heart. I didn't get a message telling me I was barred from the house - that meant there was no risk of penalty. Moreover, I couldn't shake the feeling that the strange behavior of the priestess was scripted into the scenario. I took a deep breath and ran after the herd. The goblins were about five hours ahead of me, but they moved slowly, so catching up with them wasn't too hard. The main problem would be how to deal with the six newly-hatched minions of Kartoss. Nor should I forget about the eight children. It's just in the real world children can't do anything - in Barliona even a toddler with 100 levels would thump me into the earth all the way up to my ears.

Running turned out to be surprisingly easy. Ever since I had replaced Stamina rings with Intellect rings I'd had little cause to notice the Energy decrease. It was always at the maximum, so at first I could maintain the speed of a good horse. However, after twenty minutes of running I acquired a 23-hour buff 'Run-down Horse', which slowed Energy regeneration by 20%, while every twenty minutes this percentage consistently grew - by the same 20%. This meant that by the end of the first hour of the run I decided to stop and catch my breath. Minus 60% to Energy regeneration did not permit the rings to restore this stat in sufficient amounts. The upside was that I had already run quite a long distance and even gained an achievement:

Achievement earned! Runner Level 1. The running time without acquiring the 'Run-down Horse' buff is increased by 25 minutes. The next level gained: after the buff is incurred 9 times

While I was running, I tried not to fill my head with too many thoughts, but now, as I dropped into a walk, questions began to arise in my mind. First - why didn't the goblins run for the Free Lands, where concealing the herd would have been much easier and there was plenty of space for Kartoss forces to hide? Instead, they took the road that headed straight to Farstead. They turned off it from time to time, but always came back to it. Strange behavior from the freshly-minted green minions. Have they started a migration to Kartoss or something? They won't be able to just stroll through the Empire like that: they'll be caught at the nearest settlement with any players in it.

I summoned Draco to keep me company. The last session with Clouter only raised my Totem to level 36. Looks like the idea of leveling up the Dragon with the help of the kid had played itself out. Draco was no longer a child, but a normal adolescent who would get bored with just running around the yard. What do teen dragons do? Who knows...

I entered the Spirit summoning mode and continued to go down the road constantly hitting my Tambourine. While my Energy was being restored, I could level up in Spirituality - no sense in wasting time. And I haven't even looked properly into Draco's settings, although my hands were itching to do just that.

Three hours spent with the Dragon flew by in an instant. I increased my Spirituality to level 14; if I understood the description correctly, from level 20 I would be able to summon one Spirit of a different Element without a penalty. Great. Draco flicked his tail and returned to his world and I, my Energy restored, sped after the goblins.

"Hey you, stop right there!" a rough voice brought me back to reality. I'd became so lost in thought that I'd even stopped looking around as I walked.

"Are you deaf or wot?" I finally turned around, when I realized the voice was coming from behind. The bright red glow of the names above the heads of the three players obligingly informed me who it was I ran across: PKers. From level 120 to 205. What did these goons want?

"That's him, right?" the highest level player turned to one of the others.

"He's got the right nick. But where's the red headband? The Merchant mentioned it several times!"

"Yo! You from Beatwick?" that was addressed to me now.

"No. From Farstead. Finished a quest and coming back now." Yeah, like I'll tell them all the truth this very minute. Being rude to PKers, especially of this level, is not a good idea: they'd send you for respawn at the drop of a hat and I had a herd to return. But being honest with them when they seem to have found out about my red headband somehow... My intuition told me it wasn't such a good idea. By the way, where the heck was the damned thing when I was catching Beth? Went completely shtum on me.

"Tiger, get him, don't let him slip away," said the head of this threesome, and then turned back to me. "We'll just quickly check whether it's you or not, and then let you go," Dratanian's face sported an evil grin. He could have at least written his name correctly, stupid bastard. "On the ready check."

"Ready," the player who was called 'Tiger'

replied, though his full name came up as Tigerrat.

"Then let's roll," the boss got off his horse and headed towards me. I don't get it - what kind of nasty stuff did they have in mind?

"Drat, leave a bit for me," the third player in this little show put in. Lanus. You didn't even have think of giving him a rude nickname, it was practically suggesting itself.

Everything that happened after this only took about a couple of seconds. At first I was given a buff 'Pain suppression', which reduced the sustained damage by 50% for 30 seconds and prevented me from being sent off for respawn while it was active. A useful ability to support the tank when the raid is bringing down a boss. Then Dratanian dropped on me with his entire 205-level weight and started to shred my character, hitting me with the dagger, his feet, head and armor spikes. I held out until the last, having realized what this PKer was trying to do. He wanted to check if I could feel pain or not. What a scumbag! I broke after only twenty seconds, though they seemed an eternity to me, and screamed.

"Theeeere! Now we know!" said the leader slowly, getting up. I remained lying on the ground, fitfully gulping air. Damn! "You can tell us how you got rid of the headband later, or rather, where you found that much cash. But now, listen here. I've come by information that you have a certain very interesting object. The Eye of the Dark Widow. I need it. Or do you want to find out what real pain feels like?"

There was a clap of the teleportation portal and

a Herald appeared next to us.

"Good day, gentlemen. How do you like the weather around here? Don't you find that the sun in this region has such a special glow to it?"

"My salutations, Herald," Dratanian bowed his head. "How can we be of service?"

"Oh, just a sheer trifle. Someone here mentioned pain in relation to a former resident of a mine. Regrettably for you, I cannot allow this. This is against the rules."

"Hold on, Herald. You are confusing something. This is an ordinary free citizen here. Is it no longer allowed to hunt free citizens in Barliona? Is this your official answer?" That leader's no fool. He didn't lose his nerve in front of such a high-ranking guest, is sticking to his guns and is even trying to gain some advantage from it all.

"No, not at all. Hunting is not forbidden. But torture is not allowed in Barliona. With the exception of those who descend to the torture dungeons of their own accord: they know what they're getting into. Remember this. If I find out that someone was torturing a free citizen, measures would have to be taken. Thank you for your time. Good luck with your adventures in Barliona," the Herald went back into the portal, which then vanished with a loud bang.

"Drat, what are we gonna do now?" asked Lanus, stunned. "Did we trudge all the way out here for nothing?"

"Chill it. My bad. I forgot that those that leave the mines are being closely watched. Yeah, we can't torture him, but no-one said we can't play with him a little," Drat gave me a very unpleasant look. "Tiger, don't attack him - your turn to play nurse now. And heal him to full or he'll drop at the first sneeze. If we can't get what we want this way, we'll find a workaround."

At first I didn't get what he was on about, but once I heard Drat's shout, I understood:

"Attention all players! We are planning to carry out training exercises with AoE spells within a three-kilometer radius. I politely ask everyone to leave this zone. Please accept our apologies for the inconvenience. Lan - you can start now. Show us your proficiency with Ice Rain. You can summon it over there, if you like," Drat pointed in my direction.

"All right. Just a moment," Lanus replied in the same tone. "I've had a feeling that something's been off with my rain for a while now. Take a look and tell me what I'm doing wrong."

At that moment an apocalypse began next to me. Icicles started to fall from the sky, my movement speed was reduced by 70% and my hit points plummeted.

"Careful," shouted Tiger, in the same showy manner. "I think we accidentally hit a player! Let me heal him now!"

"Guys, have you totally lost it?" when the rain stopped I got back on my feet. This was really a bit much. I couldn't jump away, since the rain froze me to the ground, I couldn't run, because it felt like someone was holding you and it hurt like hell too. The bastards. The rain left me with only one Hit Point, but the damned buff slapped on me by the 'friendly' Tiger prevented me from being sent for respawn. Well, they can kiss my ass. I started looking around for a tree or a stone. I'll crash into it and that's the last you gits will see of me.

"Tiger, patch him up. It's not good leaving a player in such a state when it's all our fault." The scumbags were having fun while they were at it, relishing their little victory. And why not? They did, after all, declare this place a test zone, asking everyone to leave it. So if you weren't quick enough, you had only yourself to blame. And when they did accidentally hit a player, they healed him up right away. That's some imaginative thinking. I'll kill these sickos.

One spell uttered by Tiger restored everything: Hit Points and Energy and removed the 'Run-down Horse' debuff too. I should experiment with the Spirits later, removing this debuff would be very useful. Right, if I could still think, not all was lost.

"Mahan. You don't happen to have the Eye on you? It would be so nice if you gave it to me as a present. My birthday is in half a year and it would make just the perfect gift."

"What on earth makes you think I have it? Try using your head for a change. I'm only level twenty one! I live in the middle of nowhere!"

"If you don't want to do this the easy way - fine. Let's continue our training. Lan, try the Ice Explosion," the earth next to me became covered in a crust of ice, bulged and exploded with a deafening bang, sending me on a riveting flight. While I flew, along with the stars flicking through my eyes came the messages that I received such and such damage and was healed that many Hit Points. As soon as I hit the ground, Tiger completely restored my health from 1, to prevent me doing anything stupidly suicidal. Quite the ace healer, not much else to say, really. Except for swear words. While the PKers laughed their heads off, I did the only thing I could at that point: I took to my heels and headed towards the forest, which I spotted a few kilometers off the road. I found myself thanking the developer who came up with the following interesting algorithm: the running speed was determined by the ratio of Stamina and Agility to the player level. Often low level players were much faster than higher level ones, but had a lot less stamina. Their Energy fell too quickly. Not wasting any time on the shouts of 'Stop or I'll kill you!', I entered the Spirit summoning mode as I ran and called a Strengthening Spirit on myself. Let me run a little faster, even if not by much.

A minute later I realized that I had miscalculated. Yes, I was faster than the PKers, but the AoE radius of the Ice Rain turned out to be too large. A wall of ice appeared right before me and I dove into it at full speed. Please, let this one-shot me... Alas, Tiger was too good at his job.

"Why'd you stop running?" By now the players had gotten on their mounts and were circling me at leisure. "Just when I was getting into the stride of things and starting to enjoy the hunt, the bunny keeled over. Onwards with the training! Lan, some AoE, please. Let's see how long he'll last. Tiger, you'd better stay on the ball."

They made me run around the area for about an hour. As soon as I stopped an icy rain began to fall next to me, forcing me to keep running. My attempts to resist by summoning Spirits of Control or Water Strike yielded nothing except a good laugh.

"Who the hell told you about the Eye?" I finally lost it and screamed at them. That's it, I just couldn't take this abuse anymore.

"Had your fill of running, eh? No biggie, you'll keep at it, I'm having a great time here. Black market, you little twerp. Black market. Heard about it? You can buy many interesting things there - from the items that high-level players sell to the Merchants, to the information that the Merchants manage to pick up. Do you know how much you cost me? Thirty thousand gold! Plus teleporting here - ten thousand each. Dude, we're talking some real money here."

The incomprehension on my face must have been very obvious, since all three broke out in laughter.

"Drat, he didn't get a word you said!" Tigerrat put in as he finished laughing. "Little girl, the Game isn't all sweetness and light. It's got nasty people in it too. Like us. Those who did time at the mines. Those who know what the red headband means. Those who have got nearly everyone and everything in this Game under their thumb. We're kings here! And those who have leveled up in Meanness, have access to this little bonus called 'Black Market'. A damn useful thing. There Merchants sell information about what they saw, identified and bought. Information is worth a lot in this game."

"Tiger, why don't you do a little dance for him too, while you're at it? You're getting way too chatty." The leader interrupted him and turned to me, "Our information is correct, NPCs cannot lie. Hand over the Eye or we'll continue with the training. You know, I still have a problem with the way Lan summons Ice Rain on the move."

"Go to hell!" I growled. "There's nothing you can do to me, stupid dipshits."

"Oh, really? This is a game, sweetheart, the gaming process of PK-hunting and training. And Tiger there, bless his bleeding heart, keeps healing you and stops you from missing out on Barliona for the next twelve hours. I really haven't a clue how you keep ending up right in the centre of our training zone. Are you doing this on purpose? I see you still don't get it. Let's continue with our session then. Tiger, Lan, let's roll..."

After half an hour of the chase I'd ran out of steam. I tried to grit my teeth and stand under the rain of icicles, but would break after two or three minutes. The pain was too much. Endurance steadily increased, having gone up by three points since we met, but it was a drop in the ocean. The mythical five hundred points were distant and hard to imagine.

I almost decided to give these scumbags the Eye and be done with it, when I saw a flicker of a silhouette in the shadow of the trees, which we had gradually reached. A goblin! A plan immediately emerged in my head of how I could give these bastards the slip at least for a few minutes.

"Help! Coordinator's envoy has been captured and sent for torture! Help me!"

The three players glanced at each other, not getting what collection of swear words I'd just thrown at them. Little wonder, since I was screaming in the language of Dark Goblins!

"For Kartoss, attack!" ten green-skinned minions of the Dark Empire jumped out of the forest. Hm... all of them only level 50. Against the three PKers these were nothing. A brief distraction. But the goblins didn't give a damn about that. A representative of the Empire requested aid, so it had to be granted. While the players got to grips with the new obstacle, I ran for the forest. Time was too precious to lose.

"Where do you think you're going?" I was once again enveloped in the Ice Rain. "We haven't finished our chat yet... What the hell is that?" asked Drat in surprise, when a drawn-out roar came from the direction of the forest. Hairs stood up on the back of my neck. Few in the game didn't know what that roar meant: the Wild Pack. The main shock troops of Kartoss in its fight against the players: ten 200-level trolls riding their raptors. Someone's not going to have a very good time in a minute.

"Drat, let's get out of here - it's the Pack!" Lanus started to shout when a hale of arrows sped towards the players. The Wild Pack had arrived.

"Tiger, get the shield up. Lan, finish off Mahan - he's the one who summoned the beasts. Faster!" once again Drat quickly grasped the situation. Clever bastard. I had nothing to deflect a level 100 Ice Arrow, so could only stand there and wait to be sent for respawn. Hiding from magic was useless, since it went through everything. A pity, I thought I had managed to outwit them.

Hit!

I was still standing and watching how ten raptors with their riders emerged out of the forest and surrounded the dome put up by Lanus, while Tigerrat, eyes widened in surprise, was sending magic arrows at me one after another.

"Arnamal dragorhalv rpanvvly?" a human dressed in black appeared next to me and was asking me something with a lifted eyebrow. He was completely unperturbed by Lanus's magical efforts to break through my incomprehensible defense. The stranger was entirely sure of himself and was trying to ask me something. But I didn't understand him in the slightest. Of the dark languages, I only knew goblin, so I made good use of it in my reply:

"The Coordinator only taught me the goblin language. I don't understand what you are saying."

The man frowned, uttered something and touched my head.

You have learned a new language: Common Language of the Dark Empire

"I'm asking you if you are all right?"

"Thank you, you made it just in time. Any longer and they would've destroyed me and I wouldn't have managed to deliver the message."

"Don't kill them," the stranger shouted to the trolls. "Mages, commence ensnarement!" Then he turned to me, "I permitted myself to be so bold as to protect you with a dome from these sentients," he pointed to the players, who had already stopped resisting after being slapped with the 'Stun' debuff. "We would not be able to hold them long, as in twelve hours they will disappear. An unpleasant trait of the free citizens. But they can lie down here until then. In eleven hours or so my warriors will send them to the Grey Lands: that way we'll gain a whole day. What does the Coordinator need this time? Did he run out of teleportation scrolls again?"

So my current theory about the Coordinator got smashed to smithereens. Teleportation scrolls! I am a blind and stupid ass for failing to think of such a simple thing! Why waste time on travelling between bases when you can jump there at any moment? And no-one would notice a thing. This means that the entire village falls under suspicion once again. Blast!

"Exactly. The teleportation scrolls have run out and there wasn't anyone else to send. You know the current situation," I began to spout out anything that came to mind. I had no idea what I was talking about, but the main thing was that I did it with a confident face! These may be advanced Intellect Imitators, but they're still programs, so could well fall for it.

"All right. Do climb on," the stranger pointed to the sharp-toothed raptor that the trolls immediately brought to my side. "I don't have a supply with me, I'll have to ask the Keeper. Let him make some new ones."

Keeper? This title is given only to NPCs in charge of a castle. Have I stumbled across something interesting? The main thing was to behave naturally, as if none of this was out of the ordinary for me.

I failed.

After an hour-long wild ride through the forest, we found ourselves in an enormous clearing with a Dark Citadel at its centre. My jaw hit the floor as I looked it over. There were 200-level ogres, goblins ranging from level 10 to level 100, dark orcs... The place was full of bustle and gave you the feeling that you were right in the middle of the Dark Empire. When we came up to the castle I got a sense of the full scale of the local Kartoss operation: enormous walls, around twenty meters high and five meters thick with a deep water-filled moat... A typical Dark Castle of about level 400. The stranger smiled, looking at my reaction.

"Impressive, no?"

"Very," was my honest answer. "I would've never thought that such a wonder could be built here."

"I agree. It was planned by none other than..."

"Who let the human in?" a terrible scream went through the castle.

"Keeper," my guide bowed his head, "this is the envoy of the Coordinator, who is in need of portal scrolls again."

"Does he snack on them or something? I just sent him a batch a month ago!"

"You know the current situation," the man in black replied with my words. Who is he? And what the heck is really going on here?

"All right, I'm coming down now. Wait there!"

"The eight free citizens and all the Heralds flying all over the place caused us a world of trouble," my guide finally explained. "We were beginning to fear that the entire plan would collapse, but the Coordinator is pretty shrewd. I would admit that even I doubted that the idea of building a castle deep in Farstead lands, so far away from the ziggurat, was at all feasible, but practice has proved me wrong."

"Keeper, that isn't all," I decided to go for the big bluff.

"What is it?" the voice sounded once again.

"The Coordinator didn't send me here just for the scrolls. This morning several of those that turned have driven away the entire Beatwick herd. However, the Coordinator believes that it should be brought back. The residents are getting too worried. It's too early to show our hand." What was I saying? I was coming out with any old rubbish, as I improvised in the 'crazy as a coot' genre.

"Arr-r-rgh!" cursed the voice. "I already sent ten of them for slaughter, to give my Warriors a feast. Will the Coordinator get very angry if these aren't returned?"

"No, but the villagers have to be compensated the cost of the lost animals. He warned me that this might happen and said that five thousand gold for a killed cow would be sufficient. Then the missing cows could be bought in the neighboring villages," that was my sense of profit, which I had no idea I had, suddenly rearing its head. I had to get as much as I could out of the dark ones.

"Arr-r-gh thrice over! Fine. Wait there, I'm coming down."

"Our master takes great care with his security," said the guide. I wasn't quite getting this bit: which 'master' was he on about now? "He is prepared to reimburse the loss of the herd, just to remain in the shade." Ah, that would be the Coordinator then. Is he the local master then? Very interesting.

"Here are thirty teleportation scrolls and fifty thousand gold," said the 300-level goblin that came out of a small building. I was wrong. This was just a 300-level castle. The level of the castle was always determined by the level of its Keeper. "What do we do with the herd?"

"Let the goblins drive it back - take it as far as the village and leg it back here," I proposed.

"That's how we'll do it then. I'll get the Wild Pack to see this through," the goblin looked at my guide. "Why are you still here? Go!"

"Who's he?" I nodded towards the departing man.

"That? Our mage. And take no notice of his appearance. He is trying to copy his previous appearence, the underbaked lich. I told the master that we should have taken a dozen ordinary battle mages, but no. Said it's easier with a lich."

"I see. How is the construction progressing? The preparation of the army? What shall I tell the Coordinator?" I was doing all I could to make some progress with the quest. I needed at least a slight hint to understand who the Coordinator was.

"We are finishing construction. Two Corrupters have been built, but have not been deployed yet. We are waiting for the third. The army is in full battle-readiness - prepared to fight off an attack of two hundred free citizens of up to and including level 300."

I don't get it - are they setting up a separate country here? In the gap of the castle entrance I saw the herd of cows being driven past. At least that quest was sorted out.

"Tell the master that we are ready to begin and are awaiting his signal," the Keeper added for a total knock-out effect. What was it they were so ready to start?

"Want to share the tactics? I'm just interested to compare it to what the master told me."

Attention! You have called the Dark Coordinator your master. If you repeat this title again in the next ten minutes, your Reputation with the Malabar Empire will decrease and your Reputation with the Dark Empire will increase by 1000 points. Make your choice!

What on earth do I need a reputation with Kartoss for? Have the developers completely lost their marbles? What kind of a scenario did they cook up here? Never mind, I already know what to do.

"It is in no way different from the one planned by the master," the goblin looked at me in surprise. "Is something wrong with you?"

"Don't mind me. I still haven't quite recovered from the chase those three free citizens gave me," I lied through my teeth.

"Yes, I was already told. What did they want?"

"Nothing in particular. They just didn't like the look of me and decided to make my life difficult. Can you show me around the castle? I'd love to see how you've put things together around here."

I spent around three hours in the castle. The keeper gave me a tour around the citadel, showing me the Corrupters being built - the things that curse the land and its inhabitants within a large radius. A similar one was standing somewhere near the ziggurat. At last it was time for me to head back. The herd would soon be arriving at the Beatwick gates, so I would have to use a portal. What if it's linked to a particular house? Then I'll figure out who the Coordinator is. The guards took me to the edge of the forest, pointed in the direction of Beatwick and returned to their posts. The time had come to act.

After disappearing into the forest and hiding myself in thick shrubbery, to make sure nothing could be seen from the side of the castle, I uttered a summons:

"I call upon a Herald. I require your assistance."

The portal opened with a subdued clap and an NPC dressed in white stepped out of it.

"You have summoned me. I hope the reason for my summons is substantial, otherwise a penalty will be imposed on you."

"Does that look substantial enough to you?" I asked, chuckling and moving away the foliage to show the Herald the Dark Castle in the distance. "I think we're doing fine in the 'substance' department."

"Great Emperor," whispered the Herald. "This completely changes..."

Your reputation with the Malabar Empire has increased by 500 points. Current level: Friendly. You are 2,930 points away from the status of Respect

"Changes what?" I looked at the Herald, who seemed somewhat at a loss.

"The citadel cannot be left unwatched. We have to know when and where the Kartoss forces are being moved. A 300-level castle on Malabar territory... This equates to an invasion!"

"The idea of keeping an eye on it is great, but I can't stay here. I will be forcibly teleported to Beatwick. Can you remove this limitation from me?" I looked at the Herald expectantly. What if it works and my debuffs get removed?

"No, taking off this limitation is beyond my power," the Herald shook his head thoughtfully. Damn, what a pity!

"Then I can recommend a couple of free citizens who would be happy to watch this structure."

"Interesting. Who would you recommend?"

"In Anhurs there are several sentients. Their names are..." I told the Herald the correct names for

Eric, Clutzer and Leite. "These sentients would do anything that's needed of them."

"These citizens of the Empire cannot be used for this task," the Herald gave me a reality check. I was all set on seeing my future team get busy with leveling up their reputation right now. "Their threshold of trust with the Empire is too low. We cannot rely on those in whom we have no trust."

"I can vouch for them," I wasn't going to give up so easy on this. "They will carry out this task better than anyone else in this world."

"No," the Herald cut me off. "We already gave you a chance to find the Coordinator. You have only four weeks left now, but there are still no results. Who is the Coordinator? What is he up to? And what are Kartoss armies even doing in these lands? You have no answers for any of this, therefore soon real heroes of the Empire will be sent here to succeed where you have failed."

"I found the castle for you!" I was almost screaming. Why was the Herald having a go at me?

"We thank you for the castle, but you weren't able to find out who is coordinating all the work. Because the task of finding the Coordinator is still currently in your hands, I ask you to choose from a list of recommended heroes the person who will observe the movements of Kartoss forces."

A really long list of players appeared before me. Every single one of them above level 260. Beginning with the strange-sounding Etamzilat and ending with Hellfire. Scanning over the list didn't reveal a single good acquaintance of mine. They all looked the same to me. So I had to choose one, eh? No problem!

"Fortieth from above. He can do it," I had no idea who that was, but he was definitely not from Phoenix.

The Herald closed his eyes, stood there for a few moments and then was with me once again.

"Unfortunately, the free citizen that you've chosen is not currently in this world. Please choose another watcher."

"How will the watcher be rewarded?" That was the question I should have asked at the start, but it only occurred to me now. It was rather fortunate that that my first choice of player was offline.

"Since this is a unique situation (Kartoss has never before risked building a castle on our lands, remote though they are), the watcher will receive his reward directly from the hands of the Emperor. The exact nature of the reward will be decided by the Emperor himself, depending on how well he regards the watcher. The list contains only those who have access to the palace."

"Will there be only one watcher, or several?"

"The primary one must stay by the castle seventy percent of the time. The other thirty percent of the time it will be watched by his deputy, chosen by the watcher himself."

"Could I take a time-out for a couple of minutes? I need to think."

"Of course. I will watch the building myself in the meantime."

The Herald turned away from me and stared at the castle. In the meantime I was hit by a crazy idea, which I immediately decided to put into action: Anastaria. She had spent her entire gaming life chasing unique items, quests and mobs, so if I chose her as the watcher, I would put her squarely in my debt. Yes, she may have promised to rip something out of me, but she's far too proud to shaft a player who helped her. She would bend over backwards to repay the debt. This could be useful should the need arise. Moreover, she should be punished for saying what she did. Four weeks of being stuck in shrubbery, away from the capital and the centre of events - would be a small kind of revenge. Let her sit here and stare at the goblins. It'll do her good. I took out the communication amulet and crossed my fingers for Anastaria to be in the game.

"Speaking!"

Yes! Hang on, Stacey, today is your 'lucky' day!

"Hello, Anastaria. This is Mahan. Do you have a minute?"

"Mahan..." Anastaria's voice became icy. If a voice could inflict damage, I would have been sent for respawn by the cold right now. "I don't have time now. Rick will call you back. He'll help you solve whatever it is."

"Fine, it's just that I have a Herald standing here right now, asking me to choose a player for some unique quest. With a reward from the Emperor. Your name is on the list that I've been given, so I decided to see if you were interested. But, it seems you're too busy now. That's fine, I'll choose someone else. Sorry to have bothered you."

"Hol...!" came the girl's scream, but I already

switched off the communicator.

The amulet in my hands immediately started to vibrate. Of course, Stacey can't let a chance like that slip by. Three magic words: 'reward', 'unique' and 'Emperor' have been uttered and now she's hooked for certain. I'll have to be sure I get something extra out of her for this.

"Yes," I responded in a detached voice.

"Mahan," the icy blizzard of the lady paladin's voice vanished, as if by a wave of a magic wand. "What's the quest? Tell me more."

"I have no idea. I just found an interesting facility here and summoned a Herald. He flew in, had a look and told me to choose a player who would carry out the subsequent instructions connected with this object."

"How do I know that this isn't a set-up?"

"Stacey, do you think I have hostile intentions towards my own wellbeing? Like I have nothing better to do than just give you a random call. As if I missed you so much, dammit!"

"Is the object in Krong?"

"Yes."

"Then I pass," the girl's voice was now a world of grief. She was sure good at playing with emotions. I just knew that hundreds of ways of solving the problem and different possible reactions were racing through her head right now.

"Hold on, let me ask the Herald about the limitations," I said plainly, playing a total simpleton. I was allowed to choose any player irrespective of their clan membership, so the clan would not be incurring any penalties. But Anastaria didn't know this and I was aiming for a good bargain here. "Herald, if the player that I choose is from Phoenix - specifically, Anastaria - will her clan incur any penalties?"

"No. Anastaria would be carrying out only my assignment. Otherwise, if the clan does not want to breach the conditions of a future quest, Phoenix members will be forbidden from showing up in Krong."

"Hear that?" I asked the girl, who was breathing heavily now. Yes, she's all mine! Now I had to gradually make her realize that I have to be paid a handsome sum for giving her the right to sit in the bushes for four weeks and practice goblin watching. Because I do not work for free. "There won't be any penalties. You will be given personal access here."

"I agree! Tell the Herald to summon me! Right now!"

"Whoa! What's the hurry? I haven't spoken to Plinto yet. I have to ask him if he wants to take part in all this. I'll give him a call right now and then make a decision. Thanks for agreeing so quickly. I will call you back."

"Stop! Mahan, no need to play hard to get. Plinto promised not to let you step off the respawn point until the Herald slaps a ban on killing you. Can you imagine what will happen if you call him now?"

"Plinto promised to waste me? Thanks for the information. But you must understand that I can't invite you just like that. Everyone and their dog will laugh in my face after that - I had a chance to get a good deal out of Phoenix, but fell for Anastaria's beautifully-designed eyes. I don't think so. We'll agree at the outset on what I'll be getting and sign a clear-cut agreement, after which I will make my decision. I have no time limitations, since the Herald said I had until tomorrow for choosing the player if need be. Think - what can Phoenix offer that would decide it for me right now?"

"Mahan, please," Anastaria began to speak in such a sweet voice that I began to shiver. "I promise that you won't regret picking me. I'll be very well-behaved..."

Reptilis was right - women can't be trusted. I could just see what Stacey was counting on right now: the action of the poison would play in her favour and I, like some obedient puppy, would eagerly fulfill her every whim. You can dream on, my pretty!

"Of course, my darling Stacey. I will choose you..." I paused and then moved in for the kill, "as soon as we come to an agreement on the price of my choice. You have ten minutes. If you do not call me back in that time, I'll choose Plinto, come what may. Maybe he'll forgive me the chess pieces. The countdown begins now!" with these words I turned off the amulet.

"Have you made your choice?" the Herald turned away from the castle and looked at me. "Please note that you have to make the choice within an hour or I will have to choose myself."

"I'll make it, don't you worry," I assured the Emperor's representative and sat on the ground. Right now Anastaria is contacting Ehkiller as quickly as she can and they are trying to decide on the best course of action. I was very lucky that she had heard the ringing voice of the Herald. It was possible to fake a Herald's voice in the game, but it could land you in a whole world of trouble.

Nine minutes later - I noted the time on my return-to-Beatwick timer - the Phoenix amulet started to vibrate.

"Have you thought of something?" I asked straight away - no point beating about the bush.

"Good day Mahan, I'm sorry, I don't think I know your real name," a male voice came from the amulet. "My name is Ehkiller. I'm the one you depicted as a King with an up-turned nose. Anastaria filled me in on the problem and I'm ready to listen to your demands."

So they brought out the big guns. I didn't quite see that coming. This was unfortunate - I'd have to improvise on the go.

"Good day. I apologize for my words: I didn't know that Anastaria would give the amulet to you. As for the problem, I don't really understand you. I offered the charming lady a chance to take part in a certain unique quest. She agreed and now I'm trying to see what I would get out of choosing her. You must understand that I can't simply offer a quest from the Herald, who represents the Emperor himself in this, for nothing. That's it, I think. No demands - on the contrary, I was expecting an offer from Phoenix. I am quite sure that your clan would be interested in this assignment."

"You are right, we do have a certain interest. I

can't deny something so obvious. But every interest has its limits. If you ask for something unrealistic, I would have to decline this quest, no matter how much I may want to get it."

"That's why I didn't make any demands. To be honest, I expected a reasonable reaction from Phoenix and a corresponding offer, but in no way a discussion about what it was I needed. I'm somewhat disappointed."

"Something tells me that money is not the thing you're after," Ehkiller dropped into thoughtful silence. "Before I make you an offer, please answer this question. As far as I know, you have Plinto's amulet and also a chance to choose any player. Why Anastaria?"

"You wouldn't believe it, but her amulet was simply closer to my hand. I really don't care which of the clans becomes first and which second. It's all purely abstract to me. My task is to serve the rest of my sentence, preferably in as much comfort as possible."

"I understand now. Are you familiar with the faction of Thricinians?"

"Of course," I swallowed. Ehkiller managed to surprise me and strike at my most vulnerable spot: these traders in Scaling Items were world-famous.

"Anastaria has leveled up her reputation with them to Esteemed and may invite another player with her, for whom she can choose and buy from the items they have for sale. I offer you any four items from the Thricinians - paid for by Phoenix. What do you say?"

The most unpleasant part was that we both understood that Ehkiller won our little duel the moment he uttered word 'Thricinians'. It is an artificial faction in Barliona, whose only purpose was to sell Scaling Items - items that leveled up together with the players that owned them. At the same time, the faction guaranteed that any player, even one lacking any reputation with them, could come and spend a crazy amount of money to buy some simple object like my Tambourine. However, as soon as you increased your reputation with this faction, the items became a whole lot more interesting. I never imagined that it was possible to gain Esteemed with them, thinking it was totally out of reach, so Anastaria had gone up quite a lot in my estimation. This was impressive stuff. Whatever she might be in real life, gaining Esteemed with the Thricinians was worth a lot. And I could choose any four objects... Eh... I sold myself down the river, completely. All right, I knew what I was getting into. The initial deal I was fishing for with Phoenix was any four wishes that could be carried out and would not be harmful to the clan. To have a look at the scroll of Karmadont, for example. But then thought better of it. Be careful what you wish for, as they say. What if a Phoenix battle group got hold of me, like those three PKers, locked me down and chased me around until I begged them for mercy? And then they'd ask: "Is that one of your wishes?" That's one way to lose them all. I think not. Everything has to be clearly set down in writing and made official according to the letter of the law. That's the only way of dealing with the leading clans.

"That's more like it. Now I understand who holds the real power in your clan. Drop me an agreement: if I'm happy with it, I'll approve it and choose Anastaria. The choice must be made today, so it would be good to get through all the formalities straight away. "

"You will get the text in a minute," said Ehkiller, satisfied. "It's been good working with you. Until we speak again.”

Two minutes later a message lit up saying that player Ehkiller, on behalf of the Phoenix clan, was offering an agreement for me to sign. The text described in detail both what I would get if I chose Anastaria for the quest and what I would not get if I did not choose her. Moreover, Anastaria's success in completing the quest in no way affected any bonuses I would receive. Great. I carefully read the text, but it didn't leave much open to interpretation: everything was written clearly and properly, so I accepted it and, turning to the Herald, made my choice:

"I choose Anastaria from the Phoenix clan to watch over the castle."

The Herald closed his eyes, checking that Stacey was present in the game, whispered something and a portal formed next to him. A couple of seconds went by and the one I considered the ideal of female beauty stepped out. Unlike our previous encounters, this time I was no longer in the grips of the desire to roll over like a puppy and start rubbing against Stacy's feet. Something else occupied my mind: how old was she really? Let's suppose she started playing when she was fourteen, as soon as she reached the legal age for playing the Game. She would have needed at least ten years to get to her current position. Thus, she was at least twenty five, if not older.

"Well, hello again, Mahan," Anastaria fixed her hair and closed her eyes. A few seconds later she lifted an eyebrow in surprise - she was probably reading the conditions of the Herald's quest - and then broke out in laughter.

"Ah, just beautiful. Oh, Mahan..." still laughing, Anastaria started to clap, "if Barliona ever has a contest for the most epic set-up, you'd win hands down! Beautiful, just beautiful! And, most importantly, it's all totally above board!"

"Anastaria, the Emperor places his hopes in you," the Herald interrupted her. "And now I must go," the Herald nodded, opened a portal and disappeared, leaving me alone with a laughing 330-level girl.

"Stacey, you really are exaggerating," I smiled. The lady paladin's laughter was too infectious.

"Like hell I am! Managing to sell a four-week-long banishment for such a price - takes some considerable skill. But you managed it! At least tell me how you found them."

That was no great secret, so I told her how the PKers hunted me and how I ran across the goblins and asked them for help.

"If I didn't see the result with my own eyes, I would've never believed it. Why on earth do you always end up in the middle of such interesting events? Is your ass a secret adventure-magnet? Hey, you can chill - I'm just kidding. What are you going to do now? By the looks of it, I'll be stuck here until you finish your quest. I wouldn't even think of offering help: it'll end up costing the clan an arm and a leg, going by your current rates," smiled Stacey.

"I'll go back to Beatwick and will try not to set foot outside it for the next four weeks. The three morons will soon be back on their feet and eager to get their own back, so I'll have a bunch of crazies on my case. Best if I wait it out in a safe zone."

"Since when is Beatwick a safe zone?" asked Anastaria in surprise.

"As far as I know, it's not. It's just conditionally safe. But that's good enough for me."

"So it is," Anastaria smiled once again and began to take out her things. "Will you help me put up the tent or do you have to go back right away?"

"I do, but I can spare a couple of minutes. What needs doing?"

Anastaria took out a big roll and handed it to me. Wow! A Frontier Ranger Tent! If you put it up in a forest, you can stop worrying about your safety - it is only possible to see the tent by walking right into it. Or if the owner has given you his permission. Or if you're a Hunter and have turned on your 'find humanoids' mode. Or... Well, there were ways, but none very easy.

After putting up the tent and hanging up alarm traps around it, Anastaria looked at me and suddenly asked:

"Mahan, I realize that you won't hand over the chess pieces just like that, but can you at least let me have a look at them? I've seen so many fakes by now and here I have a chance to see the original. I would never forgive myself if I didn't at least take a look at them."

Right. Something strange is going on here. Since when did Anastaria turn into a nice girl who tells you her wishes and desires? Something wasn't right. Should I show them? Not on my life!

"Stacey, we've agreed that you'll only get the pieces when you put together a decent agreement. We've gone over the conditions. Where is it? I haven't seen one materialize. No agreement - no chess pieces. You should understand, being a lawyer."

"I'm not a lawyer! Where on earth did you get that idea? I have two good higher educations, but neither of them is in law."

"Really? Strange. As far as I know, all of Malabar speaks of you as a lawyer. What's your degree in then?" Now things were becoming clearer with the girl's age. You cannot study for two degrees at the same time - only one after the other. So, if she has two, she's been studying for ten or eleven years, which makes Stacey older than twenty-eight... Damn, what the heck am I thinking about?

"Radio electronics and economics. Right now I'm studying for a marketing degree."

"No way! Tell me Kirchhoff's law."

"Which of the two?" laughed the girl, "Mahan, it makes no sense for me to lie."

"I'm sorry, that was stupid. I just find this totally mind-blowing: a beautiful girl in an electronics faculty... You would've seriously distracted people from studying."

"You think me beautiful?" Anastaria dropped her eyes. She was quite the actress! I'll have to train long and hard before I get this good!

"Well... I should go. Good luck in your monster fighting."

"Wait," Anastaria stood up, made a barely perceptible hand movement, as if activating an aura, then exhaled and in a syrupy voice, which I heard before from the amulet, said, "Won't you give me the Orc Warrior figurines, eh? You don't need them, and I could find a use for them."

"Stacey, we already went over this." At first I didn't get what the girl was doing and then it dawned on me. I nearly choked with indignation. She was using her poison. On me!

"Pleeeease! I would be ever so grateful!"

Yeah... Somehow I thought better of her. Does she really want the figurines so bad she'd take such a risk?

"Stacey..." a plan emerged in my head, but I had to wrestle with myself a bit before putting it into action.

"Mahan, dear, they would make such a perfect gift, pretty please with sugar on top." Stacey was trying her best, even blushing from the effort. Right, it was time to act.

"Sweetest Stacey..." I fell to my knees before the girl. Somebody stop me! So you need the figurines, eh? Let's see how much I've learned from your acting lessons. "Stacey, my darling," I started to do what I had been fantasizing about ever since I first found out about this girl: I grabbed her legs in an embrace and started to make my way up, exploring the girl's game avatar in the most brazen manner. "Stacey, baby..."

"Mahan, the chess pieces! Where are they?" Stacey's face was a picture of revulsion, but that only amused me. I was well aware that this was only a digital copy of the girl, that her filters were probably turned on and she couldn't feel my touch, but she could see everything all right!

It took me a minute to get to my feet, all the while keeping Anastaria in my embrace. The girl wasn't even trying to resist, she was convinced that I had completely succumbed to her poison. Well, the shit's about to hit the fan! Although, it's hard not to admit that this is one of the more pleasant 'adventures'!

"Mahan! The figurines!" she repeated forcefully, when just a dozen centimeters remained between our faces. I leaned over to her ear and whispered:

"In your dreams, sweetheart. If you try to do this again, I'll summon a Herald and say that you've been trying to gain control over my character. Shall I tell you what would happen next?"

And then I saw that for which I had put on this entire performance, starting with falling on my knees. Fear appeared in the lady paladin's eyes. Fear that she was just a pawn in this game. Damn, I was relishing this!

"How?" Stacey whispered "There are no antidotes to this..."

"You're smart and will have plenty of time on

your hands to figure it out. And now, farewell," I leaned over and kissed her on the lips. I'll consider that a bonus. Whatever she was like in reality, right now I had a very beautiful, frightened woman in my hands. It would've been wrong not to kiss her. Too bad it wasn't reciprocated. That would have been very nice. But this will do.

I let go of the baffled girl, took out one of the scrolls I got from the Keeper and activated the portal. It was time I got back to Beatwick - to receive the herd of cows, complete the quest, drop by Elizabeth to clear things up with her and prepare for the fight with the mist beast.

"Mahan!" Anastaria's shout caught me just as I stepped through the portal. I looked back at the girl's sparkling eyes and raised an eyebrow in surprise. "Who are you?"

CHAPTER ELEVEN
THE MIST MONSTER AND NEW DISCOVERIES

T HE SCROLLS WERE A LET-DOWN: I came out of the portal right in the center of Beatwick square, where you usually ended up if not bound to a specific spot. A pity, as it would've been good to settle the matter of the Coordinator straight away.

"Mahan! You're back already? What about the cows?" Tisha appeared next to me.

"Aren't they here yet?" I was surprised. According to my estimates, the herd should've been in place by now.

"Why on earth..." Tisha began, but was interrupted by a guard running up to us.

"There... we... the cows have come," he said, out of breath from his run. "We won't be going to fetch them though."

"Why?" frowned the girl.

"There are goblins and the Wild Pack. They're pacing around the cows, as if waiting for something."

Well, I'll be... Did the escort really have instructions to hand them over to me personally? What would the villagers think if I started speaking in goblin? They might go straight for their pitchforks. A speedy 'disengagement' was in order.

"Mahan, what are we going to do?" the Headman's daughter started to sound worried. "Father is busy, brothers are away and Slate is gone as well. We have no-one to go to the goblins!"

"I will go. I just happen to know goblin language. I'll go and ask what they want. Maybe they've come to apologize and you're all fretting over nothing. Where is everyone?" Only now did Tisha's words sink in.

"My brothers rode off to hunt the mist monster..."

"Who?" asked the guard who was still loitering nearby.

"It doesn't matter. And Slate went to travel round the villages to fix things. Will you really go?"

"I'll go, don't you worry."

The Wild Pack was pacing by the smithy, trying not to come near the gates. The poor cows, eyes wild with terror from such attendants, huddled by the stockade, threatening to topple it with their weight. There was little cause to worry, however. This wasn't reality - in Barliona even the most flimsy-looking fence could be an impenetrable wall. Not a single cow would get through.

"Here's the herd," said one of the goblins, as

soon as I came out of the gates. "We were told to hand it over to you in person, now we go back," with this they turned around and sped away from the village. Somewhat perplexed, I stood there watching the departing cloud of dust, when the gates opened and people poured out of them.

"What did they say?" Tisha started to question me right away.

"They apologized, saying they made a mistake and won't do it again," I told a blatant lie, since it was unlikely anyone else understood what the goblin had barked.

"Count the cows," the Headman finally appeared, looking like he had been torn away from his work. "We have to be sure that they all came back."

"Ten are missing," someone shouted straight away. "These green mugs pinched ten cows!"

"Tisha and the Headman were noticeably disheartened.

"That's very bad," the village boss said, "ten cows less would be a heavy blow to the village. We'll have to replace the missing ones by buying more in Farstead. But that's for us to worry about. Thank you, Mahan. You did an honest job of this assignment."

Quest 'Returning the Herd' completed. Completion percentage: 80%. You received: +100 to Reputation with the Krong Province, +300 Experience, +80 Silver

That's it? What was the point of running after

the herd for such a measly reward? I was expecting more, somehow. I read through the quest conditions once again: Variable.

"How much does a cow cost in Farstead?" I asked the Headman, as he was about to leave.

"Five thousand a head. But I can probably bargain a thirty percent discount if I buy all ten in one go. But where would we get so much money? I just don't have that amount on me right now. I'll have to think of something."

What a snag! Damned Imitator in charge of this quest! Even counted the money that was taken off me automatically. A thirty percent discount. Does that mean I fooled that goblin for nothing? And what if I didn't ask the castle Keeper for anything? Was I supposed to have volunteered my own gold? Interesting quests they have in this area!

"Wait," I stopped the Headman and handed him the all the money I got from the goblin in the Kartoss castle, "Here you go: I believe I am partly at fault here. I failed to get the entire herd back."

On one hand - easy come, easy go. But on the other hand - minus thirty five thousand gold... I tried not to even think what I was doing when I was handing over the money. And the main thing - why am I doing this if I have three people in Anhurs living on short rations? I'm acting like a major spendthrift!

"I have nothing to give you in return," the Headman visibly swallowed, as his greedy gaze fell on the money. "I can promise only one thing: if you are ever in need, I will come to your aid."

"Take it already! I'm not doing this for something, but simply because." I had no idea what I just said, but it had a good ring to it. "When the time comes, we'll square up."

You have received: +500 to Reputation with the Krong Province, +500 Experience, +2 to all the main stats

Now was the turn for my jaw to drop in surprise. Reputation is a good thing, for sure, and I've already reached Friendly with Krong, but +2 to all the main stats... That's just super! It may not be much, but it's in the stat hard currency! I thought that such quests were available only from level 90! It's so nice to be wrong sometimes! Moreover, the promise of help from the Headman... Something tells me that it will come in useful when I find out the identity of the Coordinator.

"I heard you're having problems with Elizabeth," the Headman asked when I had finally scraped my jaw off the floor. When did he get so well-informed? "Do you need a new place to stay?"

"No, I'll go visit her now and I think that we'll come to an understanding. Thank you for your concern."

"If you need anything, just drop by. I will be in," the visibly cheered up Headman went off to his house. Right, the time had now come to find out who Elizabeth really was...

"Didn't I tell you: don't come here anymore!" came Beth's angry shout as soon as I entered the gates.

"Yes, you did, I won't dispute that," I checked the level of Attractiveness just in case: '83 points'. That should be enough for a chat, and then we'll see. "I won't go anywhere until we talk. And no need to turn around so pointedly. I didn't bring the herd back to be speaking to a back."

"You... you brought back the herd?" there was now uncertainty in the woman's voice now and I decided to take advantage of it. "And what about the people?"

"The situation with the people is not as good. Those who changed can't be brought back. They've become goblins forever, but at least now the villagers of Beatwick won't be going hungry. I think I earned the right to a conversation. Let me tell you what I know and then you can decide for yourself whether to chuck me out or not. You shouldn't make decisions in a moment of passion, priestess."

The last word made Elizabeth start.

"I... I am no longer a priestess. The goddess has turned away from me."

"Of course she did. And yet in your anger you threw my reputation with the priestesses of Eluna straight into Mistrust. How can a former priestess, from whom the goddess has turned away, remove reputation? Especially to such a degree. Tell, me, were you a High Priestess?" the last phrase was intended as a joke. As far as I knew, the High Priestess is the top rank in the hierarchy and it's virtually impossible to remove her from her position.

"Yes," tears appeared in Beth's eyes. "Ten years

ago I was the High Priestess of Eluna in Anhurs. But I was removed as soon as... You're lying, I couldn't have removed reputation!" with those last words Beth was shouting.

"Mum, are you ok?" Clouter popped out of the house. "Hi, Mahan. Are you the one that's upset mum?"

"It's all right, dear. Everything's all right," said the woman, wiping away her tears. "It's just that Mahan told me a story, which I had almost believed. Everything's all right."

"A story?" Some joke that was! 'High Priestess'! It was my turn to be indignant. "Oh No! You better take a look!" I did something I would've never done with another player: gave full access to my reputation table. From it you could see straight away, whom I've met and have been in touch with. "Before meeting you Shaman Mahan never met Priestesses of Eluna. As the Emperor is my witness," I called Barliona's most dangerous arbiter as a witness. A cloud of light immediately formed around me and quickly dissipated, leaving me unharmed. Calling on the Emperor is the final argument in communications both with other players and NPCs. Only free citizens are able to call upon the Emperor, at least those not sporting a red headband. This would have come in really useful at the mine, especially when Bat set me up that first time by taking my Rat Skins. When a player calls upon the Emperor, a special Imitator is activated. It analyses the words of the summons, looks up the game logs, checks the truth or falsehood of the words and then surrounds the player either by a light dome, showing that he was right, or by a dark one, which comes with a three-month debuff of -50% to all stats. Moreover, the owner of the dark dome gets a special 'bonus': -10% to levels. All the players are informed of these facts, so there have never been any complaints. Although it did occur to me that prisoners were never told these rules, but placed directly in the mines. I should write to tech support, making them aware of this omission. How could they fail to foresee the possibility of someone leaving the mines, removing the headband and calling the Emperor as a witness? Or is it that they didn't tell me the rules because I had played before? Right, this is unimportant. A dumbfounded priestess of Eluna was now standing in front of me wide-eyed as she read my reputation table. Admittedly, there were many interesting things to see there.

"You know the Emperor?" that wasn't the question that I expected from Beth once she had come round.

"No. The Herald handed that to me," there was little sense in deceiving the lady.

"A Herald cannot increase favor with the Emperor without his knowledge, you can trust me on this one. It's not for nothing that I was... that I am a priestess of Eluna."

Your reputation with priestesses of Goddess Eluna has increased by 1000 points. Current level: Neutral. You are 995 points away from the status of Friendly

"Forgive me. We really should have spoken right at the start. Then we might have prevented all of this from happening. Come, we shouldn't repeat past mistakes. And, Mahan," the priestess turned towards me, "keep calling me Beth. I like that."

"It all started ten years ago," began the lady when we settled down in her house. "My husband was one of the assistants to Advisor Brast, and I, as you already know, was the High Priestess of Eluna. My husband stumbled upon information about a Kartoss plan for a takeover of Malabar. First we thought it was a bad joke, but gradually we became convinced of the truth of this information. We informed Brast of this, but were only laughed at and called scaremongers. None of the Advisers that we approached in a vain attempt to get the message through took us seriously. Then we approached the Emperor directly, bypassing the Heralds and the Advisers. The Emperor heard us out and then..." Beth sighed bitterly, "we were banished as panic-spreaders and as a threat to the integrity of the Empire. My husband was appointed as the Headman in Beatwick and I was stripped of my rank. We governed this village for eight years, until my husband disappeared. That's the end of our story. I already told you about the curse: two years ago I noticed that our lands - and, as I started to travel between villages looking for a new place to live, the lands of the neighboring villages too - began to be darkened. Someone was putting a curse on them. I appealed to the Headman, but there was nothing he could do for me - magic was beyond his understanding.

His main concern was that the people and the cows were safe. I didn't even bother approaching the Priest. He wasn't interested in anything except wine. I wrote letters to my former sisters asking for help, only to be rebuked for thinking up non-existent problems. I considered talking with the village residents, but then thought - to what end? They have nowhere else to go and they wouldn't even bother hearing me out. Then I decided to try and protect Beatwick all by myself. Every seven days I put Eluna's blessing on the villagers. A few months later the mist monster turned up and tried to break my concentration. One of the villagers was summoning him. This could mean only one thing: we had a traitor in our midst, someone who wanted to plunge our region into the abyss of darkness. There was no-one I could trust. So when you turned up and started running around in search of the monster... I thought all of this was arranged for your benefit. I was even glad that the Headman assigned you to live with me. I thought it would be easier to keep an eye on you. How wrong I was..."

"And I first thought that you were actually the mist monster and then that you were a demonologist who summoned it," I said, somewhat lost. That's just crazy: I had the High Priestess of Eluna - albeit a former one - sitting right in front of me. "So I decided to catch you to stop you summoning the mist beast. Very 'smart' of me too - I could've just had a chat with you..."

"I'm no demonologist!"

"Yea, I got that already. We're as bad as each other though... What are we going to do now?"

"I don't know. I plan to perform the blessing again today, since without it many have begun to succumb."

"Can you really have the entire village under suspicion?"

"Why everyone? I tried to catch the mist beast, as you call him, together with the Headman and his family several times, but we've failed each time. You know that they're..." Beth fell silent, looking at me in question.

"Vagrens? Yes, I know. We've tried working together twice before, but the first time I followed you and the second time I was hunting you."

"You followed me?!"

"How else did I find out where you were doing your sorcery?"

"I don't do sorcery! I bless!"

"Yes, my mistake. By the way, why in the cemetery?"

"The cemetery is the only area that remains untainted. The temple protects it."

"And what did you mean by saying your husband disappeared?"

"Exactly that. One day he went out of the house and never came back. The border with the Free Lands is a very dangerous place, frequently roamed by monsters. We had waited for a very long time before reporting what happened to Farstead. I tried summoning him with magic, but without the High Priestess's amulet I can only bless. And also, as it turned out, change the attitude of other sisters. So I know nothing of my husband's fate," said Beth sadly. "I've come to terms with it by now. It's been two years, after all. Avtondil is growing and I'm trying to teach him everything that I know. He has no aptitude for magic, but would excel as a warrior. Good manners would come in useful too. When he grows up he will leave for the big world. Only I am barred from returning there - the banishment has not been imposed on the children."

"Were you banished forever? Or for a certain time?"

"Forever. We will only be able to come back in one case: if the Emperor acknowledges that we were acting on his instructions. And he would never do that. Who am I that he should concern himself with me? So now I'll have to live here for the rest of my life."

I took a certain interesting ring out of the bag and looked at its properties: The person presenting this ring is acting on my instructions and for the good of Malabar.

A moment of truth.

On the one hand, I had about a million gold on my hands. That is approximately the price for which you could sell the ring to someone who was forbidden to enter the Emperor's palace. In effect - a complete 'free pass'. A correction of a mistake. On the other hand, in front of me I had a woman, even if she was just an NPC, who was in need of help, who had already given up on ever getting it and who was a High Priestess of Eluna. If she returns to Anhurs, she is bound to assume that position once again. What's better - a million gold or a High Priestess of the high goddess in your debt? A good question, to which I had no answer. I had to think this over.

"Mahan, is anything wrong?" asked Beth, concerned. "Did I upset you in some way?"

"No, not at all. I was just lost in thought," I put the ring back in the bag. This wasn't the time for it. "I propose that we try to catch the mist beast together in six day's time. We'll invite Tisha to come with us. We will come from one end of the village and the Headman and his sons from the other. This time we'll catch it for sure. What do you say?"

"You know, let's do it. I'll put up the blessing today, which should last seven days, so I should be free on the night that the mist beast will appear. It's good that you thought of Tisha. It will be easier with a Vagren. Will you speak to the Headman or shall I?"

"I'll go. So, then, can I continue to live here?"

Beth only smiled in reply. But her smile and eyes were so full of promise that I couldn't help swallowing, which provoked a ringing laugh from the pretty woman...

Next morning I decided to busy myself with the most important task for any player: leveling up. My plan was simple: if there were no mobs in the area, I would have to create them. And I was able to create a mob only from one being in the game - Draco. There was no ban on dueling between two sentients. My Totem was a sentient, so I could probably fight him. No reason why he can't do it. In any case, I had to have a proper look at his settings: what if there's something interesting there? After I made the arrangements with the Headman about the large-scale hunt for the mist beast, I headed for the forest. Aside from Beth's family, no-one knew about the Dragon, so I didn't want to show him in the open unnecessarily. He was still small.

After making sure that I was alone, I summoned my Totem and immediately went into his settings:

Stats window for Totem Draco					
Experience	1052	of	25200	Additional stats	
Race		Dragon			
Totem level		36		Damage dealt	30
Hit points		210		Damage resistance:	3600%
Mana		220		Poison resistance:	100%
Direction		Not selected		Number of carried players	0
Stats	Scale	Base	+ Items	Acceleration coefficient 1	1
Stamina	72%	3	3	Acceleration coefficient 2	1
Strength	2%	2	2	Acceleration coefficient 3	1
Agility	24%	10	10	Acceleration coefficient 4	1
Intellect	41%	4	4	Acceleration coefficient 5	1
Free stat points			72	Acceleration coefficient 6	1

Not that many settings, in the end. By level thirty six, Draco gathered 72 free stat points: this came to 2 per level. Not a lot. Playing with Clouter had only increased his Agility and Stamina. With me he leveled up in Intellect. What a 'Coefficient' was and why there were six of them - I had no idea. The same went for 'Direction'. In the hope of looking up the properties of the latter, I pressed that slot and a window popped up with the following list: Fire, Water, Air and Earth. Ah! What's this? An opportunity to choose the direction of the Totem's development? If I'm a 'water expert', then...

The chosen direction of the Totem's development: Water. Attention, Totem modification has commenced

Draco stopped flying around in circles and began to curiously examine the shield that had begun to surround him.

"What is this?" the Totem asked in slightly scared voice.

"Don't worry, it'll be fine. This will hurt a little, you'll just have to hang in there," I remembered my own modification, so I thought to warn the Dragon.

"All right, I wouldn't..." I had no time to hear what the Totem 'wouldn't', because the dome covered him on all sides.

The shape that formed rose about a meter above the ground and then turned bright red, with flashes of fire spreading across it. A couple of seconds later a burning two-meter sphere was hanging in the air. I had little time to soak up the rays of Barliona's second sun before the terrible roar of the Dragon had shaken the surrounding land. The roar was so piercing, crushing and oppressive that my feet gave way and I fell to the ground. A steady stream of messages flashed before my eyes, telling me that I was landed with various unpleasant properties. Upon glancing at the list of debuffs I was blown away. Did my Totem really do this?

Stun. Duration: 60 seconds. Does not affect the owner or a friendly group of players.

Muteness... Fear... Armor reduction...

In total, I managed to count over twenty negative effects that Draco saddled me with before they vanished. Impressive! I should use this when leveling up through hunting mobs.

After some time the Dragon's roar died away and the fire sphere began to fade. First the flames disappeared, with the surface becoming bright yellow and then just yellow, later transforming into blue with streams of water coursing through it. The sphere turned into an enormous water droplet, with water rushing all around it. Another couple of minutes went by, this time without the Dragon's wild roar, and the droplet descended to earth, crumpling and tearing up the grass. There was a subdued clap and everything vanished, leaving only my Totem on the ground, who, breathing heavily, lifted himself on his front legs and started to look himself over. If before the modification the Dragon was completely black, now I had a bright dark-blue Totem sitting before me. I breathed in deeply. It turned out that all this time I was standing there literally holding my breath - even the 'No Air' bar had almost filled to the maximum...

"If this is 'a little' what's simply 'painful' in your view?" I heard my Totem's hoarse voice.

"If I told you that it would hurt a lot, would it have made things better?"

"No, but..."

"Then let's forget it. Now you're a Black Water Dragon. Sit still, I'll have a look where you can be improved."

I allocated all the free points equally between all the four stats. Draco had to be developed in every direction. One thing that made me especially happy was the presence of a '+Items' column. This meant that I could find gear for my Totem and improve his stats. I took one of the neck-chains out of the bag and tried to put it on Draco, but got a message that the item wasn't suitable for this creature. Damn. What do Dragons wear if no-one believes in them? Where could I find armor for him?

"An interesting feeling," said my flying pet. He had grown some more during the modification and now a meter-and-a-half-long serpent was flying around me. "It's as if water is flowing through me."

"What was it like before?"

"Fire. I'm a fire Dragon," Draco stopped and became thoughtful. "I think..."

"It doesn't matter who you were, it matters who you've become," I noted, philosophically. "All right, let's not waste any time. Shall we try to duel each other?"

"All right, brother. Let's go."

"What did you call me?" I stopped and stared at the Dragon. Could his memory be coming back to him?

"Well... you've been calling me different things as well," if the Dragon wasn't so dark, I would've thought he was blushing. "You don't like it?"

"No, not at all. It's just unexpected," I looked at the embarrassed Dragon and continued: "Why are we still standing here? Time to duel!"

Damage taken...

Draco didn't wait around and attacked straight away. A sea of fire formed around me, which slowly but surely started to diminish my Hit Points. What pleased me the most (and what I secretly hoped for when starting a duel with my Totem) was the complete absence of pain. Yes, there was fire roaring all around me, my Hit Points were sliding, but the curse of the prisoner capsule failed to strike: a Totem couldn't inflict pain on his owner. Great!

Draco began with a weak wall of fire (though I couldn't help wondering if it was normal for a Water Dragon to have fire damage) so as not to give me too much of a shock. I understood this when he finally deployed his claws, teeth, roar and some strange ability spouting jets of flaming water in my direction. Draco stepped up his attack, showing everything he was capable of. As long as the inflicted damage was small, I wasn't too concerned about the outcome of the fight, but as soon as critical hits dealing 400 damage started to land on me every other second, I began to get concerned. It was time I fought back.

In the end... I lost the first fight. As soon as I entered the Spirit summoning mode to heal myself, the Totem started to hurl attacks at me that dealt 600 damage per second. If you take into account my resistances, Endurance and gear, this was a truly enormous figure. I managed to summon only one Healing Spirit, before another of Draco's 'presents' landed on me - worth 1200 damage this time! My Hit

Points fell to 1 and a message appeared before my eyes.

You lost the duel

It was now time to do some thinking.

The Totem's base damage was 210 points. Part of this damage was blocked, part of it hit me. This was the case at the start of the fight. Then something incomprehensible had happened: the damage inflicted by the Dragon began to grow almost exponentially. Why? Appealing to the manual and the forum was quite useless: as per usual.

"Listen," I decided to ask my Totem. Can you explain to me what just happened? Why at the start of the duel you fought like a little kid, and at the end of it hit so hard that I folded right away? This just isn't normal."

"You were just standing there not doing anything. I thought that I wasn't getting anywhere, so I intensified."

"Let's go over this bit again," I interrupted. "What's this 'intensification'?"

"It's a property of Dragons. I just found out about it myself, when we started to fight. I didn't have it before. It turns out that I have six levels of intensification - I had only reached the fourth one when you lost. At the first level I can intensify myself by 100%. The intensification lasts only five minutes, after which I'll have to wait an hour until it is restored. When the first intensification is active, you can activate the second level: this will give +300% to damage for four minutes. Each intensification has an independent recharging timer: for example, the second one takes two hours to recharge. It's the same with the other levels. But my head aches something terrible afterwards... And my paws are sore... And my tail feels like it's going to fall off..."

When I opened the Totem's properties, I noticed that his level of Intellect had increased by 30% and the incomprehensible lines titled 'Acceleration coefficient' (the first four, at any rate) had increased by one thousandth in value. These lines came without a description, but now I could guess that these coefficients determined the time it took for the Dragon intensifications to recharge.

The four hours I spent dueling with Draco only brought him up by one level, and the first and second level coefficients increased by another 0.001. After each intensification the Totem wrinkled in pain, but gritted his teeth and toughed it out. I could imagine how hard it was going to be for him at level 6: +1100% to damage demands a sizeable sacrifice. As for me - my Intellect hadn't increased by even one percent, despite the fact that Draco was a much higher-level opponent than me.

The timer for summoning the Totem ran out and I was left by myself. There were no mobs and no Totem. I had no idea how to level up in such a situation. Only the professions remained, which was at least something.

There was little point in going to the mines: my mining was already at maximum and I saw little sense in mining materials that would produce only Dark objects. You couldn't sell them to players or make anything good out of them - they were just too dark for that. Now, if they could be cleansed with light, then... Beth!

I couldn't restrain myself and ran straight back to Beatwick. I just happened to have Eluna's High Priestess at hand, who must know how to turn cursed things into blessed ones. Just switch their polarity somehow. If it was hard to bless neutral things, something that would take a great deal of effort, switching the sign from negative to positive, on the other hand... If this worked, leveling up could wait.

"Mahan, is anything the matter?" Beth asked me, looking worried, when I flew into her yard - out of breath and disheveled, but practically glowing from what we were about to do.

"Beth, we need to talk. Come."

The surprised woman followed me without any further ado. I shut the door and checked that no-one was watching us, making Beth nervous, then closed the shutters and sat at the table, which already had the priestess standing next to it, almost spellbound and ready for whatever I was going to throw at her.

"Mahan, what happened?" she whispered as soon as I lit a candle.

"Beth, only you and me now stand in the path of darkness. No-one knows who is summoning the monster, who is cursing the land and who wants to drown us all in corruption. But I've come up with a way of surprising them all," with an ominous tone I started to mystify an already bewildered woman.

"And what is it?" Beth's whisper became even quieter.

"Look," I took out a piece of Marble, having first checked that it wanted to be a dark thing. "If you make something out of this piece of rock, the amount of evil in this world will increase. It wants to be evil. But you are a High Priestess! Can you do something to stop this stone being cursed?"

"And that's all?" Beth's eyes widened. "You want me to bless a piece of Marble? Whatever for? Do you intend to stone the monster with these?"

"Beth, do it first, and ask questions later," my plan was threatening to come apart at the seams. "Or is it impossible to change a cursed object?"

"Ah! You want to change its polarity? Yes, that's easy. I should have enough strength for a stone like this, but then I'll have to rest for about an hour. I am, after all, a former High Priestess. But how would that help you?"

"You'll see. The main thing is for you to do it."

Beth took the piece of Marble, closed her eyes, and a bright glow surrounded the cursed material. The woman's face grew pale and haggard, blue circles appearing under her eyes, but she unwaveringly continued to hold the item I had given her.

"Here you go," the priestess said in a weak voice, handing me the Marble. "I was wrong about the recovery time - an hour wouldn't do it. There's just too much darkness in it and I no longer have my strength. I will need three hours' rest or I'll simply keel over. But that can come later. What did you think up?"

I took the piece of Marble from her, which still looked exactly the same as those lying in my bag, and used the 'Essence of Things' ability on it. There was light, lots of light, joy and kindness - not a single hint of darkness. It had to work.

Taking a moment to concentrate, I entered the design mode, moved aside the prepped Dwarf Warriors, formed an image of the piece of Marble I was holding in my hand, opened the recipe for the Rose and embodied it in stone. An ordinary Stone Rose, which I had made many times. How could this become a blessed object? By itself it didn't seem enough. Without much ado, I placed the image of Anastaria in the central round petals of the Rose. Of everyone I knew, only she could fit the description of a 'Goddess'. The only thing I changed was removing the arrogance from her eyes and adding more gentle kindness instead. I didn't even realize how I did it. Then I slightly widened the face, making Anastaria a little more plump. Flicked her nose up just a little. Corrected the slits of her eyes. And... The result was not Aphrodite, the goddess of beauty, but a homely, warm and smiling woman, which you could meet in reality as well as in Barliona. Now the Rose seemed superfluous, so I removed it, leaving just the face. I gave it an oval background and chuckled in satisfaction: I was pleased with the result and I could only hope that I didn't make a mistake during the design process. With that thought I opened my eyes.

Item created: Blessed Visage of Eluna. (Neck-

chain detail). Description: all dark beings in the radius of 10 meters will get -20% to their stats; it is impossible to hide one's true face from Eluna; a sentient wearing this item cannot be cursed. +6 Faith, +6 Intellect. Item class: Rare.

+2 to Jewelcraft. Total: 25

Recipe created: 'Blessed Visage of Eluna'

You have received the title 'The Blessed Artificer'. Do you wish to replace 'The Cursed Artificer' title?

Your reputation with Goddess Eluna has increased by 100. Current level: Neutral. You are 900 points away from the status of Friendly. The reputation with Goddess Eluna cannot be increased on account of the 'First Kill' Achievement

You received Eluna's Blessing level 1: +5% to all the main stats. Duration: until you lose reputation with Goddess Eluna

After agreeing to the change in the Artificer title, I attached the crafted Visage to a Copper neck-chain and handed the completed item to Beth, who was watching my actions with huge, lemur-like eyes.

"Something like that," I tried my best not to give away the fact that I was experiencing a great desire to jump around the room for joy. Yes! I managed to create a holy object! It might have been useless to me because I had no Faith, but there were plenty of players leveling up in this stat who would pay good money for the Visage. Now I had to get Beth to make me as many blessed stones as possible.

"This..." the priestess said, stumblingly, as she began to come to herself, "This is the amulet of the junior novice! It's lacking a few more stats, but this is it! If I am a priestess, then..." Beth put the chain with the 'Rose' on herself and immediately the big dark circles under her eyes vanished and her face regained its natural color. A small whirlwind surrounded the priestess, messing up her hair, Beth closed her eyes in delight and a smile lit up her face. It was beautiful and kind, exactly what a smile of an NPC playing the role of the priestess of the high goddess should be like.

"The Goddess has received me back," Beth said in a satisfied voice, "She never turned away from me. How blind I was..."

Your reputation with priestesses of Goddess Eluna has increased by 1000 points. Current level: Friendly. You are 2990 points away from the status of Respect

"If we give all the villagers pendants like these, Beatwick would be saved," Beth continued. "I may not be the High Priestess, but even at the level of a junior novice I can do quite a lot. It will now take me thirty minutes, maybe less, to do one stone. I'll have to think of something to restore my strength faster. The Beatwick population is small, so we should manage this in a month. Give me all the cursed Marble you've got. I'll start on it right away."

I dumped around seventy pieces out of my bag, promising to get more, and left the priestess. I didn't mention that I hoped to hang on to the stones. No point in disappointing her right now. I had just over a month until I could leave Beatwick, so I had enough time to gather more.

The idea with the Visage made me think that it might be good to get on with making the dwarves. It's not like I had anything better to do. I went back to the summer house, took out the Lapis that Hellfire sent me, re-entered the design mode and got back to making the Warriors. Or, rather, the Masters. I corrected their gear where it didn't seem to fit too well and put the figurines next to a piece of Lapis. Strange. When I was making the Orc Warriors, the Malachite was several times larger than the figurines, which allowed me to make all eight pieces out of a single piece. Now, however, each dwarf filled up exactly one stone. Could this be linked to the fact that the dwarves are Masters? Who knows...

After I embodied the last Warrior in Lapis I opened my eyes. Barliona should now be welcoming a Legend reborn.

You have created an exact copy of the Dwarf Warriors from the Karmadont Chess Set. Resemblance: 100%. Item class: A copy
+2 to Jewelcraft. Total: 27

And that's it?!

I was staring in complete incomprehension at eight large fist-sized chess pieces. Something had broken, but I just couldn't understand what exactly it was. The Dwarves were here and looked exactly like those I needed to craft, but they were simply miles away from being the Legendary figurines... Had someone already made those? I didn't have any more Lapis, so I wasn't going to repeat the experiment. It had only been two hours since I began my work. I had to ask someone about this, but apart from Anastaria I didn't know anyone who could give me an answer. Asking her was simply not worth the pain, however. Never mind, I'll figure it out myself. I'll catch the monster and get to it.

In the six days that remained until the hunt for the mist beast, Beth and I managed to get a ton of work done. Each day she blessed around twenty pieces of Marble, which at the end of the day I made into the Visage of Eluna. My reputation with the goddess didn't increase: it would seem that only the first creation of the amulet had a positive influence on the Imitator playing the role of the goddess. But, despite this, I managed to do some decent leveling up in various professions: Jewelcraft went up to level 42, Intellect and Agility increased by 2, Mining and Cartography reached their next maximum. Now I could fly to Farstead and increase the level of my specialization. As soon as I reached level 45 in Mining, I went over to the smithy and, taking advantage of Slate's absence while he was travelling around the villages, spent two days mining Iron Ore. No point in it going to waste. During breaks between gathering resources and crafting amulets I leveled up my Smithing by smelting ingots. Although these too had to be given to Beth for 'whitening', it didn't really matter which materials you used to level up in a profession.

Finally the day of the mass hunt for the mist monster had come.

Six sentients, a rapid response force of sorts, gathered at the Headman's house to discuss the plan of the capture.

"We have to split into two groups, with three people in each," the Headman began once everyone took their places. "I propose the following: I and my sons will be in one group and Mahan, Tisha and Elizabeth in the other. We will start from the side of the gates and they from the side of the forest. We will move towards the village centre and one of us is bound to spot the beast. Any objections?"

"Yes," I added my two cents, "if we walk close together, the beast may take a fright and not attack. We have to separate and move at a distance of a hundred meters from each other. This way we'll both have time to aid each other and not frighten the beast off.

"I agree," Beth lent me her support, "if we split up we'll cover more ground. The monster won't have a chance to disappear."

"Agreed. Now we need to figure out how we'll be catching him."

"First of all we need to find out what it is," proposed Beth. "The beast is covered in a mist that prevents us from doing that, so Mahan and I have prepared these things," the priestess took four Roses of Eluna from her pocket and put them on the table. "If the monster comes into the area affected by the amulet, the mist will dissipate."

As soon as they realized what was lying on the table, all of the Headman's family backed off against the wall. No wonder - they were Vagrens. In the amulet's area of effect they would turn into pooches.

"The amulets should only be worn in the evening, so that no-one in the village will see you in your original guise," explained Beth upon seeing the Vagrens' reactions. "We won't get far without these, so you'll have to come to terms with using them."

"All right, we'll put them on," the Headman submitted to the inevitable. "I have an immediate suggestion for how these amulets should be used."

"And what is it?" asked Tisha, still sticking close to the door.

"They only affect the beast at close range. If any of you run across the monster, try to put the amulet on it. It wouldn't be able to take off the holy object, will end up with many penalties and will become more vulnerable."

"A great idea!" Beth exclaimed. "That's how we'll do it! We still have an hour until it's time, so let's decide on how we'll capture the monster."

"The beast is a lot higher than level 100," I put in. "I once caught it in a level 100 Bone Trap, but it barely took any notice of it. We need something more powerful to hunt it down."

"Over 100 levels?" the Headman looked thoughtful. "This isn't very good news. All right, we'll think of something." He got up and left the room. While

Beth's gaze followed him out, Tisha came up to the table and took her amulet. As soon as she picked it up, as small cloud enveloped the girl and, after it dissipated, there was a Vagren standing next to us. Or a Vagrenette, even.

"What do you think?" barked Tisha, giving a hoarse laugh. Her low chesty voice was very unlike the bubbling stream of the girl's speech in her human guise.

"An ordinary Vagren," I shrugged. "One head, four paws, one tail. I can't be sure, but since you're not scratching yourself, you have no fleas."

"Vagrens don't get fleas, Mahan," replied the Headman who was back in the room. "Here you go. Try not to waste it - I only have six of them left. One each exactly."

I looked at the scroll handed to me by the Headman. Ice Prison spell, level 300. This was strong enough even for Anastaria. Smashing the trap from within requires the trapped person to be at least 40 levels higher. Of course, it is possible to smash it open even if the difference is just one level, but it would take a very long time. It would be easier to wait for the 12-hour ban on imprisoning a character to kick in. Barliona has the following rule: you can't imprison a player for more than twelve hours. Once this time had elapsed, the player is forcefully teleported to the closest safe zone and was given a 12-hour buff banning any PK activity against him. Neither he nor other players are able to do anything about that. Twelve hours later the buff expires and you can continue to make the other player's life hell.

With the trap offered by the Headman the night monster was sure to be captured. It took him a few seconds to smash a 100-level trap, so it looks like he's probably around level 130. A 300-level trap is a huge overcompensation. Our Headman has turned out to be quite resourceful.

"The trap lasts for a week, so we'll have time to load it on a cart and take it to Farstead. Let the High Mage figure out what kind of a creature this is," added the village leader.

Having settled our plans we took our positions. The night had fully descended.

"Mahan, do you think we'll get it this time?" Tisha's eyes were burning with the thrill of the hunt. "I'm practically shaking with tension. When I imagine catching the beast, my paws clench so eager I am to strangle the vile thing. It caused us so many troubles in the past two years, I've lost count by now."

"It won't get away from us this time. Let's get going - the beast usually appears around this time."

"Let's go Tisha," Beth pulled the Vagren after her. Tisha stood there for a moment, then slid away and ran up to me, licking me on the cheek: "For luck" Then she turned sharply and, running on all fours, disappeared into the night. She was fast, but I still managed to look into her properties: 'Attractiveness: 83 points.' I have a feeling that whatever the result of tonight's hunt, I can expect a very interesting week. Especially during night-time.

"These youngsters. A dog, but still flirting away

like the best of them," sighed Beth and went to her position, leaving me alone.

Exactly ten minutes later, as we agreed, I began to move towards the square.

"YOU'RE PERSISTENT!" the voice behind me made me jump, "DO YOU REALLY LIKE MY TOUCH THAT MUCH? MASTER IS VERY PLEASED WITH YOU. YOU'VE GIVEN HIM MANY NEW FIGHTERS FOR HIS ARMY, ESPECIALLY THE YOUNG ONES - THERE IS MUCH YOU CAN TEACH THEM. I WAS ORDERED TO KILL YOU WITHOUT PAIN."

So the bastard showed up - right on time too. I quickly turned and looked into the huge red eyes of the beast. What the heck are you? We had over ten meters between us, so the amulet didn't affect it.

"Ordered to kill me without pain? Great, here you go then," I grabbed the amulet and ran at the beast. Even if it destroys me, I'll see who this is. "It's here!" I shouted at the top of my lungs. "Everyone come to my voice!"

I needed a couple of seconds to cover ten meters. Next to nothing, you might think, but it was enough for the beast. Instead of jumping at me, it jumped about ten meters away, turned around and sped off towards the square. Run all you like, you're expected there too.

"It's running towards the square! Look out!" without slowing from my first dash, I ran after the beast. The distance between us steadily increased, despite the fact that I was giving it all I had. I was clearly lacking in the Agility department - something to remedy later on. Perhaps I should start jogging every day...

I turned into the neighboring street as I followed the monster and practically ran into someone I didn't expect to see at all on a dark night. It was Slate, in the flesh. Where did he come from?

"Mahan? What's with all the screaming? You're scaring the village and not letting people sleep. Did something happen?"

"I... What are you doing here? Didn't you go to fix things around the villages?" I was really getting confused now. What was Slate doing out here? Even if he did return, he's an NPC and should be asleep during the night! 'Nighty-night, sleep tight and don't the bedbugs bite' and all that.

"I just returned. I heard you yelling about someone running towards the square. That's why I ran all the way here."

"Mahan, what happened?" Tisha ran up to us. "Did you see the mist beast?"

"Who?" asked the smith, but I had already realized something. I remembered the first seconds after I had crashed into Slate. The same cloud had began to form around him as around Tisha when she picked up the amulet. The Rose of Eluna allowed you to see someone's true nature. Slate wasn't human.

"It doesn't matter," Tisha waved him aside and gave me her paw. And suddenly it all clicked in my head. The smith wasn't screaming his head off in terror that such a scary beast was standing right in front of him: which means it's not the first time he's seen a Vagren. But Tisha...

"Oh, Slate, you..." the girl growled, lowering her head.

"Tisha, what are you doing here?" the smith began to ask, but I chose this moment to act: I was already on the go, so with one small jump I threw the Rose of Eluna on Slate. Let's see if I was mistaken.

"Mahan, don't!" Tisha started to say, when mist started to swirl around Slate. In a couple of seconds it dissipated revealing a two-meter-high bear.

"MAHAN! NO!" this werebear managed to roar as I threw the trap under its feet. We've got you now, my pretty!

"Stop!" now it was Tisha's turn to growl in anger. Why? Didn't she see how he had transformed? "Mahan, open the trap!"

"Tisha, is everything all right with you? This is the mist beast! You've seen him yourself!"

"He's no monster!"

"Yeah, right, he's a kind and gentle two-meter teddy bear with huge fangs and claws!"

"Mahan!"

"Tisha, stop destroying my brain. We'd better go to the square and tell the others... Tisha, no!"

The girl took out her own trap and threw it under my feet. There was no way to dodge it, so time stopped for me.

"Mahan - don't make any sudden moves, or you might get hurt as well," I heard Tisha's voice almost immediately. For me, a player in a prison capsule, the time in the trap flew by unnoticed. Whether just a minute went by or if it was almost morning by now remained a mystery. An enormous bear was lying next to me, with one paw twisted at an unnatural angle. It was probably broken.

"Mahan, let me introduce Slate to you, a member of the Werebeast race. And... he's my future husband, so I trust him like myself. He cannot be the mist beast. I'm sorry I threw the trap at you, but you left me no choice."

"MAHAN," the roar of the werebear would have made my blood freeze, if I had any to speak of. "BELIEVE HER."

"I...

"Help!" the Beatwick night was pierced by Beth's scream. "Mahan! It's here!"

"Stay here," I shouted to Tisha, "Look after him! We'll figure out who's who later!"

Beth's shout came from the direction of the forest, where our hunt had begun. Tomorrow morning I'll find Slate and, ignoring the fact that he's much bigger and stronger than me, punch in his face or, in his case, his insolent bear muzzle, and he can go...

Beth's lifeless body lying by the stockade stopped me in my tracks. Anything but this! I immediately selected her and sighed in relief: she had ten Hit Points remaining. Out of... She was level 250! Who would beat a High Priestess with that many levels? I entered the Spirit summoning mode and started to send Healing Spirits on Beth. Ten Hit Points, twenty, fifty... It took me sixty seven Spirits to get her Hit Points back to maximum. And that was despite me having a crazy amount of Intellect! I somehow wasn't all that keen on running across the mist beast again. As if reading my mind the source of the peculiar smell appeared next to me. The monster had come for its prey.

The great red eyes of the beast stared at me. The swirls of mist receded a little and I once again saw the cause of my recent troubles: enormous black claws. Did that mean that today I was looking at yet another respawn? I've really had it with this bastard! What the heck are you doing in a location for 20-level players? I gripped the Tambourine and the Mallet, and naively thinking that even if I didn't manage to beat it, I'd at least heal myself, I backed off in small steps. The fence! Now it really was the end!

One had to give it to this piece of incomprehensible shit - in all our encounters it had shown considerable mastery in choosing the method for sending me for respawn. It was either the claws, or poison, or strangling. It hadn't repeated itself once, the inventive scumbag!

"Fluffy, take it down!" a melodious voice rang in the silence that surrounded us. Mist once again spread around the beast and the silhouette of a great tiger rushed past me. There was a subdued growl and the tiger crashed into the mist. Fluffy? I lifted my eyes and saw a girl right in front of me, standing on the stockade. A player! She jumped down and walked a few paces forward, leaving me behind her. An exemplary righteous defender of the presumably innocent, dammit.

"Some 'nooberhood' you have here. What the

heck is this?" she turned around to me, lifting an eyebrow in question.

"The mist obstructs the properties, so I really have no idea what sort of a mob this is," I replied, getting my breath back. She was a 93-level elf, Mirida the Farsighted. Her face looked terribly familiar, but I just couldn't remember where I've seen her before! Could our paths have crossed when I was playing my Hunter? All right, we can leave all that for later, right now we had to solve the problem at hand. "Careful! That beast can one-shot you in a flash!"

Mirida chuckled, but then grew serious when she saw the Life Bar of her pet. The tiger kept disappearing and reappearing in the mist, flicking its tail, but its Hit Points were falling with a frightening speed.

"Fluffy - armor, heal, dodge!" the elf quickly commanded and started sending arrow after arrow into the mist. For a moment I forgot about the fight and stared at the girl. Today seemed to be the day for revelations! I was looking at a high-level Beastmaster in person! To rear a pet like Fluffy you had to possess simply angelic patience - I only managed to level mine up to 20 and then gave up on this tedious business. It just took up too much gametime to feed, train, walk and rear a decent pet, so many players prefer not to make an effort with a virtual friend. Only now, when I had Draco and seven and a half years of prepaid gametime was I eager to focus on leveling him up. In this case Fluffy had even more levels than his mistress - a triple command is possible only for a level 100 pet.

That was some killing machine: a tank, a healer and an excellent fighter. With support from arrows he had an excellent chance to last until the morning when the beast would disappear.

I didn't believe for a minute that Mirida could win this one. I had gotten to know our misty opponent far too well in the recent weeks.

"Mahan!" Beth's weak groan came like a breath of fresh air. She's alive! That was the main thing! "The beast is here!"

"Don't worry, I'm on it. How do you feel."

"I'll live. Help me up. Who's this?" she pointed to Mirida, who was biting her lips in the face of her own helplessness. The beast was winning the fight with Fluffy on all fronts. If she didn't let the pet go now he was guaranteed to lose ten levels. Mirida knew this full well, so when Fluffy's Hit Points approached zero she dismissed him. The mist monster swung around itself a few more seconds, not quite believing the enemy was gone, and then once again turned to the three of us.

"What in the hells is this thing?!" shouted Mirida, still sending arrow after arrow into the mist.

"I told you, I have no idea. It has 250 levels in it!"

"THREE HUNDRED!" came a mocking voice from the beast as it lunged towards us.

"In the name of Eluna! Let there be light!" as the beast rushed towards us, Beth shouted and lifted her arms. A dome of bright light formed around us into which the monster crashed, becoming stuck as a fly in a web. "Grant us light, oh Great Mother..."

Beth began to call on Eluna to give her strength, hallow the earth and banish darkness and then switched from the common tongue to some other and I decided not to lose any time. The dome didn't destroy the monster's mist, its function was strictly defensive, but while the mist beast hung there an excellent idea popped into my head. I jumped to the monster, took a swing and smacked the Rose of Eluna straight into its forehead.

Maybe I really shouldn't have done that...

The wild roar of the beast was probably heard as far as Farstead. I was landed with a bunch of minute-long debuffs: 'Stun', 'Dumbness', 'Immobilization' and a couple more brief ones, which vanished as I was examining the others. Judging by Mirida's downcast expression she was hit by the same stuff. With a wild jolt the beast tore itself out of the dome of light and jumped over the fence. Where the heck do you think you're going? Hold it right there! I didn't manage to take a look at its properties, so now I was kicking myself for being such a slow coach.

"Quick, after it!" I started to hurry the two ladies as soon as the debuffs expired. "Beth, the secret passage that you were using must be near here somewhere. Open it! Mirida, summon Fluffy, I'll heal him. Come on, hurry. It'll get away from us!"

"Mahan! It's a Sklic! Are you crazy?" Mirida's panicked voice made me freeze. A Sklic!

"Beth - the passage!" I continued to issue commands as I fought off the panic that now gripped me head to toe. "Now! A Sklic isn't as black as he's painted! He's got an amulet of Eluna on him - we could catch him and have a chat. Beth! You have a 300-level trap, just for him. Quick!"

+1 to Charisma. Total: 7

"Yes, just a moment," hurried the priestess and I tried to remember all I knew about Sklics. Just my luck to get landed with one of these!

Malabar players really liked to go on Raids into Kartoss and attack its castles. Once a group of a hundred players made it as far as the Nameless City, the capital of Kartoss, home to the Dark Lord with his Masters and Magisters. A Master is an equivalent of a Malabar Adviser and a Magister of a Herald. The raid group laid siege to the castle and then all twenty Magisters of Kartoss joined the battle. They could teleport to any point within the borders of their own Empire, so they appeared at the attackers' rear. But they didn't come alone - they brought their pets with them, the Sklics. The 300-level beasts demolished the raid group in less than a couple of minutes, leaving no chance of escape. After this there was a wave of discontent from the players and the Corporation created the Dungeon of Fear, where the main Boss was an equivalent of a Magister with his Sklic. As usual, the Phoenix players were the first to complete that Dungeon. About a year after it had been launched. The Magister-Sklic team was very strong.

By itself a Sklic is an enormous octopus that can take on any shape. It has an insane number of abilities, a very advanced Imitator and an impressive ability to learn. The Dungeon of Fear's design was special - the level of the boss was never higher than three levels above the highest-level player in the raid, so even level 10 players could try to complete it. What can I say? I tried it myself, so know of the Sklic's strength first hand.

But what worried me even more now was the fact that a Sklic never travelled alone. It couldn't depart from its master's side for more than a few kilometers and this meant that we had a Kartoss Magister based in Beatwick.

"Done," shouted Beth, pointing to the passage. "The beast is heading towards the temple."

"How do you know?" I asked, although I could already see the answer plain enough. Dark blood, probably dripping from the injured head left burning spots on the ground: a pretty flaming path that lead towards the temple.

"Let's group up. Beth, Mirida - accept my invite! Let's go after it!" Once the girls had joined the group we dashed towards the temple.

"It went inside! After it!"

"Why in such a hurry, my children?" as soon as we ran into the temple, the priest of Vlast appeared from behind the altar. The priest's sleeves were rolled up high, showing arms that were currently covered up to the elbow in dark blood, dripping on the floor. He had probably tried to take off the amulet.

"Father..." Beth said in a subdued hoarse voice and fell on the floor. Judging by the frames, she was under the 'Petrify' debuff.

"Mahan, I'm coming!" Tisha flew into the temple, saw Beth and froze, shifting a confused gaze from the priestess to the follower of Vlast. Though some follower he was... Judging from the fact that I was looking at a 400-level NPC, this was a Kartoss Magister in person.

"And that is that," mumbled the priest, satisfied. "I was not permitted to fight a priestess of Eluna outside the temple - it would have caused such a magical din that all the Heralds would have dropped in to join us. But inside the temple I make the rules! Thank you again, Mahan. Once more you've made me a present," a chesty and gloating laugh of the Magister echoed through the building.

"But you are the one who sent me to hunt the monster," I half-whispered, almost dumbstruck, but the Magister heard me.

"So I did. You had to find the Vagren and hand it over to me. That was the point of my assignment. When you covered for Tisha I was incensed! I wanted to tear you apart with my own hands instead of using the Sklic! But I restrained myself and was rewarded! Beatwick is finished. All of Malabar is finished! Kartoss will have victory!"

"Mahan, can you explain to me how a Magister ended up this far away from Kartoss? Are the Heralds completely blind?" Mirida's words snapped me out of it, returning my brain to a functional state. When we get out of here, I owe you a drink, elf gal.

"Heralds?" the Magister laughed. "There is a ziggurat active here, my pretty. Right under this building. Not a single Herald can see what's happening here."

"You are mistaken, 'holy father'," now it was my turn to enjoy myself. "I call upon Heralds: I need your help. Preferably of at least two of you," I added, when I saw the Magister start.

There were two portal claps and two Heralds appeared in the temple.

"You called us and we came. If you... Attack!"

The quest 'Night Terror of the Village' has been completed

Lightning began to flash through the temple. Who's the stronger - a 400-level Magister on cursed ground or two 400-level Heralds on their territory? I guess we're about to find out. One of the Heralds covered us with a dome, so neither the ladies nor I had much to worry about. We could just sit back and watch the fireworks.

Ball Lightning, Cleansing Light, Suffering Darkness, Cursed Mist - the most terrible spells available in the game were being flung about. If not for the Herald's dome our game avatars would've been blown to bits. The temple interior went up in flames, stone began to melt and then the battle was over: the Heralds turned out to be stronger. At some point the Sklic flew out from behind the altar and entered the fight. However, I noted that my amulet was still shining on its head. The Heralds barely took any notice of the Sklic: a few spells and the mist beast left Beatwick for good. That's one down.

Another minute and the Magister found himself bound. The two Heralds, breathing heavily, sat on the ground and started to drink something. They were probably restoring their Hit Points and Mana. The fight with the Magister had been no pushover for them.

"Mahan, I thank you on behalf of the Emperor. Now we know who coordinated all the works..."

"MASTER!" came a wild scream from the false priest of Vlast. "MASTER, I BEG YOU FOR HELP!"

"Master? One of the four Advisers of the Dark Emperor?" I managed to ask before both Heralds froze with glassy eyes and someone entered the temple at a leisurely pace. I turned around and my jaw dropped.

'Search for the Dark Coordinator' quest completed

"I would've never thought that such a magnificent plan could fall through on account of a 20-level free citizen. Hello once again, Mahan."

Mirida looked at me in complete incomprehension and I let the extent to which I had been a total dumbass sink in. How could I not have guessed this from the start? Everything was so damn obvious!

CHAPTER TWELVE
THE FINALE

"T HAT IS SOME PLACE I'VE LANDED IN," whispered Mirida. "A 20-30 level backwater - as if! A Magister with a Sklic, a Master... It's like the Dark Lord himself might turn up any moment!"

The smiling Master was standing in the entrance of the temple, one hand raised in the direction of the Heralds. A ray of light was coming out of it, forming a sphere around them and, by the looks of it, taking them out of action. I looked up the Master's level. Finally! He was no longer 1*N, which was all I could see before, but level 450, as is appropriate for Masters and Advisors. I looked once again at the identity of the newcomer and found that I was kicking myself very hard. What a complete dolt I've been!

"Yes, dear lady, things are interesting around here. And they're set to get even more interesting in the near future. Our Lord had spent a long time preparing for the invasion and it is finally underway."

"What's the point of invading a village this far from Anhurs, and from Kartoss too, if it came to it?" Mirida just had to know. "From the point of view of common sense this is stupid."

"Why do you say that? Really, just think about it. And while you're occupied with that, with your permission, I'll get some work done in the meantime," the Master came up to the Magister, released him from his bonds and started to utter some kind of a spell. While he was thus occupied, I fitfully began summoning the Heralds. It's time they got their act together.

"Don't trouble yourself, Mahan," the Master briefly turned to me. "Before coming here I covered the temple with a dome. The Heralds can hear your summons, but they don't know where to aim the portal." An amulet vibrated on the Master's chest. "Speaking! Continue to observe! These Heralds are so predictable. Since they can't figure out where to jump, thanks to the ziggurat, they've started jostling near the fog. Like little children, honestly. Now you'll excuse me for a moment and then we'll continue our conversation."

A shimmering veil appeared in the temple entrance and then the Master turned around and continued with his incantation. The Magister, limping, disappeared behind the altar. That was probably the location of the local basement entrance. I glanced over the battle-worn group of Sklic hunters. Beth was lying on the floor - her 'Petrify' buff would last another 15 minutes. Mirida was motionless, but it was clear from her glassy eyes that she had exited full immersion and was now vigorously reading the forums. Or perhaps writing in them about the current situation. I envied her. The last member of our wipe-group, Tisha, was lying next to Beth with a 20-minute 'Stun' debuff. Strange, I just didn't remember her being frozen. Never mind, we'll put it down to the Master.

So the Heralds don't know where to jump because they can't find an anchor point? That's bad. Very bad. Are they incapable of knocking two brain cells together and teleporting straight to Beatwick? Daft NPCs!

"Mahan, am I correct in thinking that we're done for? Let's at least get to know each other a little. I'll tell you why I'm here," Mirida began to speak, but I rudely interrupted her.

"Wait! We'll get to that later!" I took out Anastaria's communication amulet and had to exert considerable willpower to avoid crushing it to pieces as I pressed the call button. Well, Stacey, pick it up!

"Speaking!" The girl's tired voice was music to my ears. Stacey dear, I love you!

"Anastaria, this is Mahan! Summon a Herald, quick! It's a matter of life and death!" I screamed into the amulet.

"Mahan, did you hit your head or something?"

"Stacey, on the double! Trust me!"

"Shaman, have you completely lost it? As if getting me stuck in the middle of nowhere wasn't enough, you want to land me in the Heralds' bad books as well?"

"Stacey, I am begging you: summon a Herald. Just trust me."

The Master took no notice of my screaming and Anastaria fell silent. An eternity seemed to go by before a reply came from the amulet:

"I call upon a Herald, I require your assistance. Mahan... You owe me. Remember this!"

"You called me and I came. If your summons was a false one, Anastaria, you will be punished. Speak."

"Herald, this is Mahan. At this moment the temple of Vlast near Beatwick contains a Magister and a Master of Kartoss, as well as two stunned Heralds. The temple is covered by a dome that prevents you from being summoned, use the village to find your bearings!" the Heralds probably would've heard my frantic screaming even without an amulet. I cared little that the Master could hear me too - he was as good as done for. Any moment now the Heralds would turn up and clean up this mess. Two against eighteen don't stand a chance in hell.

"We read you loud and clear. Thank you Mahan! Hold out for an hour. We can't open a direct portal to Beatwick, so we'll create a network of portals. We need an hour! Hold on! Anastaria," he now addressed the girl, "on behalf of the Emperor I thank you for your help. No matter how this ends, you will be rewarded."

There came a clap of the portal, as the Herald flew off on his various errands, and then it was only Anastaria's heavy breathing coming from the amulet.

"I think my debt is paid. When the time comes for the bonuses to be handed out, I will ask the Emperor for your reward to be a good one. Anyway, I have to go. Thanks," with these words I turned off the amulet. I felt that the situation called for a flamboyant remark of some kind.

"So you managed to get through after all," as soon I turned off the communicator, I saw that the Master observing me with some interest. "Bravo, Mahan, bravo! Geranika was right, you really do have a certain something."

I was about to give a rather pointed response, when an announcement appeared before my eyes.

Citizens of Malabar!

Our lands have been invaded by the forces of the Dark Empire! I ask all the heroes who have proved their valor to come to Malabar's aid. Summon a Herald and follow him to the gathering point. I forbid fighting between free citizens during the invasion - now is the time to unite and act as one

I would like to express my gratitude to free citizen of the Empire, Shaman Mahan, thanks to whom the Kartoss plot has been exposed

Hurry, the time for summoning a Herald has begun

The Emperor.

Conditions for taking part in the continental scenario: character level of at least 280, positive reputation with the Malabar Emperor

Scenario description: PVP mode has been disabled for 24 hours throughout the Empire. Participants in the event will receive + 200 to their reputation with the Malabar Emperor
Your reputation with the Shaman Council has increased by 200 points. You are 700 points away from the status of Friendly

The last part was for my eyes only, by the looks of it.

"So, it looks like I have an hour," said the Master, looking pleased. "That's even more than I expected. Now you can drag out the time all you like - everything is ready for us to receive the guests. Thank you for reminding me about the amulets used by the free citizens. To stop you warning anyone that this is a trap, I should block them too."

My eyes met Mirida's. Judging by her raised eyebrows, she managed to return to the game, had read the announcement and was now giving me a long appraising look.

"Level twenty one, eh?" It was more of a statement than a question. "And already neck-deep in the thick of it."

"I, too, was at first surprised by this," quite unceremoniously the Master slid into our conversation. "I have to admit that I had expected a higher-level envoy from the Emperor, so right at the start I made an inexcusable mistake, which could have spoilt all my plans. I was relieved that Mahan didn't take any notice of it."

I was all set to defend myself, pointing out lack of information, but was visited by an ingenious idea. It was so good that I practically beamed with happiness. The Master narrowed his eyes, somewhat puzzled, and tilted his head.

"Why the sudden look of joy, my good fellow?" he finally enquired. "Have you really found a way to spoil my plans?"

"Of course, Master," I had to put my cards on the table. As soon as I did anything, the Master could simply freeze me and my plan would fail. I had to play on his curiosity. "If you give me your word that you won't try to hinder me, in about thirty seconds your plan will fold in a most spectacular fashion."

At first the Master lifted his eyebrows, as if in great surprise, then looked around the temple, weighing up the strength of the veil at the entrance, thought about it a moment and started to laugh.

"Ha ha ha! Do you really think that you would be able to destroy me in thirty seconds? Even if all four of you tried anything together you would fail."

"What are you on about? Do you think I'm so crazy that I'd attack someone twenty times my level? No, your Lord's plan has a certain flaw, which means that I'll need only thirty seconds to disrupt it."

"The Lord's plan is perfect. It was put together by four Masters and no room was left for mistakes. We planned for everything. You're bluffing, Mahan. Your attempt at a delay has failed."

"Master, let's make a bet," I was ready for anything at this point. It's not like I had anything to lose. "Don't touch me for thirty seconds and I spoil all your plans. Without ever moving from this spot. If I win, the Dark Empire owes me one wish. If I lose... You'll think of something - you're smart enough."

"You are able to spoil our plans in thirty seconds without moving from this spot?" The Master made for quite an interesting sight. He was almost laughing, but was just able to restrain himself in some unfathomable way. "All right! On behalf of Kartoss, I Master Naahti, agree to your conditions! If you manage to spoil our plans, the Kartoss Empire will be obliged to carry out any wish you may have. I repeat - any - which is within our power. Including having the Dark Lord sing you a lullaby. But it comes with a limitation - the wish must only be connected to yourself. No world peace, end to all hatred or other social foolishness. But if you fail, you will work as a servant in the Lord's fortress. You will be teleported to our capital and end up serving food. To everyone! For a year, without any increase in levels or reputation! Agreed?" the grinning Master was looking down on me, convinced that he had presented me with conditions that couldn't be met. NPCs have become rather naive these days.

"Agreed," I was, of course, taking a great risk, but my intuition, may it be damned, told me that the plan should work.

"You have thirty seconds, future slave."

You have concluded an agreement with the Kartoss Empire. Conditions:...

"Mahan, what are you doing?" shouted Mirida, "I haven't spent all this time looking for you to see you destroy all my efforts!"

Looking for me? Why? Never mind, this can wait.

"I call upon a Herald. I need the aid of an Advisor," at this phrase the Master laughed. To be more exact: he cracked up.

"Didn't I tell you that the temple is surrounded by a dome! Ha ha ha! The Heralds can't lock on here to open a portal! Especially one for an Advisor! Welcome, new slave of the Lord!"

"Master, we've known each other for quite a while now," I returned the Master's smile, "How could you think so little of me?" I opened my bag and took out the Emperor's ring, put it on and once again looked at the Kartoss official. Just as well I hadn't given the ring away to Beth!

"I call upon a Herald. I need the aid of an Advisor. Target destination - the Emperor's ring!"

The Master froze. There was such surprise in his eyes that I even missed the moment when the portal opened and a sentient wearing a white robe stepped out of it. The Kartoss representative came to himself, made a fast hand movement and the portal exploded with a great bang. A wave of destruction went through the temple, sending cracks through the walls, but a dome appeared around all those present. The Advisor cast it on me and the ladies and the Master put up a defense of his own. Although it's not like some explosion would do him much harm.

"Advisor," the Master uttered in a hissing growl.

"You cannot stop the invasion! You are too late!"

"I too am glad to see you," the Advisor answered in a chesty voice accompanied by thundering music, "FATHER."

The conditions of the agreement with the Dark Empire of Kartoss have been met. You have a right to one wish. In order to claim your wish, summon Master Naahti

"People, can someone explain to me what the heck is going on here? There's every chance that I'll die anyway, but this way I'll at least this way I'll learn something."

"Will you tell them, father?"

"Do not dare call me that," the poison in Naahti's voice could have easily killed, had the Advisor been an ordinary NPC.

"All right, if you won't tell, then I'll try to guess," smiled the Advisor. "Would you mind first releasing the Heralds? I really don't want to start a fight. Whichever way you turn it, you're still my father. I suggest you surrender to the mercy of the Emperor and wait to be ransomed by your Lord. No? Fine. Then I'll begin," the Advisor walked around the frozen Heralds, touched the barrier blocking the exit from the temple, chuckled at the building's exquisite beauty and then turned to us.

"I won't be telling you about myself. That is a separate tale. I would only note that I didn't share my father's attitude to Malabar - I like peace and harmony and so decided to go over to the other side. Now, about the current situation. Two years ago this woman's husband," the Advisor pointed to Beth, "who was exiled here, disappeared under mysterious circumstances. A few months before that a priest of Vlast came to Beatwick and offered to build a temple. The previous Headman knew that the village was in need of protection and gladly agreed, especially since the building was to be located outside the village. Then the Headman disappeared. Not died, but disappeared. The Master of Kartoss probably knows that all the citizens of Malabar that hold a position of importance are imprinted with a special mark, which informs the Heralds whether this sentient is being controlled and whether he's alive or not. The former headman is still alive, but it was decided not to look for him. The Emperor's decree was never recalled. A new headman was appointed to Beatwick from Farstead, the nearest town. He was a representative of an industrial association. He didn't have a mark on him, so I may surmise that he is no longer in this world. From here on I'll be guessing, so you can correct me. The Magister intercepted this industrialist on the road, where they had an interesting chat, following which Beatwick received its new Headman – who also happened to be a Kartoss Master. The residents accepted him and the Herald received a message that a new person was in charge of Beatwick. In the first few months father didn't do much, making an effort to win everyone over. You can ask any villager and he'll tell you that the Beatwick Headman is the best and most conscientious man in the world. Having secured his position, the infiltrator put his plan into action. First he founded the castle which Mahan managed to find. As an aside, I should say that that castle will soon meet its end - in just a few minutes' time it will cease to exist. After the castle father began to curse the land, putting a Corrupter in each village. Heralds get very nervous when a thing like that is placed on their territory, so it was hidden by a ziggurat. The Heralds knew that a Corrupter had been built on the territory of the Empire, but couldn't find where exactly. Nice move - this one took some creative thinking. Kartoss's aim is as yet unclear, but I can suppose that some clue to an artifact hidden in these lands had been unearthed in some archive, which explains the goblin search parties. It's all finished, father. The time has come to answer for your deeds."

The longer the Advisor had been speaking, the more pleased Naahti's expression was becoming. By the end of the speech he was smiling quite openly. I was just about to stop the talkative NPC, when a message popped up in front of me:

Change in the status of the agreement with the Kartoss Dark Empire. You were unable to hinder the Kartoss plans. In view of the previous status, the agreement is considered void

"Such a pity," said the former Headman-turned-Master slowly. "I would've liked to have a slave like that. Mahan, would you like to make another bet, perhaps? The same conditions, but this time you'll have a day. A day to hinder our plans: What do you say?" The Master was having fun. I didn't really understand what just happened, but it was certainly something very unpleasant.

"Father, you've lost!"

"Foolish little Advisor. You might have stopped me if you had started to act straight away. But no, you decided to have a chat first, to relish your victory and present your point of view. That is the difference between the Dark Empire and you. You are weak! You slavishly follow the rules and never see past your own nose. The army of Malabar should appear before the village gates very soon. Enjoy the spectacle!"

With these words the walls of the temple disappeared - in the sense that the building rose about ten meters above ground and was then flung outwards in the direction of the forest. In place of the walls there remained several vertical spikes about two meters in height.

"Allow me not to pull them out completely, this would take great deal of energy, SON," the Headman sneered at the Advisor, who turned pale. "I think you know what these are."

"The Corrupters?" I intruded on their conversation. "There were similar spikes on the Corrupter that I saw by the castle."

The Advisor grew even paler, impossible though it seemed.

"Father!" Tisha, now awake, was getting up from the ground. "The priest of Vlast is not who he claims to be. He... Brother?"

"Leave him be" the Headman came up to his

daughter and straightened out the cloak on her shoulders. "Your exiled brother has other things on his mind right now."

"Naahti, a couple of days ago you said that you would give me your aid should I need it. So - I need it now. Can you explain what's going on? I've heard the Advisor's version of events, now I'd like to hear the truth."

"Why not? All the preparations have been made and now it's time for the interesting part. Nothing really depends on us anymore, so I can give you a couple of minutes. For starters, let us strengthen the Kartoss influence," the Headman said, satisfied, and indicated the Heralds to his other two sons. The Advisor could only helplessly close his eyes - he equaled the Master in strength, but could do nothing for the Heralds. Any defense would be immediately removed by the Master. Two silent Vagrens slid towards the Heralds with lightning speed... and then Malabar had two new vacancies for this position.

"Nooo!" came Tisha's scream, as her brothers carried out the order. "Father, why? Why?"

"You made your children into your assistants," whispered the downcast Advisor. "You have gone too far..."

"What would I do without them? Tisha, calm down!"

The Master waved his hand and a small chair appeared next to each of those present.

"Beth, get up. It's stupid and uncomfortable to keep pretending you're still petrified. The ground is cold. You'll catch a chill and deprive me of the pleasure of personally crushing you."

"Father, why are you saying this?" Tisha began to cry. "What are you doing? This is Beth!"

The Headman shook his head as if so show what a handful children are these days.

"Sit down and listen to me. You can scream all you like later. SIT DOWN, I SAID!" the thundering shout made everyone sit down, even the Advisor. Now we were looking at the real Master of Kartoss, without any masks or pleasantries. "EVERYONE READY?! Then I shall begin," he then returned to his previous tone.

"The Malabar and Kartoss Empires have existed for a long time. They maintained constant armed neutrality: we took turns in attacking each other, but no-one tried too hard. It was just a couple of villages going over to one side of the border or to the other - everyone was happy with such a status quo. But fifteen years ago free citizens appeared in the world. They wanted something more than just raids to grab some loot. Instead of coming and quickly taking an object that caught their eye, the free citizens engaged in genocide. How is it the fault of goblins that they were born green? Or trolls? How is it a little warg's fault that he needs meat to survive? But no, the free citizens decided that we were 'dark' and started to kill us off. I visited the castles that had gone through the hands of free citizens. Everyone was killed. Even the little werebeasts that hadn't even been weaned yet. Why? We tried communicating with the Emperor, but boys like this one," a nod in the direction of the Advisor, "dismissed our complaints. What do you say, 'light one'?" the Headman's last words were full of so much hatred that his son started.

"Us... Them... There are always casualties during a war, father."

"There can be casualties on the battlefield, but before they can become casualties, they have to be strong and able to fight back. If the casualty is a child, irrespective of the skin color, it is no war casualty. And for this you betrayed our family? Because you enjoy watching children suffer?"

"No! I left because of Kartoss's monstrous ways. You are a horror!"

"Emotions without any facts. That pretty much sums up Malabar. We decided to respond. Ten years ago we began to develop a plan. I personally acted as its initiator and main overseer. Malabar will pay for its crimes. With each raid by the free citizens our numbers dwindle, so we decided to use one interesting invention: Inverters. One of our leading mages thought of a way to furnish a Corrupter with additional powers. Aside from cursing the land, an Inverter changes all the inhabitants within its field of action. Just thirty minutes under its rays and they turn into Kartoss minions. An ordinary villager - into a goblin. A guard into a troll. A warrior into a berserker. Everyone is changed. I had to seriously dampen the effects of the Inverter to stop the residents of Beatwick and nearby villagers from transforming before it was time. Each week my sons travelled between villages to block the action of the artifact. But even they had one day off, thanks to Elizabeth, who heroically decided to protect her village. On those days we had some fun. And now the most interesting part: can you guess who was the mage that invented the Inverter?"

"Him?" I nodded towards the Advisor. If you followed the Master's logic the conclusion practically suggested itself.

"Mahan gets to score double points with this one," smiled the Headman. "Exactly. It was my rebellious son that came up with this wonder. In Malabar few know what this thing looks like, but he recognized it from a single pipe."

"Then I don't get this bit. Once a week you didn't have to do anything. But at the same time there was a Sklic running around the village, whom you were trying to catch. It just doesn't fit in with the rest of the picture," The Headman's story was interesting, but too many things remained unanswered.

"Catch it? Not in the least. We were taking him out for a walk - to stop him getting out of control and making a mess of things before it was time. Though a Sklic is sentient, in his fighting transformation he can forget himself. In order to stop anyone recognizing it, I thought up the story with the mysterious monster plaguing the village. I sent a message to Farstead and got a reply: 'You'll have to deal with the mysterious beast yourself.' This made it possible for me to give assignments to free citizens, while concealing the appearance of the Sklic. Then I handed over the issuing of assignments to the Magister."

"And what about Tisha? Why did the priest expect me to hand her over? He wanted to get hold of a Vagren, not a Sklic!"

"Tisha..." the Headman fell silent, looked at his petrified daughter and heaved a bitter sigh. "Everyone has a weakness. Tisha really reminds me of her mother, so I decided not to inform her of our plans. She received a different education - one that was too 'correct': by Malabar, not Kartoss standards. Our ways are alien to her. We had to show her that free citizens are untrustworthy and would betray anyone for money, even a beautiful and defenseless girl. When you refused to hand her over to the Magister, I was furious. I even had to fly to the castle and inflict some discipline on the workers there. And then there's her obsession with that bear..."

"You know?" a subdued squeak came from Tisha's direction.

"Who would I be if I didn't? Any more questions from you? No? Good. Then I'll continue. An Inverter was built in Beatwick and concealed by a ziggurat, to prevent any accidental discovery. And then everything ran according to the devised plan. I sent you to catch the wolves, which started to bother our workers. At the same time, I instructed the goblins to begin hunting you. We had to get our fatso captured. To prevent you finding out too much, I personally put a defense on him. This was done to get the Heralds snooping around, inquiring about what was going on in Beatwick. In total we prepared ten potential areas for invasion and in each there was a key figure which could have relayed the information about the goblins to the Heralds. You were the only one who was able to take a prisoner and launch the subsequent chain of events. In order to spur on the heroes of Malabar, I decided to build a castle, intended to become our future base of power in this region, outside the ziggurat's zone of effect. The Heralds had to have the opportunity to jump to it and observe it by themselves, without having to be summoned. As soon as the castle was ready it was shown to you. The merchant, to whom you were careless enough to show the Eye of the Dark Widow, became our man two years ago. We got him under our thumb straight away. He traded off the information about the Eye and the person who had it in his possession. As planned, the free citizens of Malabar, greedy and stupid, immediately went after such a prize. We could only thank the Herald that he didn't let them kill you. And then you fulfilled your purpose: called the goblins for help. You were shown the castle, which, as you correctly noted, has four Inverters built into it. They were put into operation four hours ago. According to my calculations, it would take Malabar forces about twenty five minutes to storm it, after which the Heralds will teleport them all to Beatwick. Around five hundred free citizens above level 280 and about ten thousand Warriors and Mages from the Emperor's personal guard of level 380 or above - that have already spent twenty five minutes in the Inverter zone of effect, and have no amulet of the kind that's hanging on Beth's neck. Shall I tell you what will happen in Beatwick in just a few minutes or can you guess yourselves? Oh yes, I forgot to add: I removed the transformation suppressors in the villages. So - there's just ten minutes left. That's it, I think. The other nine invasion points will be discarded as ineffective, and the Krong province will become part of Kartoss. We didn't need much, but we had to show Malabar our teeth. You could have changed it all, my wayward son, if you left everyone to their fate and stopped the attack on the castle. But it is too late now. The effect of the Inverter is already underway. And here come our 'great warriors'."

From the big hill where the temple once stood, you had a very good view of a portal appearing before the Beatwick gates. A Herald stepped out of it, looked around and nine more portals materialized, from which the Malabar army began to pour out. Five hundred players and ten thousand NPCs.

"It has begun," whispered Naahti, looking pleased.

On one hand I understood very well that the players, especially the high-level ones, don't have much to worry about. So what if they lose 30% experience from their current level? It's not exactly fatal. Something else was a much more acute source of worry. Ten thousand high-level NPCs which simply had to be destroyed... I couldn't even imagine the scale of the raid that would have to be organized for such an army.

Shouts started to come from the direction of Beatwick.

"Line up! First squadron - to the left, second - to

the right, third takes the centre. The free citizens should choose any direction and try not to get in the way. Army, attack!"

There came the roar of the ten thousand voices of the attackers, though I couldn't quite identify who they were. Were they determined to wipe Beatwick off the face of the earth?

"Beth, would you be able to stop the transformation?" I asked the priestess in a whisper, when the army of Malabar began to encircle Beatwick.

"No," the woman whispered. "Even if I was the High Priestess, I wouldn't have enough strength."

"So, looks like the Emperor no longer has a personal guard..." the Advisor looked thoughtful and Naahti sported a pleased smile. "But why, father? Ten thousand Warriors is quite a force, of course, but it isn't one that our heroes would be unable to beat. Your plan was doomed to fail from the start. We would not tolerate Kartoss on our territory. Why?"

"And who is guarding the Emperor's palace right now?" Mirida suddenly asked.

"The personal guard..." the Advisor started and immediately fell silent.

"The one that's here now. Or is this some kind of a small vanguard?"

"This is all of them..." the Advisor once again was looking rather pitiful. "Including all the Heralds and two Advisors. Right now there is only one Advisor by the Emperor's side..."

"And also three Masters of Kartoss and twenty Magisters; I hope that our priest is there already, and one very interesting Shaman," Naahti summed up. "Not to mention the five thousand Dark Packs. We have somewhat perfected the Inverters, my son. Among other things, they also prevent the use of portals. I permitted the entry here, but now the Heralds are in for a surprise. They won't be able to teleport around. The two years of preparations have borne their fruit. The Emperor will be overthrown and there's no-one there to help him - even all the high-level free citizens are now here, away from the capital. The rabble that remained in the city... For our army it's nothing. Everything has gone exactly according to plan. Enjoy your defeat."

A piercing scream of pain sounded around Beatwick, drowning out all other sounds. A swirl of mist formed around each of the Emperor's guards and when it dissipated, Barliona sported ten thousand more Kartoss minions. High-level minions.

"I think that's it. There's nothing left for me to do here. Although... Beth, I did promise to finish you off personally, and promises have to be kept."

"Don't you dare touch her or you're not my father anymore!" shouted Tisha, standing between Beth and the Master. "If you..."

The Advisor lost little time and, as soon as the Headman turned his back to him, attacked his brothers, enveloping them in cocoons.

"Run!" he shouted to us, when the surprised Master turned to him. "Malabar may not have dodged this blow, but you will not escape here alive! Mahan! Take them all out of here!"

Lightning began to flash around us, the earth began to boil and a great wind started to blow. The Advisor had met his match in the Master.

"Phoenix, battle stance! Tanks to the front, full-circle defense!" The shouts of the surrounded players began to be heard from the direction of Beatwick. I recognized Anastaria's voice, in command of her raid group. "Those without a clan, get out!"

"Legion! Alpha formation! Mages - the dome! Plinto - mages are in your group. We'll fight our way to the village!"

"The Dragons are holding ground! Let's fight out to the forest! Herald, open the portal!"

By the looks of it, each clan was starting to fight for itself. If there were complete raid groups present, they could hold out against such an army for some time: the transformed NPCs wouldn't have much space to maneuver and would only be able to attack the players over a limited area.

Through the clashing of swords and whizzing of spells there suddenly came a clear sound of a crying baby. How could I forget? Beth and I made enough amulets for 80% of the village population. Those should not transform, but the other 20%... A massacre was underway in Beatwick now!

"Holy Eluna, the children!" whispered Beth in horror and ran to the village.

"Stop, you can't!" Tisha managed to jump on her and the girls rolled on the ground. "You won't get through! There are berserkers all around!"

"Clouter and Mariana are in there!" this was the

first time to my memory that I had heard Beth call her son by his local nickname.

"Beth, he's beyond help now! Look!" The berserkers have begun to break down the gates! Beatwick is doomed! We have to get out of here!"

"Everyone shut it!" I wasn't expecting to come out with such a scream, but the panicking women pushed me over the edge. Our previous group had collapsed - probably as soon as the Master removed the temple walls, or even earlier, I missed the exact moment. "I'm making a group - join up quick. Now!" I dropped an invite to Beth, Tisha and Mirida. The first two accepted without any questions, but the lady player pointedly raised her eyebrow.

"What do you intend to do, small fry? Knock over ten thousand warriors?"

"My pretty," I hissed. I've really had it with everyone. Soon there'll be screaming and a flood of swearwords. "If you don't want to come with us - do us a favor and take a hike. If you ask questions and challenge my words - take a hike. If you start acting like a spoilt princess - take a hike. Over there is a crowd of players hanging out. Feel free to march over and share all your grievances with them. It's not like I really need you or have to explain my actions to you. Are you with me? No? Then off you go! Beth, Tisha, after me, quick!"

Defying logic and common sense, I didn't run for Beatwick, but to the place where the altar to Vlast had previously stood. I was really interested in the passage into which the Magister had disappeared into.

Something told me that this was the direction we should be heading in. The ball of flame that the grappling Advisor and Master had turned into, rolled towards the village, sweeping aside a large squadron of NPCs like a bunch of bowling pins. As soon as I stepped behind the altar, I noticed that my group had grown - Mirida accepted the invite.

The passage was immediately behind the altar, with a spiral stair leading into the blackness of the basement. Not allowing myself to switch on my brain, I said: "After me!" and began to descend. At the bottom of the stairs there was a narrow passage, lit by a couple of torches. After waiting for the now calm ladies, I moved ahead. After just a dozen meters the passage turned and brought us to a five-meter-long cave, with some strange device in the middle. The portal which the Magister used to depart here had practically dissipated. And, most importantly, one wall of the cave contained a niche, fenced off with thick iron bars.

"Theodore!" shouted Beth and ran to the cell.

"Beth?" the man in the niche jumped up from the ground and leaned against the bars. "Beth, my dearest! Run from here! He may return at any time! The priest of Vlast is a Kartoss Magister!"

"I know, my love..."

"Do you know how to open this thing?" I butted into the conversation of the two lovers, who apparently lost their heads with the joy of being reunited. The developers were fond of sprinkling around scenes like that: reunited families, return of the prodigal son and so on and so forth. The designers believe it makes the players think and become more tolerant of other people.

"The lever is on the other side of the hall," Theodore managed to tear himself away from Beth and turn on his brain. Finally. At this point the group could really use someone with a head on their shoulders.

"Mirida, find the lever. Theodore, what's your class? Tisha, stop crying!"

"Me? A priest and a healer."

"Great! I'm sending you an invite. All of us are in a group now, including Beth. We will quickly free you and get out of here. Are you able to walk unaided? "

"Yes. But what's the point?"

"To get the children out! There is an Armageddon in progress upstairs!"

"Beth, what's he on about?"

"Darling, just trust him. Every second is precious. Avtondil and Mariana are in Beatwick."

"Everyone after me," I shouted when the bars of the cage flew up. Waving away the message that my Charisma went up by 10%, I headed back to the surface. It was time to rescue those wearing our amulets. I just wish I had some idea of how to get through the crowd of those that transformed.

"Hel, hang in there! Rick, the right side's on you! Barrs, grab five - the left edge is yours," as soon as I emerged above ground, I was hit by a torrent of shouts and commands. I looked over the battlefield and chuckled: the players had split themselves into several modest-sized groups, about forty people in each, which were being gradually destroyed by the enemy. The loners that responded to the summons of the Emperor were mowed down immediately. Only the clan raid groups held out, but they were being pushed farther and farther from the village. One small comfort consisted of the fact that ten thousand NPCs were unable to knock down the village gates. Far though it was, I could see that the level of Durability of the gates was still at half full. If we make it into Beatwick through Beth's passage, we would be able to save all the NPCs who had not been changed. One slight problem was the enormous Kartoss detachment between us and the village, which surrounded the Phoenix and Legion players. The clan fighters weren't standing far from each other, but it looked like the question of combining their forces didn't even occur to them. Strange, this would make their lives a lot easier. Each group contained two or three Heralds that helped to repel the attacks and Phoenix even sported an Advisor in their ranks.

The ball of flame that was the Headman and his son became a whirlwind and started to race around about five hundred meters away from the village.

"Mahan, what should we do?" asked Beth, with a resigned look. "We can't fight through this crowd."

I had to decide something and quick. I whipped out both amulets from Anastaria and Plinto and activated both.

"YES?" "WHAT?" the players shouted almost at the same time. "Whoever you are, get lost, we've no time for this!"

"Now, shut up and listen here! Anastaria, are

you the raid leader? I'm sending you a group invite - join together with all your raiders. Plinto, the same goes for you!"

"Mahan, have you totally lost it?" roared Plinto.

"Mahan, do you know what to do? Where are you?" this one came from Anastaria.

"I have no time to explain. Stacey, just trust me, as usual. I'm on the hill about three hundred meters away from you. Plinto, dammit, don't decline the invite! To me, quick!"

"Phoenix is joining!" shouted Stacey and the frames of thirty players appeared before my eyes. Hellfire's Hit Points constantly jumped up and down: he was probably tanking. "Stacey, what are you doing?" Hellfire's and Rick's shouts could be heard through the amulet.

"Plinto, will we be waiting long for you?" I really didn't care anymore. High-level or not, they were essentially a gathering of disorganized idiots, each thinking only about himself.

"Plinto, this is Anastaria! Let's group up! I agree with Mahan, it would make it easier for all. We would see your frames and would be able to heal you when needed."

"Go to hell! Legion never backs down! We will win!" with these words Plinto turned off the amulet.

"Forget him! Mahan, what do you propose?"

"Stacey, give the amulet to the Advisor!"

"Mahan? " Even in the heat of the battle the voice of the Advisor was calm.

"Advisor, I know that the Heralds are unable to

form portals. In this area only Kartoss portals work. I happen to have a couple. But before I use them, I need to get people out of the village!" What am I saying? This is a game! I have immersed myself in it so much that I no longer pay any heed to high-level players, dictate my conditions to an Advisor and, in general, carry on like a 400-level character. "If we each fight separately, we will be overrun very quickly! We have to join up, but other clans won't go under Phoenix. Their pride wouldn't permit them. I'm not from Phoenix and they don't know me. Give me the opportunity to command the clans in this fight." That's it, my foot was off the brakes. I'll cook up such a fantastic mess now that I'll end up giving myself a good kicking for it all later.

"Are you sure you can handle it, twenty-leveler?" a thoughtful voice of the Advisor came from the amulet.

"We'll have to find out, won't we? It's not like we have any choice. Half the Mana's already gone - another five minutes and the Phoenix fighters will start migrating to the Grey Lands. I can't say what will happen with the Heralds and Advisors, but I doubt it'll be very pleasant."

Attention all players taking part in the battle near Beatwick! Shaman Mahan, a level 21 free citizen, will be in charge of the evacuation. He has been granted all the necessary authority. His word is the word of the Emperor. Duration of his appointment: 2 hours

"Stacey, fight your way to the left," I continued

to scream into the amulet. "Heralds, I need a communication line with the Azure Dragons clan raid leader."

"What?" a muffled tense voice of a player, probably one of the clan leaders, sounded in my amulet.

"This is Mahan. Are you the one in the red hat?"

"Yes! What did you want?"

"I'm inviting you into the group. You read the announcement, right? If yes, then it should all be crystal clear. Stacey, fight towards them and join up - you'll figure out the tactics yourself, you're a pro at this."

"Sir, yes, sir!" even through the noise of the battle, I could hear the cheer in the girl's voice. Yes, this is what having proper raid experience means! For her everything going on right now is just a game, and I'm the only one that started to confuse it with reality. Suddenly I felt the vibration of Plinto's amulet.

"So you've come to your senses, then? I'm sending you an invite."

"Mahan, this is Evolett. The Legion is ready to join you. You can send the invite to me. What do we do?"

"Great! I see you've taken one heck of a battering! Phoenix and Azure Dragons - fight your way to the Legion. They'll be getting mashed any time now," I suddenly had a bout of the damned premonition. "Stacey - bubble on Hellfire! Now! The second tank - pull those mobs! The rest - support the second tank!"

I didn't know what it was that the Kartoss

warriors had come up with, but Hellfire started to catch hits worth five hundred thousand damage. Yes, he was quite thick-skinned himself, with almost a million Hit Points after all the buffs and elixirs, but he simply wouldn't have survived damage like that. The bubble, which Stacey threw on him without any questions, protects the target from all types of damage for ten seconds. It was for this ability that paladins were a must-have feature of any raid: when the 'big boom' hits, a pally would pull you out.

With the aid of Heralds I was able to join up with three more clan raid groups. In total, including my original five members, I was now looking at a sea of about two hundred frames. They constantly jumped up and down, with numbers indicating damage or healing lighting up next to them every second - it was enough to do your head in.

"To all raid leaders!" I shouted through the Heralds. "The detail of raid management is in your hands. I'm in charge of the general strategy. Now we must all gather into one group and together make our way towards the stockade. Stacey, take out a party to pick me up. I'm on the hill. Go!"

"Why the heck are we going for the stockade? We should head to the forest!" I couldn't really make out who said that. What's with the dissent in the ranks? Such insolence must be stamped out at the root. I finally get the rare opportunity to order people around, best players of the Empire, no less, and someone's throwing a spanner in the works.

"We need to make it to the village before it's

taken by the Kartoss forces. The gates will hold out another five minutes at the most. We gather the surviving villagers and teleport out of here. Now!"

I wouldn't say they went supersonic, but the players did start running around. After we united into a group of a couple of hundred fighters and I had the ability to see the frames of each, it was considerably easier to repel Kartoss attacks.

"Beth, open the passage," I continued to shout orders left and right. "Stacey, take your lot and leg it to the gate. It'll break any time now and this horde will spill inside. Stop them at the entrance. It's a narrow space, so you won't have to fight them more than two or three at a time. Beth, where's the passage?"

Some messages constantly flashed before my eyes, telling me I was receiving this and that, but I simply had no time to read them. The only thing I noticed was that I reached level 35 in the last five minutes.

"Mahan, we're in position. The gate's about to come down, you were right," reported Anastaria when half of the players were already inside the village.

"Evolett - you take the street on the right. Go through all the houses, shout that the Emperor sent you and do what you can to gather all the NPCs together.

"Partaros," I shouted to the leader of some other clan, having only a vague idea at this point which it was. There was no time to look it up. "You take the left street. Same stuff. Beth, where are you going? Undigit, take her and go straight ahead. We gather on the central square! The Advisor and Heralds - you need to hurry to the palace. The Emperor has been or is about to be attacked. We'll manage here without you. Here, take a portal scroll - I don't know where it leads, other than out of this area." I took out the scroll, which I had taken off the captured goblin and activated it.

"If you are right, Mahan, the Empire will be in your debt," said one of the Advisors, after which the entire Malabar elite left Beatwick.

"A portal! Time to split!" Plinto's shout came from nearby. That's the last thing I need!

"EVERYONE STOP!" I never thought myself capable of raising my voice quite like that. Plinto and a band of ten players simply froze, agape. "EVERYONE - STAND YOUR GROUND!"

You have used a raid-leader ability 'Thundering Shout'. Energy of all the raid members has been increased by 20 and all the main stats by +20%. Duration: 5 minutes

Waving away another message informing me that my Charisma had once again grown by 1, I looked at the potential deserters.

"Plinto, dammit! Are you a player or a pushover? If you're a player, what the hell are you doing? Had enough of the game, have you? Want to be booted out of Barliona altogether? Back in the line and hold the passage! If Kartoss gets through, gnaw them with your teeth if you have to, but hold them off!"

"The left street's been cleaned up!"

"The right one's done!"

"Mahan," Clouter ran into me. I will probably never call him Avtondil now. "Tiny Tim attacked me! He suddenly became huge, black and scary, tore through the netting and jumped on me. He was going to tear me to shreds! But another Tiny Tim appeared from your present, a see-through one! Just imagine, two Tiny Tims are fighting in our yard right now: one evil and black and the other good and see-through. What happened to my dog?"

"Let's go dear, don't distract him. It's hard enough for him as it is," Beth dragged the excited lad away from me and I looked at Undigit, the leader of the Azure Dragons.

"How many normal ones?"

"A hundred and thirty five. It's time to bail out. Phoenix is holding the gates, but look at the walls - half of their durability's gone. Soon they'll give and we'll be mowed down."

"I agree. Attention everyone! It's time to get out of here! Undigit, take your team and get ready to receive the NPCs. The others will come after. Stacey, how are you holding up?"

"Not that great! The tanks are still standing, but we're running out of Mana. Mahan, I agree with Undigit - it's time to bail. I'm not prepared to lose experience over this, it's bad enough running around with your debuff on me."

"Roger that! As soon as half of them go through the portal, run towards us. Throw freezing spells and traps - anything to slow them down. Time's a ticking!"

Azure Dragons went through the portal, followed by the rescued residents of Beatwick. Only Beth with her family remained.

"Do you need a special invitation?"

"We can't go back. If we leave Krong, we will be immediately killed on the orders of the Emperor," Beth heaved a deep sigh. "The children will go through, but we'll stay behind. Perhaps we'll be able to slow them down..."

"Why is everything so damn hard with you guys? Here, take this," I handed the Emperor's ring to the priestess. "Get out of here - quick! Plinto, grab her and jump in the portal!"

"How did you..."

"Now! Quit it with the drama. Just go! Stacey, that's it - pack up and run to us."

"Coming. Hel, charge!"

A couple of flashes came from the direction of the gates, which was probably Stacey using something to blind the mobs and Phoenix players immediately appeared from around the corner.

"Ten seconds and they'll follow us," shouted Stacey as she ran.

"Evolett, get ready to jump into the portal as soon as Phoenix goes through," I issued the last command to the defenders of the passage and jumped in the portal. That's it. I've had my fill of fighting.

"I was the last," shouted Hellfire as he jumped out of the portal, "you can shut it the hell down!"

I deactivated the portal and slumped to the ground, exhausted, and only then looked at the map to see where we ended up. We ported to the lands surrounding the Kartoss castle! Just my luck! Only ten kilometers from Beatwick!

"What's with the castle? Did you destroy it completely?" The thought about the Inverters was really bothering me. If they were activated, the Heralds wouldn't have been unable to teleport out of here and all of this would have been for nothing.

"There's not a stone left standing of the castle," Evolett assured me. "We destroyed everything."

"What the heck is that?" came a muffled shout of some player.

A tornado was heading towards us from the direction of Beatwick. Two enormous figures could be seen at its centre: the Advisor and the Master, neither of which had yet gained the upper hand in their duel. I was about to respond when another message appeared in front of me:

Citizens of Malabar! Lament!
The Emperor is dead!
Your reputation with the Emperor is changed to reputation with the Emperor's Steward

Everyone froze. What did 'the Emperor is dead' mean? How was this possible? A minute had gone by when a new message appeared:

Citizens of Kartoss! Lament!
The Dark Lord is dead!
Your reputation with the Dark Lord is

changed to reputation with the Dark Lord's Steward

And now I had completely failed to understand anything. I got it as far as our Emperor was concerned, since the aim of the plot was to kill him, but the Dark Lord?

The tornado made up of the Advisor and the Master fell apart and both Vagrens, who had for some reason become three meters tall, froze about three hundred meters away from us, looking at each other.

"Mahan, don't even try to pretend you don't know what's going on," Anastaria came up to me and the entire crowd of players stared at me expectantly. "I would never believe it!"

"A slight disagreement had taken place here, my pretty," a pleased and imposing voice spoke in my stead. I've heard it somewhere before... That's it! It was...

"Let me introduce myself," a man appeared next to me, wearing a formal dress of the courtier, "I'm Geranika. I've come for this sentient," he pointed towards me. "And to make sure no-one gets in the way, I'll tidy up a little around here."

He waved his hand and all the players and NPCs standing nearby were landed with the 'Petrification' debuff for fifteen minutes.

"Now we can have a chat," the dark Shaman walked around me and shook his head. "When we spoke last, you were just level twenty one. But now I see that you've grown somewhat. To gain forty six levels in two weeks is a very impressive result."

What? What forty six levels? With all the surrounding mess I completely forgot to keep an eye on my character's status. I opened my properties and was struck dumb. Holy cow!

Stat window for player Mahan:					
Experience	10466	of	87100	Additional stats	
Race	Human				
Class	Elemental Shaman			Physical damage	91
Main Profession	Jeweller			Magical damage	3419
Character level	67				
Hit points	2600			Physical defence	840
Mana	8548			Magic resistance	280
Energy	100			Fire resistance	280
Stats	Scale	Base	+ Items	Cold resistance	280
Stamina	64%	30	68	Poison resistance	100%
Agility	11%	7	7		
Strength	84%	18	21	Dodge chance	14.60%
Intellect	35%	56	185	Critical hit chance	8.80%
Charisma	41%	6	6		
Crafting	0%	3	4		
Endurance	30%	10	10	Water Spirit rank:	2
Spirituality	0%	21	21	Totem level	37
Free stat points			265		
Professions				**Specialisation**	
Jewelcrafting	91%	42	42	Gem Cutter	1
Mining	1%	52	53	Hardiness	5%
Trade	25%	7	7	-	
Cooking	20%	5	5	-	
Cartography	50%	52	52	Scroll Scribe	1
Smithing	20%	24	24	Smelter	5%

You could say that the fight went well for me!

"My plan is flawless. There is now no Emperor or Lord and no Masters or Advisors on our continent.

Even all the Heralds and Magisters have perished. Although I did have to kill the Dark Lord myself - it was just as well that his personal guard had their hands full with the Emperor at the time. Now I'm the only power that remains! Everyone will fall at my feet! I offer you to join me. You are still weak and inexperienced, but I'll teach you everything I know. Make your choice, Shaman!"

Attention! You have been offered to go over to the side of Shaman Geranika as the disciple of the Emperor. Description: having set himself against both Empires, Geranika destroyed the Emperor and the Dark Lord, creating an Empire of his own. The capital of the third Empire is on the edge of the Free Lands and is now marked on your map

Do you agree to join the new empire?

To the player located in a prisoner capsule! In connection with the launching of the continent-wide scenario, the term of compulsory settlement has been revoked by court decision No.45-RS344328. Now you are a provisionally free player. Remaining limitations: presence of pain, the 30% tax, prohibition on attacking other players first. Have a pleasant game!

"I am waiting, Mahan. Do not test my patience! You will have everything that you could possibly wish for," Geranika hurried me.

To become an Emperor's apprentice? What a

brilliant idea! Soaring to such heights in a flash, it's just hard to imagine... And how long will be the fall from these great heights when Malabar raiders will come after Geranika to avenge the Emperor? Although, why worry? I'm a player and they can't really do anything to me. But then what amazing gaming abilities would open up with this offer! I almost pressed the button 'Accept', but then I remembered Kornik's words: "When the time comes to choose, make the choice with your heart and not your head." Could my green teacher have seen this coming?

"Mahan!"

I ignored Geranika's shout and listened to myself. Do I really need what's being offered by this NPC? Yes, I do. Do I want to follow him? E-eh... no, I don't and I can't explain it. My entire being screamed that I should make this bastard feel bad. And then stomp on him some more. And then jump up and down on his remains, just to be sure.

"I refuse," I decided to put my feeling into words.

"Is this your choice?!" Geranika was enraged. "You decided to oppose me? You decided that you'll have enough strength to fight me, the one who destroyed both Emperors? The one who will be the only Sovereign in Barliona! Then take what you deserve!"

Lightning bolts started to flash out of the dark Shaman's hands, but they were stopped by a dome that formed around me. What, another helper had joined the show?

"STOP, YOU FOOL!" a thundering voice nearly threw me to the ground.

"Dragons," hissed Geranika. "That's the last thing I need!"

I glanced at Anastaria, who was lying next to me and looking up with huge shocked eyes. I looked up and saw Renox, hovering above our raid.

"Hello, Renox. What are you doing in the middle of this mess?"

"We could not calmly watch what this madman was doing! Dragons had to intervene in the events of this world!"

"Know this, Mahan: we'll meet again!" Geranika spat out angrily, "And for you our next meeting will be a very unpleasant experience." With these words Geranika disappeared.

"Renox, it's good to see you. Can you remove 'Petrification' from everyone here?"

"I greet you, my son. Wait a little, first I would like to speak to the new Emperor and the new Dark Lord!

"With who?" Who was this reptile speaking about?

"Naahti, Regul," the Dragon rumbled, ignoring my question. "Come here!"

Both Vagrens, not daring to refuse, came up to the Dragon. Renox came down to the ground and stared intently into the eyes of each, as if reading their thoughts.

"Behold the result of your enmity! The Emperor and the Dark Lord are dead and you are behaving yourselves like two wolf cubs fighting over a bone! Come to your senses! Regul! Now and henceforth I dub you the Nameless Dark Lord of Kartoss. Gather the remainder of your army and rebuild the palace destroyed by Geranika. Naahti! Now and henceforth I dub you the Emperor of Malabar. Gather the remainder of your army and rebuild the palace destroyed by Geranika. I grant you the power of the Emperor and the Dark Lord, may you be worthy of this burden! Rule wisely and honorably, like your predecessors. My task here is complete!"

"The Great Dragon is mistaken..." started Regul, the only remaining Advisor and now the Lord of Kartoss.

"SILENCE!" roared Renox. "I know who you were! And who you will become!"

"I bow before the wisdom of the Great One," bowed the Emperor, the former Master of Kartoss.

Citizens of Malabar! Rejoice! The Emperor is alive!

Your reputation with the Steward of the Emperor is changed to the reputation with the Emperor!

Citizens of Kartoss! Rejoice! The Dark Lord is alive!

Your reputation with the Steward of the Dark Lord is changed to the reputation with the Dark Lord

"Mahan, I can see that a quiet life is not for you. At our last meeting you managed to surprise me, but now I am simply astonished. You are a worthy Dragon!

Unfortunately, my presence here has disturbed the balance, so in the next hundred years Dragons cannot appear in Barliona. Try not to destroy the world," with these words Renox soared up and disappeared, returning to his realm. The two Vagrens, having risen to level 500, first looked at each other and then at me.

"Mahan," began the new Emperor. "I thank you for everything you have done."

Your reputation with the Emperor of Malabar has increased by 4000 points. You are 5700 points away from the status of Esteem

"I agree," added the new Dark Lord. "You also have my thanks."

Your reputation with the Dark Lord of Kartoss has increased by 4000 points. You are 6000 points away from the status of Esteem

"Emperor, come. We have much to discuss. It's time we learned how to talk."

As soon as both NPCs disappeared, the 'Petrification' debuff was removed from all the players, but no-one broke the silence. Anastaria got back to her feet, looked me in the eye and whispered.

"Mahan... I never expected something like this. You, a Dragon?"

I wanted to respond to Anastaria with the usual - along the lines of 'you're such a fool', when another message struck me dumb:

Attention all players!

Following numerous requests, the game administration has now opened the option of making characters on the side of the Kartoss Empire. To transfer a character to the 'dark' side, please read the rules published on the official website of the game.

Welcome to the renewed Barliona!

END OF BOOK TWO

Want to be the first to know about our latest LitRPG, sci fi and fantasy titles from your favorite authors?

Subscribe to our **NEW RELEASES** newsletter:
http://eepurl.com/b7niIL

Thank you for reading *The Kartoss Gambit!*
If you like what you've read, check out other LitRPG
books and series published by Magic Dome Books:

Dark Paladin LitRPG series by Vasily Mahanenko:
The Beginning
The Quest

The Dark Herbalist LitRPG series
by Michael Atamanov:
Video Game Plotline Tester
Stay on the Wing

The Neuro LitRPG series by Andrei Livadny:
The Crystal Sphere
The Curse of Rion Castle

The Way of the Shaman LitRPG series
by Vasily Mahanenko:
Survival Quest
The Kartoss Gambit
The Secret of the Dark Forest
The Phantom Castle
The Karmadont Chess Set
The Hour of Pain (a bonus short story)

Galactogon LitRPG series by Vasily Mahanenko:
Start the Game!

Phantom Server LitRPG series by Andrei Livadny:
Edge of Reality
The Outlaw
Black Sun

Perimeter Defense LitRPG series by Michael
Atamanov:
Sector Eight
Beyond Death
New Contract

Mirror World LitRPG series by Alexey Osadchuk:
Project Daily Grind
The Citadel
The Way of the Outcast

AlterGame LitRPG series by Andrew Novak:
The First Player

The Expansion (The History of the Galaxy) series by A. Livadny:
Blind Punch

Citadel World series by Kir Lukovkin:
The URANUS Code

The Game Master series by A. Bobl and A. Levitsky:
The Lag

The Sublime Electricity series by Pavel Kornev
The Illustrious
The Heartless
Leopold Orso and the Case of the Bloody Tree

Moskau *(a dystopian thriller)* by **G. Zotov**

Memoria. A Corporation of Lies
(an action-packed dystopian technothriller)
by Alex Bobl

Point Apocalypse
(a near-future action thriller)
by Alex Bobl

You're in Game!
(LitRPG Stories from Bestselling Authors)

The Naked Demon (a paranormal romance)
by Sherrie L.

In order to have new books of the series translated faster, we need your help and support! Please consider leaving a review or spread the word by recommending *The Kartoss Gambit* to your friends and posting the link on social media. The more people buy the book, the sooner we'll be able to make new translations available. Thank you!

Till next time!

Made in the USA
Middletown, DE
18 November 2020